HOLDING OUT FOR A HERO

He found another stone and skimmed it across the water. He hadn't intended to tell her about his mother. He hadn't intended to divulge anything personal about himself that would make her question him or his relationship to Billy. He knew she valued honesty. What would she say if he told her the truth now?

She stopped walking and looked up at him with a sympathetic look in her eyes. "I'm sorry."

"What for?"

"Reminding you of unpleasant memories."

He smiled. At first he'd thought she meant for driving him crazy while she was on the dance floor. "They're not all unpleasant."

She cupped his face in her hands. He didn't resist as she brought his mouth down to hers. Her lips were soft, warm, inviting, but he pulled away almost immediately. He didn't trust himself or her motives for the overture.

"Adam," she said, drawing his attention to her mouth, made moist by its contact with his. She rose on the balls of her feet and kissed him again. And again. Light, sipping kisses that grew longer and more intense. Adam shut his eyes tightly against her onslaught. His nostrils flared, breathing in the subtle scent of her perfume and the tang of the ocean. The salt air lifted tendrils of her hair to tease his skin.

He felt himself going down, dragged into a whirlpool of sensations. For a moment, at least, he didn't want salvation. From the second she'd walked down the stairs wearing that outrageous outfit, she'd had him hot and wanting.

His arms closed around her, crushing her to him. His tongue plunged into her mouth, claiming hers. One of his hands slid down to cradle her hip, bringing her in contact with his erection. She moaned and swiveled her hips against him. He groaned as a wave of pure pleasure washed over his groin and eddied throughout his body. Immediately he pulled away from her, while he still could.

She blinked her eyes open and stared at him, confused.

He touched his knuckles to her cheek. "What are we doing here, Samantha?"

S0-BJJ-893

Books by Deirdre Savoy

Spellbound

Always

Once and Again

Midnight Magic

Holding Out for A Hero

HOLDING OUT FOR A HERO

Deirdre Savoy

ARABESQUE
★BET
BOOKS™

BET Publications, LLC
http://www.bet.com
http://www.arabesquebooks.com

ARABESQUE BOOKS are published by

BET Publications, LLC
c/o BET BOOKS
One Bet Plaza
1900 W Place NE
Washington, D.C. 20018-1211

Copyright © 2002 by Deirdre Savoy

All rights reserved. No part of this book may be reproduced,
stored in a retrieval system, or transmitted in any form or by
any means without the prior written consent of the Publisher.

If you purchased this book without a cover, you should be
aware that this book is stolen property. It was reported as
"unsold and destroyed" to the Publisher and neither the
Author nor the Publisher has received any payment for this
"stripped book."

All Kensington Titles, Imprints, and Distributed Lines are
available at special quantity discounts for bulk purchases for
sales promotions, premiums, fund-raising, educational or in-
stitutional use. Special book excerpts or customized printings
can also be created to fit specific needs. For details, write or
phone the office of the Kensington special sales manager:
Kensington Publishing Corp., 850 Third Avenue, New York,
NY 10022, attn. Special Sales Department. Phone: 1-800-
221-2647.

BET Books is a trademark of Black Entertainment Television,
Inc. ARABESQUE, the ARABESQUE logo, and the BET
BOOKS logo are trademarks and registered trademarks.

First Printing: September 2002
10 9 8 7 6 5 4 3 2 1

Printed in the United States of America

Acknowledgments

Thanks to James B. Finn, my agent, whose invaluable insight helped me to flesh out the story in this novel and whose unfailing guidance keeps me sane.

Thanks to my family, particularly my husband and my mom, for putting up with me and never letting me make them as crazy as I make myself.

Thanks to real-life hero, firefighter Paul Haney, the 2001 Arabesque Cover Contest winner. I am truly honored to have him grace the cover. Paul worked on the Pentagon for 48 straight hours after the September 11 attacks. You did a wonderful job bringing fictional hero Adam Wexler to life.

Most of all, thanks to Darlene James, my friend and fellow writer. Your encouragement, advice, humor and insight pull me through every time. This book and especially *Midnight Magic* would not exist without you. Now do what they say in New Jersey and finish the damn book!

DEDICATION

For the every day heroes—the dedicated teacher, the patient father, the uncomplaining volunteer, the neighbor on the corner, the Samaritan who lends a hand just because it's needed—those who with simple, uncelebrated courage show the rest of us the way the world should be.

And for the fire fighters and police who risked or lost their lives on September 11, 2001. It takes a special brand of courage to rush into disaster when the rest of the world is running out. We are forever in your debt.

Prologue

"Isn't she the sleekest baby you've ever seen?"

Samantha Hathaway eyed the black convertible her former fiancée, Billy Prescott, ran his hand over with all the gentleness and care of a lover. "Looks like a car to me."

"Sam, haven't I taught you anything? This is the BMW Z-eight. A hundred and fifty horses, V-eight powered, aluminum body. It goes from zero to sixty in three-point eight seconds. Ever hear of an automatic doing that before?"

Sam shrugged. She'd been this route before. Billy liked everything fast: fast cars, fast women—though she herself didn't fit into that category—the fast life. Billy jetted around the globe with all the élan his status as one of the hottest young actors in Hollywood afforded him. She'd jumped ship from his frenetic life once and had no intention of getting aboard it again.

"Is this what you dragged me out of my bed for on a Sunday morning? Your car?"

He huffed, deflated by her lack of enthusiasm. "I want you to take a drive with me. I want to show you something."

In the past three months, he'd made an absolute nuisance of himself, calling her, sending her flowers, popping up in places he knew she'd be. He'd shown up on her doorstep this morning, unannounced and uninvited, refusing to leave until he saw her. It was all she could do to keep Lupe from running him off with a shotgun. If there was a point to all this, she might as well find out what it was.

"You've got twenty minutes."

A broad smile broke out across his handsome face. "It won't take that long."

He held the door open for her and she folded her long-legged frame into the low-slung bucket seat on the passenger-side of the car. He slid in next to her as she finished fastening her seat belt. He surprised her by fastening his own, and by the sedate pace at which he pulled from the curb. The Billy she knew wouldn't have bothered with either of those things. He drove toward the hills behind her ranch-style house.

"Where are we going?" The route he chose was little more than a dirt road known as much for its mud slides in the spring as it was for the hordes of tourists that showed up every summer. The road overlooked several celebrities' homes, her own included.

"We'll be there in just a moment."

After a while he pulled off the dirt road onto an embankment that overlooked a sprawling home surrounded by acres of woodland. "What do you think?"

She took off her seat belt and leaned farther over the side of the car for a better look. "Nice house. Whose is it?"

"Mine. Or it will be in two weeks when I close on it. It's got a sauna, a gym. There's an indoor pool and a Jacuzzi out back. Four bedrooms, plenty of space for kids."

An ideal house, no doubt, but what did that have to do with her? "Why did you want to show this to me?"

"I thought it could be our house." He took her hand, rubbing his thumb over her knuckles. "I want you back, Sam. Surely you figured that out by now. I've missed you. I want to make a life with you. No one has ever been as good to me as you were."

She didn't doubt that. No other woman would have put up with half the nonsense from him that she had. She'd made the mistake of seeing the man's potential, rather than the man himself. But he hadn't changed one iota for her five years ago when she'd been engaged to him. Why would he bother to change now?

"It might surprise you to know," he added, "that I've done

the whole Betty Ford thing; I've been sober for almost six months now. I don't hang around with the same crowd anymore. In fact"—he chuckled—"I'm getting a reputation for being a stick-in-the-mud. I did all of that for you."

Sam shook her head. She would have preferred it if he'd done those things for himself. Then there might be some hope that any reformation on his part might be permanent. She had no intention of taking him back. She opened her mouth to tell him that. Before she got a word out, he placed a silencing finger over her lips.

"Just think about it. That's all I'm asking."

He leaned forward and pressed his mouth to hers. She felt no stirring of passion, no desire to reciprocate, as she might have felt only a short time ago. In that moment she knew she was completely over him. There would be no turning back.

After a moment Billy sat back, exhaling audibly as he adjusted his seat belt. "I guess I'd better take you home."

She nodded. "Thank you."

Billy pulled back onto the road, keeping to the same sedate pace he'd adopted for their drive up. But she sensed in him a desire to peel out, to burn rubber, to let his new toy run full-out and damn the consequences. He hadn't changed as much as he thought he had.

Sam stared out at the passing scenery on her side of the car. Part of her wished she could believe him. Part of her wished there were more to him than the vain, spoiled man-child she'd once loved, then hated, and now felt absolutely nothing for. In his own way, he'd been good to her, too.

Her hair whipped across her face. "Slow down, would you?" She glanced over at him. His hands gripped the steering wheel in such a way that his knuckles blanched, and a sheen of perspiration had broken out on his forehead.

"I would if I could, but Sam, baby, my foot's on the floor and the brakes aren't working."

"What?" Sam shifted in her seat, only then noticing that she'd never bothered to refasten her seat belt. She fumbled with it, trying unsuccessfully to fit the two metal pieces together. Another time, another car, another perilous ride super-

imposed itself on her consciousness. Panic, stark and hideous, rose like bile to her throat.

Traffic on the hillside was sparse, but traveling at a much slower rate than they now moved. Billy swerved several times to pass cars in their lane. Sam swallowed and gripped the frame of the open window as a tour bus barreled toward them. She screamed, but no sound made it past her constricted throat. Billy yanked the wheel to the right a second before the bus whizzed past them, close enough that the air between the two vehicles whistled.

Her pulse racing, her heart beating with the force of a jackhammer, Sam squeezed her eyes shut. She bent her head, clasping her hands together in supplication. Soundlessly she repeated every prayer the nuns at Saint Victoria's had foisted upon her. There were no atheists in foxholes, or agnostics in cars careening out of control.

"Oh, damn."

Sam's head snapped up and her eyes flew open. An SUV loomed in front of them, straddling the center line of the narrow road. They had nowhere to go. Billy veered to the right, riding so close to the edge that the wheels on the passenger-side dislodged clumps of rock and dirt that tumbled down the rocky side of the cliff.

With one hand gripping the steering wheel, Billy honked and waved at the driver. "Get out of the way, damn it," Billy yelled. Finally the driver pulled to the opposite side of the road. But the path before them curved sharply and unexpectedly to the left.

Billy spun the steering wheel frantically, but not fast enough. With nothing to hold the vehicle on course, the car pitched off the road, arced in midair, and crashed to the rocky ground below.

One

Did this woman ever plan on waking up?

Adam Wexler stared down at the woman who slumbered on, unaware of his presence. No doubt she was beautiful, with that halo of auburn hair surrounding her face, or she would be again, once some of the swelling went down and the bruises faded. He'd seen pictures of her over the years. He knew that face from countless glossy snapshots that graced the pages of magazines and billboards. He'd seen her walking and breathing, filling the big screen and the small with her presence. That face was Samantha Hathaway's stock in trade as she'd become one of the most sought-after and well-paid actresses in Hollywood.

She was beautiful, all right, but if she could manage to be conscious, too, he'd consider it a personal favor.

Didn't she realize he had murderers to catch, rapists to apprehend, not to mention all the other assorted bad guys that populated the city of New York, clogging the justice system and making the citizenry just a little bit edgy?

Or at least he would, *if* he got off disability and *if* he got his job back, two very big ifs at the moment. His hip burned as though someone had lanced it with a white-hot poker. Maybe he should have listened to his doctor about giving up the cane too soon, but he'd be damned if he'd be stuck with that thing the rest of his life.

Frustrated, he glanced around the darkened room, illuminated only by the light panel above her head and a shaft of

sunlight that peeked in through the tiny gap between the curtains
at the window. Vases of flowers, cards, elaborately wrapped
gifts, and what else he had no idea littered the floor, the small
table by the window, the dresser by the bed. Four more vases
had been delivered in the two hours since he'd gotten there.
What would any one person do with all those flowers?

"Come on, Sleeping Beauty. Wake up and smell the hibis-
cus."

When that elicited no response, he slumped into the chair
at the foot of her bed, groaning as the flimsy construction of
cheap metal and cheaper fabric barely accepted his six-foot-
seven, 245-pound frame. Not a lot of chairs did. He sighed,
resting his elbows on the arms of the chair and cradling his
head in his hands.

He hadn't slept much in the last twenty-four hours, and in
an odd way, he envied Samantha Hathaway her ability to shed
all cares and sleep. Then again, what did she have to worry
about? Whether or not her teeth would need to be recapped?
She'd survived the accident with only a faceful of bruises, a
dislocated left shoulder, and a sprained ankle.

Things would have been much worse if she'd been wearing
her seat belt. With nothing to restrain her, she'd been thrown
clear of the sports car that had literally crashed and burned a
few hundred feet below her. So much for "Buckle up for safety."

"Jarad?"

He lifted his head to find her watching him with a heavy-
lidded gaze. He tugged on the Yankee cap on his head, his
attempt at traveling incognito. "You're awake."

"What are you doing here? How's Ariel?" Her voice cracked
and she licked her lips, then winced from the pain.

He knew who she thought he was, film director Jarad
Naughton, her best friend and the man who'd gotten him into
this mess. He opened his mouth to correct her, then swallowed
his confession instead. Maybe in these first few unguarded
minutes, she might tell him something he might never get out
of her otherwise.

Modulating his voice into his best impression of the other
man, he said, "How do you feel?"

"Like someone hit me with a bag of bricks." She touched the fingertips of one hand to several spots on her face, pausing longest at the rectangular bandage on her forehead. "How bad is it?"

Just as he'd expected, her first concern was for her face. He didn't know why that annoyed him so much. "I've seen worse."

"Where's Billy? We were driving—"

Her doctor had told him she'd been informed what happened to Billy, but she'd been groggy and unresponsive. He didn't appreciate having to be the one to remind her about it.

"You had an accident. He didn't make it."

If he'd had any doubts about her feelings for Billy Prescott, they vanished as she wailed, "No," and squeezed her eyes shut. Slowly, silently, tears began to seep from beneath her lashes. They cascaded down her cheeks, but she made no move to brush them away. They had to sting, considering the number of abrasions on her face.

And what did he do now? He'd cast himself in the role of her friend, and no man worth his gonads could watch a woman cry and not comfort her. He rose from the chair, got a tissue from the box by the head of the bed, and handed it to her. Luckily she'd turned her face from him, so that here in the light he didn't have to shield his face.

"I'm sorry."

She nodded, sniffling. "I know you never liked him, but deep down there was something good about him. I just wish he'd let a little more of it out."

He said nothing to that, no words of comfort forming in his mind. Time to put the charade to an end, as he'd never get any information out of her this way. He laid a hand on her shoulder.

"I'd better go and let you get your rest."

He turned to leave, but felt her hand grasp his. "Don't I get a kiss goodbye?"

When he looked down at her, her eyes were closed and her swollen lips were slightly puckered. Did she expect a kiss on the mouth from him—or rather from her very married friend

with the very pregnant wife? Mentally, he shrugged. There
was no telling how weird these California people might get.

He bent and lightly pressed his lips to hers. She tasted sweet,
so sweet that he didn't immediately pull away.

When he did, he noticed her breathing had evened out and
her chest rose and fell in an even rhythm.

"I'll be damned," he muttered. "That's the first time I've
put a woman to sleep by kissing her."

He snorted, went back to the chair, picked up his bag that
lay on the floor beside it, and left the room.

Minutes later, stepping out into the clear afternoon sunshine,
he inhaled deeply, expanding his lungs to their fullest. L.A. even
smelled different from New York, as if someone had taken the
Bronx and run it through a dehumidifier.

He'd better get used to it. He wasn't going anywhere anytime
soon. He needed to get some food in his belly, find a place to
stay, and, if his reaction to the very battered and bruised Samantha Hathaway was any indication, he needed a woman—bad.
His stomach growled, and he decided food would be his first
stop. The other two could wait.

Sam woke to the sound of the phone ringing on her bedside
table. She picked it up, wincing at the pain in her shoulder as
she cradled it against her ear. "Hello?"

"Sam, how are you feeling, sweetheart?"

"Jarad? Where are you?"

"Home. Ariel and the girls were pestering me to call you.
You gave all of us one hell of a scare."

"You're home?" That meant New York. It must have been
a dream, then. His presence in her room had seemed so real,
though. Especially his kiss. In all the years she'd known Jarad,
she'd never once felt the slightest romantic urge toward him.
Then again, he'd never kissed her on the mouth before. At the
time, she'd wondered why he had.

She'd feigned sleep to cover her totally embarrassing reaction. She'd fallen asleep in earnest soon after he'd left the room.
At least she'd thought that was what had happened. Thank

goodness it hadn't been real, but now she wondered why she'd dreamed such a thing to begin with.

"Sam, are you okay? Is anyone there with you?"

"No, I'm here by myself."

"When are they letting you go home?"

"I don't know."

"I'm going to be sending someone out to you. A trainer."

"What for? I don't think I'm in any shape to make the Boston Marathon this year."

"A police officer."

"I don't need a bodyguard, if that's what you're thinking. Lupe will be with me."

"Yeah, the original female pit bull. Does she still bite the leg off every man that comes to the house?"

"Everyone but you. The other day someone tried to give me a puppy. She wouldn't let it in the house because it was a male."

"Well, the person I'm sending you is a New York city cop to help you prepare for your role in *Guardian Angel*. You do remember that part you begged me for? We're set to shoot in less than four months, and I want you to eat, think, and breathe cop by the time we're ready."

Sam sighed. She knew when she was licked. As a friend, Jarad was the biggest sweetheart in the world; as a director, he was a royal pain in the butt. "All right, all right. As long as it's someone unobtrusive. No one named Helga or Brunhilde who'll think they're going to tell me what to do."

"I promise, no Helgas." She suspected she heard a note of humor in his voice, but dismissed it when he spoke again.

"You know that Billy didn't make it."

So that much of her dream had been true. She'd probably heard the nurses talking and incorporated it into her dream. "Yes."

"I'm sorry, Sam. You know I wish I could be there with you, don't you?"

"I know, and I'm fine. Don't worry about me, okay? Kiss the girls for me, and tell Ariel I'll be out to help her with the new baby as soon as I can."

"I'll tell her. You take care of yourself."

"I will."

She leaned over to place the receiver in the cradle. But one question plagued her after she hung up the phone: If Jarad hadn't been there, why was there a wadded-up tissue in her right hand?

Adam sat on the bed in his hotel room, his legs stretched out in front of him, his dinner—the latest offering from the local McDonald's—spread out beside him. The news filled the TV screen with the usual murder and mayhem. Some things didn't change, no matter what city you were in.

Finally the report focused on the subject that interested him. A picture of Billy appeared in the corner of the screen above and to the right of the anchorwoman's head. If the news report could be believed, the police's preliminary report assumed Billy's death to be an accident. No surprise there, given Billy's penchant for crashing, burning, and otherwise mangling expensive pieces of machinery, most often with himself inside them. He had to be the unluckiest guy in America, or somebody had it in for him.

That was the crux of it, the suspicion that had brought him to Samantha Hathaway's room that morning, the bug that had been successfully planted in his ear less than twenty-four hours ago by none other than Jarad Naughton.

He'd been packing, getting ready for the inevitable trip to California, when his doorbell had rung.

Disgruntled, already in a foul mood, he'd opened the door to find a stranger standing before him. Dressed in a navy sport coat and khaki trousers, he looked like one of his neighbor's clients. He didn't know what kind of business Rhonda was running over there, but as far as he was concerned, he didn't need to know. He operated on a strict "don't ask, don't tell" policy with his neighbors.

"If you're looking for Rhonda, she's in apartment eight-F."

"If you're Adam Wexler, I'm looking for you. I'm Jarad Naughton."

The name sounded vaguely familiar, but right now he wasn't in the mood for guessing games. He stared at the hand the man extended toward him, but made no move to shake it. "I'm kinda busy right now, so I'll speed this up. I'm not looking to buy anything, sell anything, or have my kitchen remodeled. I like my phone service the way it is, and I already have insurance. Did I hit you somewhere in there?"

"I wanted to talk to you about your brother."

It was a struggle to keep his features immobile, to give away nothing. That was the last answer he would have expected. Though not a state secret, few people knew of his fraternal connection to Billy. How did this man know? "What about him?"

"Can I come in?"

Adam stepped back, allowed the other man to enter, then closed the door. He waited as the other man's gaze scanned the disarray of his living room, the beer cans that, in a moment of artistic inspiration, he'd piled into a pyramid atop his coffee table. "What did you want to tell me about Billy?"

"First, let me offer you my condolences. I worked with your brother a while back—"

"And?" Adam interjected. He recognized the look of someone searching unsuccessfully for something nice to say.

"And my friend Samantha Hathaway was the woman in the car with him. I'm afraid the police will dismiss it as an accident. That means they aren't going to offer Sam any protection."

"Why would they, if it was an accident?"

"I'm not so sure it was. Due to the fire, tests will probably be inconclusive as to whether the car had been tampered with."

"If it had been, that would point more to someone wanting to harm Billy than Ms. Hathaway. They were in his car."

"All the more reason for you to want to be involved."

Adam gritted his teeth. Score two points for the man in the khaki pants. He'd walked right into that one. "What kind of involvement are you talking about?"

"I need someone to look after Sam. She's all alone out there, and I can't go. My wife is about to deliver any day now. I can pay you whatever you ask."

Inwardly, Adam stiffened. "I don't need your money, Mr. Naughton. And I'm not a baby-sitter. I'm a New York City detective. If you're so worried about your friend, why don't you hire some L.A. muscle to look out for her?"

"Because if she so much as smelled bodyguard on the man, she'd send him packing. She's very independent."

"Look, Mr. Naughton, I appreciate the offer, but Billy was on a self-destruction kick long before you ever met him. If it weren't this, it would have been something else. I've got better things to do with my time."

"Like what?" He gestured in a way that encompassed the room. "Sit around here drinking beer and wondering, Why me? I know you are on disability leave right now, and an investigation of your last assignment is pending."

His last assignment. He made it sound like something out of *Mission Impossible*. It wasn't an assignment; it was a bust, one that self-destructed as surely as one of Mr. Phelps's weekly instruction tapes. In their own way, everyone involved was paying the consequences for it.

"Find somebody else. If you want to know how good I am at protecting women, why don't you ask my ex-partner? She's accepting interviews at Woodlawn Cemetery. No lines. No waiting."

"I read the newspaper reports of what happened. It seems to me your partner was little more than a rookie who barely passed the height requirements to get on the force. She had something to prove and rushed into a dangerous situation while you kept your head."

Adam snorted. Leave it to the media to give the public an accurate picture of police operations. "How much do you want to bet she wishes I were a little less cautious and she were a little less dead?"

"Your captain doesn't think it's such a bad idea. In fact, he recommended you for the job."

Adam shoved his hands in his jeans' front pockets and rocked back on his heels. "Did he now?" Considering the brouhaha presently playing out in the media, he doubted Captain Fowler would mind if he were shipped to Timbuktu right now. Anywhere where he couldn't incite a reporter's curiosity. His last "assignment" had left a thirteen-year-old kid and a member of one of the oldest police families in the city DOA. If there was any hell to pay for that fiasco, Adam was the only one left standing to pay it. "How did my name come up in the conversation?"

"I'm set to shoot a film set in the Bronx, the story of a female police officer. I need someone to help Sam get ready for the role. And since you were on your way to California already . . ."

"You figured I wouldn't mind extending my stay to accommodate you."

"Something like that. Sam was in your brother's car."

Adam shook his head. "I'm not responsible for my brother's actions."

"Maybe not, but the fact is, Sam needs your help."

"The fact is, you want me to rearrange my whole life for some bimbo Billy probably should have known better than to hook up with in the first place."

"Use that word and Sam's name in the same sentence again, and you'll be able to interview your partner face-to-face."

For the first time in days, Adam felt a smile lift the corners of his mouth. "Are *you* threatening *me?*"

"If that's what it takes."

Adam shook his head. The guy had guts; he'd give him that. But the intensity of his words bespoke more than a casual relationship between director and star. If he did what this man wanted, what exactly would he be walking into? "What is she to you?"

"Sam is my best friend. She's more than that. When she was sixteen, her father died and my family took her in. Her mother had died a couple of years before that. She didn't have anyone else. She's like a kid sister to me. She needs me, and I can't be there. You know how that feels?"

Grudgingly, he admitted, "Yeah." Every time he heard about some stupid thing Billy had done. The shrink on the job said Billy's extreme lifestyle was a call for help. Most of the time Adam had been too busy or too fed up to answer.

"All I'm asking is that when you go out there, see how she's doing, see what you can find out. Maybe I'm being paranoid. Maybe I'm worrying over nothing. But I feel in my gut that something isn't right with her. I can't just sit here and do nothing."

Unable to resist, he asked the obvious question: "Why me?"

"Because I trust you."

That raised Adam's eyebrows a fraction of an inch. "Mind if I ask why that is?"

"For one thing, you're Billy's brother. I assume you'd want to get at the truth."

"And the other thing?"

"You don't have anything to lose."

He had that right. Adam sighed. If someone had succeeded in killing his brother, he did want to know about it. He wanted to make them pay. But knowing Billy, the only person to blame was himself. "I tell you what; I'll visit Ms. Hathaway, make sure she's all right. If I decide to stay, then we'll talk."

A picture of Samantha Hathaway flashed across the television screen, drawing Adam back into the present. She was hawking that lipstick she sponsored. He didn't know what brand. He never got past looking at her, listening to her saying that one line he could recite in his sleep: "Make your lips feel wonderful!"

It was a play on a movie role she'd had a few years back. She'd played a waitress, and in one scene she'd been behind the counter putting on her lipstick. His brother, her costar, had asked her how she could get it on so flawlessly without checking in a mirror. She'd answered that she knew what her lips felt like. The way she'd said it was a dare to kiss her, and on-screen his brother had done just that.

Adam must have watched that movie a dozen times on videotape. Or a certain scene of it, anyway. One of the cops at the precinct had pointed out that if you watched in very slow motion this one scene where she was startled while dressing, you could see one of her breasts. It took a cop, or a genuine pervert, to ferret out stuff like that. He'd tried it, just out of curiosity, he'd told himself. She whirled around and her hair lifted from her shoulders, and there it was. A very nice breast—firm, rounded, with a large, dark areola the color of unsweetened chocolate.

In his heart of hearts, he had to admit he had his own little obsession thing going for Ms. Samantha Hathaway. Nothing that would stand in his way or cause him to make an ass of himself. The attraction was purely physical. He knew the kind of women his brother dated. Billy had always been more concerned with what was between a woman's thighs than what was between her ears. Despite her friend's insistence to the contrary, he couldn't imagine this Sam being much different. But it didn't hurt a man to fantasize, did it?

Not much, anyway. But in his mind's eye, the most compelling image of her was of her face contorted with grief upon hearing that Billy was dead. She had loved his brother, a feat he hadn't always managed himself. If she was in trouble, he couldn't turn his back on her.

He picked up the hotel phone, dialed the number he already knew by heart, and waited. When the other end was picked up, he barked two words into the phone; "I'm staying."

Two

Standing at the precipice, Adam focused the zoom lens of his 35-millimeter camera and rattled off a few shots of the charred woods and shrubbery that marked the spot where Billy Prescott had met his end. Adam shifted, turning to his right to photograph the rocky ledge that lay a few feet below. Samantha Hathaway's landing there, as well as her surviving without a single broken bone, were equally miraculous.

Sighing, Adam lowered the camera. Aside from the burned shrubbery, there was nothing here: no guardrail to possibly forestall the accident, not even a skid mark to denote that Billy knew what was about to happen. Due to Billy's notoriety and history of substance abuse, an autopsy had been performed posthaste. The ME hadn't turned up so much as a trace of drugs or alcohol in Billy's system to explain such a tragic end.

So why hadn't he tried to stop, to turn? Had he been so preoccupied with his lovely passenger that even impending death hadn't drawn his attention back to the road?

Or maybe he hadn't been able to stop.

A familiar nervous energy crackled through Adam, a sure sign that he'd stumbled onto something that bore further investigation. Jarad Naughton's words came back to haunt him. Adam understood gut reactions. In the fifteen years he'd been a policeman, those instinctive feelings had proved right often enough for him not to doubt them. And right now his gut told him that more existed to Billy's death than the scene before him could explain.

Adam huffed out a breath. He'd wasted enough time here. Only one person could give him the answers he needed as to the last moments of Billy's life. His need to know had nothing to do with the cop in him and everything to do with the brother in him, the part of him eaten up by guilt and sorrow. If he'd reached out to Billy just one more time, would that have been the instance that made a difference? He didn't know and he would never know. It was time for him to go.

He wasn't supposed to be here now, anyway. He was supposed to be at the elaborate funeral planned to mark his brother's passing. Someone had "leaked" the time and location of the service to the press. The last Adam had heard, hundreds of Billy's fans, almost all female, had lined up outside the church hoping to get inside. Adam could do without that sort of scene, or the inevitable platitudes and falsehoods that would be spouted about Billy's short and tragic life.

What was it about death that made everyone so forgiving? Why couldn't people simply say, "The guy was no angel, but we loved him," and leave it at that? Adam knew what Billy was and what he was not; that was enough for him.

After taking one last look at the landscape below, Adam turned toward the tiny red sports car he'd rented—the last remaining unclaimed car, according to the girl at the Hertz counter. Such a car, which lacked an antitheft deterrent of any kind, wouldn't last two minutes on the streets of New York before some enterprising youth stole it outright or stripped it for parts. In broad daylight.

Adam stowed the camera in the trunk of the car, then folded himself into the most comfortable position he could manage and started the ignition. He had just enough time to make it to Foxwood Cemetery for whatever brief ceremony would take place at Billy's burial site.

A crowd of women mobbed the outside gate, demanding entrance, but only a select group of mourners stood on the hillside grave site where Billy would be interred. Adam walked up the slight incline, his eyes focused on one woman as he advanced. He sensed her awareness of him as he drew closer, but she didn't acknowledge him. She continued her conversation with the woman beside her. She wore a navy blue silk dress. The sapphire-and-diamond jewelry that adorned her ears and throat could pay his salary for a good five years.

He stopped right in front of her, towering over her five-foot-six-inch frame. He waited until she deigned to throw a glance up at him.

"Hello, Mother," he said.

She pressed her lips together the way some women do after applying lipstick. Long ago, he'd learned that was a sign of disgruntlement on her part. Then she squared her shoulders and glared up at him, resting one hand on her hip. "You didn't come to the funeral."

Adam snorted. Rather than an accusation of a lack of brotherly devotion, her words served as a reprimand for dashing her hopes that he'd stay away altogether.

"It's good to see you, too."

She pursed her lips, glancing around at the other mourners gathered around them. "Don't embarrass me, Adam."

"I wouldn't dream of it." His gaze slid to the woman standing beside his mother, sensing an anxiousness in her to catch his attention. A mousy thing with nondescript brown hair and dark brown eyes that lacked the sparkle of an intelligent mind, she offered him a faint, tremulous smile. "Hello, Adam."

He said nothing, only nodded. He'd never met her before, but he knew of her, Sandra Something-or-other, and the four-year-old child who stood beside her. His gaze traveled over the little girl. How could anyone look at this child and not know Billy had fathered her? She had the same dark brown eyes shaded by long lashes that curled up at the tips, the same square-shaped face and cleft in her chin. Her hair was the same jet black, styled into two pigtails at either side of her head. She was a beautiful child, but then he doubted his brother capable of siring anything less.

He squatted down next to her and held out his hand. "Hi, sweetheart. I'm your uncle Adam."

Predictably, she scooted behind her mother's legs, only her forehead and eyes peeking out at him. Her little mouth formed one word: "Big."

Adam grinned. At least the kid was on the ball.

"Leave the child alone, before you frighten her to death."

That imperious command came from his mother. Slowly and with purpose, Adam rose to his full height. He glanced around the well-tended cemetery with its nearby duck pond and ornate headstones, then down at his mother. "This is some eternal resting place you've got picked out. But last I heard, Billy wanted to be cremated."

She swallowed and looked away from him. "Under the circumstances, I thought it would be a bit morbid."

"Not to mention redundant."

She glared up at him, her hand flexing at her side, as if she longed to slap him. If they'd been alone, she probably would have slapped him. Part of him wished she would. It would be the most emotion she'd shown toward him in his lifetime. Whatever maternal feeling she possessed extended only to Billy, the lone child produced by her second marriage to famed defense attorney Barrington Prescott.

But Adam knew she'd never resort to something as mundane as violence here in the presence of the rich, the glamorous, and those intimately connected with the local television stations. Despite never having held an acting job in her life, Adele Wexler Prescott was always "on," always conscious of the impression she left on those around her.

A tall, gray-haired man wearing a stark black suit and tie approached them. Adam hadn't seen Barrington Prescott face-to-face in a good ten years, but he recognized him immediately from his occasional stint on the nightly news when the clients he represented were of the particularly heinous type: the type Adam worked equally hard to put in jail.

Prescott reached Adele's side and draped an arm around her waist. He extended his right hand toward Adam. "It's good to see you, son."

"Thank you." Adam shook the extended hand. Although Prescott had never tried to exert much of a paternal influence over him, a call from the older man's secretary had kept Adam from finding out about Billy's death on the nightly news.

"Will you be stopping by the house later?"

"No. I have something I need to take care of."

Automatically, Adam's gaze slid to his mother, and the expression of profound relief that flooded her features. He shook his head, wondering how a man like Barrington Prescott, known as "the Barracuda" in legal circles, had managed to stay married to his mother for more than thirty years. Maybe his mother possessed charms a son would have no cause to know about.

Prescott lifted his shoulders slightly as his hand tightened on Adele's waist. "It looks like we're about to start."

Adam hung back while the others gathered around the casket and the minister began to speak. Adam tuned him out, focusing on the steel-gray casket suspended over the artfully concealed open grave.

"Good-bye, Billy," he whispered, but he knew his presence here had nothing to do with his brother. He'd come to see her, his mother. In some secret place, he'd wondered if the loss of her golden child had changed her feelings toward him. He didn't know why after all this time it mattered to him, but it did.

But since Billy's death changed nothing between them, he no longer had a reason to stay. He turned and silently walked back to his car and drove away.

"Lupe, would you please stop fussing over me." Sam shifted as Lupe shoved another pillow behind her back, then gritted her teeth as pain shot through her left shoulder. "I am not an invalid, you know."

Lupe snorted and frowned, continuing to adjust the pillows behind Sam's back. That was Lupe: never one to waste words when a gesture or an expression would do. At the moment, Sam wasn't in much of a position to argue the point. In the past two days, the swelling in her face had gone down considerably, but it had taken all her skill with a makeup brush to conceal the remnants of the bruises that marred her face. If it weren't for Jarad's trainer showing up any minute now, she'd have spent the afternoon in bed.

Lupe placed a large cushion on the coffee table in front of Sam, propping her injured ankle on the table. "Don't you have a meal to prepare or something?"

Lupe straightened, adjusting the white apron that covered her pale yellow uniform—a garment uniquely unsuited to Lupe's olive complexion and jet-black hair. But Lupe insisted that if she were going to play the role of housekeeper, she was going to look like one, too. Sam had given up arguing with her a long time ago.

"Why should I worry about lunch when you didn't touch your breakfast?"

"I wasn't hungry this morning." Truthfully, she hadn't had much desire to eat, much desire to do anything, since she'd woken up in the hospital to find out Billy had died.

Lupe rolled her eyes, then settled her gaze on the stack of notes Sam had written to the fans who had wished her well during her stay in the hospital. Sam had donated the gifts and flowers to the hospital to be distributed to the other patients. That left her with the task of signing the countless thank-you notes she'd had printed up.

"Why don't you let that fancy secretary of yours do that?"

David could sign her name better than she could, but Sam felt an obligation to answer her fans personally, at least with her own signature. Some of these people were very devoted to her and had spent hundreds of dollars on gifts they probably could ill afford to part with. She placed the fingers of her injured arm to hold a note in place so she could write with her good one. "No one sent anything to David: they sent it to me."

Lupe frowned and gave one last pat to the pillow underneath Sam's foot. "I hope you're in the mood for fish, because that's what we're having."

After Lupe left, Sam leaned back against her pillows. If it didn't hurt so much to simply breathe, she'd probably give in to the urge to pace the floor, an activity completely alien to her.

Sighing, she set her pen down next to the stack of stationery at her side. She should have been at Billy's funeral that morning. She should have said good-bye. She owed him that much. But she'd spent the morning waiting for her doctor to show up to check her out one last time before discharging her from the hospital. If it hadn't been for Lupe's threatening her with further bodily harm, she'd have left anyway, against medical advice. Sometimes Lupe's overprotectiveness could be a pain in the neck.

So now she sat here, trying to busy herself with note writing to keep her mind from focusing on what really bothered her. Unfortunately, it wasn't much of a distraction. Only a twist of fate—Billy wearing his seat belt the one time she hadn't—had saved her from meeting the same fate he had. Only a fluke—her being thrown from the car—allowed her to be here, now, instead of in a hole in the ground, like Billy. What few injuries she'd suffered were a small price for her life.

The sound of the doorbell chiming reached her. Sam pushed her morbid thoughts from her mind and straightened the white caftan she wore. Concern for her appearance was a habit borne of a lifetime in the public eye. If you didn't look good, you didn't work. Hollywood was one of the few places where un-mitigated vanity was actually a career asset.

A few moments later, a mountain of a man strode into the room and stood before her. Lupe scurried in behind him like a chihuahua hot on a bulldog's trail. As Lupe came to stand beside her, she focused her gaze on his face. That and the slight crook-edness of his nose that suggested it had been broken.

Nonetheless, the man oozed sex appeal like a fountain spouted water. The ill-fitting black suit he wore accentuated rather than camouflaged the muscular body beneath it.

For an instant a crazy thought popped into her head. Last Christmas she'd hired a "secret Santa" to deliver her gifts to Jarad and his family on Martha's Vineyard. At least, she'd thought she'd hired a "secret Santa." What had arrived was a "stripping Santa." The poor man had barely made it out of the house alive. But in Sam's mind, anyone idiotic enough to start disrobing in a room full of children deserved what they got. Returning the favor would have fit with Jarad's skewed sense of humor.

But the expression in this man's dark eyes—a cool, steady gaze that gave away nothing—sent a shiver through her. With his dark clothing and shaved head, he reminded her of a bullet: cold, hard, and deadly. Whoever this man was, she doubted shaking his money maker was on the agenda.

"How can I help you, Mr. . . ."

"Wexler. Adam Wexler. Jarad Naughton sent me."

"To do what?"

"I understand you have a movie role to prepare for."

Sam almost laughed. This behemoth was going to help her prepare for a movie role portraying a *female* police officer? Not bloody likely.

No wonder she'd detected a hint of amusement in Jarad's voice when she'd said, "No Helgas." He'd never had any intention of sending a woman at all. And only one reason for Jarad's sending a man when a woman would serve so much better popped into Sam's mind: He wasn't here to train her, but to protect her. As enlightened as Jarad might be about some things, he would still assume that a man would better suit that job. But what exactly did he seek to protect her from?

"If this is some sort of joke, it's not funny."

"There's no joke, Ms. Hathaway. Jarad Naughton asked me to—"

"Please, Mr. Wexler," she cut him off. "Spare me." She brushed her hair over her shoulder with her good hand in a distracted motion. "I regret whatever time and trouble you've gone through to come here, but I won't be needing your . . . services, shall we say. And don't worry about your money. I'll make sure Jarad pays you every cent he promised you." She glanced at Lupe. "Please show Mr. Wexler to the front door."

"Look, Ms. Hathaway, I *am* a New York City detective, and I *am* here to help you. If you have a problem with that, maybe *you* should take that up with Mr. Naughton."

She didn't miss his implication that he didn't recognize her power to fire him. Knowing that, she didn't made her eyes narrow and her back stiffen. "I intend to." She gestured toward her foot. "Unfortunately, I'm not as mobile as I'd like to be at the moment. If you'll excuse me, I will get this straightened out." She glanced at Lupe. "Please show Mr. Wexler to the green room."

A faint smile graced Lupe's face as she gestured toward Adam Wexler. "This way."

As soon as they'd left the room, Sam picked up the cordless phone that sat on the end table next to the sofa. She pressed the speed-dial number that would connect her to Jarad's house in New York.

"Hello?"

Hearing Ariel's cheerful voice on the other end of the line, Sam gritted her teeth. Ariel would want to chat, and Sam was not in the mood for small talk. "Hi, Ari. Is Jarad home?"

"He took the girls to the movies. I take it you met Adam Wexler."

"How did you know?"

"You spoke to Jarad this morning. You had no reason to call back unless something new happened. How are you two getting along?"

"We're not. Who exactly is this man?"

"He's an NYPD detective. From a precinct in the Bronx, I think. Not too hard on the eyes, either."

Without thinking, Sam said, "For a minute I thought your husband was trying to pay me back for the fiasco at Christmas."

"Now there's an idea," Ariel chimed in. "Any woman lucky enough to get Adam Wexler to take off his clothes would certainly get an eyeful."

For one brief moment, Sam let her mind conjure up an image of a very nude, very virile Adam Wexler. But only for a moment. In a teasing voice, Sam asked, "Ariel Naughton, does your husband know you fantasize about other men?"

"I am married, not dead, which you would have to be not to notice that man. Besides, I've only seen his picture in the newspaper. You have him there in flesh and blood."

Ariel let her words hang there, obviously waiting for Sam's appraisal of Adam Wexler. Not on her life would she venture further in that direction. She'd made the mistake of throwing Ariel a crumb of information, and her analytical mind had cooked it up into a gourmet meal. "That's exactly the problem," she said finally.

"What do you mean?"

"No way do I believe Jarad expects that man to help me prepare for a role playing a *female* police officer. You and I both know a female officer's motivations and daily experiences would be far different from a male's, which is what I need to tap into to understand my character. Mr. Wexler might be a cop, but he has *bodyguard* written all over him. I'm not in any danger."

Ariel sighed. "I know that and you know that, but try telling that to Jarad. He's been a total pain in the neck ever since the accident. Personally, I think his guilt about not being there with you is making him paranoid."

"Is that a professional opinion?"

"No, just a wife's observation."

"Did you know about this?"

"Only after the fact. For the record, I don't agree with him sandbagging you like that."

"Then you won't mind informing your husband that I gave Adam Wexler his walking papers."

"Actually, I would." Ariel sighed. "Sam, there's something we haven't told anyone else because we didn't want them to worry. I'm expecting twins again. It appears that's the only thing my husband knows how to make."

Remembering Ariel's difficult recovery from the first set of twins, Sam asked, "Are you okay?"

"I'm fine, but please, for my sake, let Jarad have his way this time. I know I'd be furious with him, too, but between worrying about the babies and his guilt that he can't be there with you, he's driving us all crazy."

Sam rolled her eyes. She knew when she was licked. "All right. All right. You win. I will give the man two weeks. If no one's tried to bludgeon me or drown me in my swimming pool, he goes home."

"Fair enough. I'm glad you gave in so easily. It's bad luck to refuse a pregnant lady anything. I wouldn't want anything to happen to you on my account."

Sam snorted, knowing just how unsuperstitious Ariel was. "Anything else I can do for you, pregnant lady, while I'm at it?"

"You can let Adam stay with you while he's there."

Sam stiffened. "No way." Allowing the man to check up on her was one thing. Having a man underfoot was another. Besides, Lupe would never stand for it. Lupe would lock herself in her room for the duration if she did that. Sam wasn't about to alienate her for some man she didn't know from Adam.

"Why not? Your guesthouse is lovely, maybe not to a man's tastes, but certainly large enough."

Sam exhaled. She hadn't thought of the little bungalow that adjoined her house. She couldn't remember the last time anyone had used it. Just airing out the place would probably take the better part of a day. "Is that all? Why don't I name my first child after him, too?"

"There's no need to be sarcastic about it."

"Of course not. You got what you wanted."

"Seriously, Sam, on the off chance that Jarad *isn't* wrong, be careful. Promise me you'll let Adam protect you if it should come to that."

Sam made a disgusted sound in her throat. Apparently both Jarad and Ariel had gone nuts. Though she had no intention of letting Adam Wexler do any such thing, she didn't want her friends to worry. "I promise."

"Thanks, Sam. I'll let Jarad know you called."

The line went dead. Sam clicked off the phone, certain Ariel had flexed her psychologist muscles to get Sam to agree to everything she wanted.

Sam groaned, letting her shoulders droop. Immediately, sharp pain flashed through her left side. Trembling slightly, she rose to her feet and headed toward the Green Room. Her ankle didn't hurt nearly as much as it had right after the accident. She hobbled two doors down the hallway to the green room, pausing in the doorway. Both Lupe, who hovered near the door, and Adam Wexler, who stood near the fireplace examining the selection of old photos arranged on the mantel, looked up at her.

"Lupe, Mr. Wexler will be staying in the guesthouse. Please see to getting it ready. Mr. Wexler, you are welcome to use any of our facilities, if you like. Lupe will give you a tour. If you'll excuse me, I'll be in the Angel Room."

Not waiting for a reaction from either of them, Sam pivoted on her good foot and headed down the hall.

Three

Adam glanced from Samantha Hathaway's receding back to the gilt-framed photograph in his hands. A young Samantha Hathaway smiled back at him—an image so different from the woman who had stood before him a moment ago. Her face bore an open, friendly demeanor, not the hauteur she exhibited today. And, if he wasn't mistaken, Samantha Hathaway's current packaging didn't include her original nose, either.

An image of Samantha Hathaway flashed in his mind, of the instant she'd looked up to see him walking toward her. Heavy makeup coated her skin, probably an attempt to camouflage the healing bruises that still marred her face. The white, gauzy thing she'd worn, combined with the brace on her left arm, completely concealed the shape of her body. Even her eyes were a different color, not the warm, inviting brown he'd grown used to, but a cool, pale amber. He would have been crazy to expect the siren of the silver screen to welcome him into her home, but aside from the auburn hair that skimmed her shoulders, physically she'd been nothing like he'd expected.

And besides that, the one brief kiss they'd shared in her hospital room had suggested a softness in her that he had yet to witness. She'd allowed him into her home, but hadn't so much as offered him a seat. Like a queen holding court, she'd kept him standing there, dismissing him when the whim pleased her. No one he knew, not even his captain, would dare treat him in such an offhand manner.

Despite his promise to Jarad Naughton, he'd walk right out

the front door and leave her to her own devices if he didn't need
to know what she knew about the last few minutes of Billy's
life. Having seen his mother that morning, he'd already reached
his quota of abuse from rich, spoiled women for the week.

Mentally, Adam shrugged and returned the photo to its place
on the mantel. What difference did any of that make, anyway?
He'd come here for two things: to help her prepare for her movie
role and to find out what he could from her about what had
really happened to Billy. Nothing else mattered.

But he supposed he'd learned his first lesson in Hollywood
politics: what the director says goes—even if the star is not
too happy with it. He'd have to remember that should Samantha Hathaway give him any trouble.

He glanced at the diminutive housekeeper. If it weren't for
the perpetual frown on her face and the severe way she'd pulled
her hair back into a bun, she might be pretty.

Just to be perverse, he rocked back on his heels and crossed
his arms in front of him. "I believe you owe me a tour."

She shrugged in a way that said the only thing she'd like to
show him was a view of the front door from the outside. "This
way."

Despite her obvious Hispanic heritage, her speech lacked
any noticeable accent. She led him out of the Green Room
down the wide hallway to the next room and opened the door.
"This is the Lotus Room."

Adam peered inside. Delicate black-lacquered furniture off-
set the pale peach walls. A pair of samurai swords and an
authentic-looking suit of Japanese armor dominated the far
wall. A low table surrounded by several large pillows commanded the center of the room. A curio housing a collection
of dolls in traditional dress stood in one corner; a life-size
statue wearing an elaborate red kimono stood in another.

Abruptly Lupe shut off the light. "Next is the music room,"
she informed him. She led him to a room across the hall and
opened the door. The room was dominated by a stark-white
grand piano. But there were other instruments as well. Most
were housed in glass cases, which suggested they'd been

bought for show, not play. But an open book of sheet music rested on the piano's music stand.

The housekeeper led him to several other rooms, each with its own name and distinctive decor. The entire house, or at least what he'd seen of it, spoke of understated opulence and the kind of wealth he could never acquire if he worked for the NYPD for a hundred years.

Was that the point of this tour he'd been foolish enough to insist upon? To put him in his place? To remind him he was a mere public servant and she a star? Not being able to fire him must have rankled her more than a little.

Adam stepped into the room. Every exercise machine imaginable, including a treadmill, a minitrampoline, and a pair of cycling machines, sat on the white-padded covered floor. A set of silver weights stood in a rack in one corner. All four walls were mirrored, their glass gleaming in the early-afternoon sunlight. It appeared Ms. Hathaway was as obsessed with looking at her image as was the rest of the population.

A small door on the other side of the room attracted his attention. "What does that lead to?"

Lupe glanced at him over her shoulder, then slowly opened the door. "The sauna and the indoor pool are downstairs."

"Where's the Angel Room?" he asked, to see what reaction he'd get out of her.

"You will not go there."

Her softly spoken words made him all the more curious. Especially since she turned and exited the room without bothering to turn out the light. He did so, then shut the door behind him.

She led him to the back of the house, through the solarium, to a set of double doors. A white stone path led from the doors and split several feet ahead. Neatly trimmed hedges obscured the view of what lay in either direction.

"To the right is the hot tub and the outdoor swimming pool. To the left is the guesthouse, which I must go make ready. If you want to eat, breakfast is at six o'clock sharp, dinner is twelve hours later, and lunch you can get on your own."

With that, she pushed through the doors and headed down the path to the left.

For a moment Adam watched her go, shaking his head. Her dislike of him had been immediate and intense from the moment she'd opened the door to find him on the doorstep. Did she greet every guest in the same manner, or was he the only one who merited such special treatment? If it was the former, it didn't surprise him that there wasn't a waiting list for Ms. Hathaway's guesthouse.

Adam shrugged. Staying on the Hathaway property was a boon he hadn't anticipated. Right now he needed to take care of a few things and get back. He'd worry about Ms. Hathaway's crazy housekeeper another time.

The first thing Adam did after leaving Samantha's house was to use his cell phone to call Jarad Naughton.

"Good afternoon, Detective," came Jarad's voice over the line.

"How did you know it was me?"

"The wonders of caller ID. How'd it go with Sam?"

"Didn't you talk to her?"

"No, my wife took the call. I take it you'll be moving into her guesthouse this afternoon."

"Something like that." Annoyed at the humor he heard in the other man's voice, he said, "I thought you were supposed to tell her about my coming."

"I did. But somehow she'd gotten the impression I'd be sending a woman."

Adam drew to a halt at a red light. Yeah, he'd bet that if Samantha Hathaway had that impression, Jarad Naughton had given it to her. No wonder she'd been surprised to see him show up at her door. "I'm sure she figured out my other purpose in coming out here."

"Sam's a smart girl. I'm sure she would have figured it out eventually. It's better this way, don't you think? Now everything is out in the open."

Not everything. Neither of them had told her about his being

Billy's brother or their now mutual suspicion that Billy had been the victim of foul play. He wondered if keeping that a secret was a mistake. Wouldn't she be more willing to cooperate if she thought she was helping one of Billy's relatives find his killer?

"There's one catch."

Why was he not surprised? "What's that?"

"She'll only give you two weeks."

It figured. Why make his life any easier? With any luck he'd have figured out what happened to Billy and be back on a plane to New York by then. "Not a problem."

Jarad cleared his throat. "You sure you won't take me up on the offer to at least pay your expenses while you're out there?"

"No, thanks. That would mean I worked for you. And frankly, I don't like the way you operate."

He disconnected the call and dialed the number of the only cop he knew in L.A. Adam had worked with Joe Martinez when both had been rookies at the Four-seven. A good guy, funny, fair, a little rough around the edges, but he could say that about half the cops he knew. Joe's wife had gotten a job with one of the studios out here, and Joe had done "the *Die Hard* thing," as he put it and left New York. Joe wasn't in, but Adam left a message for him to call, then eased into freeway traffic that would take him to his hotel.

Lying on the divan in her Angel Room, Sam opened her eyes slowly, sensing the presence of someone else in the room. Her gaze settled on the opening doorway and Lupe's hunched figure peering in at her. "Are you awake?" Lupe asked in a hushed voice.

"I am now." Sam stretched as best she could with one good arm.

"Want me to let you sleep?"

Sam shook her head. She'd come here, to her sanctuary, to think and to put the last few days into some sort of perspective in her mind. But not two seconds after she'd lain down, she'd fallen asleep, to dream of something vague and threatening. That in itself disturbed her. Usually nothing touched her in this room, the one place where she felt totally safe, totally at peace. "It's all right. I have to get up anyway. Richard is coming for dinner."

In less than an hour, Richard Russell, her business manager and longtime family friend, would be here. Richard had been out of the country at the time of her accident and insisted in his fatherly way that she allow him to come over and make sure she was okay.

Lupe clomped to the windows and threw open the curtains. Late-afternoon sunlight washed into the room, making Sam squint until her eyes adjusted.

"Which one is that?" Lupe nodded toward Sam's lap.

Sam looked down, using; her right hand to pick up the figurine cocooned in the folds of her gown. She ran her thumb over the crystal Cupid perched on a rock made of solid platinum. The eighteen-carat gold bow and arrow in his hands gleamed in the sunlight.

Billy had given it to her the day he'd proposed. A small, rueful smile crossed her lips. Billy never did anything by half steps. He couldn't even die without creating a sensation. Billy had gone out in a literal blaze of glory—in all likelihood exactly the way he'd have wanted it.

"I don't like the look on your face," Lupe said.

Sam glanced up. "I'm not mooning over Billy, if that's what you think. It's just . . . I should have been there this morning to say goodbye to him. I owed him that much, didn't I?"

Lupe took the figurine from her fingers and plunked it in its place amidst the others. "I'm going to start your shower."

Sam sighed as Lupe headed into the adjoining bathroom.

Everyone she knew had expressed anger at Billy for nearly taking her to her death with him. Everyone believed he must have had something in his system his powerful father had bribed the coroner not to find. But she didn't blame Billy—not for that, anyway. A few bumps and bruises were a small price to pay for her life.

She wished she could remember. She wished her memory

hadn't snagged and robbed her of the last few minutes of Billy's life. The last thing she remembered was climbing into Billy's car and starting off on the road behind her house. He'd wanted to show her something, but what? Had he ever gotten the chance or had he sailed off the edge of the road before they'd arrived at their destination? She didn't know, and she would probably never know. The one person who could tell her had been buried that morning.

The sound of water running reached her, but she had no desire to get up. As much as she cared for Richard, she didn't want to see him, didn't want to see anyone, Lupe included. She wanted to be left alone. But that was impossible, not only because of Richard, but because Jarad had saddled her with Adam Wexler. She would put up with him for Jarad's and Ariel's sake, but at the moment, she couldn't care less about the movie role she'd once begged Jarad to award to her. She couldn't seem to care about anything.

She stood anyway, knowing that if she looked too helpless, Lupe would fuss over her like a mama hen with a recalcitrant chick. A certain amount of dependence had been forced on her since the accident, but she managed to undress herself, shower, and redress herself, this time in a burnt-orange caftan with an African print. But when she lifted her hand to run her brush through her hair, her body protested.

Lupe, who'd been standing over her the whole time, scowled at her, her perpetual expression of late. "Why don't you let me do that for you?"

"Because you are the Torquemada of hair care." Sam stuck her tongue out at Lupe in the mirror, but conceded the brush.

Lupe made a face in response and pulled the brush through Sam's hair.

"Ow," Sam protested. "Take it easy, would you? I'd like to have some hair left when you're through."

"What was it your mother used to say? 'Beauty knows no pain.' "

"Then I'd rather be ugly. Ouch!"

"You should be taking the medication the doctor gave you."

"I should be doing a lot of things. So should you. Is the guesthouse ready?"

Lupe tossed the brush onto the vanity. "Are you really going to let that man stay here?"

She considered telling Lupe what Ariel had said about Jarad and the babies, but decided against it. Apparently Lupe had bought that nonsense about Detective Wexler helping her with her movie role. Lupe would only worry more if she thought Sam was in any danger.

"I don't have much choice. You know how Jarad gets over his movies." Sam stood with a little of Lupe's help. "So is the house ready or not?"

"All except for the bedding. The tulle curtains are still on the windows. I wanted to know whether I should have the matching sheets put on the bed or if I should pick something else."

Then Sam remembered who'd last stayed in the little bungalow out back—her friend Winona, a soap-opera queen with a penchant for drama. Sam had redecorated with her friend's comfort in mind. For the first time in days a genuine smile formed on Samantha's face. Even petty revenge could sometimes prove sweet. "No, the matching sheets will be fine."

"Yes, boss," Lupe said, and for a moment, she smiled, too.

The sun had begun to set by the time Adam made his way back to Samantha Hathaway's house. His cell phone rang, playing the first few bars of the theme song from *Hawaii Five-O*. "Wexler," he said once he got the phone turned on and in place.

"Mr. Wexler, this is Alex Winters, Billy Prescott's attorney."

Adam stiffened. He had as much use for most lawyers as he had for a third eye in the middle of his forehead. "What can I do for you?"

"I need to meet with you to discuss the contents of your brother's will."

What a waste of time. At most, Billy had probably left him the Harley Adam had once admired—the only possession of Billy's Adam had ever coveted. "Why don't you stick whatever papers you need me to sign in an envelope and mail them to me?"

"I'm afraid not, Mr. Wexler. Can you meet me in my office tomorrow morning at nine?"

Resigned to the inevitable, Adam said, "Sure. Where is it?" The other man rattled off an address and directions, which Adam had committed to memory by the time he hung up. Having reached the turnoff for Samantha's house, he pulled into the front drive and parked behind a silver Mercedes. Apparently Samantha Hathaway was not alone.

Lupe greeted him at the door when he got back to Samantha's house, scowling at him as if he'd disappointed her by remembering the address.

"Where's Ms. Hathaway?" he asked, ignoring her animus.

"Ms. Sam is in the solarium."

"Thanks, Lupe. I know the way." He found Samantha on the same sofa she'd occupied earlier. A man sat beside her, his body facing hers, his hand draped on the back of the sofa. Judging by the gray hair at his temples and the lines around his eyes and mouth, Adam would put him in his early sixties. Neither of them noticed him.

"Ms. Hathaway."

Slowly, her head turned toward him. The man beside her stood, not as a gesture of politeness but as if to guard her from the intruder—a possessive gesture that made Adam wonder exactly what his relationship was to her.

From her spot on the couch, Samantha said, "Richard, this is Adam Wexler. Adam, this is Richard Russell, my business manager."

The older man extended his hand toward Adam. "Please, call me Dick. I'm here today in the capacity of family friend, not financial adviser."

Adam shook the man's hand, scrutinizing him. His breath smelled of alcohol and cigar smoke. But any grown man in this day and age who actually wanted people to call him Dick had bigger problems than halitosis.

"Okay, *Dick*," Adam said, not doing a great job of keeping the derision from his voice. He felt Samantha's eyes on him and shifted his gaze to look at her. She glared at him, but sent a glowing smile in Russell's direction.

"Adam is a New York City detective," Sam said. "He's here to help me get ready for my role in *Guardian Angel*."

"Really? A policeman?" Dick stuck his hands in his pants pockets. "Have you taken a look at the script yet? I'd be interested to know what you think."

For the life of him, he couldn't imagine why this man would give a rat's behind what he thought. He might just be making conversation, but Adam doubted it. Russell's lips bore a broad smile, but his eyes held the sort of slyness that bore watching. Crocodiles grinned while they ate their prey, too.

Sam said, "Adam just got here. He hasn't had time to review anything yet."

"I see." Dick returned to his seat on the sofa. "Will you be joining us for dinner?"

Adam met Samantha's gaze, looking at her in a way that said he left the decision up to her. For a moment she frowned at him, probably trying to come up with some excuse for him not to stay. Finally she waved toward one of the chairs, indicating he should sit. "I'm sure Lupe has made more than enough for all of us. In fact, if you'll excuse me, I'll see what's keeping dinner."

She rose from the sofa, demurring Russell's attempts at helping her. For a moment, Adam watched her walk away. Despite the slight hitch in her gait, her hips swayed provocatively, riveting his gaze to her. For a moment his mind filled with images of what she hid beneath the gown she wore.

Then Russell turned toward him, leaning forward as if to whisper to a coconspirator. "It makes your teeth hurt just to look at her, doesn't it?"

Adam sat back and crossed his arms over his chest, saying nothing. Yeah, even bruised from her accident and as frigid toward him as a full-blown nor'easter, Samantha Hathaway did something hot and wicked to his insides. But Russell was fishing, and Adam wouldn't give him the satisfaction of catching anything.

"Of course, Sam is like a daughter to me," Russell continued. "Her mother, Theresa, and I grew up together, and eventually her father and I became partners."

"So she said." Adam knew Russell's type, the kind of man who talked you to death, inviting confidences while he divulged none of his own.

"I'm sure you heard about the accident. I was no fan of Billy's, but he didn't deserve to go that way—and nearly take Sam with him on top of it." Russell glanced in the direction of the doorway. "I swear, I never knew what she saw in him. Despite being Barrington Prescott's son, he was never in her league."

For a moment Adam wondered if the man didn't somehow know about his connection to Billy and sought to provoke a response from him. But Russell rambled on without waiting for him to answer.

"What do you think of the way policemen are portrayed on-screen? What do you think is the most egregious error in portraying police activities?"

Adam leaned back in his chair. "I never really thought about it, Dick. I don't pay much attention to movies."

"The small screen then. What about the current lineup of police shows?"

Adam shrugged. "The way every crime is solved in one hour. The only crime I ever solved in an hour was who stole the stapler off my desk."

Russell made a creaky sound that could pass for a laugh. "Very funny, Detective, and quite true, I would guess. So what brings you out to California?"

"What do you mean?"

"Well, it doesn't seem you have much regard for what we do here. I wondered what motivated you to want to help Sam with her role."

"A profound desire to escape August in New York. The heat's not so bad, but the humidity will kill you."

Russell shook his head. "Now, *Detective*," he said, as if he were discussing some rare and reviled species of bug, "you don't expect me to believe that you were not a little taken with the idea of working with Samantha on such an intimate level?

You have no personal feelings about having access to one of the most beautiful women in Hollywood, if not the world?"

Adam leaned forward and rested his chin on his hand. For a man who professed to view Sam as a daughter, Russell had an odd preoccupation with her feminine charms. "My personal feelings are just that, Dick—mine and personal."

Russell sat back and crossed his legs, issuing another creaky laugh. "I didn't mean to pry, Detective. Both Jack and Theresa are gone. Sam has few people to look out for her interests. Sometimes she isn't as careful as she should be."

Adam assumed he was making another allusion to her involvement with Billy. Was this Russell's way of warning him off of any similar involvement with her? On that score, Russell didn't have a thing to worry about. He had as much intention of making a play for Samantha Hathaway as he did of winning a gold medal in rhythmic gymnastics. He liked his women warm, willing, and well endowed. From what he'd seen of the real-life Samantha Hathaway, she didn't fit in any category.

Lupe chose that moment to appear in the doorway. "Ms. Sam is waiting for you in the dining room."

"You're in for a treat." Russell smiled, as if the previous conversation had never taken place. "Lupe makes her crème brûlée whenever I come to dinner."

Sam sipped from her glass of wine, the only alcohol she allowed in her house. Lupe had prepared broiled salmon in a dill sauce with wild rice and asparagus as a main course. The meal was divine; the company left much to be desired.

Her gaze slid from Richard on her left to Adam on her right. Could she find two more different men to share her dinner? Richard was older, dressed in a hand-tailored suit, and Adam was younger, dressed casually in jeans and a black T-shirt. Richard was cultured, almost to the point of being effete; Adam exuded a sort of primal sexuality that called to her on some basic, unwelcome level. Involuntarily her gaze wandered to him time and again, riveted, for some unknown reason, to his arms and the powerful muscles that bulged there.

Richard blathered on about something she'd tuned out five minutes ago; she doubted if Adam had said five words since he'd sat down at the table. If Lupe didn't get in here with that blasted custard soon, she was going to scream.

Before she resorted to that, Adam Wexler saved her. He tossed his napkin on the table and pushed back his chair. "Don't think this hasn't been fun, but I need to get settled." With a nod to her, he rose from the table and left the room.

Sam envied him his easy escape. Knowing Richard, he'd prattle on for another half hour about nothing in particular while he savored a helping or two of custard. Dining with Richard was like being trapped in a bad *Frasier* episode with no hope of a commercial break.

"Is something the matter, Samantha?" Richard asked, drawing her attention. "You look drawn."

"I'm just tired, I guess." Despite the long nap that afternoon, she did feel ready to drop. "I guess I am not as recovered as I'd like to think I am."

Richard reached across the table and took one of her hands in both of his. His hands were soft and moist, comforting. "Of course you're not. You need your rest." He patted her hand. "I'll tell Lupe to make my crème brûlée to go, as long as you promise me you'll head straight to bed."

He'd get no argument from her there. "I promise."

"Good girl." He rose and placed a paternal kiss on her forehead. "Are you sure you'll be all right with that policeman staying here? I don't entirely trust him."

That made two of them. "I'll be fine. Besides, Lupe still has her shotgun."

Richard laughed. "All right, then. Call me if you need anything."

"I will."

As Richard left the room, Sam hid a yawn behind her hand. Normally she would have helped Lupe clear the table, but tonight she lacked both the wherewithal and the equipment to be of any use. She was about to rise from the table herself, when Adam Wexler appeared in the doorway. She took one last sip from her wineglass, wondering if he'd seen his sleeping accommodations yet.

She set down her empty glass. "What can I do for you, Mr. Wexler? I thought you were getting settled."

He folded his arms across his chest and leaned against the doorjamb. "That's a nice maneuver you pulled there."

Feigning innocence, she said, "What are you talking about?"

"Siccing your guard dog on me, while you retreated to another room. Very clever."

Sam blinked. "So clever, I didn't even know I'd done it. I repeat, what are you talking about?"

"I'll give him this; he does have a nice interrogation style: attack, circle around, and attack again. Unfortunately, he didn't get much information out of me, but I'm sure you already know that."

"You are delusional, Mr. Wexler. Richard is harmless, unless you consider someone boring you to death a hazard."

"If you wanted to know something about me, why didn't you ask me yourself?"

"The only thing I need to know about you is that you will be gone in two weeks. But while we are on the subject, why *are* you here? I didn't know the NYPD was in the habit of granting its officers summer vacations."

"They do if certain movie directors happen to be making a film that will portray New York City cops in a favorable light."

Was he implying that his presence here was somehow her fault? "So what did you do to get yourself exiled to the hinterlands of California? Sleep with your captain's daughter? Shoot the police commissioner in the foot?"

"Nothing so mundane as that."

"Somehow I didn't suspect it would be." Sam rose from her seat, leaning her weight on the ankle that didn't hurt. "Don't think *this* hasn't been fun, Detective, but I'm tired and I'm going to bed. I trust you will find some way to amuse yourself while you are here without disrupting my household."

She walked toward the door as gracefully as she could, hoping to slip past him and into her bed. As she reached him, his hand darted out to span the doorway, blocking her exit. She looked straight ahead, ignoring him.

"Despite what you think, I would like to help you."

"No, you are here to spy on me and report back to Jarad."

"Partly."

For the first time she glanced up at him. At least he hadn't lied to her and tried to deny it. He earned himself a couple of brownie points for that.

"I am also here to give you any help you need with your movie."

His voice was soft, deep, compelling, as were his eyes, a warm brown shaded by long, thick lashes that made them almost pretty and somehow familiar.

Sam blinked and took a step back. Detective Wexler didn't lack in the technique department himself. In another minute he would have had her believing he cared one way or another what happened to her. If he hadn't become a cop, she suspected he'd have made a great con man, the type who lured lonely women into parting with their life savings.

"The only thing I need right now is to be left alone."

He dropped his hand and she slipped past him. Remembering the fate that awaited him, she paused at the door to the Angel Room and turned to face him.

"One more thing. Sweet dreams." Then she disappeared inside.

Adam rubbed the back of his neck with his palm, wondering about the abrupt change in her mood. Then he shrugged, picked up his bag, and headed out the back door toward the guesthouse. He unlocked the door, groping along the wall for the light switch. Finding it, he flicked on the light.

His eyes widened, and it was an effort to keep his chin from dropping down to his chest. The walls, the carpet, and the curtains were various shades of pink. Delicate antique white furniture accented the combined living/sitting area, most prominently a king-size four-poster bed. A ruffled quilt and about a million frilly pillows covered the bed. A white flounced canopy hung overhead.

It was the most overdone display of femininity Adam had ever seen outside a drag queen's apartment he'd once raided for cocaine.

No wonder she'd smiled when she'd told him good-night. She knew what awaited him. He glanced back toward the house. A solitary figure stood at one of the upper windows, backlit by a lamp in the room. Definitely not Samantha. Lupe, then, observing him to report back to the boss.

Shaking his head, Adam closed the door behind him. No, Samantha Hathaway wasn't anything like he'd expected. Definitely not the bimbo he'd first suspected her of being. She had a brain and a sense of humor. She also had absolutely no use for him.

Honestly, he couldn't blame her. What competent, rational person would want someone dogging her every step and reporting back to another?

But he knew two things she didn't: He had no intention of going anywhere until he was certain what had happened to Billy, and he didn't plan on telling Jarad Naughton one thing.

Four

Alex Winters was exactly what you'd expect a high-powered attorney to be: wealthy, white, and wearing a hand-tailored suit that probably cost more than Adam's entire wardrobe. The only thing Adam had in common with this man was the same set of initials. Yet Winters welcomed him into his outer office with an effusiveness Adam found surprising.

"William has told me so much about you," Winters said, shaking his hand, "I feel like I know you. Please come in. The others are already here."

It took Adam a moment to realize who Winters meant. No one ever called Billy anything but Billy, except maybe their mother. "The others?"

"I called the whole family together. I didn't see any point in doing this more than once."

"Great," Adam muttered under his breath as he followed Winters. If he'd known, he would have stayed in bed, such as it was. No motorcycle was worth seeing his mother again so soon.

As they entered the room, Prescott stood. Sandra smiled up at him, while his mother did her best to avoid his gaze.

Winters gestured toward the only empty chair beside the one behind his desk. "If you'll have a seat, we can begin."

Winters sat, shuffled his papers for a moment, and began. "This is a task that gives me no pleasure. William was my friend as well as my client. I hope you all know you have my sincerest condolences on his untimely passing."

Adam nodded, more to move things along than anything else. He couldn't imagine what this man and his brother might have in common besides a hell of a bank account.

"Mr. and Mrs. Prescott, William has made provisions to donate two million dollars in your name to Actor's House, your charity of choice. He has also left you some personal articles, a list of which I will provide for you separately."

Adam looked from Prescott to his mother. Each of them nodded their response, but surprisingly his mother appeared moved to tears. Prescott handed her a handkerchief, which she used to dab her eyes. Had Billy disappointed her by not leaving her personally any portion of his fortune? He doubted even his mother could be that avaricious. Between Prescott's income and her own family's wealth, she certainly didn't want for money.

"Ms. Paige," Winters continued.

"Yes?"

Adam's gaze turned to Sandra. She sat up straighter, clutching the child in her arms more tightly.

"William has provided you with an allowance of twenty thousand dollars a month in perpetuity, the title for the house on Chatham Drive will be signed over to you, and he has set up an irrevocable trust for little Brianna in the amount of five million dollars."

Sandra shook her head. "I don't understand. An allowance? For what? An ir-revoking trust? What does that mean?"

Winters threaded a hand through his graying hair and spoke as if he were addressing four-year-old Brianna, instead of her mother. "The allowance is for your upkeep, my dear. To maintain you in the style to which you have become accustomed. The trust will secure Brianna's future. William has stipulated that the trust will be administered by the major beneficiary of the estate."

Adam froze as Winters's gaze came to rest on him. "That would be you, Mr. Wexler."

For a moment Adam said nothing, gripping the arms of his chair as the room and its occupants spun momentarily. When the world righted itself, he asked, "Would you mind running that by me again?"

Winters coughed, obviously trying to mask his own humor. "William has left the bulk of his estate to you, which includes roughly five million in liquid assets, several homes, interests in several businesses, a collection of antique auto—"

"Hold it." Adam put up his hand to halt any further recitation of Billy's property. Not only would Adam have sworn that Billy must have frittered away most of what he made with his extravagant lifestyle, finding himself the recipient of such largesse blew his mind. Two minutes ago he'd been a poor working stiff; now, if what Winters said could be believed, he was a multimillionaire. He needed a drink and he needed to lie down. It didn't matter in which order.

"There are some papers for each of you to sign in the other room," Adam heard Winters say through the fog that clouded his brain.

In a haze, he heard the others depart. He felt a masculine hand on his shoulder and heard Barrington's voice asking him to call. He barely registered nodding in response to that or answering Sandra's whispered good-bye.

Adam pressed the heels of his hands to his eyes. Why had Billy done this? He'd never taken a cent of Billy's money while he was alive. Now Billy had foisted it on him from the grave. Billy had to know that Adam was a cop through and through. As much as he might complain about the long hours, the hard work, the lack of respect he encountered from the very people he was supposed to protect and serve, he didn't want to be anything else. Having that much money changed things. The force wasn't chock-full of millionaire cops, rich guys who just wanted to do their civic duty.

"You look like you could use this."

Adam lifted his head to find Alex Winters standing beside him, holding out a glass of what looked like scotch. Adam downed three quarters of it in one gulp. Since he hadn't bothered to eat breakfast that morning, it burned all the way down and settled in his stomach like a banking flame. "Thanks." He set the glass on Winters's desk. "Sorry to take up so much of your time."

"Think nothing of it, Mr. Wexler. Believe me, I've seen all

kinds of reactions to sudden wealth, and yours is one of the mildest."

Adam snorted. He supposed abject shock beat full-blown hysteria any day. "What if I don't want it? What if I don't want Billy's money?"

"Have you ever heard of Marcus Roundtree?"

"Who hasn't?" Marcus and his brother Samuel went on a crime spree in the Midwest that left four policemen and more than a dozen civilians either wounded or dead. Samuel had been killed in the takedown. Marcus was on death row appealing his conviction once again. But what did either brother have to do with Billy?

"If you renounce your portion of the estate, every cent of it, including the donation to your mother's charity and the allowance for the girl's mother, goes to Marcus Roundtree's defense fund. The only thing unchanged is the trust for the little girl, which you would still have to administer."

Adam's throat worked, but no words that didn't contain four letters seemed to want to make it out of his mouth. Finally, with a disgusted sound in his throat, he gave up.

Winters chuckled. "You seem to think of this as some sort of punishment. It isn't. Your brother thought very highly of you, Mr. Wexler. I don't know if you know this, but Billy kept a scrapbook of your exploits, starting with the day you were inducted into the police force. He wanted you to have it."

Winters pulled out the side drawer of his desk and extracted a thick white envelope. He extended it toward Adam.

"Thank you." Adam took it and laid it across his lap. He was tempted to look at it, but wondering what memento Billy might have been able to cull from his last, disastrous assignment kept him from opening it.

"Think about it, Mr. Wexler. Either you accept your brother's fortune and do with it what you like, or it ends up in the hands of a killer."

Some choice. But he supposed his younger brother knew him better than he'd thought. Billy had known Adam would want to refuse his money, and how much it would kill him to see it go to someone like Roundtree. But Adam wasn't ready to commit himself to taking it, either. He stood, clutching the envelope in one hand. "I'm sure you'll understand if I take some time to think about this."

Winters nodded, rising. "But not too long. I can't proceed with anything else until I know what you're going to do."

Adam shook Winters hand, thanked him again for his time, and turned to leave.

"Maybe I shouldn't tell you this, but if Billy had lived another two days, the point would have been moot."

"What do you mean?"

"Billy had drafted another will; all he had to do was come in and sign it. In it, he provided for you generously, but another person was named the major beneficiary."

"Who?"

"I'm sure that if you don't know her, you know of her. His former fiancée, Samantha Hathaway."

Adam drove back to Samantha's house, then pulled to a stop behind a white van parked in the drive. He kicked the car door closed. The very first thing he was going to do was buy a car he actually fit into.

He took the path around the house that led to the guest cottage rather than tramping through Samantha's house. He wasn't in the mood to see her anyway. He'd nearly needed another drink when Winters had told him she was Billy's intended beneficiary. Why would Billy have been about to make that change unless the two of them had reconciled?

He didn't know why that realization bothered him so much, but it did. He'd known her only one day, but Samantha struck him as too intelligent to buy into Billy's usual line of BS. What didn't Adam know about her that would lead her to commit to his brother, not once but twice?

Adam shrugged. Well, that let her off the hook as far as suspects went. Not only was she in the car at the time of the accident, which may have been nothing more than poor planning on her part, but she stood to lose a considerable fortune. If anything, the fact that Billy had intended to change his will

made Adam look more suspect; that was if he'd known anything about it.

"Damn, you, Billy," Adam muttered. What little buzz he'd
gotten from the drink in Winters's office had faded, leaving him
melancholy. That and the package he held in his hands. He sat
on the bed and slid the album from the envelope. *My brother,
the cop,* was written in gold script letters across the black surface. Underneath the words, a picture of himself in dress blues
the day he'd taken the oath stared back at him. He hadn't even
thought about that picture in years. It surprised him that Billy
had held onto it all this time.

Adam opened the cover to reveal a page that read, *The Early
Years,* in the same fluid script. A half dozen photos surrounded
the words, ones taken those few summers when he and Billy
were boys and Prescott had talked his father into letting Adam
stay with them for a couple of weeks. Those were good times,
good memories, even though he'd known Billy was the one their
mother bought presents for, focused her attention on, praised
and petted, all while he looked on silent and uncomplaining.
He certainly hadn't understood then how she could love one
son so lavishly while abandoning the other. Even today, he
couldn't fathom what he had ever done to make her hate him.

Maybe he wasn't supposed to understand it. Maybe it was
like having big feet or diabetes: an unpleasant fact you simply
had to learn to deal with.

Adam's cell phone rang, ending his opportunity for reflection.

"Wexler."

Joe Martinez's jovial voice crackled over the line. "Hey, bro.
How's it hanging?"

"Not too bad. And you?"

"Así así. What brings you out to La La Land? Man, you
hate this place."

"Long story. Can I meet you somewhere?"

"I'm on my way home, but I can make a detour. You know
where Bailey's is?"

"I can find it."

"Where are you coming from?"

"The Hills."

"Excuuuuse me. Sounds like you got yourself a sugar mama out here."

"I wish. Tell me how to get there."

Joe rattled off the directions. "See you in twenty minutes."

Adam clicked off the phone and reattached it to his waistband. Before he left, he wanted to check on Samantha. He entered her house through the back door. As he did so, he noticed that the alarm panel on the side of the door had been switched off. He hadn't noticed that before, nor had he bothered to check the property either—slipshod police work on his part. If anyone were trying to get to Samantha, they could slip in right under his nose. He'd have to talk to Samantha about taking her safety more seriously.

Adam followed the dull hum of a vacuum being run to the front of the house. He expected to find Lupe cleaning the carpet in the large front room. Instead he found her sitting on the sofa, her attention centered on the big-screen TV and a Julia Child look-alike demonstrating how to bake bread. Another woman, tall, blond, dressed in spandex shorts and a crop top, ran the vacuum.

"Lupe," he called over the noise of the machine.

Lupe started, rising to her feet, nervously brushing at the apron tied around her waist. "Yes?"

Humor rose in Adam. He supposed even crazy housekeepers didn't want to be caught loafing. "Where's your boss?"

"Ms. Sam is sleeping."

At two o'clock in the afternoon? He wondered if she'd gotten up at all or if she'd gone back to bed. "I'm going out for a while, but I'd like to talk to her when I get back."

Lupe nodded, docile for the first time since he'd known her.

He winked at her. "Don't worry. I won't tell her if you don't."

Adam let himself out of the front of the house, got into his toy car, and drove away.

Adam spotted Joe as soon as he walked into the restaurant. A smattering of gray salted Joe's jet-black hair, and he'd put on a few pounds, but the boyishness of his features hadn't changed. Joe rose from his seat at the bar as Adam approached. For a moment they indulged in the familiar male ritual of whacking each other on the back in what might pass for an embrace.

Reclaiming his seat, Joe asked, "Hey, man, what happened to your hair?"

Adam slid into the seat next to Joe's, resting his elbows on the bar. "I started working on that male-pattern thing, so it was either Rogaine or this."

"Yeah, right. Chicks don't go for that Homey the Clown look too much." Joe ran a hand through his hair. "I still have all mine, just a lot grayer."

"How's Sheila?" Adam asked, inquiring about Joe's wife.

"I wouldn't know. Six months after we got here she divorced me. Took up with some actor who plays a cop on TV. Go figure. But you didn't get me out here to discuss my love life."

The bartender came over and each of them ordered a beer. Adam took a long draft of his before speaking. "Are you familiar with the Prescott case?"

Joe shrugged. "Who isn't? As far as I know, the case is officially open, but not active. It didn't make the Sunday papers or anything, but Billy got picked up a few times for DWI. He was seen driving erratically right before the accident. You know what everybody thinks—that he was on something, but his pops put pressure on the ME to come up with a clean slate."

"What about forensics?"

"Man, that lab is so jammed up, it could be next September before they get to it."

By then, whatever trail a killer might have left would be cold. "Didn't anybody find it odd that there were no skid marks or any other sign he'd tried to stop?"

"Yeah, that did bug me, but between you, me, and the lamppost, the guys working it were told to leave it alone. That came from on high. My take is, Daddy doesn't want anybody digging around in sonny boy's affairs. Even if foul play was involved, the poor bastard is dead anyway, so what's the point?"

Adam didn't remember Joe ever being so cynical. It didn't suit him. "A murderer going free?"

"Yeah, like that never happens. Like I said, he was all over the road. Probably didn't know what hit him. The one I feel sorry for is the girl who was in the car with him. She got pretty banged up." Joe shrugged. "But what do you expect when your main squeeze is a speed freak in more ways than one?" Joe lifted his beer bottle, poised to take a drink. "Why do you care so much?"

"Because Billy Prescott was my younger brother."

Joe gulped and sputtered and coughed up what had gone down the wrong way. He wiped his mouth with the back of his hand. "Damn, man, you could have told me before I went shooting my mouth off."

Adam shrugged. "I wanted your honest opinion."

"Well, I'm still sorry. Were you guys close?"

"Not really. We weren't raised together. Same mother, different fathers."

Joe said nothing to that, probably contemplating the obvious question: Why hadn't his mother kept him with her? But Joe had enough class not to ask. "Must have been rough," he said finally.

Adam lifted his beer bottle to his lips, saying nothing.

"Maybe you should try to get your step-pops to call off the dogs and let the boys in blue do their jobs."

Adam inhaled and let his breath out slowly. There was a thought. But he'd bet if Prescott had exerted any pressure on the LAPD, it had been on his wife's behest not his own idea.

"I've got to go." Adam stood and tossed enough bills on the table to cover his beer. "Give me a call if you find out anything else."

Joe nodded. "You do the same."

Five

"Face it, Sam, you're going to have to call a press conference."

Alana Morris, Sam's publicist, tossed one newspaper after another onto the coffee table in front of Sam. Every one of them had her picture splashed across the front of it. "Since you were so adept at sneaking out of the hospital without a single press photo, speculation is rampant that you died in the crash with Billy or were so hopelessly disfigured you refuse to be seen in public."

Sam leaned forward and picked up the top paper. "I should care what the *Weekly Sun* has to say? Alana, these are tabloids. If they weren't printing that I was dead, then I'd be pregnant or have two heads. They don't care what they print as long as it sells papers."

Alana tossed one last paper on the pile. "How about today's *L.A. Times?* Their entertainment section questions your readiness to start filming *Guardian Angel* and the effect that will have on the production."

"That's ridiculous. Jarad hasn't said anything about it. He knows I'll be ready."

"I know he's your friend, but he's not the only one you have to consider. You know how these financial types are. They back out the moment it looks like they don't have a sure thing going. Jarad could find himself out of a deal and you could find yourself out of a job."

Sam sat back, considering that.

"Look, I know how much you hate the press. Who doesn't these days? But we have to face certain realities here. Besides, as soon as the press realizes you are home, not still in the hospital, as I have very adeptly led them to believe, they'll swarm all over you like bees at a honey convention anyway. Wouldn't you rather do it in a way you can control?"

With a sigh, Sam conceded Alana's position. She couldn't jeopardize the film, which would employ several hundred people, for her own personal wishes. Nor did she want the nuisance of reporters hounding her for interviews. "Where do you want to hold it?"

"How about here? We'll keep it small, only about a dozen or so reporters. That will be enough to dispel the rumors."

The thing she dreaded most, the press overrunning her home. "No tabloids, only legitimate newspapers. And no TV."

"Come on, Sam. Nothing beats a moving, breathing Samantha Hathaway to give the story credibility."

Sam rolled her eyes. "Oh, all right. Who do you want to invite?"

Before Alana had a chance to answer, the sound of the front door opening caught both women's attention. Sam froze as Adam Wexler appeared in the doorway. Sam's eyes narrowed and her shoulders tensed. Did the man think he owned her home because she let him stay in her guesthouse?

"What can I do for you, Detective?"

"I didn't know you had company. We'll talk later."

Sam eyebrows lifted. Now he thought he was going to tell her what to do? Not in this lifetime. But since she didn't want to create a scene in front of Alana, she said nothing as Adam turned to leave the room.

"Who's that?"

Sam waved her hand dismissively. "A policeman Jarad hired to help me prepare for my role."

"Why didn't you tell me about him?" Sam could sense the wheels in Alana's mind whirring. Alana was one of the best in the business, the reason Sam paid her exorbitant fees. Yet her methods were sometimes questionable, even if she ended up getting her clients the exposure they wanted. She dreaded what Alana would say next.

"What's his name?"

"Adam Wexler."

"Ooh, even better. I'll be right back." Alana hopped up from the sofa. "Detective Wexler," Alana called from the doorway.

Sam put her face in her good hand. What on earth could Alana be up to now?

A few moments later, Alana came back to the room with Adam in tow. "Look who's agreed to help us," she announced. Sam noted Alana's hold on Adam's arm. Alana was a natural flirt, a toucher. Men fell all over themselves to impress her. She glanced at Adam, wondering if he'd be the next to fall. She waited for Alana to take her seat, but she should have known better. Alana would have had to release her hold on Adam to do that.

Sam shifted in her seat. "What are you suggesting?"

"Here's what I'm seeing. The press sees you; that instantly proves the reports of your death have been greatly exaggerated. You answer a few questions about the accident—we'll go over what questions to put in the press packet later."

Alana patted Adam's shoulder. "Then we introduce the good detective here. He tells all about how Jarad hired him to help you get ready for the film, inspiring confidence that the production is not in jeopardy. Yadda, yadda, yadda, end of press conference, we all go home. How does that sound to you?"

It sounded like a three-ring circus in her home. "Are you sure this is the only way to handle this?"

"I'm afraid so, Sammy, or I wouldn't suggest it. If you doubt me, think of what happened to Halle Berry a couple of years ago. She was in that car accident, but she didn't speak to the press for months. Remember how much trouble she had getting her career back on track?"

"Okay, here's what I agree to. I will talk to one reporter, an exclusive. I don't really care who. When do you want to do this?"

"Two days from now, three o'clock. That way we give you a little more time to heal and we make the evening news and the papers the following morning. I'll e-mail you the questions later today and we can go over responses." Alana shone her best smile on Adam. "Is that all right with you, Detective?"

Adam extracted his arm. He looked from Alana to her and back. "Thanks for the invitation, ladies, but I'll have to pass."

Alana blinked. "Why?"

Sam almost laughed at the dumbstruck expression on Alana's face. Although Sam appreciated Adam's desire to stay out of the public eye, she knew Alana couldn't understand anyone not wanting their fifteen minutes in the spotlight.

"All we'd need you to do is answer a few questions," Alana continued. "No one's going to break out the bright lights and rubber hoses."

"That's good to know, but my answer is the same. Excuse me."

He headed out of the room before either woman had a chance to respond. "I guess that settles that," Sam said. "We don't need him, anyway."

"No, but it would be better if we had him."

"Alana, he doesn't want to do it."

"Leave him to me, Sam," Alana said, staring off in the direction Adam had gone.

"Leave him alone." Sam warned, but from the faraway look on the other woman's face, she doubted Alana was listening.

Lupe poked her head in the room the minute Alana was out the door. "What did that one want?"

"An interview here tomorrow afternoon. I'll understand if you don't attend."

Lupe snorted and adjusted the apron around her waist. "Dinner's ready."

Sam's stomach immediately growled. She had slept through lunch and hadn't wanted to bother Lupe to heat something up. "Where's our houseguest?"

"Out at the guesthouse."

Sam stood and heaved out a heavy breath. She had some

issues to settle with the good detective, as Alana called him. She might as well get it over with.

She stalked out to the guesthouse, as best as one could stalk with a sprained ankle, and rapped on the door. A second later Adam pulled open the door. His shirt was open, the collar bent back in an odd position, as if he'd thrown it on to answer the door.

For a moment her eyes fastened on the strip of bare, dark skin between the two flaps of his shirt. From what she could see, not an ounce of fat marred the hard planes of his chest and abdomen. He started to adjust his shirt, pulling the two sides together in order to button it.

Sam swallowed and brought her gaze back to his face. The smug expression on his face told her he'd noticed her perusal of him.

"What can I do for you, Ms. Hathaway? Don't tell me. Barbie called. She wants her dream house back."

"What I have to say will only take a few minutes."

He stepped back, allowing her to enter. As she did so, she looked around, nearly wincing at the garish hot pink walls and yards of lace everywhere. She'd forgotten how atrocious Winona's taste in decorating was. She turned around to face Adam, wrapping her good arm around her injured one.

"Let's get something straight right off, Detective. I offered you the use of my guesthouse. I did not give you permission to traipse through my front door whenever the mood strikes you."

"I shouldn't have been able to do that, should I? At the very least, the door should have been locked, which it wasn't. And what braniac turned off the alarm system?"

She glared up at him. "That braniac would be me. It kept sounding every time someone breathed too hard. My friendly neighborhood patrol was getting downright testy about it. I've been meaning to have it serviced, but I've had other things on my mind." She lifted her shoulders in a way that denoted her injuries.

"Are you that unconcerned for your own safety?"

"Come on, Detective, do you honestly think I'm in any

danger? I've lived here my entire life. We've never had a single break-in, not so much as a crazed fan trying to get an autograph."

"Or a tenacious reporter?"

"Honestly, I'm not that newsworthy. I don't throw any wild parties or sunbathe in the nude or do much of anything anybody would want to see. Besides they're all terrified of Lupe."

"I'll take care of it tomorrow."

Her eyes narrowed. *"If* I decide to have the alarm system fixed, *I* will handle it."

"While I am here, I am responsible for your safety, and I damn well will do whatever I feel is necessary to ensure it." He expelled a breath. "Look, I understand how you feel b—"

"No, Detective," she cut him off. "You don't." No one understood how she felt, least of all this . . . this pigheaded policeman who wanted to order her around like one of his suspects.

Without waiting for him to respond, she whirled and left the cottage.

"Ms. Hathaway," he called after her. "In case you've forgotten, I'm also here to help you with your movie."

"So?"

"Since I'd just as soon not see another caricature of a cop parading across the screen, I take that job seriously. We start tomorrow morning, ten o'clock."

She said nothing to that, but simply continued walking toward the house. He could think whatever he liked. It wasn't her job to argue with him. As she entered the larger house, she saw Lupe standing at the kitchen window watching her. She slipped past her, going to the Angel Room and shutting the door. Not two seconds later, Lupe came in behind her without bothering to knock.

Sam continued to the window, pretending interest in the night sky. "If you're coming in here to fuss at me, I'm not in the mood."

"I brought you some dinner."

Sam glanced over her shoulder to see Lupe set a tray down on the side table near the door. "I'm not hungry."

"You're wasting away."

"And you are being melodramatic. I'll eat later, okay?"

Lupe snorted, letting Sam know how likely she thought that was. "It's not like you to be ungracious to guests either. That's my job."

Sam smiled, humor getting the better of her. "Don't tell me *you* want me to be nice to him?"

"I want you to start acting like yourself. You're not eating; you're sleeping all hours of the day. . . ."

Sam brushed her hair over her shoulder in an distracted motion. "You'll have to forgive me if I'm a little off my game. A few days ago I was in a hospital bed having narrowly escaped becoming a carbecue."

"And I was here, not knowing if you'd lived or died."

Sam ran her hand over her face, exhaling a heavy sigh. It had taken rescue workers a while to notice that Sam had been thrown from the car and survived. The first news reports had stated that both Billy and his passenger had crashed to the valley below. She'd been so wrapped up in her own misery, she hadn't realized how much the accident had affected Lupe. For the past fifteen years they'd been all the family either of them had.

Sam walked to Lupe and embraced her. "I'm sorry. I know I haven't been myself lately." Sam drew back from Lupe. "Just give me a little more time to pull myself together, okay?"

Lupe nodded and left the room. Sam supposed Lupe wasn't finished with her yet, but for the moment she'd been mollified.

The Prescott family mansion boasted over forty rooms and sat on twenty-five acres of prime California woodland. Elaborate ten-foot gates marked the entrance to the property. Adam stabbed the button on the intercom that summoned a lanky kid to open the gate.

Up at the house, a busty young woman in a maid's uniform opened the door for him. Her eyes traveled upward until she met his gaze. Then a broad, suggestive smile spread across her face. "Well, what can I do for you?"

As a younger man, Adam might have found such outrageous flirting a turn-on. Now it simply annoyed him. "Is Mr. Prescott at home? You can tell him Adam is here."

"Just one moment."

She disappeared around a corner, her heels clicking on the marble floor. Adam surveyed the high-ceilinged entranceway and the elaborate Baccarat chandelier that illuminated the foyer. To his right, a sloping staircase led to a gallery above. Not bad for a kid from the slums of Watts.

"Mr. Prescott is in the den. I'll take you to him."

Adam focused on the young woman who'd rejoined him. "Don't bother. I know the way."

What Prescott called his den was actually a large, open room, the outer wall of which consisted entirely of bullet-proof glass, facing the artificial lake built onto the property.

"Adam!" Prescott put down the drink he'd been sipping and extended his hand toward Adam. "What brings you out here?"

Adam shook the older man's hand. "I need to talk to you about something."

"Come on in." Prescott gestured toward one of the over-stuffed chairs. "Have a seat. I was just about to mix myself a little drink. Would you like one?"

Noting the glassiness of Prescott's eyes, Adam wondered exactly how many little drinks he had made himself so far. Adam rested his hip on the arm of the chair. "Sure."

"Scotch and soda okay for you?"

"Neat would be better."

While Prescott poured the drinks, Adam surveyed the room. He and Billy had played in this room as children. Nothing much had changed in the intervening years. The same dark-wood paneling covered the walls; the same cream-colored carpeting covered the floor. The furniture had been reupholstered a lime green instead of the sandy beige he remembered. The same photograph of his mother hung on the opposite wall.

As a child, he'd thought she looked about a hundred years old in that picture. As an adult, he realized she must have been younger than he was now when the photo had been shot. She had been young and pretty, with her black hair down around her shoulders. And happy, judging from the smile on her face—a smile he couldn't remember ever being sent in his direction.

Prescott came up beside him, extending a drink. Adam accepted it and took a token sip, watching Prescott slide into a seat facing his. "She doesn't hate you, you know."

He and Prescott had never discussed his relationship with his mother, but Adam supposed the alcohol had loosened Prescott's tongue. "Then that's a hell of an impression she's got going there."

Prescott shook his head. "You remind her too much of him. Your father. He was a demanding man, an army colonel who expected his home to run as smoothly as his platoon. And your mother . . . well, a woman like her needs to be pampered and appreciated. I'm surprised she lasted as long with him as she did."

Adam shook his head. Long? Four lousy years, that was all she'd lasted. He'd barely been out of diapers when she'd gone AWOL, jumping ship for a better life with the man who sat across from him.

"Of course, Adele and I have an understanding. She has her life and I have mine. I actually walked in on her once. I thought I would feel anger or at least jealousy seeing her with another man. Actually, I was curious. You see, I'd never thought of Adele as a particularly passionate woman, but there she was panting away over some young stallion, the gardener, I think. Nothing I had ever done had inspired half that much reaction in her."

Prescott shrugged, glancing at him as if he had just realized whom he was speaking to. "I don't suppose this is the kind of thing you want to hear about your mother."

Adam offered him a tight smile. "Not particularly."

"Then what did you come to see me about?"

"What was Billy up to lately?"

Prescott looked down into his glass, swirling its contents with a flick of his wrist. "I honestly don't know. He didn't come to me. Your mother spoiled him to the point that every time I tried to intervene the two of them shut me out. I'm ashamed to admit

I eventually gave up trying. If you want to know about your brother you'll have to ask your mother."

Just the news he didn't want to hear. "Is she here?"

"She went to bed with a sedative an hour ago."

"Is she the reason you don't want the police investigating Billy's death?"

Prescott nodded. "You and I both know how self-destructive Billy was. How likely is it that anyone beside Billy was responsible for his accident?"

"Not very," Adam admitted.

"What good would poking around in his life do? Our son is dead, Adam. Maybe one day, when you have children, you'll understand how devastating even the prospect of that is. But the reality . . ." Prescott downed a large gulp from his drink.

"I would think that would make you more intent on finding out what happened, not less."

"Right now, all the public knows about Billy is speculation printed mostly in the tabloids. You and I both know an investigation into Billy's life would turn up some pretty unsavory activities. I honestly don't think she could handle seeing Billy's exploits paraded on the front page of the *Los Angeles Times*." Prescott paused, again looking down into his glass. "I'm not sure I could either."

Adam drove back to Samantha's house, beginning to feel like the boy who cried wolf. Maybe he was the one who had it wrong. Maybe he wanted someone, something, to be responsible for Billy's death, outside of Billy's own death wish being played to the obvious conclusion. Maybe then he could rid himself of some of the guilt that haunted him.

Adam inhaled, letting his breath hiss out through his teeth. All he knew was that something had to give. Either that, or he'd end up going home empty handed, and that failure would torment him for the rest of his life.

Six

"Hey, bro, rise and shine. Guess who just got himself transferred to the Prescott case?"

"Joe?" Adam groaned and pulled himself to a sitting position. The clock on the bedstand read seven forty-five. "What are you doing up so early?"

"The early bird catches the worm, but then who the hell wants worms?"

Adam ran his hand over his face, trying to banish sleep. "You're disgustingly cheerful this morning."

"That's 'cause I got myself a lead in your brother's case. Some broad out in Compton claims her old man had it in for Billy over her being a bit too friendly. The guy happens to be a mechanic."

"I thought upstairs told you to leave it alone."

"So who's going to tell 'em I'm not?"

Adam chuckled. "Not me, man. Just don't want to get you in trouble."

"No sweat. Listen, I'm going to meet the woman this morning. You want in?"

"Yeah. How likely do you think it is?"

"Not very, but you know how it is. A good cop follows every lead, no matter how small. I'll swing by and pick you up around ten. Where are you staying?"

"You know where Samantha Hathaway's house is?"

"I drive past once a week and drool. Don't tell me you're staying at her place. How'd you manage that?"

"I'll tell you when I see you. I'll meet you out front at ten."

"See you then, bro."

Adam returned the phone to its cradle and threw off his covers. Naked, he padded to the revoltingly pink bathroom and turned on the shower. He stepped under the warm spray, closed his eyes, and let the water rain down on him. Immediately a picture of Samantha formed in his mind, the expression on her face when he'd answered the door last night. That look, one of blatant feminine appraisal, had lasted only a second, but had revved his heartbeat into overdrive. It had made him wonder if the rampant lust he felt for her didn't run on a two-way street.

But he'd also seen the pain in her eyes when she told him no one understood how she felt. Considering that the Prescotts were more concerned with protecting Billy's image than with finding Billy's killer, Adam probably was the only one who *did* understand what she was going through.

After shaving and dressing, he called the alarm company. He expected some geeky-looking technician to show up, but the guy who rang the doorbell half an hour later looked like he'd been putting a lifetime membership at Gold's Gym to good use.

Once he'd set the man to work, Adam went to find Sam. Failing that, he confronted Lupe in the kitchen.

"Where's your boss?"

Lupe continued wiping down the spotless stainless-steel cabinets. "Ms. Sam is sleeping in."

"I'll bet." She'd sleep in until the precise moment he gave up and did something else. "Go tell her Cop One-oh-one starts in fifteen minutes."

Lupe ignored him, scrubbing at a nonexistent spot on the counter. Silently he counted to ten. Damn obstinate females. Didn't either of them realize that if Samantha was in any danger, her safety or even her life might depend on both of them doing as he said? Josie hadn't listened to him, and it had cost her everything. He wasn't about to go through that again.

Still, he sensed that Lupe's animosity came from a different source than Samantha's. "You don't want me here. Why"

She darted a glance at him. "You have a Y chromosome, don't you?"

"Last time I checked."

She shrugged as if that explained everything. "Is it just me or is it all men?"

She flicked another glance at him. "I have work to do."

"Fine. I'll find her myself."

He'd said that only to see what reaction he'd get. The wide-eyed expression of horror that crossed her face both surprised him and aroused his curiosity even further.

Lupe dropped her sponge to the counter and glanced toward the door. "I'll get her."

"Too late." He took a step back as if he'd leave the room. Lupe scurried around the corner and down the hallway. Adam followed her to the door Samantha had gone into the other night. Lupe tried to make it inside and shut the door, leaving him on the other side. A strategically placed foot prevented her from succeeding.

He pushed the door open and froze. A combination of artificial light and the sunlight washing into the room illuminated pale blue walls depicting angels frolicking on a bed of clouds. Tables and cabinets of all sizes and shapes filled the room, and angels—some crystal, some porcelain with lifelike faces, one almost three feet high—stood against the wall. Whoever had named this the Angel Room wasn't joking.

As he suspected, she was fully awake, dressed in one of those ridiculous robes, lounging on the divan in the room, reading. Lupe had gone to stand next to her, partially blocking her from his view.

"We had an appointment, Ms. Hathaway. You're late."

"Didn't Lupe tell you? I canceled."

"I didn't." He stepped into the room, stopping by the table nearest the divan. He picked up a gaudy specimen of angeldom with what appeared to be a solid gold halo above its head. Looking down at the figure in his hand, he said, "Someone got their religions mixed up on this one. Cupid was a Greek, god not an angel."

He lifted his gaze to Samantha's face. Her openmouthed expression of indignation lifted one corner of his mouth. "Where'd you get it?"

She leaned forward and snatched it from his hand. "Billy Prescott gave it to me. I'm sure you've heard of him."

She hoped to put him in his place by mentioning his own brother's name, and in a way she succeeded. Both outrage and pain mingled in her gaze. Adding to her grief hadn't been on his agenda.

"I have to go out anyway. We'll pick it up later." Adam turned on his heel and left the room.

Sam ground her teeth together, watching Adam leave, wishing she had something heavy throw at him, like a house. "I'm really beginning to hate that man."

"I could always poison his food. I wonder what they have on the market for really big rats."

Sam glanced up at Lupe. Having Adam here was more of a strain on Lupe than it was on her. She patted Lupe's arm. "Twelve more days. That's what I'm going to keep telling myself. Twelve more days. Then that beast from the east goes home."

"My way is quicker."

Sam snorted. "Don't think I'll be sneaking any files to you in prison."

"What are you going to do?"

Sam sighed. "I have no idea." Beside she had bigger worries than Adam Wexler. Alana had scheduled the interview for the next afternoon. Already a mass of knots had tightened in her stomach. Talking with the press always gave her an attack of nerves, but this seemed different somehow, foreboding. She considered canceling the whole thing, but decided against it. Alana's dramatics aside, Sam understood the necessity of the interview. She wouldn't let a case of media cold feet stop her from doing what needed to be done.

"Did Alana ever send over that list of questions?"

Lupe pulled a folded sheet of paper from her apron and handed it to her. "Anything else?"

"No. I'm fine."

After Lupe left, Sam unfolded the paper and surveyed the list—how was her recuperation coming along, her intentions of keeping the role in *Guardian Angel*. She could answer any of them in her sleep. But Barbara Mitchell, the reporter with whom Alana had scheduled the interview, had a reputation for ruthlessness in scoping out a story. The likelihood that Barbara would stick to the approved questions was practically nil.

Sam leaned back on the divan, closed her eyes, and inhaled deeply. She'd swear she still smelled the remnants of Adam's aftershave, still felt his overwhelming presence in the room. In her mind she saw him standing in front of her holding the statue Billy had given her in his hand. When she'd snatched the statue away from him, he'd crossed his arms, revealing bulging muscle and hard sinew.

What did a man have to do to get arms like that? Arms that seemed capable of holding the world up on its axis? What would it be like to be held in those arms? What would it feel like to simply lean on someone else, to rest?

Sam squeezed her eyes tight to forestall the tears that threatened to fall freely. She'd been on her own since fourteen days after her sixteenth birthday. Although Jarad's parents had taken physical custody of her, she'd forged her own way. She was the one who'd arranged her father's funeral and overseen the payment of all his debts. She'd been the one to accept the first movie contract, an offer that she hadn't pursued but that had fallen into her lap at a time when she'd needed it most.

The day she'd turned eighteen she'd moved back into her parents' house and sent for Lupe, who'd been shipped off to an aunt in New York. Even Jarad, as good a friend as he had been to her, didn't know everything.

Sam sniffled and wiped away the lone tear that trickled down her cheek. Life, at the moment, didn't offer her any shoulders to lean on, especially not the broad and powerful ones possessed by Adam Wexler. What would be the point? He'd be gone in twelve days anyway.

Twelve more days, she reminded herself. Then maybe life could get back to normal.

Once in Compton, Joe turned onto a block of town houses that had once been painted an olive color but now gave new meaning to the word drab. Tasha Benson met them at the door wearing a pair of Daisy Dukes and a T-shirt emblazoned with the name of a popular downtown restaurant. Both articles of clothing could have stood to be a size or two larger. Her gaze traveled from Joe to Adam while a salacious grin turned up her lips.

"What can I do for you boys?"

Adam remained silent while Joe flashed his badge and said, "You have some information on Billy Prescott's death?" The less attention Adam drew to himself, the better.

She sucked her teeth and brushed her stringy dyed blonde hair back from her nut-brown face. Her nails were long and curved, painted black. They reminded Adam of a hawk's talons. "Like I said, my old man had it in for Billy. Talkin' 'bout how he was going to get back at him. And nothing even happened."

"What do you mean?"

"Billy used to come into the restaurant where I work. I was nice to him, you know, and he was nice to me. One time he came in, he tipped me a hundred dollars. Rufus, that's my old man, his last name is Jenkins. Rufus said nobody tipped that much unless they were getting something other than food. I tried to tell him nothing happened, but he didn't believe me."

"What makes you think Rufus had something to do with Mr. Prescott's death?"

"He said if he ever caught us together, he'd fix Billy. The night before Billy died, he came into the restaurant. Billy was in a good mood and liked to kid around. When I brought him and his friends their order, he grabbed me around the waist and pulled me onto his lap, just fooling around, you know."

Tasha sighed, giving her hair another swipe with the talons.

"I had forgotten my purse in Rufus's car, and he came down to bring it to me. You should have seen the look on his face when he saw me sitting on Billy's lap. He threw my purse on the floor and stalked out. The next morning I heard about the accident and figured Rufus must have done something to Billy's car in the parking lot. People just don't go sailing off the edge of a cliff for no reason."

Adam glanced at Joe, whose expression told him he'd drawn the same conclusion Adam had: the odds were looking just a little bit better.

"Where can we find Mr. Jenkins?"

"He's got his own place a few blocks over. He should be at work now, anyway."

Joe wrote the name of the body shop and address she gave him on his notepad. "Thanks, ma'am. Can we contact you again if we need to?"

"Sure thing. I'd invite you in, but the place is kinda a mess."

"Thanks anyway."

Once they were back in the car, Adam said to Joe, "What do you think?"

"Scar-ee. I'd like to haul in her hairdresser and her manicurist for defacing private property." Joe pulled away from the curb. "You think this Rufus has anything to do with your brother's death?"

Adam shrugged. "Only one way to find out."

Seven

Rufus Jenkins was a no-show at his apartment, and his boss at the body shop said he'd taken a few days off without offering any explanation. After Joe dropped him off at Samantha's, he contemplated going into the house but decided against it. He'd put off what he needed to do long enough.

When he got to the Prescott house, the same housekeeper greeted him and told him that his mother had gone for a walk on the grounds. He saw her almost immediately, sitting on one of the wrought-iron benches that stood around the lake at precise intervals.

Adam walked along the gravel-strewn bank of the lake until he stood before her. She'd pinned her hair up, exposing her long neck and delicate shoulders. She reminded him of one of the swans that glided through the calm water before them— haughty, proud, and cold. Still, she struck him as something else that the swans did not—sad. Melancholy etched lines around her mouth and dulled her eyes. He wished that he could reach out to her, to offer her comfort. He also knew that was the last thing she'd accept from him.

She pursed her lips in a way that said he'd not only interrupted her solitude, but he blocked her view of the lake. "Barrington told me you want the police to investigate Billy's death."

"It's their job."

"And mine is to protect my son."

Adam huffed out a breath through his teeth and shoved his hands in his pants pockets. Even after death, she couldn't give up playing the overprotective mama. He was tempted to tell her that all her coddling had done Billy more harm than good.

"You'd know if you ever returned his phone calls, ever came to visit him. He idolized you, Adam, and you turned your back on him."

A slow, malicious smile spread across his face. If he'd abandoned his brother, what had she done to him? But his mother's treatment of him wasn't the issue. "Are you going to help me or not?"

She shook her head and looked down at her lap. "No."

Adam's breath whooshed out, leaving him deflated in more than one way. With Billy gone and her refusal to help, he had no need to see her anymore. "Sorry for wasting your time, then." He turned to leave. "Have a nice life."

"Adam."

He paused, but didn't look at her. "What?"

"Billy's gone. Nothing you do can change that."

As if Adam needed anyone to point out his impotence in making sense of Billy's death. "Thanks for reminding me."

"Another marriage proposal," Lupe said, stapling the envelope to the back of a five-page handwritten note. "He's looking for a spring wedding."

"Put it in the pile with the others." Sam returned her gaze to the letter on her lap, written by a fifteen-year-old girl seeking advice on entering the movie business. Whenever she got letters like these, the temptation to tell the writer to reconsider such a career choice assailed her. If she'd known what awaited her after accepting her first role, she'd have run to the nearest McDonald's and applied for a job. As quietly as she lived, the luridness of the business still touched her. Still, the girl deserved an honest answer. She set the letter aside in the pile of correspondence she would answer personally later.

The doorbell sounded. Although she wasn't expecting anyone, Sam welcomed the reprieve. She'd made it her policy to at least look at every piece of mail sent to her by fans. David usually sent her a package once a month, but with her recent accident, her mail had doubled. On top of the usual marriage proposals, death threats, long, gossipy epistles, and requests for money, many of her fans had sent her gifts as well. It would take forever to sort through all this stuff.

Sam set aside the letters in her lap as Lupe went to answer the door. A few moments later, Richard came into the room with Lupe following behind him. He leaned down to kiss her cheek before settling in the seat Lupe had occupied. He sat back, crossing his legs at the knee. "You're looking much better."

"Thank you." And Richard, dressed in an immaculate black suit, looked more prepared to spend a night on the town than an evening in her company. "What brings you out here?"

"How are you getting along with that . . . that . . . policeman?"

Sam ground her teeth together, resisting the urge to tell Richard his snobbery was showing. He wouldn't appreciate the comment and it wouldn't change his outlook any, so she didn't bother. "Why do you ask?"

"You know I was suspicious of him from the beginning. I've had someone checking into his background."

Sam blinked. "You didn't."

"You should be glad I did. I've learned a few things, none of them savory. Haven't you wondered why he's free to keep company with you?"

"Of course."

"It turns out he's on disability leave from the police department after both he and his partner were shot while on assignment. His partner didn't survive."

"That sounds tragic, Richard, not tawdry."

"It is if you consider that his negligence is believed to be responsible for the incident."

She shook her head. He irritated the liver out of her with his overbearing attitude, but she didn't see him as the careless type. He'd not only fixed the existing alarm system, he'd had the man install a video camera at the front door, all at her expense, no doubt. Those were not the actions of a man who left things undone. And if nothing else, Jarad had sent him here. Surely he would have checked the man out before sending him to her.

"If you don't believe me, you can read for yourself." He

pulled a sheaf of papers from inside his jacket pocket. Sam took them and unfolded them—Xerox copies of articles with unflattering headlines from New York newspapers. All bore the same grim-faced picture of Adam at what appeared to be a police press conference.

She tossed the papers onto the coffee table. She'd read them later, after Richard had gone, when he couldn't try to color her judgment. For now, she'd change the subject. "Do you want to stay for dinner?"

Richard stood. "No, I have an engagement." He bent and kissed her forehead. "I'll see myself out. You take care of yourself. You know I worry about you."

Sam suppressed the urge to roll her eyes. Despite Richard's theatrics, he meant well. "I will."

After Richard left, she relaxed against the sofa, but the papers on the table called to her. She picked them up and read.

Adam pulled up in front of Samantha's house in time to see that business manager of hers climb into his car and drive away. With his narrow face and thin nose, Russell reminded him of a weasel—furtive, shifty, and cunning. He didn't trust the man as far as he could spit. What mischief had he been up to today?

Adam got out of his car and slammed the door shut. No time like the present to find out.

Adam knew the moment Samantha arrived in the dining room. A subtle floral fragrance he'd begun to recognize as uniquely hers accompanied her entrance, one that filled his nostrils and spoke sonnets to his libido. She had on another one of those robe thingies, which left him oddly disappointed. She hesitated before moving into the room to let him know she hadn't expected to find him here.

He stood and held out her chair for her. She sat, her back stiff, her eyes downcast. "Thank you, Detective," she said in a formal voice.

Adam returned to his seat, his eyes on her. She managed to unfold her napkin with one hand, then took a sip of water. Adam sat back in his chair, watching her. She darted a glance at him, and for a moment their gazes locked. Surprisingly, he found her natural eye color, a light sherry brown, oddly compelling. So why did she hide it under a pair of contacts?

He never got a chance to ask her, as Lupe chose that moment to enter the dining room. She served Samantha by delicately placing a bowl of salad and a plate of lasagna in front of her; she served him by plunking his food in place. She turned and stalked from the room.

Inwardly, Adam shook his head. She must have been a New Yorker in a former life. Only a New Yorker could make you feel like dirt without saying a word.

He sampled the salad, a combination of greens in a savory dressing flavored with mustard and peppercorns. He had his fill of it after two bites. He probed the lasagna with his fork. He noted flecks of green and orange in the sauce, but nothing brown. He sampled a corner of it, chewing slowly. "Doesn't this thing have any meat in it?"

"Of course not. I'm a vegetarian."

Why was he not surprised? Anyone who collected angels probably thought tofu was one of the four major food groups. "Don't tell me you're one of those 'I can't eat anything that once had a face' people."

"And what if I were? There's something to be said for not destroying life needlessly."

"Isn't that just a little hypocritical? Plants are living things too. And which is worse; eating an animal, which at least has some natural defenses against attack, or some poor plant that can only sit there and let you pick it? At least my food has a chance to run away."

She tilted her head to one side, considering him. "I suppose you're a big consumer of animal flesh, blood-rare no doubt."

"It can still be mooing when you bring it to the table."

She cast him a disgusted look before lifting her water glass to her lips. He would have laughed if their little foray into culinary delights didn't divert them from whatever bee she had in her bonnet, probably planted there by her business manager. For now he would bide his time. One way or the other she'd tell him eventually.

"We never did start your cop lessons." He let his words hang there like a gauntlet for her to pick up.

She laid her fork on her plate and sat back in her chair. When she looked at him, the glint of challenge was in her eyes. "All right, Detective. Let's start with you. Why did you want to become a cop?"

"I passed the test and they gave me a gun, so I said, 'What the heck.' " He leaned back in his chair, watching her as she lifted a forkful of lasagna to her lips. "Why do I get the idea you are not taking this the least bit seriously?"

She laid her fork on her plate and sat back. "Because the whole idea is ludicrous. I expected Jarad to send a female officer so that I can learn from her experiences. Can you tell me what as a woman motivated you to go into such a dangerous line of work? Or how you cope with sexism on the job? Or how about dealing with men who don't take you seriously because you're a woman? Are you an expert on any of those things?"

"No, but my last partner was a woman. That's given me a little insight."

"Your last partner? What happened to her? Did she run screaming from the force after working with you?"

There wasn't a trace of humor in her voice, which led him to believe she already knew the answer. "What did Russell tell you?"

He'd been guessing, but when she averted her eyes, he knew he'd hit the mark. "He showed me some newspaper articles that blame you for your partner's death and that of a thirteen-year-old boy."

Acid churned in his stomach. He should have known it wouldn't take her forever to ferret out that information, especially not with Russell on the case. "And you believed them?"

"I don't trust newspapers to get the date right on the top of the page."

He gave his standard answer to the question. "The department cleared me of any wrongdoing." Of course, everyone assumed it was just another case of the police protecting their own. What the people vilifying him in the papers didn't realize was that if there were any way for the department to hang him out to dry, they would have done it.

"Were you negligent?"

"Probably."

She blinked and looked away from him, saying nothing for a long time. He ground his teeth together, regretting the sarcastic bite in the one curt word he'd spoken. Despite being cleared, the entire subject made him edgy for exactly the same reason her question made him tense: he hadn't been in top form that night, and two other people had paid for that with their lives.

Finally she lifted her eyes to him and spoke. "The papers said you'd been shot, but didn't say where."

"Why do you want to know? Want to see my scar?"

"Hardly. Just wondering if the reason you're so testy is that they shot off something vital."

The mere thought of it made his insides seize. "I won't be singing soprano anytime soon."

"Then maybe you can manage to improve your disposition." She stood and dropped her napkin onto the table. "You told me if I wanted to know something about you, I should ask. I asked. Excuse me, Detective. I seem to have lost my appetite."

Adam sat back in his chair and let his breath hiss out through his teeth. So she could give as good as she got. He'd deserved that and probably more. Especially after she'd been willing to give him the benefit of the doubt when it came to those newspaper stories. Most people, even those he knew personally, hadn't done that.

He'd deliberately baited her with his flippant responses. He didn't have to search far for his own motivation. He'd seen her vulnerability twice—three times, if you counted her bout of tears in the hospital, and he didn't like it. Not only did he suspect that it defied her normal persona, but he doubted he would have seen it at all if he hadn't pushed her to it.

If worse came to worst, the time might come when he would need her to trust him in order for him to keep her safe. In that regard, he'd figured he'd lost any ground he'd gained.

Eight

"Are we almost ready in here?" Hearing Alana's cheerful voice, Sam ground her teeth together. Alana treated every instance in the public eye as if her client were about to receive an Academy Award. "Barbara Mitchell is setting up in the front room as we speak."

Sam already knew that. Lupe had disappeared the instant the press van had driven up. Knowing Lupe, she wouldn't make another appearance until the following morning.

"Can you tilt your head back a little, Ms. Hathaway?"

Sighing, Sam did as the makeup artist Alana had hired suggested, parting her lips slightly so that the other woman could line her lips with a thin red pencil. Out of the corner of her eye, Sam watched the hairstylist selecting a brush from her bag with the same care with which a golfer selected an iron from his bag. In the meanwhile, the pins holding the electric rollers in her hair dug into her scalp, giving her one more reason to regret ever agreeing to this interview in the first place.

The makeup artist stepped back, viewing her handiwork. "What do you think?"

Sam took the mirror Alana extended toward her. She gave a cursory glance at her reflection and handed the mirror back. "Lovely."

Alana looked at her closely. "Are your contacts in?"

Sam widened her eyes and stared at Alana.

"Good." Alana motioned toward the hairstylist. "Bobbie."

Out of the corner of her eye, Sam saw the hairstylist, a

woman as round as the makeup artist was thin, approach. Sam tapped her fingers on the arm of the chair as the woman began to unwind the rollers from her hair.

"Relax, Sam," she heard Alana say. "It'll all be over in half an hour, tops."

Sam stilled her fingers, willing away the disconcerting bout of nerves that flapped around in her stomach like a flock of startled birds. Usually she breezed though public appearances, the picture of serenity. Today a nervous energy seized her, making it difficult to keep still. If she were the sort to believe in premonitions, she'd go back to her bed and stay there. But something told her this afternoon did not bode well for her at all.

"I'm going to get you some tea," Alana announced on her way out of the room. She returned a few minutes later carrying a cup and saucer. "Make sure you keep the left side down to cover the scar at her hairline." To Sam she said, "Drink this."

Sam lifted the cup and sniffed its contents. "What is this?"

"A new herbal blend. Unstress Success or some nonsense. Try it."

It smelled like nail polish remover and tasted like old shoes. Sam tried another sip. The hot liquid hit her empty stomach like a hot, heavy weight. She handed the cup to Alana. "They need to work on their recipe."

"That bad?"

"I'm on the verge of suing both you and the manufacturer."

Alana snorted, setting the cup down on a nearby table. "How do you feel?"

"Slightly better."

"Where's the good detective?" Alana asked.

Sam did her best impression of a shrug. She too, wondered where Adam had disappeared to. She hadn't seen him since she had walked out of the dining room last night. For a man supposedly concerned with her safety, he'd been remarkably absent while a camera crew set up camp in her home.

"I'm going to check on how things are going in the other room. We should be ready to start in five minutes."

"Great." Sam let out a heavy sigh. Just great.

* * *

Adam claimed a spot at the entranceway to Samantha's front room and leaned his shoulder against the wall. The furniture had been arranged so that a single chair faced the cream-colored sofa. One camera sat on the floor facing the sofa; another faced in his direction toward the chair. Several people hurried around the room, while a technician fitted a tall blond woman with a microphone. Barbara What's-her-name, he presumed.

"Why, Detective," Alana Morris said. "I thought you weren't going to be joining us today."

He looked down at the manicured hand on his biceps and followed the trail up her arm to her face. She struck him now as she had the first time he'd met her—as a woman who worked so hard at being beautiful that it made her less attractive. "I'm not."

"That's a shame, Detective. We could really use you."

And he could use the kind of exposure Alana Morris provided like he could use a full frontal lobotomy. Being subjected to the New York press had been bad enough. All he needed was his face plastered on the national news scene.

"Tell Ms. Hathaway I said to break a leg." He turned his attention to the scene in the front room. After a moment Alana took the hint and walked away.

Sam walked into the front room on unsteady legs via the side entrance, flanked by Alana. A smattering of applause came from those assembled in front of her, as did several camera flashes. While the film from the interview would be aired on Barbara's weekly entertainment show, the still photographs would be sent to print media, along with a press release Alana had written.

She greeted Barbara with the obligatory air kiss and plastic smile, then took her position on the sofa. As the technician fitted her with a microphone, she scanned the room. Adam had said he wouldn't show up, so the disappointment that swept through her when she didn't find him there was completely irrational. Despite the numerous times she'd told him she didn't need him, she sensed an innate protectiveness in him that she could use at the moment. She wanted someone there in her corner. And despite the fact that Alana worked for her, Alana mostly served herself.

"Are you ready to go, Sam?"

Sam focused on the blond, blue-eyed rattlesnake sitting across from her. If you wanted exposure, you couldn't ask for a better person than Barbara. Her show had a rabid viewership in the millions, and her network connections would ensure that the story got national news coverage, but Sam wouldn't have minded dealing with someone with a little less clout and a lot more sensitivity. Especially since her stomach had begun quivering like a volcano about to erupt. Considering she'd skipped lunch earlier, her belly didn't have anything to complain about.

Sam nodded. Maybe if they hurried she could get through the interview before she either passed out or threw up. "Let's get started."

Barbara sat back in her chair, smiled into the camera facing her and began. "I'm here in the home of Samantha Hathaway, star of *Summer's End,* and the upcoming *Guardian Angel.* As many of you know, Samantha was in the car accident that claimed actor Billy Prescott's life. Samantha has offered this exclusive interview to discuss the accident, her recovery, and her plans for the future. Samantha, how are you feeling?"

She had gone over what she would say with Alana. She let the words spill from her mouth without thinking. "I'm just happy to be here with you, Barbara. And I would like to publicly extend my sympathy to the Prescott family. I know that they must be going through a difficult time right now, and my thoughts and prayers are with them."

Sam drew in another long breath. What a laugh that was. Not one member of Billy's family had tried to contact her in any way. She'd found out about Billy's funeral arrangements from the television in her hospital room. Any thoughts and prayers she had about Billy's family consisted of their continued absence and lack of concern.

"So, Sam, how are you feeling? You look a little thin."

"Barbara, have you ever tried eating hospital food? I assure you, now that I'm home, I've been more than making up for it. The next time you see me, I may need to go on a diet."

"What is the extent of your injuries? And does this mean you'll be giving up your role in *Guardian Angel?*"

"I have no plans to give up my role in *Guardian Angel,* even though I may have a bum wing at the moment. I bruised the rotator cuff in my left arm and I sprained my ankle. According to my doctor and my physical therapist, I should be back to normal in a few weeks."

"Any truth to the rumor that you and Billy were getting back together?"

And now it started. That question definitely had not been on the list, because she never would have agreed to discuss her relationship with Billy. "That's a moot point now, isn't it, Barbara?" Let her stew over that one if she wanted to.

The room grew warm and the air seemed to thin. Her head felt as if a spider had spun a web around her brain. For some reason a dark shape beyond Barbara's shoulder caught her attention. Adam stood framed in the doorway, his shoulder leaning against the jamb, his arms crossed over his chest. How long had he been standing there?

"I would think so," Barbara said, drawing her attention. "Especially since I hear there's a new man in your life. . . ."

She left her words hanging there as if Sam should know what she meant. "Unless you mean the gardener I hired last month, I have no idea who you're talking about."

"Don't be coy, Samantha. A little birdie told me that a certain New York City police officer has caught your fancy. In fact, my sources tell me he's living with you."

Sam's gaze immediately went to Adam. For once she had no trouble discerning the expression in his eyes: white-hot anger. Surely he couldn't think she'd fed Barbara that lie herself. Without a doubt, Alana had been the planter of that particular seed. At the moment, Sam lacked the wherewithal to figure out why.

Samantha turned her head and gave Alana a narrow-eyed look that caused the other woman to fidget. "I do have a policeman staying in my guesthouse. He's helping me prepare for my role in *Guardian Angel*."

"Is that what they're calling it these days? Perhaps Detective Wexler would like to give us his side of the story?"

A dull pain throbbed at Sam's temple, and her head swam. Her stomach seized up, forcing bile to her throat. For a moment she squeezed her eyes shut, fighting a wave of nausea.

When she opened her eyes, she saw Adam striding toward her, an intense expression on his face. What did he intend to do? He couldn't be taking Barbara Mitchell's offer seriously. She glared at him, hoping he'd get the message to stay away. But he kept coming. The room seemed to hold its breath, waiting to see what he would do.

He stopped when he stood beside the sofa facing Barbara. "This conference is over."

He turned and offered her his hand. For a moment she stared at it dumbly. What was wrong with this man? She couldn't leave now. His actions, though chivalrous, gave the lie to every word she'd just said about their not sharing a romantic relationship. Or at least, that was the way Barbara and anyone else watching this footage would interpret it.

To her, he whispered, "You're sick. Let me take you out of here."

The softness in his voice surprised her, considering the venom in his gaze just a few moments ago. She wanted to stay, but the cramping in her stomach changed her mind. Passing out on-camera wouldn't do her cause any good either.

She nodded and pushed to her feet, but her ankle nearly gave way. She didn't balk when Adam steadied her and led her from the room with an arm around her waist.

He led her to the solarium and she gratefully fell into a seat on the sofa. "Are you going to be all right?" he asked.

She touched her fingertips to her temples and nodded. "Where's Alana?"

Getting no answer, she looked up to catch the tail end of Adam's exit from the room. Alana chose that moment to enter. For a moment the two of them eyed each other like two pit bulls about to tear each other to shreds. Then Adam moved off and Alana breezed into the room, obviously pleased with herself.

"What's his problem? I just made him the most famous houseguest since Kato Kaelin."

Samantha narrowed her gaze on Alana, but Alana seemed not to notice. "The problem is, he didn't want to be part of this circus you created in the first place. What the hell was that out there?"

"Don't be angry with me, Sam. Both of you were wonderful. I couldn't have planned it better myself. When he took you out of the room, I thought every woman in attendance would swoon."

"I nearly swooned myself. What did you put in my tea?"

"A little shot of brandy to loosen you up."

Which Alana had undoubtedly brought with her, since Sam didn't keep any liquor in the house. "You know I don't drink."

"You were wound tighter than a Swiss clock."

"And now I'm going to be sick. Why would you do this?"

"It's been so long since your name has been linked with a man's, people were starting to wonder if you'd gone over to the other camp. No one would dare say that with the very hunky Detective Wexler in the picture."

Sam couldn't argue with her there, so she didn't bother. "I could care less what lies you tell to reporters. That's part of the game. But I do expect you to be honest with me."

"Don't get so bent out of shape. Do you have any idea how difficult it is to drum up publicity for a woman who sizzles on screen but in reality is the biggest wet blanket in history? You don't drink, don't smoke, don't fool around. Tell me, Sam, don't you have any vices?"

"Just one: I trust people I shouldn't. But I'm about to rectify that. You're fired. Take your things and your people and get out of my house."

"Fine." Alana picked up her purse and her date book from the coffee table. "When you change your mind, you know where I'll be."

As Alana stalked from the room, Sam leaned back against the sofa and closed her eyes, willing her stomach to quiet.

What a mess Alana had created. She couldn't blame Adam for not only being furious with her but for abandoning her to her own devices as well. Considering how poorly she'd treated him thus far, he'd probably never believe she had nothing to do with Alana's scheme.

Lupe was right: she needed to get herself together. If she'd been herself, she would have foreseen what Alana had in mind and thwarted her before Barbara Mitchell even thought to ask the question. She would have realized that Alana would find a way to pay back any man who had the nerve to rebuff her.

Sam dragged air into her lungs and squared her shoulders. She would have to hope that he accepted her apology. His anger had been formidable. She doubted he'd cooled off by now, but she wouldn't put off what she had to do any longer.

She went to the guesthouse and knocked on the door. Adam answered almost immediately. Seeing her, a sardonic expression came into his eyes. He leaned against the doorjamb. "Ms. Hathaway, we've got to stop meeting like this."

Sam forced her eyes to focus on his face. "I want to apologize for that scene out there."

"Really? And I was coming to thank you for announcing to a national audience that I'm a cop. Maybe the next time I arrest some lowlife, he'll ask me for my autograph."

"Look, I can understand you're being angry with me. But I had no idea Alana was going to do that."

"Of course not. She only works for you."

"Worked. If it makes you feel any better, I fired her."

"Why?"

"Because she lied to me. That's one thing I won't tolerate in the people around me."

Sam sighed and leaned her hand against the door frame, close to his. "I know I've given you a hard time, but the truth is, I do need your help. I am facing a role I don't understand. I can say the words, but that's not the same as being able to understand the motivation behind them. Despite what you think, I am interested in giving an accurate portrayal. Will you help me?"

"What do you want to know?"

"Everything. Everything you ever wanted to know about cops but were too chicken to ask."

"You don't want much." Adam sighed. "Do you have a copy of the script?"

"There's a copy in the desk in the solarium." For a long moment he said nothing, and she held her breath, waiting for him to respond.

"We'll start tomorrow morning."

Sam nodded and walked back to the house. Lupe was in the kitchen washing vegetables in the sink. "How did it go?"

"You don't want to know. I'm going to lie down for a while. Call me when dinner's ready, okay?"

Once inside the Angel Room, she picked up the statue Billy had given her and lay down on the divan. She couldn't argue with Adam's assessment of the piece; it was ghastly. She closed her eyes, hoping to get back some of the sleep she'd lost worrying about the press conference.

After fifteen minutes she gave up trying. Although the afternoon's fiasco was long over, her feeling of foreboding remained.

"What the hell is going on out there?"

Adam settled the phone against his ear as Jarad Naughton's irate voice crackled over the line. He'd been expecting the call ever since the story of Samantha Hathaway's mystery man hit the evening news in California. Adam glanced at the bedside clock. The numbers burned bright red in the darkness: four-fifteen, which meant it was a little after seven in New York. "Good morning to you, too."

"Imagine my surprise turning on the morning news and finding Sam's face and yours plastered on my television screen. I nearly choked on my cornflakes. I thought you were taking care of her."

"Strange species of piranha they've got out here. Goes straight for the jugular. Between the reporter and that publicist of hers, it was my pleasure to show both of them the front door."

"How is she?"

He had the urge to tell him she had more guts than he gave her credit for. Although Adam had put an end to the interview, he suspected she'd have mopped the floor with Barbara Mitchell in another minute. Judging from the look she'd sent Alana, he believed that she had no idea what her publicist had planned to do, even though he took his anger out on her for it. But instead of backing down or shrinking away, she'd asked him for help.

Still, it wasn't his job to school anybody on Samantha Hathaway's character. "She's hanging in there."

"Have you found anything out about Billy?"

"Maybe."

"Let me know if there's anything I can do."

"How about waiting for a decent hour to pick up the phone?" Adam replaced the receiver in the cradle and tried in vain to settle back down to sleep.

Nine

"It can't be that bad, can it?"

Adam looked up from the copy of the script he'd been reading to see Samantha framed in the doorway of the room. She wore a sleeveless white blouse that wrapped around her body and tied at her waist, and a pair of skintight white pants. She walked toward him, and he realized her ankle must be better. The hitch in her walk had been replaced by a sexy sway that revved his heartbeat up a notch. "Excuse me?"

Although he stood to make room for her on the sofa, she sat in the chair across from him and propped her feet on the table. *"Guardian Angel.* The script." She gestured toward the script in his hands. "You were frowning."

He tossed it on to the table between them. "Not bad." In fact, the quality and authenticity of the writing had surprised him.

"The screenplay was written by an ex-New Yorker, a former NYPD cop. She's a consultant for *NYPD Blue.*"

"An ex-New Yorker?"

"Someone who lives out here who still thinks of New York as home."

"Smart woman."

"Why do you say that?"

"I don't trust a city that boasts a perennial ring around its collar."

"You have something against wholesome L.A. smog, I take it."

"Air should be smelled, not seen."

"Even if it smells like sweaty socks left in the gym bag too long?"

"So you have been to New York."

"A long time ago." She bit her lip and shifted in her seat. She settled a cold, brittle gaze on him. "I thought we were supposed to be discussing the movie."

He said nothing for a moment, wondering what he'd said to suddenly make her so touchy. Maybe she'd been mugged. "Okay, if you answer a question for me first."

She considered him warily. "If I can."

"Why is this role so important to you?"

She lifted her undamaged shoulder in a shrug. "For one thing, it's the first real leading role I've had. I've been the female lead, you know, played off whatever man is the true star of the film. For the first time I'd be carrying the picture on my own."

"Tired of playing the female sidekick?"

She shook her head. "It's not just that. I'm thirty-four. The next thing you know they'll be offering me 'mother of' roles, and then probably none at all. The movie industry isn't particularly kind to women, especially not where age is concerned. The number of roles for women over forty is a crime, when you consider how many roles are written for older men. Harrison Ford is over sixty and still considered a romantic lead. And who does he play against? Certainly no one his own age. His costars keep getting younger and younger. The only actresses who have any longevity are those who prove they can handle a meatier role."

Adam hadn't thought of it that way, or considered that she felt the need to prove herself. "Is that why you agreed to the press conference?"

She nodded. "Partly. In this town, you're only as good as your last movie, and my last two tanked. I can't afford to let the next one get any bad publicity on my account." She dragged in a breath and let it out slowly. "As much as I hate to admit it, Alana's stunt actually worked. My agent called this morning to tell me he's got three decent scripts for me to look at."

"Did you always want to be an actress?"

"No, I wanted to be a veterinarian. Acting sort of fell in my lap. Comes with the location, I guess. Everyone in Hollywood is either an actor, a waiter dreaming of being an actor, or a fan hoping to meet an actor."

Adam snorted. "On the job, if we refer to someone as an actor, we mean they're the one who committed the crime."

She smiled. "Sometimes so do we, Detective."

Why did the way she said "Detective" rankle him so much? Though not as condescending as her business manager, he suspected she used the word as a means of distancing herself from him. "Adam."

"Excuse me?"

"I have a name. I would prefer that you use it. Being a detective is what I do, not what I am."

She shook her head. "I don't think so."

"What does that mean?"

She tilted her head to one side, considering him. "I bet you wanted to be a cop since you were five years old."

"Really?"

She tilted her head in the opposite direction and narrowed her eyes, apparently only warming up to her topic. "I bet all your friends are cops, with the possible exception of a woman or two. You signed up for the police academy the day you graduated high school. I read that it takes the average patrolman three to five years to make it to detective. I bet you were on the low end of that figure."

"Is that all?"

"You used to skip the first half hour of *Columbo,* so you could figure out the crime without knowing who committed it first. How close am I?"

He shifted in his seat, acknowledging to himself at least that her assessment had been dead-on. "Why? Auditioning for the Psychic Friends Network?"

"Just curious. Cops and shrinks aren't the only professions where it pays to know what makes people tick. So?"

"You're right on all counts, except I made a brief pit stop

at John Jay. I majored in theater, though when I graduated I had enough credits for a second major in criminal law."

Her eyebrows lifted and a look of disbelief crossed her face. "Really?"

"Surprised I graduated or surprised at my choice of major?"

She pressed her lips together in a way that gave him his answer: both. How much of a Neanderthal did she think he was?

She shook her head. "Why theater?"

He shrugged. "Mostly to tweak my old man's nose. He thought any man who even knew Broadway existed needed a testosterone injection."

"You two didn't get along?"

For a moment Adam let memories wash over him, both good and bad. "He was a good guy; we just didn't agree on much. Though he did come to see me in my one and only acting role—in *Streetcar.*"

"You must have made an impressive Stanley."

"I might have, if the student directing the production had known anything about casting to type. I got stuck playing the bumbling, sensitive Mitch. To make things worse, the girl playing Blanche was about five-foot-nothing, with curly blond hair. Together we looked like a clumsy Mr. Bojangles trying to put the moves on a pubescent Shirley Temple."

She giggled, a sound so alien and captivating that all he could do was stare at her. Then she smiled at him, not one of those plastic numbers that looked back at him from billboards or magazine covers, but a genuine expression of humor.

"Tennessee Williams must have rolled over in his grave a couple of times over that abuse of his literary talents."

He never got a chance to respond, as Lupe chose that moment to appear in the doorway. She glared at him for a moment before focusing her gaze on Sam. "Mr. Clean is here."

Adam lifted an eyebrow, but with supreme effort managed to say nothing.

Sam rolled her eyes. "That's Lupe's name for him, my therapist." She waved her hand dismissively. "Don't ask."

Malign her therapist? He wouldn't dream of it. Especially

since a moment later, a tall, Caucasian man dressed head to toe in white appeared in the doorway. His bald head gleamed in the morning sunlight. For a fleeting moment Adam wondered if his own scalp ever gave off so much glare.

"Sam, darling, how are you?" the man said in a voice that reminded Adam of Mike Tyson—all brawn, no vocal cords to speak of. He stopped at Sam's chair and the pair exchanged the greeting of stars—air kisses to both cheeks. "This is so awful. How do you feel?"

"Much better." She sat back and darted a glance in Adam's direction before returning her attention to her guest. "Though I have to confess I forgot about our appointment today. Teddy, this is Det. Adam Wexler. Detective, this is Teddy."

Teddy extended his hand in a way that left Adam in doubt whether he expected him to shake his hand or kiss the dainty silver ring on his pinky. In the end, Adam ignored it.

Teddy seemed not to care. He waved his hand as if swatting at a fly. "I know who you are. You were plastered all over the TV with our dear Sam. I hope you're taking good care of her."

"Passably." Adam folded his arms across his chest, surveying the other man. Something about Mr. Clean's routine, like everything else in this town, seemed phony, put on. Either that or Adam had succumbed to an odd brand of paranoia, but he didn't think so. "Exactly what kind of 'therapy' do you practice?"

"Physical, mostly. Though I've gotten into reiki lately."

"Ricky who?" Adam said, just to be perverse.

"Reiki is an ancient Japanese healing art," Sam said in a patient voice.

Teddy looked him over the way a housewife eyed a piece of steak at the butcher's. "I could tune the energy in your chakras," Teddy volunteered.

"Thanks, but I like my chakras the way they are. Excuse me." Adam went back to the guesthouse, changed into his swim trunks, and headed out back in the direction of the hot tub. But once he got there, the cool, artificially blue water of Samantha's pool called to him instead.

Instead of stewing in his own juices, he needed exercise,

something to work off the layer of frustration that enveloped him like a second skin: frustration at his lack of progress in his brother's case, frustration at his mother's indifference.

And most of all, frustration at being so close to Samantha Hathaway. She'd haunted his dreams the night before, and this afternoon, for a moment there, he thought he'd glimpsed the woman behind the façade, and he'd liked what he'd seen.

Adam shook his head. Why was it every time he started thinking of her as a flesh-and-blood woman, something less ethereal than the celluloid images and more real than the angels she collected, she had to zap him with some new bit of California weirdness? Another reminder that he didn't belong in her world any more than she belonged in his?

After a half hour in Samantha's kidney-shaped pool, Adam emerged from the deep end, grabbed his towel off the bench, and slung it over his shoulder without bothering to dry himself. He walked back to the guesthouse, his leg sore, his gait stiff, despite his doctor's claim that swimming would be good for his injury. He heard the phone ringing and hoped it was Joe on the other line. Adam wanted to get somewhere on this case. Samantha Hathaway had given him one more reason to want to get done what he had to do and get himself back to the Bronx where he belonged.

"Guess who just surfaced?" Joe said without bothering with a greeting."

Adam eased down to a sitting position on his bed. "Jimmy Hoffa?"

"Nah, he's still holding up the Meadowlands. This Rufus guy. His boss called me to say he showed up for work today. Claims he went to visit a sick aunt."

"How convenient. Are you heading over there?"

"I'm in your neighborhood. I'll see you in ten minutes."

Adam was standing at the curb when Joe pulled up. Joe got out of the car, opened the passenger door, and made a show of dusting off the seat with a whisk brush.

Adam's brows drew together. "What is your problem?"

Grinning, Joe stepped back gesturing for Adam to sit. "Can't have no celebrity riding in a dirty car."

Obviously Joe had seen Barbara Mitchell's report and didn't plan to let it slide without comment. "Don't start." Adam gave Joe a hard stare as he got into the car.

Joe walked around to the driver's side and got in. "Too bad they didn't catch your good side."

"I don't have a good side."

"Well, watch yourself out here, man. The people out here smile in your face and stab you in the back as soon as you look away."

Adam studied Joe's profile, wondering if he spoke from observation or personal experience. As they lapsed into silence, Adam stared out the window, watching the freak show that was Los Angeles pass before his eyes.

"That's him over there." Rufus Jenkins's boss, a short, round man with squinty eyes, buckteeth, and blue-black skin, reminded Adam of a gopher. He pointed to a dark-skinned young man in neat overalls. He stood beneath a hydraulic lift, examining a yellow convertible. Adam took a position against the wall while Joe confronted him.

"Rufus Jenkins?"

He answered without looking at them. "Yeah."

"Can we have a word with you?"

Rufus focused on them then, first Joe, then him, a wary expression coming into his eyes. Even if Joe hadn't pulled Jenkins's file, Adam would have known this wasn't the man's first brush with the police.

Rufus stepped around the car, wiping his hands on a rag. "What can I do for you?"

"You know a girl named Tasha Benson?"

"Yeah, I know her. What's that bitch said I done now?"

Adam slid a glance at Joe. "According to her, you visited In 'n' Out, where she worked the night before Billy Prescott died."

"Yeah, so? She left her purse in my car. I gave it back to her. She saying I stole sumthin' off her?"

"She says you made threats toward Billy Prescott."

"Yeah, I said I'd like to rip the guy's throat out. That's when I thought he was trying to make a move on her."

"Something changed your mind?"

"I walked into where she worked and saw her throwing herself all over the guy. I just walked out."

"What did you do after that?"

"I ran into one of my boys who works at one of the hotels in the parking lot. We hung out for a while; then I went home. He saw me get in my car."

Joe wrote down the name and number Rufus provided. "Just ask him," Rufus reiterated. "I didn't do nuthin to no Billy Prescott."

As Joe closed his notebook, Adam pushed off the wall. He had a feeling Rufus's story would check out. That would leave them right back where they started—at square one without a clue where to look next.

"Good Lord, not another one." Ever since Barbara Mitchell's report had graced the entertainment section of the nightly news, the phone had been ringing off the hook. Barbara's story had intimated that Sam hadn't been out of the public eye due to grief over Billy's death or due to injury, but rather that she'd holed herself up in her house with a new lover.

A few of the calls had come from friends or acquaintances calling to gossip. Most came from reporters who had ferreted out her home phone number, hoping to scope the next juicy tidbit.

Sam responded by politely declining the interviews; Lupe blew a police whistle in their ear and slammed the phone receiver on the cradle.

Sam snatched up the phone a moment before Lupe would have grabbed it. "Hello?"

"Tell me the news story isn't true," Richard said without

preamble. "You are not involved with that . . . that . . . policeman. Not after what I told you."

Sam ground her teeth together. "No, the story isn't true. Alana decided to spice up my life for the press. She didn't tell me what she planned to do beforehand."

"I have to tell you I'm relieved to hear that. He hasn't made any advances toward you, has he?"

She remembered the feel of his arms around her yesterday—gentle, supportive, but impersonal. "Not one." If anything, he seemed oblivious to her as a woman. Most men tripped over themselves trying to impress her. Adam Wexler couldn't care one whit. She found that as refreshing as it was unusual.

"I have half a mind to call Naughton myself and find out what he was thinking, involving you with such a man."

And try to get him fired, no doubt. Sam huffed out a breath. "Richard, really. I'm fine. There's no need for you to worry."

"If you say so, I'll stay put. But promise me you'll phone if you need me."

She promised, simply to get him off the phone, but the call left her with a cold ache at the pit of her stomach. She'd always tolerated Richard's elitism because of his friendship with her parents, and because she'd never sensed any malice in him. But she suspected he had it in for Adam, and that neither Adam's work history nor his attitude toward Sam was at the root of it. But that left her to wonder what was.

It was nearly midnight when Adam let himself into Samantha's guesthouse. He hung his jacket and holster on the back of the desk chair. He'd spent the last few hours on Venice Beach, staring at the water. He'd always found the rolling of the ocean soothing. As a kid he'd ridden his bike to nearby Orchard Beach when life with his father or whatever female relative he'd be shipped off to got to be too much. Although the water was murky and smelled only slightly cleaner than the average sewer drain, he found the relentless march of the waves calming.

Tonight had been no exception. He'd stood on the boardwalk, his elbows resting on the railing as the fading sun painted the water orange, then crimson, and finally black. Despite everything, his mother's words had gotten to him, churning the guilt he felt up a notch.

Adam's stomach growled. He'd bought a hot dog and a soda from one of the beach vendors, but aside from that he hadn't eaten since breakfast. He'd never get to sleep with all that rumbling going on. Adam patted his stomach. Whether Samantha liked it or not, he intended to make a late night raid on her refrigerator.

He let himself into the house through the back door and switched on the kitchen light. Chrome gleamed from nearly every surface, giving the impression more of an industrial workspace than the life center of someone's home. The house was deathly quiet; not even the characteristic hum of a working refrigerator disturbed the silence.

Nor did the refrigerator contain much of anything appetizing: a tray of leftover vegetable lasagna, the obligatory containers of tofu and bean sprouts, and some other things he wouldn't begin to guess what they were. He opened the freezer. Not one package of anything that resembled meat. Resigning himself to the only bit of protein he found, he made himself a poor man's grilled cheese sandwich by toasting two slices of bread and no-fat mozzarella under the broiler and slapping the two together.

With the sandwich in hand, he decided to check out the rest of the house. He paused at the Angel Room door. With his luck the door would be locked—or worse, she'd be on the other side, sleeping.

Not that catching a glimpse of Samantha soft and warm in slumber would be the stuff of nightmares. But she had gotten to him, too, in a different way. He popped the last of the sandwich in his mouth and took a step away from the door.

"Nooooo." A high-pitched, tormented wail came from the other side of the door. "Nooooo."

"Samantha?"

"Nooooo."

Obviously she was having a nightmare. He tried the doorknob, surprised it wasn't locked. He pushed open the door. She thrashed about, still in the grip of her dream. He sat on the bed next to her and shook her uninjured shoulder.

"Samantha, wake up. You're having a bad dream. Samantha." Slowly she opened her eyes and gazed around her, as if she didn't know where she was. For a moment their gazes locked and he could see the dawning recognition in her eyes. "You were dreaming," he repeated.

She melted against him, her wounded arm pressed against his chest, her free arm grasping his biceps as if it were a life preserver. "Thank God."

He couldn't help himself. He slid his arms around her, letting his hands travel over the soft flesh exposed by her skimpy nightgown. She smelled of lilacs or some other delicate flower he couldn't name. Without thinking, he touched his lips to the healing wound at her temple. "Are you okay now?"

Before she had a chance to answer, he felt the unmistakable imprint of a shotgun digging into his spine. "Take your hands off her."

Adam did as she said, lifting his hands in a classic surrender position as he slowly rose to his feet.

In an exasperated voice, Samantha said, "Lupe, put that thing away before you hurt someone."

The pressure on his back immediately eased, but Adam wasn't taking any chances. While her attention was diverted he turned and snatched the gun out of her hand by the barrel. Startled, she took a step backward, tripping over her own feet. He caught her arm before she fell, and attempted to right her onto her feet, but she went wild on him, pounding him with her fists, clawing at him with her nails, while Samantha pleaded with him from the bed to let her go.

"What the hell . . ." He finally did let her go, only because she didn't leave him any choice. She stumbled backward, her eyes wide and horror-filled, her long hair wild around her face. For a moment she reminded him of a wounded animal staring up at her tormentor.

"Lupe," Samantha called.

Lupe ran past him and threw herself into Samantha's arms,

sobbing with the intensity of a child. "I thought he was hurting you."

"Shh, sweetie. It's all right. I was having a bad dream. He woke me up, that's all. He didn't hurt me."

"I couldn't let him hurt you."

For a moment Adam watched the two of them, unsure who was comforting whom. What on earth had he stumbled into? For sure, more existed to their relationship than housekeeper and employer. At the moment he didn't want to delve into that too deeply, for fear of where he'd end up.

He backed out of the room. For now he'd leave them alone, but tomorrow morning he'd damn sure better get some answers.

Ten

Sam awoke the next morning to the feel of something warm beside her. It took her a moment to realize it was Lupe, who'd cried herself to sleep in Sam's arms last night. They hadn't shared the same bed since they were girls together, when Lupe would have one of her nightmares and seek out Sam's protection.

But that had been a long time ago. Even then, Sam had never seen Lupe as she had been last night. Part of her reaction, Sam knew, had been the instinct of fight or flight in the presence of perceived danger. Lupe had naturally chosen fight. But the expression in Lupe's eyes had gone beyond fear into terror.

That knowledge both frightened and worried Sam. She'd known that Lupe disliked Adam, that she didn't trust him or want him here, but she'd never suspected that Lupe was afraid of him, as well.

Sam sighed, feeling as if her life were slipping out of control. Ever since the accident, things had gone from bad to worse. She never should have agreed to have Adam Wexler here in the first place, and never would have if Jarad and Ariel hadn't pressured her into it. She hadn't wanted them to worry about her. But if it came down to Lupe's peace of mind or Jarad's, Adam would have to go.

The aroma of brewing coffee reached her. Only one person could be responsible; Adam.

She didn't want to face him. Lupe's behavior demanded an explanation, but she had no idea what she'd tell him. The full, gory truth was definitely out of the question. Lupe would never forgive her.

And aside from that, the memory of being held in his arms the night before burned in her consciousness and stirred her senses. His touch had been far gentler than she would have expected from such a big man—a hard, cold New York cop, at that. He'd kissed her, just a brief caress of his lips on her skin. But in that moment she'd wanted more, wanted him. She hadn't craved a man's touch since Billy. The knowledge that she did now only added to her anxiety. She wondered what she might have let happen if Lupe hadn't burst in when she had.

With a weary sigh, Sam rose from the bed, pulled on one of her caftans over her nightgown, and went to the kitchen to find Adam.

She paused in the doorway a moment, watching him. He sat at the small kitchen table sipping from a cup of coffee. The morning paper lay on the table in front of him. Even at this distance she could see deep scratches along his neck. So much for hoping the night before would pass without comment. Not when he bore the evidence of Lupe's violence for everyone to see.

Adam's head turned, and upon seeing her he stood. His brown-eyed gaze traveled the length of her, from her face on down and back again. There was nothing sexual in his appraisal, only detached concern. Surprisingly, that disappointed her. Had she been the only one moved by their embrace last night?

"Did I wake you?"

She shook her head, motioning for him to sit. Instead he held out a chair for her to sit in.

Seeing no other choice, she sat, though she would rather have said her peace and beat a hasty retreat to her room.

As she sat, he went to the counter and poured her a cup of coffee. He set it in front of her. "How is she?"

"Sleeping."

He retook his seat, saying nothing more. Sam sipped her coffee, wanting to feel as detached as he appeared to, but she couldn't. The yawning silence tautened her nerves, making her want to scream, if only to hear a human sound in the room.

Their eyes met, and she recognized that what she'd sensed in him was deliberation, not detachment. He was simply waiting her out, knowing that most people found silence disconcerting. Most people would fill that silence with their own words—a technique straight out of Policeman 101.

Sam swallowed in a dry throat. She wasn't any different from anyone else. "I have to apologize for last night. Lupe is very protective of me."

"No kidding." Adam sipped from his coffee cup. "Does she pull a gun on every man who touches you?"

"She wouldn't have hurt you. I don't allow her to have any bullets."

He put down his cup and stared at her in shocked disbelief. "That's one hell of a way to get yourself killed."

"What are you talking about? I told you the gun wasn't loaded."

"And it took me all of two seconds to get it away from her. Suppose that happened with someone without such a forgiving disposition? Or what if she pulled that on someone who was armed? They might not think twice about shooting, and she'd be defenseless."

A chill of alarm rushed up Sam's spine. "I hadn't thought about that."

Adam lifted his eyebrows in a way that said she should have known better. "So why the wildcat routine if it wasn't loaded?"

"Lupe doesn't like to be touched."

Adam snorted. "Do tell."

That was just the point; she didn't want to tell him anything. Deciding the best defense was a good offense, she pushed back her chair and stood. "Look, Detective, what Lupe does or doesn't do is none of your business. It was late; she must have heard me cry out the same way you did, and when she saw you in my room, she assumed the worst. End of story. If you'll excuse me, I'm going to check on her."

Adam let her get two steps away from him before he rose from the table to follow her. Though she wanted to downplay last night's events, he knew more had to exist to the story than she told him. He'd seen the haunted expression in Lupe's eyes. You didn't see that look every day, and he wanted to know why he'd seen it last night.

By the time he reached her, she'd made it to the doorway of the room. Grasping her arm, he pulled her back, though he was careful not to hurt her. With his free hand he gestured toward his neck. "This right here makes it my business. If I have to worry about her going postal every time I get near her, I want to know now."

He sensed the defeat in her as her shoulders slumped and she released a heavy breath. At the same time, she glared up at him, the sheen of tears glistening in her eyes.

"If you must know, Detective, if your precious hide is that important to you . . ." She inhaled and let her breath out in several short bursts. "Lupe's stepfather had the unfortunate habit of forgetting which female in the household he was married to."

Slowly, as her words sank in, he released her. An expletive escaped his lips before he had the time or the inclination to stop it. Sam winced at the harshness in his voice, but didn't move away. "What happened?"

She shook her head. "She's never told me the details and I never asked. But when Lupe came to live with us, I was the only person she allowed near her. She was ten years old at the time."

Adam shut his eyes as a wave of white-hot anger flashed through him. He'd suspected mistreatment by some man was at the root of Lupe's animosity, but he hadn't expected that. Some cop he was. Despite working in one of the most crime-ridden and whacked-out cities in the world, some part of his brain still rebelled against accepting the brutality and depravity of the human psyche.

He opened his eyes and looked at her. She'd lowered her head. With a hand under her chin, he tilted her face up to his. A single tear trickled down her cheek. He brushed it away with the pad of his thumb. His hand lingered to cup the side of her face. "What happened to him?"

"My father made sure he was prosecuted." A slow, satisfied grin spread across her face. "He lasted two years."

A similar smile flickered across Adam's face; he hadn't missed her implication. Even the most heinous criminals despised pedophiles. Getting a taste of their own medicine was often the least of their worries.

He brushed his knuckles across her cheek. "I'm sorry."

Sam shook her head. "It's not your fault. You couldn't have known. I didn't know. I have never seen her like that before."

"Surely she's seen you with other men?"

"Never here."

That surprised him. He didn't know about the other men in her life, but she'd been engaged to his brother. Sam had never brought him here?

"Look, I've told you something that no one else knows, at least no one who hasn't taken that knowledge with them to their grave. I would appreciate it if you didn't let on that you know."

"No one knows? Not even a therapist?"

"She won't go."

"You're her employer. Couldn't you make it a condition of her employment?"

"It's not that simple. You try getting Lupe to do something she doesn't want to do. Then you can talk." She sighed, shifting her weight. "I have to go. I have a doctor's appointment this morning. I need to call my driver."

"I'll take you."

He expected her to argue with him, but she didn't. "Thank you. I need to get changed and tell Lupe I'm going. I'll meet you out front in fifteen minutes."

As Sam walked down the hallway, Adam pulled out his cell phone and dialed Joe's number. When Joe answered, Adam said, "See what you can find out for me about Samantha Hathaway and her housekeeper, Lupe. I don't know her last name."

"Will do," Joe said, "But why?"

"Tell you later." Adam hung up the phone and went back to the guesthouse to get ready to go.

* * *

After showering and dressing in a black-and-white top and matching shorts, Sam sat on the edge of the bed and nudged Lupe's shoulder. "Lupe, wake up. It's me, Sam. Are you okay?"

Lupe turned on her side to face her. Her eyelids were red and puffy from crying, but her eyes were alert. Just as Sam had suspected, she hadn't been sleeping. "You didn't tell him, did you?"

"Not everything. Just about your stepfather." She brushed Lupe's hair from her face. "You scratched him. I had to tell him something."

Lupe turned her face into her pillow. "I'm sorry."

"Don't be." If anything, Sam was more to blame for indulging Lupe's fears rather than forcing her to seek help. "Adam is taking me to the doctor. We shouldn't be gone too long."

Lupe nodded.

"You might want to think about making some lunch. Adam made coffee this morning. He might actually try to cook this afternoon."

Lupe's head snapped up, exactly the reaction Sam expected. She knew Lupe would mope for the rest of the day without some reason to get out of bed. The idea that someone else might be fiddling around in her kitchen was enough to do the trick.

"I'll see you when I get back." Sam stood and left the room.

When Sam emerged from the front of the house, she nearly burst out laughing. Adam, dressed totally in black from his jacket to the boots on his feet, and wearing a pair of reflective sunglasses, his arms crossed over his chest, gave off an aura of danger and power.

Yet he leaned against the hood of a tiny red sports car. The incongruity made her laugh. "This is what you're driving?" she asked.

He lifted one shoulder. "I figured since I was living in Barbie's house, I might as well drive her car."

He might look dangerous, but she appreciated his humor. After last night and this morning she needed humor. Sam nodded in the direction of the garage. "You know, you could drive

my Mercedes while you're here. It's a convertible, but much
roomier."

"No, thanks. I've gotten used to driving with my knees in
my chest." He pushed off the car hood and opened the passenger door. "Your chariot, such as it is, awaits you, Ms.
Hathaway."

She allowed him to help her into her seat, then waited for
him to take his seat before speaking. "Sam."

He revved the engine. "Excuse me?"

"Everyone calls me Sam. The only people who ever called
me Samantha are Richard, because he's pretentious, and my
mother, and then only when she caught me doing something
I wasn't supposed to."

She watched his profile as he pulled out onto the street. A
little half smile turned up his lips. "You expect *me* to call *you*
Sam?"

"Is that a problem?"

"When I was a kid we had a dog named Sam. The com-
parison does not compute."

Her brow furrowed. "What does that mean?"

He glanced at her, but his sunglasses prevented her from
seeing the expression in his eyes. "You figure it out."

Sam lowered her head, a slow smile spreading across her
face. So he didn't think she was a complete dog. He might even
be attracted to her. She didn't know why his opinion mattered
to her when he'd be gone from her life in little over a week. If
she were smart, she'd wish for the opposite. That would mini-
mize the chance she'd do something stupid before he left.

A flood of warmth cascaded through her as she remembered
the tenderness of his touch, both last night and this morning.
Would he be a sensitive lover, as his caresses suggested?

"Where are we going, anyway?"

Sam's head snapped up. Heat stole into her cheeks. She was
grateful Adam's attention was focused on the road. What had
she been thinking? Was she so sex-starved that a couple of
caresses from a man revved her libido into overdrive? Until
now, she hadn't thought so.

As they pulled to a stop at a light, Same gave Adam rudimentary directions to her doctor's office in downtown L.A. Another car pulled up beside them. Bob Marley wailed from its speakers. The blond, blue-eyed driver bopped along to the beat, sending the shoulder-length braids that popped up at odd intervals on his head bouncing.

Sam pressed her lips together to keep from laughing at the incongruous sight. She turned to Adam to gauge his reaction.

"Nice head," Adam said, then roared ahead as the light changed from red to green.

Adam sat in the doctor's office while Sam was being examined in a nearby room. His eyes scanned the walls, which were cluttered with diplomas and certificates and commendations. Framed photographs of Dr. Jerry Daniels with some of his more famous patients hung in one corner. The orthopedist of the stars, Samantha Hathaway included.

To pass the time, he imagined unholstering the gun at his hip and taking target practice on the good doctor's face. Adam resented any man who looked like Billy Dee Williams's younger, more attractive brother and bore even the remotest possibility of having seen Samantha naked.

Besides, he suspected the good doctor had more than a professional interest in his patient. Jerry had greeted Samantha as if she were his long-lost lover returning from the war, and had been almost hostile toward him. Samantha apparently hadn't noticed.

Hearing someone approach, Adam stood. Jerry entered alone and sat behind his desk, a concerned expression on his face. Adam retook his seat. "Where's Samantha? How is she?"

"She'll be joining us in a minute. I wanted to talk to you for a moment first. Sam's injuries are healing nicely. Much more quickly than I expected."

The doctor let his words hang there. Adam nodded, encouraging the doctor to go on. Somehow Adam sensed a *but* coming on.

"But whether or not she wants to admit it, she's still fragile. She's lost weight and her blood pressure is up." The doctor's gaze slid to the scratches on Adam's neck. "I wouldn't want her condition to deteriorate because of undue stress or unwarranted physical activity."

In other words, sex. Adam folded his arms across his chest and glared at the man across the desk from him. "Is that a personal or a professional recommendation?"

"It's no secret that I'm very, um, fond of Sam. But I do think it would be wise if you encouraged her to rest."

Adam decided to take it easy on the other man. "I don't know what you've seen in the media, but I'm only the hired help. She doesn't listen to me."

"Listen to you about what?"

Both men's heads turned as Samantha appeared in the doorway.

Adam stood. "About what station to put on the radio. Are you ready to go?"

She nodded. "I'll see you in two weeks, Jerry."

Jerry grinned, showing even, white teeth and a dimple in each cheek. "I'm looking forward to it."

With some effort, Adam managed not to deck him. Adam took Samantha's arm and led her from the room. "Let's go."

When they got back to the house, Sam took the mail and headed off to the Angel Room to find Lupe. The bed was made and Lupe was nowhere in evidence. She hoped that meant Lupe hadn't found somewhere else to hole up.

Sam sank down on the bed and thumbed through the mail. Most of it was the usual nonsense, but one letter caught her eye. It had no return address and something about the stamp seemed odd. Inside the envelope was a single sheaf of paper.

Sam had seen messages like this in movies or on TV shows, but never in person. Letters cut out from magazines had been pasted together to spell a cryptic message.

You made me kill once. Please don't make me kill again.

Eleven

After dropping Samantha off at her room, Adam continued on through the house, intending to head out to the guesthouse. He stopped short upon finding Lupe in the kitchen. After the events of last night and Samantha's revelation that morning, he didn't know how to approach her, or if at this point he should. Maybe he should back out of the room and leave her in peace for the time being.

She looked up at him, taking the option away from him. Her eyes widened and her grip tightened on the paring knife in her hand.

"Just passing through," Adam said, but he didn't move right away. She shrugged, but he noticed that her gaze traveled from his face to his neck, where she'd scratched him. Her brow furrowed and she pressed her lips together, then lowered her head again. She seemed to be merely staring at the vegetables she'd been cutting, because her hands remained still.

Adam wished he had some words to say to her to put her at ease. None sprang to mind, so he figured the best thing to do was to get out of her way. In a few strides he made it to the other side of the kitchen with his hand on the doorknob.

"I didn't mean to hurt you."

Hearing Lupe's whispered words, he paused. "I know."

"I want my gun back."

Adam suppressed a smile. Like her boss, she wasn't afraid to step into the fray. He turned to face her. "On one condition."

The wariness returned to her eyes. "What's that?"

"Agree to let me teach you how to shoot it."

She shook her head. "Why would you do that?"

"To prevent you from taking it upside my head should the mood strike you. Being shot I can handle, but a whack to the cranium might actually do some damage."

For the first time since he'd known her, she smiled, lighting up her eyes and softening her features. "You like that idea, do you?"

Lupe's expression immediately sobered. "You hurt Sam, you'll find out exactly how much."

"I have no intention of hurting Samantha. I'm here to help her."

She cast him a look full of skepticism. "Lots of things happen nobody intends."

He couldn't argue with her there. "Let me know what you decide about the shooting lessons."

Adam opened the kitchen door into brilliant late-morning sunshine.

Samantha looked down at the letter in her hands. She'd spent the last ten minutes with her eyes riveted to the missive, as if staring at it would change its meaning.

You made me kill once. . . . Immediately Sam thought of Billy. Had the accident that claimed his life not really been an accident at all? She shut her eyes tightly, wishing she could remember more than the vague, terrifying images that haunted her dreams. Maybe then she'd know if there were any portent to this letter other than a prank designed to torment her.

In the past week and a half, she'd received at least a score of letters blaming her for Billy's death. Some of them had been filled with such vitriol they'd frightened her. But none of them had borne the type of threat this simple message had.

Please don't make me kill again. But kill who? Her? Or was someone else involved, and if so who? And what was she supposed to do to avert the threat?

She rose from the bed, intent on showing the letter to Adam, but sank back down again. If she showed this to him, he'd probably order her to her room and put the house on lockdown. He'd have the LAPD here faster than she could say the word *cop*. If she'd learned anything about him, she knew he took his job seriously.

Ordinarily she wouldn't complain. She'd heard of other celebrities who were hurt or even killed by people obsessed with them for some reason. She had no interest in becoming another statistic. But she thought of the effect this news would have on Lupe. Lupe hadn't really recovered from the shock of Sam's accident, and now this business with Adam. Could Lupe handle any more?

Sam's gaze fell on a silver-framed photograph that sat on her dresser showing Jarad, Ariel, and their girls frolicking in the waves at their home on Martha's Vineyard. Maybe she should concoct some story about a friend of a friend and ask Ariel what she thought. Yeah, and what were the chances Ariel wouldn't see through that? Practically nil.

Sam picked up the telephone next to her divan and dialed Ariel's number anyway. She hadn't heard from either Jarad or Ariel since the day after the press conference. At the moment it wouldn't hurt her to hear a friendly voice or two.

The phone rang only once before Ariel picked up and said, "Where are you?"

"California. Ari, are you okay? It's me, Sam."

"There's nothing wrong a few more hours of labor won't cure. I just beeped Jarad on location to tell him I'm ready to go to the hospital. I thought you were him calling me back."

"Oh, God, Ariel, I'm sorry. I'll get off the phone. I'm so happy for you guys. Tell Jarad to call me the minute the babies are born."

"If he survives that long."

Sam laughed. "You know you won't kill him."

"Probably not. I've gotten soft in my old age. Was there something you wanted?"

"To check on you. I got the answer I was looking for. Don't forget to call me."

"I won't."

Sam clicked off the phone and tossed it onto the bed. If she needed another reason to keep her mouth shut, she'd found one. Adam would undoubtedly tell Jarad about the letter. Neither he nor Ariel should be worrying about her right now. They should be together enjoying the two precious lives they were about to welcome into the world.

Sam folded the letter and replaced it in the envelope. For now she'd bide her time and say nothing.

"I got bad news, worse news, and truly messed-up news. Which one you wanna hear first?"

Those were Joe's first words when Adam picked up the phone, not even a hello. "Hold on a minute while I do eenie meenie miney mo."

"Don't bother. Some of what I have to say is best said in person. I'll swing by in a few minutes."

"Where can I meet you?"

"I'll come to you. I've got some things I need to take care of before I sign out tonight."

"Don't come here."

"Why not? You and Ms. Hathaway too busy playing house?"

"Hardly."

"Then I'll see you in a few minutes."

The line went dead before Adam had a chance to protest. Despite what Joe said, Adam suspected that getting a peek at Samantha close-up was the only reason Joe had volunteered to come there.

With a growl of annoyance, Adam clicked off the phone, slammed it back on the cradle, and reached for the T-shirt he'd tossed on the bed. With any luck he'd catch up with Joe before he rang the bell.

Lupe was standing at the stove stirring a giant pot when Sam walked into the kitchen. She took a deep breath to calm herself. If she intended to keep the letter a secret, she'd have to do a better job of controlling her nerves. She reminded herself that she was a trained actress, though this was the first time she'd had to put her skills to use in her own home.

Sam forced a normal-looking smile to her face. "Something smells delicious."

"Just some minestrone. It'll be ready in a few minutes."

"Good, I'm starving." Sam leaned her elbow against the counter. "How are you doing? Have you seen Adam?"

Lupe nodded. "He won't give me my gun back."

And Lupe obviously expected her to intervene. After all these years of trying to wrest the damn thing away from her, Adam could bury it in the backyard for all she cared. "Can you blame him? I would think cops in particular would get a little testy having a gun held on them."

She shrugged. "He said he'd give it back if I let him show me how to use it properly."

"What?" The man was nuts. Either that or he was so gun-happy he couldn't see the craziness of what he suggested. She wasn't blind; she'd noticed the gun strapped to his hip on the drive home from her doctor's office. She doubted a weapon that size was department-issue. Whatever the case, under no circumstances could she let Adam's offer stand.

Sam stood. "I'll go tell Adam lunch is ready." Sam felt Lupe's eyes on her as she crossed to the door. Let Lupe think whatever she wanted.

Sam stalked out to the guesthouse. She flung open the door. "Are you totally insane?"

Adam stood in the middle of the room, tucking his shirt into his waistband. "That depends. What did I do now?"

"Offering to give Lupe shooting lessons. She's dangerous enough without them."

"I agree with you, dangerous to herself. I thought we went through that this morning."

"And giving her a box of bullets and saying, 'Have at it' is going to make her safe?"

"That's not what I was offering to do, and you know it."

"Don't you know how many people are killed by their own guns every year? How many kids shoot themselves or others with guns they 'find' in their own homes?" She stopped short of rattling off statistics he probably knew as well as she. "Haven't you ever heard of gun control?"

"Sure. Gun control is hitting what you aim at." He walked to the desk, picked up the holster, and clipped it to his belt. Her eyes followed the path of the gun, transfixed. "Besides, I'm not the one who let her have it in the first place."

Sam bit her lip. He had her there. At first she hadn't known Lupe had kept the thing. Once she'd found out, nothing short of wrestling Lupe to the floor and confiscating it would have gotten it back.

Aside from that, she recognized this as an argument she couldn't win. "Fine. Then whatever happens to her is on your head."

She turned to leave, but Adam grasped her arm, preventing her from leaving. "Let me ask you a question now. What do you really have against Lupe learning to shoot?"

She turned to face him. "I don't like guns, okay?"

"That's obvious. How do you expect to play a policewoman if you're afraid of guns?"

"I never said I was afraid," she protested. But she was. Part of the appeal of the role was the necessity of confronting the one fear she'd harbored for the past twenty years. "The gun I'll carry will be filled with blanks. It can't hurt anybody."

"Tell that to Jon-Erik Hexum."

"Who's that?"

"I'm surprised you haven't heard of him. A television actor who labored under the same misconception you do. Fooling around, he put the gun to his head and it went off. Even a blank fires a cartridge. Needless to say his show went on hiatus."

Sam let her eyes drift closed as her brain swam. "I see."

She felt Adam's strong hands at her shoulders, gentle, soothing. "Sweetheart, I'm not trying to scare you, but you need to face some realities here."

Sam's eyes flew open. Adam didn't strike her as a mushy, kissy-face sort of man, so hearing the endearment on his lips surprised her. The comment on her lips died when she heard an unfamiliar male voice behind her.

"Ding-dong, Avon calling."

Sam spun around, backing into Adam. Luckily his hands caught her waist, steadying her. She dragged air into her lungs in short gasps and willed her heart to stop racing. That stupid letter had made her jittery as hell.

"They shoot Avon ladies, don't they?" Adam replied. "Samantha, this is a friend of mine, Det. Joe Martinez from the LAPD."

Detective Martinez smiled back at her with an expression bordering on awe. Still, she couldn't stop trembling. Undoubtedly Adam noticed that, too. His hands still rested at her waist, his fingers moving in a soothing manner. In the periphery of her vision, she noticed him watching her closely, but he said nothing.

"Pleased to meet you, Detective." She didn't extend her hand, fearing both men would see her tremble. She moved away from Adam and his hand fell to his side. "We'll be serving lunch in a few minutes. You're free to join us."

Without waiting for a reply, Sam slipped past him, went back to the house, and locked herself in the Angel Room. Leaning her hand against one of the tables, she dragged in air, willing the trembling to stop. Logically it didn't make sense for someone to go to the trouble of fabricating that note to simply show up at her house in broad daylight, but when she'd seen that man approaching, terror had seized her and reason had flown.

She went to the dresser and pulled out the letter. Maybe she should tell Adam about it. That would make her feel better. She realized she trusted him completely—with her safety, at least.

Then she reminded herself about Ariel and Jared and Lupe. None of them needed to worry about her right now. For the second time that day she folded the letter and buried the envelope in her underwear drawer, wondering if she would live to regret her decision.

Or if she'd live long enough to regret it.

Twelve

"Nice crib you got here." Joe tested the bed a couple of times before settling back against the pillows and drawing his feet up on the comforter. "Soft. My only question is, what time is Ken coming over?"

Adam turned the desk chair around and sat. "Cute, now get your shoes off my bed."

Joe sat up. "Spoilsport. And after I've busted my hump finding out information for you."

"Yeah, right. What did you find out, anyway?"

"Rufus What's-his-name's story checks out. According to his buddy, they hung out for a while. He stayed around after Rufus left. Never saw him touch Billy's car."

Adam shrugged. He'd thought as much. Why tell a lie so easily checked? "Is that it for the bad news?"

"Not quite. I did like you asked and had someone look into your lady friend's and her housekeeper's backgrounds. I couldn't turn up anything on the housekeeper. I don't know what financial arrangement she has with Ms. Hathaway, but there's no record of her employment, and neither of them is paying proper tribute to Uncle Sam for it."

Adam sat back, rubbing his chin, not knowing what to make of that. "What about Ms. Hathaway?"

"Now we're venturing into truly messed up territory." Joe paused, and Adam held his breath wondering what he'd say. "When she was fourteen, she and her mom went to the Big Apple on vacation. They wander down the wrong alley and get mugged by some lowlife. Mom refuses to turn over her wedding ring, or maybe she can't get it off fast enough. The son of a bitch shoots her right in front of her kid. According to a witness who tried to come to their aid, the bastard would have shot the kid, too, but the gun jammed. The shooting made all the papers, as there had been a rash of crime against tourists at the time."

Adam ran his hand over his face. At the moment he felt about two inches high. He'd assumed her dislike of guns was just another example of West Coast weirdness, never imagining a more personal root to her fear. "Is that all?"

"Afraid not. After Mom's death, Dad climbs into the bottle and stays there, runs up some debts. One night while in a drunken stupor, he wraps his car around a tree trunk, sending Ms. Hathaway into the windshield. It seems one of the most faces in the world owes her fortune to Plastic Surgeons R Us."

Adam lowered his head to cup his forehead in his palm. "Damn."

"Are you all right?"

Adam raised his head. "Hope you've still got that good news for me."

"Word came down this morning that your brother's case is back on. I don't know what you said to your step-pops, but it must have done the trick."

Adam doubted anything he'd said to Prescott had made an iota of difference. His mother must have changed her mind. But why? "Where do you stand?"

"As far as leads go, nowhere. You know how it is with a case like this—every crackpot and his mother phones in some bit of information we have to track down. So far nothing even as substantial as the Rufus business. The lab has the car. We should have a prelim report by tomorrow."

"What do you think they'll find?"

"Not much. Not to be insensitive, but between the crash and the fire, there's not much left to examine."

Adam nodded. He'd figured as much. He'd have to content himself with whatever results the lab came up with. At least he'd know he'd done his best to figure out what had happened to his brother.

Adam stood and extended his hand. "Thanks, Joe. I appreciate it."

"De nada, bro. But I don't work for free. Didn't I hear something about lunch?"

Adam grinned. "Anybody ever tell you how transparent you are?"

"As clear as Saran Wrap."

Adam shook his head. "Come on."

The kitchen was deserted when they got there. Adam assumed Samantha had warned Lupe that Joe was on the premises and she'd disappeared somewhere. He doubted Samantha would make an appearance, either. He'd seen the horrified look on her face when Joe showed up. He'd felt her trembling in his arms. It seemed way too much of a reaction for being startled. Something was going on with her that she hadn't confided to him. As soon as Joe left, he intended to find out what it was.

Adam motioned toward the kitchen table. "Have a seat. I'll see what's on the menu." A lone pot sat on the stove. He picked up the spoon that lay on the rest on the center of the stove and gave the soup a stir. "Looks like minestrone."

"Yummy. Vegetables."

Adam got two bowls from the cabinet and began to ladle out the soup. "You wouldn't be growing that gut if you ate more of them."

He'd expected some snappy comeback from Joe. When he got none, he glanced over his shoulder. Lupe stood on the second step of the back staircase, directly across from Joe, a basket of laundry in her arms. The two of them stared at each other, Lupe with a wary glare, Joe with interest.

Lupe looked away first, glancing at him. "I'm sorry, Mr. Adam. I didn't know your guest was still here."

Adam blinked. If someone had blown on him, he'd have fallen over. Mr. Adam? Since when had he earned any respect from her?

"Lupe this is a friend of mine, a cop, Joe Martinez."

Lupe turned in Joe's direction and frowned.

Joe grinned. "Don't worry. I don't bite. Not unless I'm asked."

Adam was about to intervene when Lupe speared Joe with a withering look. "Good thing I won't be asking."

With supreme confidence and a dash of cockiness, Joe said. "Not yet."

Lupe glared back at him with all the contempt of a bishop regarding a sinner. "Why don't you hold your breath while you wait?"

Laughing, Joe got up and held the door open for Lupe's departure. As she walked through the door, Lupe cast a speculative look back at Adam as if to ask, Who is this idiot?

Adam wondered that himself. He'd never actually seen Joe come on to a woman before. Joe was like Billy when it came to the female portion of the population: both men had women falling into their laps; they didn't have to go looking. Even when Joe had been married, women with no respect for a wedding ring had tried to tempt him. To Adam's knowledge, Joe had never succumbed.

So what was the deal now? Maybe Lupe intrigued him because she didn't immediately fall at his feet.

Whatever. Adam waited until Joe retook his seat before saying anything. "What the hell is your problem?"

"I was just being friendly."

"Don't even think of hitting on her."

"Why not? You got the lock on all the women in the Hathaway household? By the way, which one of them left her calling card on your neck?"

Annoyed with Joe's humor, Adam plopped a bowlful of soup in front of him. "Much as I'd love to see you make an ass of yourself, find some other way to get your kicks and leave her alone."

"Come on, man. Haven't you ever indulged in that whole French-maid fantasy? A woman at your beck and call, seeing to your every whim, preferably dressed in something skimpy with garters and those stockings with the seam down the back?"

"I'm serious."

Joe sobered. "All right. I'll behave myself. You plan on telling me why?"

"She's not exactly a cheerleader for the male half of the species. A stepfather with hand problems."

Joe muttered the same word Adam had when he'd heard the news.

"Of course, you don't know that."

"My lips are sealed."

Joe left a few minutes later, claiming to have lost his appetite. Adam wasn't much in the mood for food himself. It had been a long day already, and it was barely two o'clock in the afternoon.

Hearing the cell phone on his hip ring, Adam suspected the day was about to get longer. "Wexler."

"Adam, is that you?"

Adam searched to place the familiar voice. "Sandra?" Why would she be calling him? And how had she gotten this number? "What can I do for you?"

A long pause, then: "It's so silly really. Can you come over?"

"I can't leave right now." Until he heard the verdict on Billy's car, he didn't want to leave Samantha alone.

Sandra sniffled and let out a heavy sigh. "I used to be able to call Billy."

Her words trailed off. He'd had her pegged as one noodle short of a casserole, but she'd played the guilt card just right.

"Where are you?" Adam wrote down the address and directions she gave him. "I'll be there in half an hour."

Adam clicked off the phone and latched it to his belt. He went out to the guesthouse to retrieve his jacket, then went to find Samantha. He wanted to check on her before he left.

She didn't immediately answer when he knocked on the Angel Room's door. He was about to knock again when he heard the latch turn. He'd never noticed her locking the door before and wondered why she'd done so now.

She opened the door and peered up at him. "What can I do for you, Adam? I was trying to take a nap."

He doubted that. Her rumpled clothing and tumbled hair suggested she'd been in her bed. But she didn't look sleepy; she looked worried.

"I'm sorry about Joe startling you before. I should have warned you that he was on the way over."

"It isn't your fault. I overreacted."

"Why did you?"

She stepped into the room, turning her back on him. "I heard from Ariel and Jarad this morning. Ariel's in labor."

"Shouldn't you be happy for them?"

"I am, but they're expecting twins again. They don't talk about it, but it was hard on Ariel the first time."

She expected him to believe that concern for her friend put that anxious look on her face? He wasn't buying it. He didn't have time to argue with her about it, though. He wanted to get out and back before nightfall.

"I have to go out for a while. No one gets in or out until I get back."

Samantha spun around to face him. "I beg your pardon?"

"You heard me. You and Lupe stay here and don't let anyone in until I get back."

Her eyes flashed amber fire. "First off, this is my home—"

That was as far as he let her get before placing a silencing finger against her lips. "Do as I say, or I'll call your friend Jarad in the delivery room and tell him you're being uncooperative."

Her eyes narrowed and her mouth compressed into a thin line. He had her and she knew it—and more important, she didn't like it. Good. He preferred the fire in her eyes to the haunted expression he'd seen before.

On impulse, he cupped his palm around her nape and lowered his lips to her forehead. "I won't be gone long."

He turned and sauntered from the room, leaving her gaping openmouthed behind him.

Sandra met him at the door to her house in Brentwood, wearing a short, clingy robe, high-heeled slippers and, apparently nothing else. She clutched the collar of robe in one hand. Her brown eyes fastened on him. Gone was the vacant look he'd seen at the cemetery, replaced by a sloe-eyed, seductive expression.

"I didn't expect you so soon."

Adam raised one eyebrow, but didn't comment. Due to traffic on the freeway, it had taken him longer to get there than he had planned. If it weren't for the little girl standing beside her mother, he'd swear he'd walked in on the beginning of a bad porno movie. "What's the emergency?"

She motioned him inside the house and closed the door behind him. "It's the sink in the bathroom upstairs. It won't stop running."

She got him all the way over here to fix a broken washer? "Why didn't you call a plumber?"

"I couldn't afford to call a plumber. Billy used to bring me money every month. Since his death . . ."

Her words trailed off. Adam filled in the rest. Billy hadn't been around to see to her financial needs. And since Billy's estate remained in limbo due to his indecision, she'd been cut off. The temptation to tell her to get a job, like the rest of the normal population, rose in him. But then he looked down at the little girl plastered to her leg, Billy's child. One dependent woman raising her daughter to be another one—or trying to. Adam knew he would do whatever he could to prevent that from happening.

In ten minutes he had the washer fixed. Sandra tried to convince him to stay for coffee, but he declined, not only because he suspected her motives, but because he wanted to get back to Samantha.

At the door, he reached into his front pocket and pulled out whatever money he carried there, probably no more than two hundred dollars. He extended the bills toward her. "If you need anything else, call me."

She took the money from him. "Thank you." She leaned a hand on his chest, going on tiptoe. Adam took mercy on her and leaned down for the peck he assumed she planned to give him. But her lips lingered on his cheek and she withdrew slowly, gazing up at him with a seductive gleam in her eyes. "Thanks for everything."

Adam rocked back on his heels and shoved his hands in his pockets. *Jesus. Not too obvious.* "I'd better be going."

"You know, Billy thought the world of you, Adam. He talked about you all the time. If he were here, he wouldn't understand your not accepting his money."

Adam shrugged. Undoubtedly she couldn't understand it either. She didn't seem to have trouble accepting anyone's money. "I didn't say I would refuse Billy's legacy."

"But you didn't say you wouldn't. Please think about it."

And he realized her purpose in getting him over here: to convince him to sign the papers that would allow Billy's estate to continue paying her. The seductive outfit served only as a distraction. Or maybe it was an invitation for Adam to take over where Billy had left off. Either way, he wasn't interested.

He consoled himself with the knowledge that Sandra could be let off the hook as a suspect in Billy's death. She'd have to be crazy to kill off her only source of support. Conniving, maybe, gold digging, definitely, but crazy? The jury was still out on that.

Adam went out to his car and drove off. He drove out to the Prescott estate, but once he parked outside the gate, he remained in the car staring up at the house. What had made his mother change her mind? That question ate at him, begging to be answered. But he feared that if he confronted her with it, she'd do a turnaround and clamp the case shut again. He'd be better off leaving things as they stood—for now. Once the police did their job, he'd be back. He roared off into the burgeoning darkness and headed for Samantha's house.

When he pulled into Samantha's drive to find not only the white van that had been there the other day, but a blue sports car with the top down, Adam ground his teeth together. He wondered if these visitors had stopped by, or if she'd called them over just to thwart his wishes.

Adam slammed the car door shut, entered through the front door and went to find Samantha.

Thirteen

Finding the front rooms empty, Adam headed down to the solarium. The same woman he'd seen vacuuming a few days ago now dusted the piano in the green room. Figuring she'd more likely know the whereabouts of the housekeeper than of the mistress of the house, he shouted, "Where's Lupe?" over the din of the CD player blasting in the woman's ear.

The woman blew a bubble and popped it. "Kitchen."

He should have figured, as that was the only spot in the house she actually seemed to do any work. He wondered if Samantha realized that the money she paid Lupe was misspent.

When he walked into the kitchen, Lupe jumped up from her seat at the table and shoved the book she'd been reading into her uniform pocket. "D-dinner isn't ready yet."

"Where's your boss?"

"Miss Sam is in the gym, but you can't go there."

He'd already headed back toward the hall by the time she finished her sentence. The last of it was spoken in a near shout. He heard her scurry up behind him and asked, "Why not?"

"Miss Sam won't like it."

Too bad. Miss Sam seemed particularly gifted at flouting his wishes. Maybe she ought to taste her own medicine. He paused at the gym door, debating the wisdom of simply barging in. Then Samantha's dreamy voice reached him: "Oh, God, that feels marvelous."

Without thinking, he pushed through the door, then drew up short, finding Samantha lying on a massage table. Mr. Clean hovered at the base of the table, holding Samantha's left ankle

An important message from the ARABESQUE Editor

Dear Arabesque Reader,

Because you've chosen to read one of our Arabesque romance novels, we'd like to say "thank you"! And, as a special way to thank you, we've selected four more of the books you love so well to send you for FREE!

Please enjoy them with our compliments, and thank you for continuing to enjoy Arabesque...the soul of romance.

Karen Thomas
Senior Editor,
Arabesque Romance Novels

Check out our website at
www.arabesquebooks.com

SPECIAL OFFER!
4 FREE BOOKS

ARABESQUE ®

A PRODUCT OF

BET BOOKS™

3 QUICK STEPS
TO RECEIVE YOUR "THANK YOU" GIFT
FROM THE EDITOR

Send this card back and you'll receive 4 FREE Arabesque novels! The introductory shipment of 4 Arabesque novels – a $23.96 value – is yours absolutely FREE!

There's no catch. You're under no obligation to buy anything. You'll receive your introductory shipment of 4 Arabesque novels absolutely FREE (plus $1.99 to offset the costs of shipping & handling). And you don't have to make any minimum number of purchases—not even one!

We hope that after receiving your books you'll want to remain an Arabesque subscriber. But the choice is yours to continue or cancel, anytime at all! So why not take us up on our invitation to receive 4 Arabesque Romance Novels, with no risk of any kind. You'll be glad you did!

Call us
TOLL-FREE
at 1-800-770-1963

THE EDITOR'S "THANK YOU" GIFT INCLUDES:

- 4 books absolutely FREE (plus $1.99 for shipping and handling)
- A FREE newsletter, *Arabesque Romance News*, filled with author interviews, book previews, special offers, and more!
- No risks or obligations. You're free to cancel whenever you wish... with no questions asked.

BOOK CERTIFICATE

Yes! Please send me 4 FREE Arabesque novels (plus $1.99 for shipping & handling). I understand I am under no obligation to purchase any books, as explained on the back of this card.

Name _____

Address _____ Apt. _____

City _____ State _____ Zip _____

Telephone ( ) _____

Signature _____

Offer limited to one per household and not valid to current subscribers. All orders subject to approval. Terms, offer, & price subject to change. Offer valid only in the U.S.

Thank you!

AN092A

Accepting the four introductory books for FREE (plus $1.99 to offset the cost of shipping & handling) places you under no obligation to buy anything. You may keep the books and return the shipping statement marked "cancelled". If you do not cancel, about a month later we will send 4 additional Arabesque novels, and you will be billed the preferred subscriber's price of just $4.00 per title. That's $16.00 for all 4 books for a savings of 33% off the cover price (Plus $1.99 for shipping and handling). You may cancel at any time, but if you choose to continue, every month we'll send you 4 more books, which you may either purchase at the preferred discount price. . . or return to us and cancel your subscription.

THE ARABESQUE ROMANCE CLUB: HERE'S HOW IT WORKS

PLACE
STAMP
HERE

ARABESQUE ROMANCE BOOK CLUB
P.O. Box 5214
Clifton NJ 07015-5214

in his hands. Both of them glared back at him as if he were the fox invading their henhouse.

Every ounce of annoyance he'd felt vanished as a bolt of white-hot desire flashed through him. A large blue towel covered her from the middle of her back to midthigh, but his imagination filled in all the blanks. His gaze scanned down her impossibly long legs and back up to her face. He couldn't think of a single coherent thing to say.

Sam eyes narrowed, and an arch expression formed on her face. "We have a little custom here in California. It's called knocking before you enter a room."

He ignored her jibe. "I need to speak to you. And if you don't want Mr. Gladhands over here hearing what I have to say . . ."

With a withering glance in his direction, she gathered the towel around her more tightly. "That's all for today, Teddy," she called over her shoulder.

To Adam she said, "If it's not too much trouble to turn your back, I'll get ready." He did as she asked, but as the mirrors reflected back on one another, he might as well have stayed the way he was. If he were any sort of gentleman, he'd have closed his eyes or stared down at his shoes or busied himself with something safe, the way Mr. Clean set about replacing his things in a black leather bag.

Adam didn't do any of those things. He tried to pull his gaze from her reflection, but his eyes refused to go along with the plan. As Sam slid the towel from beneath her robe, he caught the briefest glimpse of what he'd only imagined before.

"See you next week," Mr. Clean said, slinging his bag over his arm.

She finished cinching the robe at her waist, and her gaze lifted as she called out, "Thanks, Teddy," but the masseur was already out the door. Adam drew in a quick breath as her gaze locked with his for an instant. Her mouth dropped open and her gaze narrowed. Obviously it hadn't occurred to her that he could see her. He couldn't help himself; he winked at her.

She snapped her mouth closed and whirled around to face him.

"I hope you enjoyed the peep show, Detective, since it's the only one you're going to get." She stalked past him and pushed through the door.

After a moment he followed her. He supposed he should feel some remorse for partaking of the little sneak preview of Samantha Hathaway's charms, but he didn't. She visited his dreams every night to torment him; it seemed only fair that she oblige him during waking hours as well. And she was right: that was the closest he'd ever get to satisfying the lust she inspired in him.

"Samantha," he called, just as she reached the Angel Room door.

She stopped, but she didn't turn to face him. "What now?"

"If you are so concerned with your modesty, why didn't you ask me to leave?"

"If I had would you have done it?"

"Probably not."

"There's your answer."

In other words, she wouldn't ask for anything she knew she wouldn't get. "Is that why you didn't ask a certain director to yank a certain scene out of a certain movie you made a few years ago?"

Her lips curled and she ground her teeth together. "Has *every* man in America seen that?"

"Only the ones with red blood and a heartbeat."

"I should have sued Jarad's butt off for that."

"Maybe he didn't know it was in there."

"Detective," she said in a patient voice, "Jarad is the most conscientious director in the business. He probably knows every frame that goes into his movies. He knew it was in there, but didn't want to lose the scene. He didn't tell me about it because he hoped nobody would notice. But I never authorized him to breach my contract. I don't do nude scenes."

To Adam's thinking, it never paid to underestimate the perversity of the male mind. "So those Internet photos of you are fakes?"

"They'd have to be. I've never taken any nude photos."

"Never?" He couldn't believe some old flame hadn't convinced her to pose for him.

Her cheeks pinkened, and she glanced away from him. "That's none of your business."

Maybe not, but she'd just answered his question, whether she'd wanted to or not. "So why didn't you sue him?"

"He sicced his wife on me. She'd just found out she was pregnant with the girls at the same time I found out about the scene."

"So you're a soft touch?"

"No, just easily manipulated."

If she was he had never seen it. "So it's only me you enjoy giving agita to."

She nodded. "Pretty much."

"Why? Because I asked you not to let anyone in the house?"

"Funny, I don't recall your asking me a thing. I remember you barking a few orders at me. . . ."

She trailed off, looking away, and he suspected she also remembered his impulsive kiss. He rubbed his knuckles across her cheek. "Did it occur to you I might be concerned for your safety while I couldn't be here?"

Her gaze traveled upward to lock with his. "Why, Detective, I didn't know you cared."

He should have pulled away from her. He should have walked away, or barring that he should have ignored the allure of her amber eyes or the seductive lift of her smile. He should have done anything other than what he did, but this seemed to be his day for doing things he shouldn't.

He lowered his head to claim her mouth. With a sigh she sank against him. Since that first ill-fated kiss in her hospital room, he'd wondered if he'd imagined the softness of her lips, the sweet taste of her. If anything, the reality far outstripped the memory. He stifled a groan as her lips parted beneath his, seeming to invite him in.

But suddenly she pushed away from him, an expression of horror on her face. She took a step back from him and wiped her hand across her lips as if to erase his touch. "It was you," she accused.

Confused, he reached toward her, but she backed away. "What are you talking about?"

"In my hospital room. It was you who kissed me." She

touched her fingertips to her temple, shaking her head. "You had me thinking I was losing my mind. I thought Jarad . . ." She trailed off, turning troubled eyes to him. "Why didn't you tell me?"

For one thing, he hadn't expected her to remember their encounter. When she hadn't recognized him at their first meeting, he'd considered it a blessing and never mentioned it.

"Sweetheart, listen to me." He took a step forward, reaching for her. She backed away from him, trembling, not with anger, which he would have found reasonable, but in fear, which he could not. What had he ever done to make her fear him?

He dropped his hand and stood rooted in place. "Yes, I kissed you. You were so out of it, you thought I was your friend. When you didn't seem to remember, I didn't remind you, thinking it was for the best."

She shook her head, denying his words. "What do you want from me? Why are you really here?"

"Just what I told you. To help you with your movie, and to keep you safe."

"Nonsense. How did you trick Jarad into sending you here?"

"I didn't. He came to me." Adam sighed. Ever since he'd figured out she wasn't the brainless bimbo he'd first expected, he'd known it would come to this, his having to tell her the truth about his being there, about his relationship to Billy. If anything, he felt relieved to put an end to the charade. Knowing how much she valued honesty, guilt had eaten at him knowing that he'd lied to her, if only by omission.

But he also couldn't simply blurt out the truth. He'd ease her into it rather than dump the news in her lap. "Jarad knew of my connection to Billy's family. He knew—"

Her eyes narrowed and she held up a hand to silence him. "Don't you dare talk to me about Billy's family. After the accident, did I receive one visit, one phone call, one note from them asking if I was all right? That mother of his had the nerve to believe *I* was a bad influence on *him.*"

With her index finger, she pointed to her own chest. "I was the one trying to get him to clean up his life, while all she did was coddle him and let him believe that everything he did was all right. Maybe if she'd been a little more concerned when Billy was alive, no one would have to worry about how he died now."

He couldn't argue with her assessment, so he didn't try. "Billy had a brother. An older brother."

"Yes, I know. He mentioned him once. I don't even know his name. Billy spoke about him with the same reverence Catholics reserve for the pope.

"But where is he? I'd like to know. As far as I know, he didn't bother showing up for the funeral. And where was he when Billy was growing up? Why didn't he ever try to exert some brotherly influence over Billy?"

"They weren't raised together. They're half brothers, really."

"And which half was that? From the waist up only? Or maybe only on the left side? Either you are brothers or you're not. And obviously Billy and his brother were not. Billy and I were together for nine months. In all that time, this man never called, never wrote, never visited, not that I'm aware of. And now he wants to get involved?"

Suddenly her mouth dropped open and her back stiffened. "Is that who sent you? Billy's brother? Don't think I'm going to help you assuage his guilt over abandoning his brother. Pack your things, Detective. You're going home."

So much for telling her he was Billy's brother. If she was willing to kick out his brother's supposed friend, he hated to imagine what she'd do knowing that brother was standing here in the flesh beside her.

She turned away from him, heading for the door to the Angel Room. As she reached for the doorknob, he covered her hand with his own, preventing her from opening the door. "Didn't you love him?"

She snatched her hand away and looked at him over her shoulder with eyes liquid with unshed tears. "Yes, I loved him."

"Then don't you want to find out the truth? You said yourself that you don't remember what happened. Are you so sure it was an accident?"

A shudder passed through her and reverberated through him too, even though they weren't touching. "You believe somebody wanted to kill Billy?"

"I don't know. But if I were in your position, I'd want to find out."

She lowered her head, and he tensed, waiting for her reply. If she threw him out he would lose both her cooperation and his ability to protect her.

She lifted her head and met his gaze. "What do you want me to do?"

"I need to know who Billy knew, what he was up to."

"The who he knew part is easy. What he was up to? That I'm not so sure." She pressed her lips together and shrugged. "Billy and I hadn't exactly been in touch lately."

"Then let's start with who he knew."

"If you haven't got any plans for tonight, we're going to a party."

"Just like that? How do you know what's going on?"

"This is Hollywood, Detective. There's always a party."

Adam snorted. "I thought you were going to call me Adam."

A hint of a mischievous smile turned up her lips. "Just as soon as you start calling me Sam." She turned and went into the angel room shutting the door behind her.

Adam headed out to the guesthouse. He opened the door and stopped short for the second time that afternoon. Gone were the frilly curtains and bedspread that had dominated the room, replaced by unadorned counterparts in beiges and browns. The cooler colors tamped the brilliance of the walls to a manageable level.

Who would have done this? Certainly not the lady of the house. He glanced over his shoulder to the upper floor. Lupe stood at the same window she had the other night. This time she didn't move into the shadows when he looked up at her. He'd swear she smiled at him, though the distance made it impossible to know for sure. Shaking his head, he stepped into the room and closed the door.

Only after he went to the closet to hang up his jacket did he find the reason for Lupe's smile. The shotgun he'd left there was missing.

Fourteen

Fifteen minutes later, when Sam emerged from her shower, she wasn't entirely surprised to find Lupe waiting on her bed. Lupe sat with her arms folded and her legs crossed. One leg bounced impatiently, as if she'd been sitting there for hours. Sam's gaze darted to her dresser; she wondered if Lupe's anxiousness stemmed from finding the letter among Sam's things. Almost immediately she dismissed the thought. If Lupe knew about the note, she wouldn't keep it to herself.

Sam sat at her dressing table, arranged her robe more comfortably, and picked up her brush. "You know, you could give vultures lessons on waiting for their prey to die."

"I was waiting for you to hand that policeman his head, but that never happened. I saw what he did in the gym."

"No kidding." Lupe had been standing right outside the room when Sam had exited, not even trying to pretend she hadn't watched the proceedings through the cutout in the door. Sam had to admit that had it been anyone else, she'd have done just what Lupe suggested. But somehow, when he'd walked into the gym and scorched her with his hot, hot gaze, her body had responded as if he'd touched her with his hands instead of his eyes.

She'd forgotten the mirrors in the gym reflected back on one another; most of the time she ignored them, ignored her own image on-screen, on billboards, and especially when reflected back at her from a mirror. It had shocked her to find him watching her, but rather than being repulsed or even angry, she'd felt a thrill race up her spine. Now what did that say about her?

Sam forced her prurient thoughts from her mind. She had bigger problems than whether Adam Wexler had seen her naked. For one crazy moment, when her imagination had gotten the better of her, she'd thought he might be the one responsible for the note. Rationally, she knew that if he intended to harm her, he'd already had plenty of opportunity to do so by now. But he'd lied to her twice, both times by omission. What else did he keep hidden from her?

She couldn't worry about that now, either. She had to come up with some plausible excuse for leaving with Adam tonight, one that wouldn't arouse Lupe's suspicions. She hadn't kept silent with Adam only to put Lupe on alert with uncharacteristic behavior.

Sam ran her brush through her hair. "Do you know where my black leather skirt is?"

"In the closet upstairs with all your other clothes." Lupe's eyes narrowed. "Why?"

"I'm going out tonight."

"Where?"

"Out to Malibu. A party."

"Are you taking *him* with you?"

"I need a driver, and he's here."

Sam's gaze met with Lupe's scrutinizing one in the mirror. Clearly she wasn't buying a bit of what Sam said. Then Lupe's eyes widened, and her mouth dropped open. "You like him," Lupe accused, her tone a mixture of surprise and condemnation.

"For heaven's sake, we're not in junior high school. I'm not going to ask him to carry my books home from school."

"You want him then."

She couldn't deny that. Having Adam Wexler underfoot had awakened a sleeping appetite in her; the desire to be touched, to be held, to seek release. She had no intention of acting on it, but she acknowledged its existence. "Making love is *not* the worst thing that could happen to a person."

At Lupe's horrified look, Sam turned to face her. She wondered if Lupe's experience with her stepfather had ruined forever any chance she would have of enjoying a relationship with a man.

"You don't have to worry. I'm not going to do anything stupid. I recognize that what I'm feeling is a simple biological urge. I'm not in love with the man; I just want the use of his body for a couple of hours."

She'd hoped her humor would cheer Lupe, but her frown stayed firmly in place. Sam sighed; she knew Lupe feared a repeat performance of her relationship with Billy. Lupe had recognized, long before Sam had figured it out for herself, that what she and Billy had shared was more mutual need than mutual love. Billy had needed a mother figure, someone to keep him in line, since his own mother proved so lacking in that department. Sam had needed someone to mother, an innate drive that had exerted itself first with Lupe, then her own father, then finally Billy.

Sam had finally realized that you couldn't save anyone unless they wanted you to save them. Something in Billy had wanted to drag her down to his level rather than his aspiring to raise himself to hers. Luckily she'd extracted herself from the relationship before he'd destroyed her.

Although Adam appeared to be a hard-nosed, badass New York cop, she suspected the old adage proved true with him: scratch a pessimist and you found a disappointed optimist. Someone or something had wounded the good detective. But whatever his problems were, he'd have to figure them out for himself. Sam had had enough of trying to fix other people. He wouldn't be here long enough for her to try, even if she wanted to.

Sam twisted around to look at Lupe directly. "If I ever give my heart to someone, it won't be to some cynical, overbearing, meat-eating excuse for a cop. I'm holding out for someone who truly appreciates me and loves me. Someone worthy of my love, whom I can love and respect in return. Adam Wexler does not fit the bill."

Unmollified, Lupe pulled away from her. "I have to make dinner."

Sam's gaze followed Lupe to the door. Only when the other woman's hand rested on the doorknob did Sam turn away. She went to the divan, lay down, and closed her eyes. If she intended to stay awake tonight, a nap now couldn't hurt.

"What does it feel like? To want someone?"

Sam opened her eyes and pushed up on her elbows, surprised both by Lupe's still being there and even more so by her question. In the fifteen years she'd known her, Lupe had never asked her about sex before. "I don't know." As an actress she made her living recalling emotions viscerally, not verbally. "Why?"

Lupe shrugged, but her dark eyes were intense. "H-how does it feel?"

This time, Sam figured, Lupe meant the act, not the desire for it. "Sometimes it can be good. Sometimes it can be very, very good."

Lupe appeared to digest that information for a moment. "I-I had better make dinner," she said finally. Lupe backed out of the room, shutting the door behind her.

Huffing out a breath, Sam relaxed on the divan. All this talk about things carnal had her mind racing and her body overheated. She'd never sleep in her present state of mind. Sam shifted onto her side and closed her eyes.

"What are you doing to me, Adam Wexler?" she whispered to thin air. But she already knew the answer.

Standing at the base of the stairs, Adam tugged at the collar of the black jacket he wore. After eating dinner alone in the guesthouse, since Samantha was resting and wouldn't be making an appearance, he'd answered a knock at the door to find Lupe standing on the other side of the threshold, a garment bag hanging from her fingertips.

"Ms. Sam said to wear this." She'd thrust the bag at him, and once he'd taken it, she'd turned to leave.

He'd tossed the bag onto a chair and called to her, "Lupe, wait."

She paused on the path, turning to face him.

"Thanks for the change in accommodations. I was beginning to sing 'I Feel Pretty' in my sleep."

He'd expected her to laugh, or roll her eyes in her inimitable fashion. Instead she looked down at the ground, toeing a stone with the tip of one shoe. "I didn't want to embarrass you in front of your friend."

He couldn't help smiling. Did that mean embarrassing him in private was okay? "There was an item missing from my room, though."

"I decided to take you up on your offer, so I figured it was okay to have my gun back." She smiled wickedly. "As I remember it, you said I had to agree to let you teach me how to use it. You never said I actually had to go through with it."

"So you're going to hit me on a technicality?"

"You bet."

Adam laughed. "Have you been taking semantics lessons from your boss?"

Lupe shook her head, humor dancing in her eyes. "I taught her." She turned and hurried back to the house before he could say anything else.

He'd gone back inside the house, hooked the hanger on the garment bag on the closet door, and unzipped it. Inside hung a black jacket, black pants, and a black mock turtleneck shirt, all in varying textures of silk. Unzipping the front pockets of the bag produced a pair of Italian loafers he wouldn't be caught dead in on the streets of New York. Inside the shoes were a pair of rolled-up designer socks that someone had left the price tag on. Seventy-five dollars? For socks?

Adam rocked back on his heels. She expected him to wear this? And how had she magicked up this ensemble on such short notice? He supposed when you had money to burn and a famous face, all sorts of doors opened to you that were closed in the common man's face. How did she even know his size?

Out of curiosity he'd showered, shaved, and dressed. Aside from a slight lack of breadth in the shoulders, the clothes fit perfectly, even the damn shoes.

And now, waiting for Samantha at the proscribed time and place, Adam found himself doing something he never did: fidgeting.

"Why, Detective, you do clean up nicely," he heard a voice from above say.

Adam glanced in the direction of the voice and froze, his eyes riveted to Samantha as she descended the stairs. What little she wore was made from black leather: a bustier on top that barely contained her breasts and a miniskirt on the bottom that barely covered anything at all. A pair of scarlet snakeskin pumps completed her outfit and nearly undid him. She stopped on the third step from the foot of the stairs. His gaze traveled upward over her long, bare legs, skimming her body to settle on her face. A knowing smile turned up her lips.

He said, "Where's the other half of your clothing?"

She put her hands on her waist and canted her hips to one side. "I thought you of all people would approve. It's my submissive outfit."

He snorted. "I never asked you to be submissive. I said I wanted you to do what I tell you."

"If there's a difference between the two, I'd love to know what it is."

In no mood to argue, he gestured toward the upper floor. "Go upstairs and change. Put on something that has some actual fabric to it."

Affecting the guise of innocence, she asked, "Why should I?"

If she thought he'd bring her out in public in that getup, she'd lost her mind. He had no intention of touching her himself. That kiss before had been a mistake. He didn't need his feelings for her clouding his judgment. He wouldn't go back and change things if he could, not only because that little bit of a kiss would probably haunt him for the rest of his life, but because her reaction to it had allowed him to come clean with her, if only a little bit.

But he'd be damned if he had to watch a roomful of men ogle what he would not allow them to touch either. "Because half your assets are hanging out the back of that skirt."

"Tsk, tsk. I never would have pictured you as a prude, Detective. Actually more of the adventurous type."

"Who, me? I'm as kinky as a straight line." He nodded toward the upper floor. "Go change."

She shook her head. "Don't you see, Adam, no one would

ever believe that I, Samantha Hathaway, the wet blanket of the
Western world, would show up to the type of party we're going
to, unless I were a little bit off the deep end. If I show up
looking like the same old Sam . . ."

He frowned. She had him there. The men and women who
would have traveled the same circles as Billy wouldn't be playing canasta out by the pool and sipping sherry. They would
be a hard-drinking, hard-living bunch. If there was a killer
among them, he or she would be playing for keeps. He didn't
know how to impress that on her without scaring her, but
maybe she needed a dose of reality. Maybe then she'd change
her mind and stay home.

He grasped her elbow and pulled her the rest of the way down
the stairs to stand beside him. Even with her in four-inch heels,
he towered over her. "Look, Samantha, I want you with me at
all times. Do not leave my sight. Do you understand me?"

"Yes."

Her simple answer surprised him into releasing her. "Let's
go."

Her heels clicked on the tiled floor as she preceded him toward the doorway. With each stride his heartbeat seemed to
accelerate just a little more. He should tell her he'd changed his
mind or make her stay home and go on without her, or even
better, sit back and let Joe and the rest of the LAPD do their
thing.

All she was supposed to do was point out the people who
figured prominently in Billy's life, those who would most
likely want him dead. An ache in his gut told him that tonight
would not go off as smoothly as planned.

Once they were seated in his sports car with their seat belts
on and the top down, he turned to her. "Are you sure you want
to do this?"

"Why not? You can't think we're in too much danger. You
don't have your gun with you."

Adam revved the engine and pulled off into the dark, moon-
less night. Maybe he should warn her not to look in the glove
compartment.

Fifteen

Adam glanced over at Sam as they drove toward Malibu. She'd been extraordinarily quiet during the ride. Her hands were gripped together in her lap, and she'd been gnawing on the inside of her lip for the past fifteen minutes. Wherever they were heading, she wasn't looking forward to it any more than he was.

He slid another glance in her direction. "You never did tell me where we're going."

"To Johnny Maxwell's house."

Adam snorted. "Johnny Maxwell? Sounds like a pimp."

"Close. He was Billy's connection, if you know what I mean. I'd heard rumors about Billy getting sober, so I can't say how long ago that relationship ended."

She looked out the window, effectively closing the subject. Not for the first time he wondered how a woman like her had ended up engaged to his ne'er-do-well brother. He wouldn't ask her now, though. He didn't want to draw her emotions to the surface. He wanted her cool and detached and using her head instead of her heart.

"So what's with the clothes? Didn't trust me to dress myself?"

"No." She grinned up at him. "And I'd advise you not to spill anything on yourself tonight. You're wearing close to forty thousand dollars' worth of clothes."

He almost drove the car off the road. "For a jacket and a pair of pants?"

"It's the shirt, actually. It has real gold filaments woven into the cloth. And the diamonds on the belt buckle are real."

Adam's hand automatically went to his waist to finger the W inlaid into the gold buckle. "Jesus."

She laughed, a sound he realized he liked hearing. "I couldn't have my 'boy toy' showing up in jeans and a T-shirt."

His eyebrows lifted. "Excuse me?"

"Don't sound so shocked, Detective. I didn't cast you in that role; the media did. After those reports aired, do you think anyone would believe there's nothing going on between us?"

"Probably not."

"So rather than fight it, I plan to exploit it."

"How so?"

"Just follow my lead."

Right. He glanced over at her profile. This was her world, not his, but he couldn't help feeling that she was out of her league dealing with these people. Something about her remained untouched, unsullied by the pervasively hedonistic L.A. lifestyle. Billy might have moved with ease in these circles, but the two of them would stick out like a pair of sore thumbs: an honest cop and a Goody Two-shoes. What the hell were they getting themselves into?

"Is there anything else you've forgotten to tell me?"

"Tonight's event is by invitation only. We're crashing."

Johnny Maxwell's house, stark white and massive, rose from the cliff above the beach like a giant specter. Samantha had been here once before in the daylight, before she knew either the owner of the house or how he made his living. But now the house and its eerie outdoor illumination sent a shiver through her.

Adam pulled up to the gate, a twelve-foot-high iron monstrosity with an elaborate M woven into its metallic design. The whole night would be shot if they were refused admittance. Sam pushed up her breasts and smoothed down her hair, which had been blown into a tangle by the night air. She noticed Adam watching her with a sober expression on his face.

"What are you supposed to be doing?" he asked.

"Greasing the gates, so to speak." Sam wet her lips with her tongue and focused on the dark-skinned man who emerged from the guardhouse inside the gate. Although he stood no taller than she, his neck was probably thicker than her thigh. A gap-toothed grin split the man's face when he got a good look at the tiny car.

"Hey, man." He laughed. "What happened? Somebody stole the rest of your car?"

The guy guffawed, finding his own humor hilarious. Sam felt Adam tense beside her. Before he got out of the car and decked the man, she leaned over Adam in a way designed to give the guard a spectacular view of her cleavage. "Hi," she said, affecting an alien throaty voice.

The man immediately sobered. "Oh, Ms. Hathaway, I'm sorry." He raised the clipboard in his hands and fiddled with the papers attached to it. A few times his eyes darted back and forth between Sam's chest and whatever was written on those papers. "You're not on the list."

She pouted and fluttered her eyelashes. "You're going to turn me away because of a piece of paper? I'm sure Johnny wouldn't mind having me here."

The man's throat worked, and she could see the ambivalence in his eyes. She tried to think of something to say to persuade him. She glanced at Adam, but he was no help, doing his usual interpretation of a brick wall.

"I'll call the house," the man said finally.

Great. All they needed was to alert Johnny to their presence and have him turn them away. As the man retreated to the guardhouse through a cutout in the gate, Sam crossed her arms over her chest and gazed out her window.

"Nice vamp impersonation. Do you trot that out often?"

Turning to look at him, she cocked her head to one side. The same grim expression darkened his features. What was his problem? "Only when necessary."

"Don't try that on me."

"Why not? Am I not your type?"

He looked her up and down, a hint of a sardonic smile on his face. "Too skinny."

She rolled her eyes and stared out the window in the direction of the house. When she'd caught him staring at her in the gym, his eyes hadn't registered anything close to "too skinny."

The guard returned a moment later. "Mr. Maxwell says he'd be delighted to have Ms. Hathaway join him."

Sam winked and flashed an "I told you so" smile. "Thanks."

The man stepped back and pressed a button inside the guardhouse. Slowly the gate swung open. Adam eased the car up the path, out of sight of either the guard or the trio of kids parking cars up at the house.

"Why are you stopping?"

Adam leaned over and flicked open the glove compartment. Inside lay a black handgun. She gazed at him wide eyed as he tucked the gun into his waistband at the small of his back.

"What are you planning to do with that?"

"Hopefully nothing. But I don't intend to leave either of us unprotected."

She looked down at her hands, which she gripped together in front of her. "I don't like guns, Adam."

"I know." His fingertips, cool and gentle, touched her cheek. She lifted her head and focused on the warmth in his dark eyes. "I am not a careless man or a hothead. Nothing is going to happen that somebody else doesn't start first."

She shut her eyes, inhaling deeply, drinking in the salty smell of the nearby ocean and the citrusy aroma of Adam's cologne. She'd deliberately been vague with Adam about where they were going and who they'd be seeing, partly because she thought he never would have agreed to take her on this outing in the first place. He would never have allowed her to endanger herself by confronting a criminal in his own home, a criminal who might also be a murderer. Partly she hadn't wanted to think of the danger herself.

But without her entrée into this world, he would never find out anything. Thanks to Alana, all of the Western world knew he was a cop. Adam would never have made it past the gate.

"Changed your mind about going inside?"

She opened her eyes and squared her shoulders. "No. If Johnny had anything to do with Billy's death, I want to find out. I want to help you."

Adam released a harsh, exasperated breath. "All right. But you do exactly as I tell you. I want you to point out Maxwell to me. I'll do the rest." He revved the engine and pulled up to the front of the house.

Adam took Sam's elbow as they walked the short distance from the car to the front door. To the eye she gave no sign of being nervous, but he felt her tremble when he touched her. When they paused in front of the door, he turned to face her. "Are you sure?" he asked one last time.

"It's too late to turn back now. He already knows we're here."

He couldn't argue with her there. "Are you going to be all right?"

"I'm fine." She busied herself adjusting the collar of his shirt, the front of his jacket, brushing imaginary dust from his shoulders.

Ordinarily he wouldn't have minded her fussing over him, but it spoke of an anxiousness in her he needed to quell. "Gee, Mom, do I look all right?"

At first her shoulders slumped; then she grinned. "You'll do."

"Then let's go in."

She nodded and reached for the doorbell. Immediately the door was swung open and a wave of pulsing sound hit them. A pair of guards stood by the door, dressed all in black. Each was the first guard's twin in girth, but both possessed a height the other had not. "Welcome, Ms. Hathaway," the man on the right said. "Mr. Maxwell told me to tell you he wants to speak with you later."

"Please tell him I'm looking forward to it."

With a hand on her waist Adam led her past the guard into the spacious, populated foyer. He leaned down to whisper in her ear, "You're not going anywhere alone with that man; do you hear me?"

"Yes, Dad. We went over it in the car."

He squeezed her waist. No matter what he threw at her she never backed down. He glanced around the foyer, which was decorated in an elaborate Egyptian motif.

Sam shrugged. "I hear he had a past-life regression done a few years ago and found out he was Ramses the Second in a former life."

Adam snorted. "Ever notice that no one is ever Hans the stable boy or Bobo the court jester in a former life?"

"Even quack psychics want to get paid."

The foyer led to a eight-foot black marble statue of Horus, the god of the dead. It reminded him of the monstrosity in the movie *The Ten Commandments.* "A friend of yours?" Adam asked.

"Blame it on Cecil B. DeMille."

"Sam," a female voice called. They both turned in the woman's direction. Adam focused on Barbara Mitchell making her way through the crowd toward him. During Sam's interview she had come off as the consummate professional. Dressed now in a short black skirt and minuscule sequined top, she struck him as a pro of another variety.

"I can't tell you how surprised I am to see you here," Barbara said when she reached Sam's side. "And with the delectable detective in tow." Adam stiffened as Barbara's lustful gaze traveled over him. "I really must applaud your taste—in men and in clothes."

"Thanks, Barbara." Sam leaned into him and placed her hand on his chest. "Two things that should never disappoint a girl—men and clothes."

"I'll drink to that," Barbara said, lifting her champagne glass in salute. The two women laughed, attracting the attention of others. Soon a crowd had formed around them, all either consoling Samantha on the "terrible ordeal" of her accident, or inquiring what had prompted her to make an appearance here. Many of the faces he recognized from the entertainment or music industry or from ESPN. An overpaid, underworked bunch out to anesthetize themselves with their drink or drug of choice. The lot of them made Adam's stomach turn.

And none of these people could know Samantha very well. If they did, they would have seen through her thinly veiled act of gaiety. Her mouth smiled, but her gaze was brittle, flitting from one of them to another as if she couldn't stand to look at them any more than he could.

One woman pushed her way to the front to confront her. "Well, if it isn't Miss High and Mighty herself."

Sam tilted her head to one side, her smile broadening. "Hello, Alana. How's tricks?"

"Why are you here, and why did you bring your cop friend with you? Is he here to bust up everyone's fun?"

"Why, Alana, you of all people should know." Sam grasped the hand that rested on her waist and placed it on her stomach. Automatically his hand flexed, encountering soft, bare flesh—the reaction she'd hoped for, no doubt. "Adam's here to guard my body."

That comment elicited oohs and laughter from the women in the crowd.

"And to think, I have you to thank for the idea. I had the man living under my roof and I hadn't given him a second thought until you concocted that news story for Barbara."

Alana looked ready to spit, and Barbara glared at Alana, obviously put out that the story had been fabricated.

Sam gazed up at him and winked. "Come on, Adam. Buy me a drink now and I'll let you frisk me later." She looped her arm with his and started to lead him from the room.

Alana's voice called after them. "Make sure to let us know when you're through with him, Sam. Lord knows, you never did like to share."

Sam froze mid-stride. For an instant a pained expression came over her face, but it disappeared by the time she turned to stare down Alana. "It's not the sharing I'm opposed to." She gave Alana a disgusted once-over. "It's the caliber of person with whom I'm asked to share."

Adam stifled a grin as Sam turned back to him. If Alana knew what was good for her, she'd give up trying to get the best of Samantha. He had no idea what that last exchange was about, but by the snickers and guffaws that followed Samantha's comment, she had obviously emerged the victor.

He pulled her closer with an arm around her waist and whispered in her ear, "Come on, sweetheart. I still owe you that drink." She nodded and allowed him to lead her from the room.

Sixteen

The foyer led to a large, open space. A bar had been stationed by the double doors that led off to the pool.

"Two scotches, neat," she told the bartender when he asked her what she wanted.

Adam studied her for a moment. "Aside from the fact that I'm driving tonight, I don't usually engage in two-fisted drinking."

"One of them is for me."

"You don't drink."

"I don't do a lot of things I plan to do tonight, but how did you know?"

"Lupe informed me after I had the misfortune of asking if you girls kept any beer in the house." She accepted with a demure "Thank you" the glass the bartender extended toward her.

"Let's see if you're still thanking him after that alcohol hits your stomach. Don't think I'm going to hold your hand while you're hugging the porcelain throne later."

"You don't have to worry. I occasionally have a glass of wine with dinner. I can hold my liquor if I have to."

She gulped down half the drink in one swallow. For a moment her eyes squeezed tight and she grimaced, but she swallowed the caustic liquid. Lowering the glass, she shuddered. "I swear I don't know what people find so appealing about this stuff."

Adam shrugged, then took a swig from his glass. "Is Maxwell here?"

She shook her head. "Not yet. His thing is voyeurism, not participation. Rumor has it that he has every room wired with cameras. He watches the whole scene from some room upstairs. Later in the evening, he'll make a grand appearance, followed by a lot of fawning and adulation."

"Anybody else of interest here that I should know about?"

"Not really. Not unless you want to play Name that Bimbo, and guess all the women here that Billy supposedly slept with."

"I'll pass. By the way, what was that with Alana before?"

"Alana's nose is out of joint because I fired her."

"I figured as much. But was that sharing business about?"

She shifted so that she leaned her back against the bar. "It's pretty much common knowledge that I broke off my relationship with Billy after I found him with another woman." Her eyes darted up at him and she shrugged. "The fiancée is always the last to know."

She tried to sound cavalier, but Adam sensed the pain his brother's infidelity had inflicted on her. *Damn Billy.* Had he been insane? He'd jeopardized his relationship with Samantha, and for what? An image of Sandra flashed in his mind. Had she been the woman Samantha had found him with?

Adam recognized that he no longer maintained complete objectivity in regard to Samantha. She got to him, made him wish for the impossible, that he would someday know her in more than the fleeting way he did now. And although he wanted her more than he could ever remember wanting another woman, his feelings ran deeper than that. To what he wasn't sure. But he felt pretty damn sure that if he'd ever earned this woman's love, he wouldn't throw it back in her face as his brother had done.

She put down her glass. "Then let's go. It's showtime."

"What do you mean?"

"Believe it or not, this is the tame crowd up here—people who like to boast they've been to a Johnny Maxwell party, but not brave enough to do anything truly risqué. If Billy were here, he'd have been downstairs."

Adam tossed back the rest of his drink, set the glass on the bar, and followed her.

She led him from the main room to a long staircase that led to the floor below. As they descended, the pulsing beat of the music grew louder. The staircase led into a large, open room. The decibel level of the music and the flickering colored lights rivaled that of any dance club Adam had ever been in. At one end, a glass deejay's booth rose above the crowd, parallel to a gallery lined with two dozen or so small round tables.

Standing on the fourth step from the bottom, Adam scanned the gyrating crowd that filled the room. No wonder there were no secrets in Hollywood. Everyone was busy letting it all hang out, both figuratively and literally. Any vice squad in America would have a field day with this crowd—everything from drug use to indecent exposure. If these people were Billy's friends, it didn't take a genius to imagine why Billy's life was so screwed up.

Adam thought back to Samantha's condemnation of Billy's brother for abandoning him. At the time her words had stung, but he'd never felt worse about his lack of involvement in Billy's life than he did now.

Adam glanced over at Samantha. "Welcome to Gomorra," she said, then descended the rest of the stairs and disappeared into the undulating crowd.

For a moment he stood where he was, watching her. It didn't take long for the men to gravitate to her, like sharks sensing fresh meat in the water. He couldn't blame them. With that outfit and the wild auburn hair around her shoulders, she gave the impression of a party girl out to have fun. Apparently none of the men around her minded obliging her. A drink magically appeared in her hand and she drank deeply.

If she kept that up, she really would make herself sick. Adam entered the crowd, intent on putting an end to this performance of hers. Before he reached her, one of the men took her hand and led her to the dance floor.

What followed was a bump and grind so erotic as to draw the attention of others. Sam had herself plastered against this guy, closer than a stamp on an envelope. She didn't even attempt to keep the guy's hands from roving freely over her body.

Did she really expect him to stand here and watch this? If

she did, she'd lost her mind. He pushed his way through the crowd to where she stood, grabbed her arm from the other man's neck, and pulled her toward him. "We're getting out of here."

She looked up at him, but didn't seem particularly surprised by his actions. He led her to the nearest door, which opened out onto the beach. The shore was illuminated by a series of floodlights embedded in the sand. Once they'd gotten far enough away from the house that the music faded to a quiet roar, he turned to face her.

"You mind telling me what the hell that was back there?"

"What are you so bent out of shape about? I was just dancing."

"Is that what you call it? If you had wedged yourself any closer up under that guy you'd be pregnant right now."

"Oh, please. Larry is harmless. Why do you think I picked him?"

From where he'd stood, it had looked the other way around. "I wouldn't know."

She ran her fingers through her hair that the salt breeze had stirred around her face. "What do you want from me? I am trying to create an impression here—Sam Hathaway off the deep end. You're not helping standing around like Father Time waiting for the New Year to change."

What did he want from her? At the moment he wanted her in his arms, assuaging some of the lust she inspired in him.

With a growl of frustration, he turned away from her and headed down the beach. He stooped to pick up a stone and skimmed it across the surface of the water. He felt her come up beside him. He glanced over at her. Without her heels, she was considerably shorter. He linked his arm with hers and led her down the beach. For a long while neither of them said anything.

Eventually Adam broke the silence. "You know what's wrong with you people?"

"What people would those be?"

"Los Angelenos. You're surrounded by all this majestic water, yet everyone owns a pool."

She laughed, looking out at the water. "How did a city boy like you develop an appreciation of the ocean?"

"Contrary to popular belief, New York is on the eastern seaboard. We have beaches. Most of the decent ones are on Long Island or up in Westchester. My particular fondness is for Orchard Beach in the Bronx."

"What's so special about it?"

"Proximity. I lived close enough so that whenever my father or my aunts got on my nerves, I could ride my bike there and watch the waves."

She tilted her head to one side, watching him with a thoughtful expression on her face. "What about your mother?"

"She wasn't in the picture. She lived out here, actually."

He found another stone and skimmed it across the water. He hadn't intended to tell her about his mother. He hadn't intended to divulge anything personal about himself that would make her question him or his relationship to Billy. He knew she valued honesty. What would she say if he told her the truth now?

She stopped walking and looked up at him with a sympathetic look in her eyes. "I'm sorry."

"What for?"

"Reminding you of unpleasant memories."

He smiled. At first he'd thought she meant for driving him crazy while she was on the dance floor. "They're not all unpleasant."

She cupped his face in her hands. He didn't resist as she brought his mouth down to hers. Her lips were soft, warm, inviting, but he pulled away almost immediately. He didn't trust himself or her motives for the overture.

"Adam," she said, drawing his attention to her mouth, made moist by its contact with his. She rose on the balls of her feet and kissed him again. And again. Light, sipping kisses that grew longer and more intense. Adam shut his eyes tightly against her onslaught. His nostrils flared as he breathed in the subtle scent of her perfume and the tang of the ocean. The salt air lifted tendrils of her hair to tease his skin.

He felt himself going down, dragged into a whirlpool of

sensations. For a moment, at least, he didn't want salvation. From the second she'd walked down the stairs wearing that outrageous outfit, she'd had him hot and wanting.

His arms closed around her, crushing her to him. His tongue plunged into her mouth, claiming hers. One of his hands slid down to cradle her hip, bringing her in contact with his erection. She moaned and swiveled her hips against him. He groaned as a wave of pure pleasure washed over his groin and eddied throughout his body. Immediately he pulled away from her, while he still could.

She blinked her eyes open and stared at him, confused.

He touched his knuckles to her cheek. "What are we doing here, Samantha?"

"I was kissing you, or hadn't you noticed?"

"You know I noticed. I meant, where is this going?"

She tilted her head to one side. For a moment she said nothing, biting her lip as if deciding what to say. Then she squared her shoulders and looked at him levelly.

"I want you, Adam. If I'm not mistaken, you want me. What would be the harm in . . . in . . . indulging ourselves?"

His eyebrows lifted and his stomach dropped. She couldn't have surprised him more if she'd told him she used to be a man. "What exactly are you offering?"

"I'm offering me, Detective. With no strings attached, no guilt, no promises."

He unwound her arms from his neck and took her hands in his. "You can't even bring yourself to call me by my first name."

"What has that got to do with anything?"

"How much of this sudden offer has to do with the amount of alcohol you drank up at the house?"

She snatched her hands from his. "None of it. If you're not interested, just say so."

"Interest has nothing to do with it." If that was all that mattered, his shoes wouldn't be the only thing on him full of sand. His fingers itched to pull her to him, but then he'd be no better than the men inside waiting to prey on her.

He rubbed his knuckles against her cheek before dropping

his hands to his sides. "But I've still got some self-respect left, and I'd like to keep it."

She stepped back from him, her mouth dropping open, her chest heaving. "Heaven knows, Detective, I wouldn't want to damage your precious self-respect by asking you to touch me."

"That's not what I meant."

He reached for her, but she smacked his hand away. "I think you said exactly what you meant. Well you know what, *Detective?* You can kiss my too-skinny ass."

Sam whirled and ran back toward the house. Her ankle hurt, but she didn't care. She heard Adam calling after her, but she ignored him. If he wanted to, he could easily overtake her, but he didn't.

When she got back inside, she threaded her way through the crowd without speaking to anybody. She'd had enough of this charade for one night. She'd had enough of making a fool of herself.

Damn Adam. She'd reached out to him, sensing an emptiness in him similar to her own. Losing a parent was always painful, even if it was from neglect. But once he'd taken her in his arms, her own needs had risen to prominence. Her flesh still crawled from Larry's drunken touch. Had it been so wrong for her to want him to wipe it away, to hold her, to make her feel all right again?

Obviously Adam thought so. He'd made no secret of his disdain for the people here. She couldn't blame him; they disgusted her, too. But until that moment, she hadn't realized he lumped her in with the rest of them.

If she had to walk home barefoot, since she'd left her shoes on the beach, she intended to leave now. When she reached the base of the stairs, she turned back to search for Adam. She spotted him easily. He'd never made it past the doorway.

Samantha hurried up the stairs, bumping into the guard who had spoken to her at the front door. "Excuse me," she said, taking a step back.

"I've been looking for you, Ms. Hathaway. Mr. Maxwell will see you now."

For a moment Sam thought of the promise she'd made to

Adam not to go anywhere near Johnny without him. But what choice did she have? If she waited for him, she'd blow the flimsy cover story they'd concocted for being there in the first place. Besides, given his opinion of her, he probably wasn't concerned for her safety. More likely he figured she'd blow the only shot they would have of talking to the man.

Sam plastered a fake smile on her face and turned toward the guard. "I'm looking forward to seeing him."

Seventeen

After pausing long enough to retrieve Sam's shoes and empty his own, Adam reentered the house through the same door Sam had used. He scanned the room, not finding her anywhere. Where could she have disappeared to so quickly?

"Damn." He'd thought that other man had heated her up and she was looking to him to cool her down. Not in this lifetime would he have let that happen—and not only because he would not take advantage of her vulnerability, even if it were physical and not emotional. If he ever made love to her, it would be out of a mutual desire to be together. Regardless of the couple of times he'd caught her watching him, until that moment he hadn't realized she saw him as anything more than an albatross around her neck imposed by her friend Jarad.

"Damn," he said again. He began to thread his way through the crowd and ran smack into Alana. Or rather, she threw herself in his path and he almost mowed her down.

"Excuse me," he said, both as an apology and as a request for her to get out of his damn way. She stayed put, blocking his progress, then crossed her arms underneath her breasts and *tsk*ed.

"Well, Detective," she shouted at him over the din of the music, "seems our Sam has disappeared, leaving you holding the Ferragamos."

"Have you seen her?" He hoped the desperation he felt didn't come through in his voice. If it did, Alana probably wouldn't tell him anything. Adam suspected the catfight up-

stairs had more to do with his lack of interest in Alana than
with her losing any job, no matter how lucrative.

"A couple of minutes ago, heading upstairs with one of
Johnny's men. She'll probably be busy for a while, if you know
what I mean."

That was what Adam feared: that Johnny had lured Samantha upstairs alone for God knew what purpose. Knowing
Samantha, she would have gone, figuring she could handle
him, or worse, out of spite for that disastrous scene on the
beach. Either way, she'd put herself in a dangerous situation
he might be too late to get her out of. Maxwell could be doing
anything to Samantha up there, and with the noise of the party,
no one would ever know.

Alana linked her arm with his. "I'm not busy at the moment."

"Some other time." He detached her arm from his and made
his way back to the foyer, where a winding staircase led to the
upper floor. One of Maxwell's goons stood at the top of the
stairway. Was he there to keep Samantha in or to keep Adam
out? Only one way to find out. Adam started up the steps.

Samantha followed the guard to the second floor and down
a long, dimly lit corridor to a room at the back of the house.
Every step added to her trepidation, but she refused to show
it. Besides, it was too late to turn back now. She'd have to
tough it out and wait for Adam to find her, if need be. No
matter what he thought of her, he would do his job. That much
she knew about him.

And maybe, while she had him alone, Johnny might let slip
something that he would never say in front of Adam. She could
hope, anyway.

Pausing at the doorway, Sam focused on Johnny. Given the
elaborate display downstairs, she'd expected to find him holding court with a hook and cross and a pharaoh's triple crown
on his head. Instead he wore a simple black crew-neck sweater,
which she suspected cost a fortune nonetheless. His only con-
cession to his Egypt obsession was the large gold ankh on a
thick chain around his neck. With his long, thin frame and his

slicked-back, jet-black hair, he reminded her of a snake. He
sat behind a massive black desk stroking the Pomeranian on
his lap. Somehow she'd never pictured him as a dog lover.

"Come in, Sam," he said, gesturing to the leather sofa parallel to the desk. "Have a seat."

"No, thanks." She crossed to the opposite wall, which was
made entirely of reflective glass. The one way mirror looked
down on the dance floor. At least part of his reputation as a
voyeur proved true. Quickly she scanned the floor below for
a sign of Adam. Finding none, she turned to face Johnny.

She'd refused a seat, as it put her at too much of a physical
disadvantage. Besides that, her nerves had tied themselves into
such knots, she'd never have been able to sit still. She identified
with the Pomeranian on Johnny's lap that shook nervously every
time he touched it. She didn't want to think about what he'd
done to that dog to make it so terrified of him. "Thank you."

"Can I get you anything? A drink? Some candy?"

Sam shook her head, sure he referred to candy of the nose
variety.

"Still the good little girl?"

"Not quite as good as before, but not that adventurous yet."

"Then why are you here, Sam? Why did you bring a policeman to my home?"

She hadn't expected him to be so blunt, but that didn't bother
her. "I'm not responsible for Detective Wexler. Jarad hired him
to make sure I don't have any more accidents before we start
filming *Guardian Angel.*"

Sam shrugged. "He's amusing, but too possessive for my
liking. I ditched him and my shoes on the beach." She tossed
her hair and let a suggestive smile spread across her face. "As
for why I'm here, I came to have a good time."

His gaze traveled from her face down her body to her bare
feet. "And it appears you are." He let the dog go and it scram-
bled from his lap and out the open door. "A lot different from
that time you came with Billy and you demanded that he take
you home."

She shrugged, tilting her head to one side. "Things change.

There's nothing like narrowly escaping death to give a girl a new perspective on life."

He nodded, as if considering that. "I wanted to offer you my condolences on Billy's death. He didn't deserve to go like that."

"I appreciate it, but I think Billy went exactly as he would have wanted to go; in a fast car with a woman by his side. I was grateful not to make the entire trip with him."

She turned her back to Johnny, pressed her hands against the glass, and sighed dramatically. She inhaled and let her shoulders droop, waiting for Johnny to take the bait. Now that they'd steered to the topic she wanted to discuss, she'd do her best not to let him off the hook.

"What's the matter, Sam?"

"A touch of survivor's guilt, I guess. Billy had wanted to get back together." A fact confirmed for her by Larry during their tête-à-tête on the dance floor. She had dismissed the rumors in the paper or from Barbara Mitchell as pure speculation, but if Billy had told his friends, that made it real. "He told me he'd straightened out, but I didn't believe him."

She glanced over her shoulder at Johnny. "He wasn't still buying from you, was he?"

"Nah, he'd cleaned up as far as that goes. But then, he'd never really been addicted to chemicals. For him, rehab was more of a public declaration, a way to get people to take seriously that he'd changed. It was the life that had Billy hooked, knowing what he did was just on the other side of the law. Most of the time he gave away whatever I sold him, wanting to play the big man with the big bucks to burn."

"Then you hadn't seen him in a while?"

"Billy and I still hung out. He served other purposes." Johnny smiled malevolently, leaving her to wonder to what purposes he referred. Before she had the chance to ask, Johnny waved his hand, dismissing the subject.

"Enough about Billy." Johnny rose from his chair, rounded the desk, and came to stand beside her at the window.

Even without her shoes they stood eye to eye. Still, panic flooded through her as he cupped her chin in his palm, forcing her to look at him.

If not for the rigid control under which she kept her body, a tremor of unadulterated fear would have passed through her. Sam's gaze darted toward the door. Where the hell was Adam, her supposed protector, when she finally needed protecting?

Her gaze was drawn back to Johnny when he leaned in closer to whisper in her ear, "Now I have another proposition to discuss."

As Adam approached, the behemoth at the top of the stairs turned in his direction. Adam almost wished the man would try to stop him. After all that had gone on tonight, he was spoiling for a fight. This guy was big enough to make it interesting.

Gaining the landing, he asked, "Where's your boss?"

The behemoth had the nerve to smile at him. "At the end of the hall."

Adam's eyebrows lifted. So Maxwell wanted him to find them? What kind of game was he playing? Why lure Samantha to his inner sanctum, if he didn't plan to take advantage of her in some way? But he supposed Samantha couldn't be in too much danger if Maxwell was expecting him. At least not yet.

What had he been thinking when he brought Samantha here, to the house of a man whose activities were unknown to him? In general, people willing to dabble in drugs were capable of doing a lot of other things as well. Still, it didn't make sense. What could he want from Samantha?

Adam glanced down the hallway to the one door under which glowed a faint light. He supposed it was time to find out.

Sam ran her tongue along the seam of her dry lips and met Johnny's gaze. "What sort of proposition did you have in mind?"

"You're a beautiful woman, Sam."

Folding her arms in front of her as a means of protection, she tilted her head to one side. "What's your point?"

"I just wanted to offer you a little gift." Johnny produced a little plastic Ziplock baggie from somewhere. He held it between his middle and index fingers.

A tiny amount of dull white powder shifted inside the bag. "In case you're feeling adventurous."

Sam held her breath, her eyes riveted to his hand as he tucked the bag into the valley between her breasts.

"If you want more, you give me a call. I'm sure we can work something out." His hand lingered, traveling up the side of her breast.

She swallowed convulsively and her mind whirled. What the devil did she do now? Should she play along until Adam showed up? Would he ever show up? What if one of Johnny's men had made it impossible for him to show up?

Sam swallowed and met Johnny's gaze levelly. She was letting her imagination run away with her. Johnny might be a sleazebag drug dealer, but she'd never really suspected him of having anything to do with Billy's death, at least not the way he'd died. Why go through all that trouble when he could slip something in his drink or replace one bit of powder with something even more deadly?

As for Adam, she couldn't think of anything outside of a nuclear explosion that would stop him from getting to her. She just wished the man would hurry up about it. Johnny's fingers traced the swell of her breast. Any second now she was going to have to do something before Johnny took his exploration any further.

"Hands off, Maxwell."

Sam's gaze flew to the open doorway, where Adam stood with one shoulder against the doorjamb. Her shoes dangled from his fingertips. Despite his indolent stance, anger radiated from him, searing her with its intensity even at a distance.

With a mocking grin, Johnny turned toward Adam. "The cavalry has arrived, and just in the nick of time. What took you so long, Detective?"

A shiver of alarm shot up Sam's spine as Adam fastened his gaze on her. "Someone forgot to leave me a trail of breadcrumbs."

"No need to be upset. Sam and I were just talking."

"Oh? What about?"

"I assure you, Sam gave me a thorough going-over. Why

don't you ask her what I said?" Johnny glanced back at her, sending a shiver racing up her spine. "I'll leave you two kiddies alone. I'm sure you have a lot to . . . discuss."

Johnny slithered past Adam. From the venomous look in Adam's eyes, it must have taken all his strength not to beat the crap out of the man. When Johnny had gone, Adam tossed her shoes to the floor, slammed the door shut, and walked toward her. The expression in his eyes made her back into the glass wall. She expected him to be angry with her for going off with Johnny alone, but the look on his face bordered on fury.

She licked her lips nervously, searching for something to say to abate some of his anger. "I-I've never been so glad to see another human being in my life."

He stopped a few inches in front of her, his hands rising to grip her shoulders. His face hovered a few inches above hers. "Didn't I tell you not to go anywhere alone with him? Didn't I?"

"What did you want me to do? Refuse? If I hadn't gone with him, we would have blown our reason for being here in the first place. I played it okay, though I don't know what I would have done if you hadn't come in when you did."

"This is not a damn movie, Sam. I spent the last fifteen minutes going out of my mind when I couldn't find you."

Sam winced and pushed against Adam's chest as pain sliced through her shoulder. She doubted he realized he was shaking her. "Adam, please, you're hurting me."

He blinked and the harshness of his features receded. "Oh, God, baby, I'm sorry." He pulled her into his arms and held her, running his hands over her back in a soothing manner. She burrowed her nose against his neck, inhaling the remnants of his cologne mixed with his own natural scent, absorbing the warmth of his big body. His breath against her bare skin warmed her too, but the soft kiss he placed on her shoulder sent a shiver though her.

His fingers tangled in her hair, tilting her head back. "Are you all right?"

She nodded, but kept her eyes closed, knowing he would see in them how much his embrace affected her, how much she wanted him. He'd already made it clear that a dalliance with her didn't fit into his agenda.

His hands cupped her face, and the featherlight touch of his kiss flicked over her eyes and her cheeks, and then his mouth was on hers again. She dragged in a heated breath as his tongue slid past her parted lips to find hers.

Her head told her she should stop him, for the sake of her pride. She didn't need anyone's pity kisses, least of all his. But at the moment she couldn't make herself care about anything, except that he was here and he was holding her and she was safe.

One of his hands lowered to cup her breast. Unable to help herself, she moaned and arched against him as his thumb brushed over her nipple. Then his hand moved so that two fingers delved into her cleavage and extracted the packet Johnny had placed there.

She pushed Adam away from her. "If that's all you wanted, why didn't you say so?"

Adam shot her a quelling look, but said nothing. He opened the little baggie, wet his pinky, and dipped it into the white powder. "Are you going to arrest him?" she asked as he brought his finger to his mouth.

"Not unless they've made dispensing powdered sugar a crime."

Sam's eyes narrowed on the bag. "What would Johnny be doing with confectioner's sugar in the first place? He definitely doesn't strike me as the baking kind."

"Dealers cut heroin with it. It's cheap, white, and most users are not concerned with those extra pounds on their hips." Adam closed the bag and put it in his pocket. "In this case, he was sending you a message."

"Oh?"

"What are little girls made of?"

"Sugar and spice . . ." She trailed off as realization dawned. "In other words, he didn't buy my act for one second."

"Nope." Adam took her arm. "We've done as much damage as we're going to do. Let's get out of here."

Eighteen

Pulling up in front of Samantha's house, Adam slid a glance at her. Since leaving Johnny's room, she hadn't said one word to him. She'd spent the entire ride sitting with her arms crossed in front of her, her eyes closed, though he doubted she'd slept. He wished he knew something to say to break the tension between them. He wasn't even sure of its cause. Was she still upset with him for what he'd said on the beach or the way he'd kissed her in Johnny's room, or had the events of the evening simply worn her out?

"How much were the shoes?"

She opened her eyes and focused on him as if he were a Martian. "Excuse me?"

"I asked you how much the shoes cost."

"About fifteen hundred, I think. Why?"

Jesus. "I think they're ruined."

She shrugged. "I can have another pair sent out if you want."

Adam sighed. No, he didn't want. He wanted her to snap out of this funk she'd settled into. He cupped his hand over her knee. "Are you all right?"

She glanced down at his hand, then met his gaze with a look of disdain. "Be careful, Detective. You're touching me." She opened the door and slid out of the car.

He caught up with her halfway up the walk. "We need to talk."

"Can't Johnny's ramblings wait until tomorrow?"

At the moment he couldn't care less what Johnny had told her. Johnny's real message had been for Adam, not Sam—Maxwell's way of challenging him. The only question Adam had was why Maxwell would bother.

"No." He took her keys from her, let them into the house, and tossed the keys onto the foyer table.

"If you want to talk you'll have to do it walking. I'm going to bed."

She turned, but instead of heading for the angel room, she headed for the stairs. "Where are you going?"

"To my room. I was only staying down here while my ankle healed." She reached the bottom step and turned to face him. "This is as far as you go, Detective. You wanted to know what Johnny said, here it is: he told me that Billy had stopped using. Larry told me the same thing. That Billy had straightened out because he wanted me back. Billy knew he could have that life or me, but not both."

"When did Larry tell you that?"

"On the dance floor. That's why I was 'pressed up under that guy,' as you put it. It was the only way he would talk to me."

Adam wanted to laugh. He'd thought she was enjoying herself with that guy, while in actuality she'd been pumping him for information. "Is that all?"

"No. Johnny also said that although Billy wasn't a customer anymore, he served other purposes. What do you think he meant?"

Feigning a nonchalance he didn't feel, Adam shrugged. "I wouldn't know." Whatever it was probably was illegal, immoral, or both. At this point there wasn't much he would put past his brother. And even if Maxwell had nothing to do with Billy's death, he was up to something. Samantha didn't need to know either of those things. From now on, he intended to keep her out of the loop and out of harm's way.

"What do we do next?"

"We don't do anything. *I* will tell Joe what happened, and then *we* let the police do their job."

"You're the police."

"Yes, but since I have jack jurisdiction to do anything, we'll leave it to the local boys."

"If that's the way you want it." She brushed her hair over her shoulder. "I guess this is good night then. Sleep tight and all that other jazz."

She turned to leave, but he couldn't let her go like this. He tried to grab her hand to stop her, but she pulled her arm out of his reach.

"Don't even think about it."

"What is with you, Samantha? Talk to me."

"What's with me? Did it ever occur to you that you weren't the only one concerned with his self-respect? Remember me? I'm the woman who offered herself to a man who finds it repugnant to touch her unless he wants something. And you know the worst part? I let him."

She turned and hurried up the stairs, but not before he saw the sheen of tears in her eyes.

He pounded the banister with his fist. "That's not what I meant," he said to thin air. With a growl of frustration, he stalked back to the guesthouse, stripped, and got ready for bed.

But after an hour of tossing and turning with the only vision in his head that anguished look on Sam's face when she ran up the stairs, he got up. He considered going to the gym to work off some of his frustration, but his hip ached, making that idea impractical. Instead he'd settle for a soak in her hot tub. Maybe the warm water would make it easier to sleep.

He changed into his swim trunks, grabbed one of the towels from the bathroom, and headed in the direction of the hot tub. The lights that illuminated the area were already on, though, and he could hear the hum of the bubbling water. As he drew closer, he saw Samantha leaning back against the rim, her eyes closed, her hair pinned up, exposing the long column of her throat. Her face was scrubbed clean of makeup. It hadn't occurred to him before that other than that one time in the hospital, he had never seen her without it.

As if feeling his gaze on her she opened her eyes and frowned. "What can I do for you now, Detective?"

"You said I was free to use the facilities."

"So I did. I was just leaving anyway." She reached for her towel on the bench beside the tub. He snatched it out of her reach a second before she would have grabbed it.

"Don't lie to me, Samantha. You had no intention of going anywhere. This tub easily fits six people. Is it too much for you to share it with me?"

She shot him a disgusted look. "Fine. You stay on your side; I'll stay on mine."

She settled back in the water and closed her eyes, ignoring him. Adam hid an amused smile, in case she was watching him surreptitiously. He climbed into the tub, hoping he didn't groan too loudly when the warm water hit his hip. *The hell with it.* He settled back with a loud sigh of contentment.

"What are you so happy about?"

"The part of me that got shot off appreciates the temperature of the water."

"Which part of you is that?"

This time he let his grin show. "If I showed you my scar, you'd probably slap me."

She did open her eyes then and glared at him. "Do you enjoy making me feel uncomfortable in my own home?"

"No, baby, I don't." He inhaled and asked the question that had been bothering him since she'd left him standing on her bottom step. "Were you crying before?"

"When? On the stairs? Almost. I twisted my ankle on the carpet. That's why I came out here. And don't call me baby."

So she hadn't been hurt by what he'd said; he'd made her mad. Mad he could handle.

"Sweetheart, listen to me. About what I said on the beach. You never let me explain what I meant."

She crossed her arms over her breasts, giving him an arch look. "If you think you can neaten that up, go ahead."

He heaved out a heavy breath. Now that he'd opened his big mouth he didn't know what to tell her. "What I said had nothing to do with you, but with me."

"It's not you, it's me?" She touched her index finger to her temple as if she were thinking. "Hmm, now where have I heard that line before? Go to hell, Detective."

"Too late. That's where I've been since I met you. Being so close to you and never touching you has been driving me out of my mind. I haven't had a clear thought in my head since I walked in the door. If I had, I never would have taken you to Maxwell's place to begin with. You'll never know how hard it was for me to say no to you on that beach."

"Then why did you?"

"Because I watched you with that pack of piranhas at the party. I saw the melancholy look in your eyes. If I hadn't said no to you, I'd have been no better than the others, waiting for a vulnerable moment to strike. That's what I meant by holding on to my self-respect. I'm willing to pretend to be your 'boy toy,' but I'm not willing to behave like one."

She lowered her head, apparently considering what he'd said. He knew he should leave it alone and make himself content with the knowledge that she no longer appeared to be angry with him. But he couldn't. "Do you want me, Samantha, or was that just the alcohol talking?"

Her head snapped up. "You can't honestly expect me to answer that question."

"But I do. Come whisper it in my ear. I won't tell anyone."

She shook her head, not in denial, but in the way one does when dealing with a crazy person. He felt a little crazy at the moment, waiting for her answer. "Come here," he repeated.

He held his breath as she slowly rose and walked the short space that separated them to stand between his legs. He noticed the tiny tremors that shook her body. His hands held her hips to steady her. Gazing up at her, he asked, "Do you want me, Sam?"

"Yes." That one breathless word sent a flood of desire coursing through him. He leaned forward and kissed the small mole next to her belly button. His tongue delved into her navel and she jerked.

"Adam." Her voice was a heated sigh, urging him on. He let his hands rove upward to span her rib cage, his thumbs resting just below her breasts. Her head tipped back, arching her spine.

He unhooked the clasp of her bathing suit top and pulled it

away. He leaned back enough to look at her seminude body. Lord, she took his breath away. One hand slid up to cover her right breast. "God, you're beautiful, Sam."

He heard her inhale as he stroked his thumb over her nipple. "You said I was too skinny."

Adam exhaled. "I do remember saying something stupid like that."

"You said I wasn't your type."

Did she plan to rub his nose in every bonehead comment he'd made? She shivered in his arms, not the tremors of passion, but some other emotion he didn't understand. He stroked his hand over her back. "What's the matter, baby?"

She pulled away from him, and this time he was certain he saw tears in her eyes. "I can't go through with this, Adam. I'm sorry. I thought I could handle this, but I can't. I'm sorry."

She bolted from the tub before he had a chance to stop her. She grabbed a towel from the bench as she ran past, wrapping it around herself as she went. Adam sat back in the tub, for the moment too stunned to do anything.

By the time he found her room, she'd already changed into one of those gauzy things and had started pacing the floor in her sitting room with her back to him. He paused at the doorway, waiting for her to acknowledge him.

She stopped and turned to him, her arms crossed over her breasts, her hair loose around her shoulders. The sadness in her eyes tore at him, but he had to know why she'd run away from him. "You want to tell me what went on back there?"

She nodded. "Come in."

He stepped into the room, closed the door behind him, and leaned against it. "I'm listening."

She remained silent so long, he thought she'd changed her mind about telling him. Then she sighed and her shoulders drooped and she turned her back to him.

"I've never told anyone this, but Billy and I were not exactly compatible in the sexual arena. Once upon a time, I used to like sex. I used to think I was good at it. Then Billy came along."

She glanced up at him to gauge his reaction. He struggled to keep his expression neutral, but his heart had begun to pound, and a dull ache throbbed at his temple in dread of what she might say.

"It's no secret that Billy did everything to the extreme, sex included. No matter what I did, it was never enough for him. Like a greedy child, he always wanted more or different or better. After a while he stopped pressuring me, and I suspected he'd turned elsewhere for those things I refused to do. When I found Billy with someone else, it was only the last of very many straws."

She sniffled and offered him a weak smile. "You know, absolutely everyone asks me what I was doing with him in the first place. I wish I had a better answer. I only know that in the beginning he was sweet and romantic and he made me laugh. Everyone warned me against seeing him, but I didn't listen. He was the first man to see beyond my looks or star potential or whatever to care about the real me. It was a powerful aphrodisiac."

She sighed. "It took me a couple of years in therapy to realize that I'd wanted to save Billy, like I'd wanted to save my father. After my mother died, he started to drink. I begged him to stop; I even thought he had until the night . . ."

She trailed off, turning her back to him, but he already knew what came next. She thought her father had stopped drinking until the night he'd almost gotten both of them killed.

"So now you know all about me. Pretty pathetic, huh?"

He went to her and wrapped his arms around her from behind. "Don't you think you're being a little hard on yourself? You were a child when your father died, and Billy was a grown man responsible for himself." He rested his head on top of hers, and rubbed his knuckles across her cheek. "If I told you how screwed up my life is, you'd be glad to be you instead of me."

She snorted, rubbing her fingertips along his arm. "I suppose you're wondering what any of this has to do with you."

"That thought had crossed my mind."

She smacked his arm, and he squeezed her waist, grateful to know that her humor was returning.

"Believe it or not, I haven't been with a man since Billy. I hadn't wanted to risk the . . . I don't know, the humiliation of being with a man and not pleasing him. I couldn't bear to have to face that person again and have to wonder if the world knew I stank in bed. I never gave anyone the chance to get close enough to find out. For all his faults, Billy never badmouthed me to anyone.

"I'm not proud of it, but one of the reasons that I offered myself to you is that I wanted to prove to myself I'd put the past behind me. And even if it was a disaster, I wouldn't have to stare you in the face forever. You'd be going home in a few days anyway. So maybe I did deserve what you said to me after all."

He turned her in his arms until she faced him. He brushed away the remnants of her tears with his thumb. His finger lingered to trace her lower lip.

"Sweetheart, stop beating yourself up about this. If you want to know the truth, I'm immensely flattered you'd choose me for your little sexual chemistry experiment."

She lowered her forehead to his shoulder, but he could tell she was smiling. Her arms wound around his back and her fingers gripped his bare flesh.

For a moment he held her tightly to him, burying his face in her auburn hair that smelled of lilacs. But he had to get out of that room. As he'd listened to her story white-hot anger had begun to burn in him so strongly that now it begged for release of some kind. He didn't know how much longer he could keep it from her without exploding.

He pulled away from her and forced a smile to his face. "We'd better get you into bed."

She nodded. "You don't have to stay with me. I'll be all right."

"Are you sure?"

She nodded again, offering him a weak smile. "Thank you, Adam."

He cupped her face in his palms and kissed her forehead. Then he ruffled her hair. "Sleep tight and all that jazz."

Adam left her then, pulling shut both her room door and the outer door. Once in the hallway, he leaned against the wall and put his head in his hands as the wave of anger washed over him full-force.

He could handle his brother's drug use and anything else that affected only himself. He could not handle what he'd done to Samantha. He'd taken a beautiful, desirable woman and destroyed every morsel of self-confidence she had. And all for his own selfish needs. Knowing Billy, he could imagine what sort of perversity he'd tried to force on Samantha. Adam wanted to smash something, smash someone, anything to replace the brother he could no longer reach.

Somehow he found himself in the Angel Room with Billy's gaudy statuette in his hand. Billy didn't deserve Samantha's remembrance or her regard or even space on her mantel. "Damn you, Billy," he muttered, fingering the delicate filigree halo over the statue's head.

He hurled the statue at the marble fireplace. The glass shattered, splintering shards in every direction. "Damn you to hell."

Nineteen

After a restless night of turning and tossing, Adam threw off his covers and stretched. He'd left the windows open rather than turn on the air-conditioning. Somewhere nearby he heard voices; one male, one female with a tinkling, intoxicating laugh.

He checked the clock beside his bed. Barely seven o'clock. Who was Samantha entertaining at this hour of the morning?

He showered, shaved, and dressed in record time. He found Samantha reclining on one of the padded lounge chairs that ringed her pool. She looked very much the star in dark sunglasses with her hair spread around her like an auburn halo. She wore one of the tiniest black bikinis he'd ever seen. His pulse raced and his nostrils flared and his heart thudded a wild tattoo in his chest.

"Good morning, Detective," she said, a hint of a smile on her face. He grunted in response.

"Hey, bro. About time you dragged yourself out of bed."

Only then did Adam focus on Joe, fully dressed, seated in the chair beside Samantha. Joe grinned at him, showing even, white teeth and a dimple in his chin. He looked from one to the other, and both Samantha and Joe looked ready to burst out laughing any second. That didn't sweeten his mood any.

Adam turned to Joe. "What brings you here so early in the morning?"

"You do. You want to adjourn to the powder room to talk?"

After excusing themselves, Adam led the way back to the guesthouse.

"Hey, what happened here?" Joe asked as he stepped inside. "Ken got tired of you and you decided to redecorate?"

"I've got two words for you, and they are not Merry Christmas. What were you and Samantha getting so chummy about before?"

"For one thing, your attire, buddy. Didn't anybody teach you how to dress yourself properly?"

Adam glanced down at his shirt, which he'd buttoned incorrectly. "Hilarious." Adam went to work righting his clothing. "What are you, in first grade or something?"

"Okay, so it wasn't that funny. Sue me." Joe sat on the bed, leaned back, and propped up his feet. "What is with you this morning?"

Adam sat at the desk chair. "Aside from your feet on my bed? Nothing."

"If you say so, man," Joe said, but his feet stayed where they were.

Adam sighed, rubbing his palm over his aching forehead. "What have you got for me?"

"Nothing good. I talked to the lab guy this morning. All the tubing in the car was incinerated. No way to tell if the brake line had been cut. Tests were inconclusive as to whether the car had been tampered with in any other way."

That was what Adam had expected to hear from the report, but for some reason, depression flooded through him. Probably because he'd never know what really happened to Billy, but mostly because without an investigation and without Samantha in any real danger, he had no reason to stay.

"Anything else?"

"Nah, man, that's it. I'm sorry."

Adam shook his head, realizing that in effect he'd been hoping someone had murdered his brother. As angry as he was with Billy, he didn't really wish that were true.

With Billy out of the way, Adam brought up his other concern. "Have you heard of a man named Johnny Maxwell?"

"Lowlife who likes to pretend he's connected. The only thing he's ever been connected to is Mommy's umbilical cord. His moms is Congresswoman Josephine Maxwell. Every time we think we've got this joker, Mommy pulls some strings and gets him off the hook."

That scenario sounded too familiar for Adam to comment on. He went to the dresser and retrieved the packet Maxwell had given Sam. "See if you can do something with that."

Joe sampled the bag's contents. "Where'd you get the H?"

"From Maxwell. We were at his place last night. He scared the shit out of her."

Joe sealed the baggie and tucked it in his breast pocket. "I'm not even going to ask. But thanks for the present." Joe grinned wickedly. "Seems like someone is due a visit from the LAPD."

"Thanks," Adam said. He knew the paltry amount of heroin Maxwell had given Samantha wasn't worth the time or trouble of an arrest. Maxwell would be back on the street while Joe was still filling out the paperwork. Then again, Adam doubted an arrest was what Joe had in mind.

Joe shrugged and rose from the bed to stand by the window. He brushed the curtain aside to reveal Samantha still seated by the pool. Lupe stood beside her, wiping her hands on a towel. Both women were laughing.

Joe nodded toward them with his chin. "She's something special, you know."

Adam said nothing, wondering where this turn of conversation was headed.

"I say if the chance comes up, you go for it, man. Or is that what's got you growling like a bear today? You had your shot and you blew it?"

"What it is, is none of your damn business."

Joe let the curtain fall. "Have it your way, bro. Just trying to be helpful."

Adam huffed out a breath. "I've got a lot on my mind."

Joe grinned. "I bet you do. I have to be heading out anyway. They got me working a triple homicide. Real gory stuff."

The kind of case Joe loved best. "Try not to enjoy yourself too much." Adam opened the door and the two men stepped out into the bright morning sunlight.

"Hey, I'm not making any promises."

As they walked by the pool, both women pretended not to notice the men pass. Adam remained silent, not knowing what, if anything, to say to Samantha. Joe wasn't as circumspect.

"So, *muñequita,* how's she running?"

Lupe, who stood with her arms crossed in front, twisted to face them. "I've one word for you: tune-up. Get one."

"That's three words," Joe shot back.

"Here are two more: get lost."

Lupe turned to face Samantha, showing her back to Joe.

"What was that about?" Adam asked as the two men continued around the side of the house.

"The Green Ghost overheated on the freeway. It was still smoking when I pulled up. Lupe volunteered to fix it for me." Joe grinned up at him. "I think she likes me."

He'd bet Lupe volunteered to fix his car the same way Pearl Harbor volunteered to get bombed by the Japanese. "More than likely she's rigged your car to explode. How does she know anything about cars?"

"She lived with her aunt for a while, some crazy feminazi mechanic, according to Sam. She taught her how to fix cars."

"A mechanic?" An uncomfortable thought formed in his mind. Given Lupe's general hatred of men, she couldn't have been thrilled with Billy's treatment of Samantha. But had she hated Billy enough to want to get rid of him permanently? Had she hated him enough to kill him?

Joe scrutinized him for a moment. "What are you getting at, man?"

"Nothing." No use speculating in front of Joe, who he suspected was becoming infatuated with Lupe. Adam hoped his friend wasn't expecting that a few sweet words from him would transform Lupe's attitude toward the opposite sex. If he was, he was likely to be disappointed.

Adam shook Joe's hand. "Thanks for everything."

"De nada, bro. If anything else comes up, I'll let you know."

Joe got into his car, an ancient green Chrysler, and drove away.

* * *

When he got back to the pool area, Sam had gone, and Lupe sat at the edge dangling her feet in the water. She slanted a glance up at him, a sly grin on her face. "So when do we start shooting lessons?"

"Why? Found someone you want to shoot?"

"Maybe. I heard Sam crying last night. You wouldn't know anything about that, would you?"

Adam lifted his eyebrows. What happened to the "Ms." part of that sentence? "I was there, but I wasn't the cause, at least not completely."

Lupe tilted her head to the side, a gesture that reminded him very much of Sam. "Seems like someone had a little party in the angel room last night."

"Are you going to tell her?"

"I wouldn't have cleaned it up if I planned to tell her. If she notices it's missing, I'll tell her I broke it. She'll believe that."

Adam snorted. "Thanks."

Lupe shrugged and rose from the pool, dusting off her backside. "Ms. Sam told me to tell you she's getting dressed. Breakfast is on the sideboard in the dining room."

Adam nodded and headed back to the house.

Samantha was already seated at the dining room table when he got there. She glanced up when he came in, laying aside the copy of the *Times* she'd been reading. "Good news, Detective. Ariel had the babies last night. Two beautiful boys. They named them Robert and Steven, after each of their fathers." She lifted her shoulders and let out a contented sigh. "I'm an aunt again."

She beamed at him, and an image coalesced in his mind of Samantha nursing her own child. Her child and his. He blinked and shook his head to chase the picture away. "Congratulations."

He went to the sideboard, picked up a plate, and stared in wonderment at the half-dozen strips of crispy bacon that lay on the tray in front of him. He loaded them and some eggs onto his plate and sat next to Samantha. He picked up one of the strips and brought it to his mouth. "If this is one of those baconesque things made from ground-up bean curds, please don't tell me." He bit into the rasher and chewed.

"No, that's real, honest-to-God animal flesh. I had Lupe order some meat for you. The butcher nearly died of shock when she called."

He snapped off another bite. "A thousand times, thank you. But why?"

"I didn't think it was fair to deny you food you like simply because I don't eat it." She sipped from her cup, then returned it to its saucer. "But if you don't mind, could you hurry up and eat? We should be going."

"Where? It's barely eight o'clock in the morning."

"Billy Prescott's house. Johnny said Billy served other purposes. I figured we'd find some clue there."

"Absolutely not. You're not going anywhere."

"Why not?"

"Because you haven't the faintest idea how to follow orders. God only knows what or who we'd find at his place."

"We can go later if you like, but I am going. I possess the one essential thing for exploring Billy's house."

"What's that?"

"Keys. Unless the locks were changed after his death, I still have the keys to Billy's place."

She would have had him there, if he didn't possess his own set. He held out his hand. "Give them to me."

"You have got to be kidding."

He didn't understand her. After all she'd told him last night, he couldn't imagine her wanting to help Billy, even if he was in his grave. "Why do you want to do this?"

"I know Billy wasn't the perfect specimen of humanity, not even close, but if our situations were reversed, I know he would have done his damnedest to find out what happened to me."

Adam sighed. He'd finished all of the bacon, and the eggs didn't interest him. "You do exactly as I tell you."

"Cross my heart." She made an X on her chest and held up her hand as if being sworn in.

Adam growled in his throat. He'd probably live to regret this. He pushed his chair back and stood. "Let's go."

Twenty

"What exactly are you expecting to find at Prescott's?" Adam asked as they pulled out of the driveway.

Sam shrugged. "I don't know." But considering the note sent to her, she suspected they would find something—something worth killing over.

Sam slanted a glance at Adam's profile. He focused his gaze on the road ahead, oblivious to her scrutiny. Maybe she should tell him about the note. Maybe he could assure her that it was written by some harmless crackpot, but she couldn't chance it. Until this morning, she hadn't heard Lupe really laugh since the accident. She didn't intend to do anything to louse that up.

Adam shot a glance at her. "What? Is my nose on crooked or something?"

"No."

"Then why are you staring at me like that?"

"I don't know."

"You're starting to repeat yourself." Adam laced his fingers with hers, lifted her hand and turned it to kiss her knuckles. "Are you sure you're okay?"

She pulled her hand out of his grasp. "Would you mind keeping your hand on the steering wheel?"

He grasped the steering wheel with his right hand, while leaning his left on the window frame. He grinned at her like a naughty little boy. "Is that better?"

"No. Keep both hands on the steering wheel. And both eyes on the road."

"Yes, ma'am."

Sam folded her arms and stared out the side window. Honestly, she didn't know what to make of the man seated beside her. Despite his gruff exterior, he possessed a gentleness and humor that surprised her. Last night he'd held her with such tenderness that even the recollection of it made something inside her go soft. She'd poured out her soul to him, and he hadn't judged her. He'd taken care of her in a way no one had since her mother had died. His concern had made her feel stronger afterward instead of weaker, dependent. How rare a thing was that?

And when he'd touched her, she'd shaken in his arms like a leaf. What a laugh. If the world only knew that the siren of the silver screen was afraid to sleep with a man. No, that wasn't quite true. It wasn't any man that scared her, just this man. His passion frightened her, as it called to something feminine in her in which she'd lost all faith.

She sighed and shifted to a more comfortable position in her seat. She'd behaved like a coward, and that disturbed her. Then she'd topped it off by wearing that damn string bikini that morning, hoping to tempt him, hoping to test whether her behavior last night had killed his desire. Judging by the expression on his face and the hostile way he'd treated Joe, it hadn't. But he deserved better from her than head games and schoolgirl antics. He deserved as much honesty from her as she'd gotten from him.

Adam's fingers twined with hers again. "You're awfully quiet over there."

She heard the concern in his voice, and sought to allay it. "Both hands on the steering wheel, bub. I was wondering if I should tell you what Lupe's making for dinner."

"Tell me."

"Steak. She got hold of some aged beef. As we speak it's marinating in the refrigerator. She plans to grill it over the barbecue in the back. A relic of my misspent youth."

"Grilled animal flesh. Be still my meat-eating heart."

She laughed and returned her attention to the freeway. "Get off at the next exit," she said pointing. "We're almost there."

* * *

Like every home he'd visited in California except Samantha's, Billy's estate was guarded by tall gates.

As he pulled to a stop out front, Sam offered him her keys. "Wave the card in front of the sensor," she instructed.

He did as she suggested, then pocketed her keys as the gates slowly swung open. Perhaps he should tell her he'd been here before, that he'd scoured every inch of Billy's house before he'd shown up on her doorstep, and found nothing. If the staff was here, they were bound to give his identity as Billy's brother away. Maybe that was what he really wanted—for someone else to tell her, since he couldn't seem to tell her himself.

The drive up to the house was lined on the right by a garden of exotic flowers he couldn't begin to name, and on the left by a topiary—huge hedges cut into animal figures: a seal, a dolphin, a bear, a tiger. While the grounds were beautiful, it must have cost Billy a fortune to maintain them. Why not donate the money to save some real animals rather than immortalizing them in shrubbery? If he had Billy's money, he wouldn't waste it on such nonsense. Then he reminded himself he did have Billy's money—if he accepted it. Alex Winters had left another message for him last night urging him to take it.

"Pull around back," Samantha instructed him as they reached the house.

He followed the trail that Samantha pointed to around the side of the house, which led to a drive that spanned the length of the house. Samantha got out of the car the moment he'd turned off the ignition. She looked up at the immense Tudor structure. "Where do you want to start?"

"Why not right here?" One of the garage doors stood open. An elderly man in overalls wearing an applejack askew on his head was polishing a Bentley from the twenties or thirties, while casting surreptitious looks at them. The same man had taken care of Billy's collection of vintage cars and motorcycles for years. He was here the last time Adam had visited L.A. to see Billy. Adam had met him briefly then, but he hadn't been here when Adam had come recently. Would this old man be the one to spill the beans?

Adam waited for Sam to round the car and together they approached the house. "Hello, George," Samantha said when they stood under the archway of the garage.

"Ms. Hathaway." The old man beamed. He pulled off his cap and bowed slightly. "It's a long time since I seen you around here."

"It's good to see you, too."

The old man dragged his eyes away from Samantha to cast a disparaging look at him. With the barest of nods, George said, "Mr. Wexler."

So much for Adam's hope of George doing his dirty work for him. George probably figured Samantha already knew he was Billy's brother since they showed up here together.

As for Samantha, she eyed him as if she were wondering how George knew him, but before she had a chance to question him, George turned sorrowful eyes to Samantha. "I'm so sorry about what happened to Mr. Billy. And that you was hurt too."

"I know, George, but I'm fine." The old man twisted his hat in his hands. "What's wrong?"

"I heard what people be saying. That something was wrong with Mr. Billy's car and that's why he went off the road. You know, Ms. Hathaway, that I didn't let Mr. Billy go out of here with no car that needed fixing. I takes good care of all these cars. That automobile was fine when it left here. Besides, Mr. Billy'd had it less than two weeks. He'd had it serviced before he had it delivered. You believe me, don't you, Ms. Hathaway?"

"Yes, I do, George." She patted the older man's arm. "I know you always took excellent care of Billy."

The old man let go a cautious smile. "Thank you, Ms. Hathaway."

Samantha smiled in answer. "Is any of the other staff here?"

"Nah, you know Mr. Billy used to give the regular girls off at the end of the summer. I stayed on to look after things."

George cast another derisive glance in his direction. "Well, I'll leave you two to do whatever you're doing."

Samantha turned to him after George had gone.

"You've been here before?"

"Yes." He let that one word hang for a moment to see if she'd question him further. When he didn't, he asked, "Why?"

She lifted one shoulder. "Because I don't think George likes you."

That was an understatement. George had such little use for him that he'd never voiced to Adam the concerns he'd just shared with Samantha.

"More likely he doesn't like seeing me with you. I have the feeling he had better hopes for you and Billy."

"Then you'd be right." She moved away from him through the rows of cars, stopping by an antique white Rolls-Royce. She turned to face him, leaning her back against the passenger-side front door. "Did you recognize him?"

"Should I?" Adam asked, wondering what she meant.

"George was a character actor forty years ago. One of those people credited with opening doors for blacks in the movies and at the same time reviled for accepting roles that presented blacks in a bad light." She shrugged. "His career dried up shortly after it began. Billy found him in an alleyway one night, cleaned him up, gave him a job and a place to live."

Adam looked down at his boots, kicked away a piece of gravel that lay at his feet, and shrugged. Billy had never mentioned how George had come to be in his employ.

Sam tilted her head to one side. "I know so many celebrities who think they're doing something wonderful by donating an insignificant portion of what they own to some charity. Rarely do they ever do anything that affects someone on such a personal level. When people ask me what I saw in Billy, I think of George. He probably would have died penniless and in obscurity if it weren't for Billy."

She lifted her shoulders and fastened a rueful look on him. "The ironic thing is, I think Billy saw himself in George, or maybe what he might have become—a used-up actor with no one to catch him if he fell."

Adam glanced down at his feet again, wishing he had more gravel to kick. Right now, his guilt meter registered in the critical range—guilt most of all that he hadn't told Samantha the truth about his relationship to Billy.

Samantha broke the silence that stretched between them. "You know, I absolutely believe George. He never let Billy drive out of here without checking the condition of the car first. If someone had tampered with Billy's car, they did it away from here."

Though logical, that bit of advice didn't help him any. No one who Billy knew claimed to have seen him that morning before he showed up at Samantha's. That left only Lupe with motive, inclination, and possibly opportunity to sabotage the car. But he couldn't believe that Lupe would take the chance of something happening to Samantha while in Billy's car, not as close as the two women appeared to be. Or maybe Lupe hadn't figured on Samantha's actually leaving with Billy. Adam sighed. He was no closer to reconstructing his brother's last day than he had been the day he arrived in California.

"Come this way, Detective." Sam beckoned to him with a wave of her hand. "I bet what's in here will be more to your liking." She walked to the adjacent garage, then stopped. She turned her head and glared at him, hands on hips. "You stole my keys."

"I'm holding them for safekeeping."

She rolled her eyes. "Wave the card in front of the panel." He did and the door slowly opened to reveal a collection of Harleys, all chrome and leather, gleaming in the morning sunlight. The one that caught his eye was a custom-built LXH painted fire-engine red three rows back.

"You like that one?"

For a man accused of wearing a poker face twenty-four hours a day, he hadn't done a great job of keeping his emotions to himself. When had she learned to read him so well? "It has a certain charm."

She walked to the far wall, to a metal cabinet obviously designed to hold keys. When she turned to face him, she dangled a pair from her right index finger. "I think these are the right ones. Why don't you try it out?"

She didn't have to ask him twice. He straddled the big Harley and held his hand out for the keys. She tossed them to him and within instants he had the bike roaring with life beneath him. He grinned up at her. "Want to join me?"

"No thanks. I'm a bona fide chicken where those things are concerned. But don't let that stop you."

With a wink at her, he took off, zipping over the length of the length of the garage and back. Knowing she was watching him, he couldn't help showing off a little by popping a wheelie he was too out of practice to execute perfectly.

Finally, he drew to a stop beside her. "Not bad." He put his feet on the ground, and cut the engine. She stood with her hands behind her back, an amused smile on her face. "You're as bad as he was, you know that? Or is it a man thing—little boys playing with toys?"

"Maybe." He'd never bothered to analyze his and Billy's shared love for motorcycles. Maybe it was genetic. "Why?"

She lifted one shoulder. "It's no secret Billy was a thrill seeker—race cars, bungee jumping, skydiving—anything fast and deadly, Billy couldn't wait to try it. I never understood that about him. I read that some policemen have that same kind of urge—the adrenaline rush of jumping into a dangerous situation, the uncertainty of knowing the outcome or whether they would come out of it alive."

He wasn't interested in analyzing himself at the moment, either. If he could, he'd take Samantha on the bike with him, hit the open road, and content himself with the sun on his face and the hum of the bike under his body and Samantha's arms wrapped around his waist. He didn't want to examine himself or his motives or the fact that everything he wanted at the moment had once been his brother's—Billy's money, Billy's motorcycle, the woman Billy had loved. Wasn't it a sin to covet thy brother's possessions? Fortunately for Adam, he'd lost his religion a long time ago.

Adam knocked the kickstand into place and stood. "Enough fun and games. We've got work to do."

Twenty-one

With everyone out of the house, Lupe indulged herself in her second and third favorite pastimes beside cooking: she took a long swim in the pool, then curled up on one of the lounge chairs and pulled out her copy of Gwynne Forster's *Scarlet Woman*. She identified with the heroine, a woman maligned by small-town gossipmongers for doing nothing more than being kind to an old man.

Even Sam didn't know about her stash of romance novels, and would probably be shocked to know she read them. She knew Sam believed her to be a complete cynic where men were concerned, but she wasn't. She still harbored the faint hope that somewhere in the world men existed who were honorable and strong and loving. If such men existed, she had never met one of them. All the men she knew lied and cheated on the women who loved them and hurt little girls who didn't deserve it. The exception that proved the rule was Sam's friend Jarad, who'd been nice to her when she'd first come to live here.

Lupe sighed and tossed her book on top of the towel in the chair next to her. The words might as well have been written in Chinese for all the sense she'd made of them in the past fifteen minutes. She leaned back and closed her eyes. Maybe she needed a nap. She hadn't slept well in days, not since Adam Wexler showed up on their doorstep.

But it wasn't Adam's face that now superimposed itself on her consciousness; it was Joe's. And like every other time she thought of him, the same restlessness invaded her body, the same feeling of, for lack of a better word, incompleteness. For the first time in her twenty-seven years, she felt like one of the women in her novels—hot and yearning.

But unlike the heroines in her stories, there would be no happily-ever-after ending. In real life, men were just men, not heroes. From what she'd seen, women only made themselves vulnerable by allowing their desires and tender emotions to get the best of them. She'd be better off forgetting she'd ever met Det. Joe Martinez.

"Lupe?"

Lupe's eyes flew open. Joe loomed above her, and the look in his eyes made her tremble. She'd seen that look before, first in her stepfather's eyes when she should have been too young to know what it meant. She saw it in Adam's eyes when he looked at Sam. She'd seen it in Billy's eyes for anything with two legs and the right thing between them. She never wanted to see that look again. It meant a man was on the prowl and some woman was bound to get hurt.

She snatched the towel from the chair beside her, sending her book flying. She paid it no attention as she covered herself from chin to ankles. When she focused on him again, the look had gone from Joe's eyes, replaced by something softer that she didn't understand. Well, he could look any way he wanted; she still didn't want to be alone with him.

"Mr. Adam isn't here now."

"I didn't come to see him. I came to see you."

She clutched the towel to her more tightly. "Why?"

"Muñequita, you could cover yourself with the Shroud of Turin and I'd still know what's under there."

After getting hamstrung in the towel and nearly tripping over her own sandals, Lupe struggled to her feet. "What do you want, then?"

"To thank you for fixing my car this morning."

He reached toward his right pocket and she realized it was moving. She took a step back, but he'd piqued her curiosity. "What do you have in there?"

"Ouch." Joe pulled his hand out of his pocket and sucked on his thumb. "She bit me."

Lupe couldn't help the grin that spread across her face. "She who?"

He reached into his pocket again and pulled out a tiny gray-and-white-striped furball. Joe cradled it against his chest. "My neighbor's cat had kittens. I thought you might want one."

She shook her head. The man was insane. He'd brought her a cat?

"If you want her, you'll have to come and get her. I'd put her down, except she's fast and we're by the pool."

Lupe swallowed. She didn't know why it hadn't occurred to her until that moment that Adam must have told him about her. As much trouble as she went to to protect her privacy, she didn't know why that realization didn't anger her. But she did understand Joe's promise not to crowd her. She almost felt sorry for him, as the kitten was having a good time sinking her teeth into his fingers.

Lupe wrapped the towel around herself and walked toward the cat. She did her best to avoid thinking about the man holding her. She stopped a few inches away from him, bending toward the kitten. The animal stared back with curious, alert eyes. She raised her hand and stroked the kitten's head. The kitten rewarded her with a closed-eyed purr of contentment.

"Oh, Joe, she's precious." Their hands brushed as she took the cat from him. Something—electricity, maybe—rushed up her arm at the contact. Shocked, she gazed up at Joe. He blinked and backed away from her.

"What are you going to name her?"

Lupe tickled under the cat's chin. "I think I'll call her Jo."

"After me?"

His tone, half surprised, half cocky, almost made her laugh. "Of course not. After Jo March from *Little Women*.

Joe shrugged. "Can't blame a guy for trying."

Having no idea how to make small talk with a man, Lupe exhaled, half smiled, then frowned. "I-I guess I'd better find her something to eat or something."

"I bought her a few things while I was at the pet store."

Lupe cocked her head to one side and narrowed her eyes. "I thought you said your neighbor's cat had kittens."

"She did. The store owner is also a vet. I wanted to make sure she wasn't a he."

"Oh."

He left her standing there while he went around the front to his car. Lupe rushed through the house to open the front door to him. Not only had he brought food, but also a dish, a little bed, and the obligatory litter box.

Once he'd set everything in the hallway by the front door, he stood back. "I'd better be going. I guess we're even now."

Even? He'd brought her a cat and all she'd done was check the oil and pour some water in his car. She told herself she wanted to thank him properly, but mostly she wanted to know if what she'd felt had been real or a trick of her imagination.

She leaned up and kissed his cheek, a bare instant of her flesh touching his. But heat stole into her cheeks, and the nether regions of her body flooded with warmth. Her mouth dropped open and she did the only thing that flashed into her mind: she stepped back and slammed the door in his face.

From the other side, she heard Joe's laughter. "Enjoy the cat, *muñequita.*" A few seconds later, the roar of that old rattletrap he called a car reached her ears, then the crunch of gravel as he drove off.

Lupe sighed and looked down at her new pet. "I'd better get changed before the others get back," Lupe told her. The cat meowed her agreement.

When Samantha had suggested they search Billy's house, he'd suspected she had a certain spot of interest in mind. They'd spent the morning going through the rest of the house, but why, of all places, did she have to bring him here—to Billy's bedroom? Like every other room in the house, its decor screamed the wealth of its owner—from the Royal Bokhara carpet on the floor to the Baccarat chandelier overhead.

Although other furnishings occupied the room, the massive black platform bed dominated the space, the bed he now knew Samantha had shared with Billy. In his mind he saw Samantha lying on that bed, her and Billy. Bile rose to his throat, but with some effort he tamped it down.

For her sake, he'd decided to back off and let things between them cool down. Maybe he ought to make sure he kept that promise for his own sanity as well. Samantha Hathaway would never be his in any way that truly mattered. Torturing himself with thoughts of things that could not be wouldn't get him anywhere and would only drive him out of his mind besides.

He hadn't moved from the doorway of the room, but Samantha had crossed the room to the desk where Billy's laptop sat and turned it on. He could have told her not to bother. Billy seemed to use the machine as if it were a device for retrieving e-mail. From what Adam had read of Billy's mail, most of it was ribald jokes, messages from his agent or from friends. Not one pertained to his whereabouts the morning he ended up dead.

And then she did the unthinkable: she kicked off her sandals and climbed onto Billy's bed and kneed her way up to the headboard.

Adam swallowed. "What are you doing?"

"You'll see in a minute." She lifted her hands to the edge of the gilt-framed portrait, apparently searching for something with her fingertips. "I discovered this by accident."

He didn't even want to think of what she'd been doing at the time to have discovered anything. But a few seconds later, she glanced back at him over her shoulder, an impish grin on her face. "Watch and be amazed."

She pressed something on the portrait, and slowly a panel in the wall across the room slid open. An interior light automatically switched on, illuminating a deep, narrow room. From his vantage point, he saw a long mahogany cabinet with a multitude of drawers in varying sizes standing against one of the walls. He could have searched for a hundred years and never come up with this place.

"Two things that most people didn't know about Billy," Samantha said, climbing down from the bed. "One, he was a pack rat—couldn't throw anything out—and two, he was meticulous about his finances. He was paranoid about getting cheated. He had this room built to accommodate both neuroses."

He followed her to the entrance of the room. As it turned out, both walls were lined with cabinets that spanned the depth of the room. Each drawer was labeled with a placard set in a brass holder: *Contracts, Media clippings, Scripts,* and on and on. Adam had wondered how Billy had managed to save all those pictures for the album he'd left for him, but at least three of the drawers were marked *Photos*.

"Here we are." Sam pulled out one of the smaller drawers and rummaged through the dozen or so zip disks housed there. Finally she pulled one out and held it aloft. "Billy's records for this year. Come on." She beckoned to him as she stepped from the room, but Adam stayed put.

Obviously Sam suspected that a financial arrangement of some sort existed between Billy and Johnny, but in his experience, most people killed for reasons more personal than that.

He opened the first drawer of photos. Mixed in with the photos was a single manila envelope. He pulled it out and read the blue Post-it note stuck to the front of the envelope: *Hope she's worth it.*

He slid out the enclosed photographs and darted a glance toward the room's opening to make sure Samantha hadn't come back to look for him. Each of the five-by-seven pictures were of her on a beach. In the first two, she clearly didn't want her picture taken, as she held her hand up to block the shot. In the four succeeding ones, she mugged for the camera, making funny faces and posing outrageously. In all six, she was stark naked.

Adam swallowed. So much for her claim of never having posed nude for the camera. Not that these were exactly the type of shots he'd had in mind when he'd asked her that question. These pictures were of a carefree woman being silly. they weren't designed to arouse, though they had that effect on him anyway.

He slid them back into the envelope rather than torturing himself any further. But the note and the pictures didn't jibe. Given what he knew about her, he figured Samantha had known and trusted whoever had taken the pictures. Assuming that person was Billy, why was someone else sending him pictures of Samantha? *Hope she's worth it.* One obvious conclusion popped into his mind: someone had gotten hold of the pictures and blackmailed Billy to get them back.

The why of it was easy to figure out. If Billy was trying to get back together with Samantha, having those photos become public wouldn't help his case any. But who? Maybe Samantha wasn't the only one to discover Billy's secret stash accidentally.

He pocketed the photos, left the room and shut the door behind him.

Sitting at the computer, Samantha heard Adam come up behind her. Without taking her eyes off the screen in front of her, she asked, "Find anything interesting in there?"

"No."

She did glance up at him then. Ever since his ride on the motorcycle, she'd sensed something different in him, as if he'd closed off a part of himself to her. Considering how self-contained he was to begin with, she felt as if she were on the wrong side of an iron curtain—no way to get in, around, under, or through.

He leaned against the desk beside her, crossing his arms in front of him. "How about you?"

She lifted one shoulder and turned back to the screen. "Not really. I didn't know that Billy was in HSE, though."

"What's HSE?"

"I can't remember what the H and the S stand for, but the E is Enterprises. Some company that went public a year ago. Richard tried to talk me into investing, but I wasn't interested. I guess he succeeded with Billy."

"Richard was Billy's business manager, too?"

"Why does that surprise you? Because Richard hated Billy or because Billy thought Richard was an uptight prig? This town is all about image, and after that it's all about money. I never knew liking someone was a prerequisite for doing business."

"So why didn't you invest?"

"Too risky. I like my money where it is, in nice, safe T-bills and blue-chip stocks. Risk is for people who expect to gain a lot. Frankly, I'm not that greedy. Besides, HSE never panned out. The company went chapter eleven and everyone involved lost their money."

"Anything else?"

Sam bit her bottom lip, glancing from Adam to the portrait of Billy on the wall. The two men were entirely different, though there was a similarity about the eyes, not the color but the shape. They were different on the inside, too. Billy wore his every whim, every emotion, like a garment for everyone to see. Adam held everything in, letting out only what he wanted to be seen. Their only link was that both of them had appealed to her, albeit for different reasons.

Sam bit her lip and turned to face Adam. There was another difference, too. Adam possessed a character and integrity that Billy never had. If Adam were Billy's brother, wouldn't he have told her by now?

"I noticed something while I was looking through Billy's records. He made a pretty hefty donation to the Guardians, an association of black police officers in New York, a couple of months back. Is Billy's brother a cop? Is that how you got involved with this—you knew his brother from work?"

Adam cleared his throat. "You could say that. Look, Sam, I—"

He was cut off by the whirring of the mechanism opening the gates outside. Adam moved to the window, brushed aside the curtain, and looked out. A black Lexus was pulling up the drive toward the house. Obviously Billy knew this person, since they would have had to have a key to get in without a problem. The car pulled into the garage, out of sight. A second later he heard a car door slam. Adam ran over the possibilities of who might have gotten out of the car, everyone from Johnny Maxwell to his mother. None of them were welcome at the moment.

"Who is it?"

Adam glanced over his shoulder at Samantha. "I don't know. Stay here. Lock the door after I leave and don't come out until I come to get you."

Her eyes widened and her throat worked, but she nodded. "Be careful."

He winked at her. "Got it covered." He stepped out into the hall.

Twenty-two

Adam stepped out onto the landing. A second later the front door opened. Sandra walked in carrying her daughter. She pushed the door closed and set the baby on the floor.

Adam loped down the stairs. Sandra looked up as he descended toward her. "Adam, what are you doing here?"

"I could ask you the same thing."

"Some of Brianna's things are here. Did I come at a bad time?"

What an understatement. Samantha would take one look at that child and know who had fathered her. After last night, Samantha didn't need to know how far Billy's betrayal of her extended.

But the little girl was his niece, a relationship he'd neglected long enough. She stared at him with an expression that reminded him of the one on Samantha's face when he'd pulled out his gun. He squatted down to be closer to her height. "Hi, sweetheart. Don't you remember me? I'm your uncle Adam."

She stepped closer to him, enough to touch his cheek. "Your face tickles," she said, stepping back.

He ran his hand over his chin. He'd done as good a job of shaving as he had of dressing. Wiping his hands on his jeans, he stood. He had to get them out of the way so he could get Samantha out of here.

"Look, Sandra, I'll be out of the house in five minutes. Wait in another room until you hear the door close."

Sandra shook her head, confused. "I don't understand, Adam. If we already know you're here—"

"Who's this, Adam?"

Adam ground his teeth together. Couldn't the woman do one damn thing he asked? Come to think of it, he hadn't heard the bolt turn on the lock, either. He turned to see Sam leaning against the wall halfway up the stairs, her arms folded in front of her. His gaze met her icy one. What he saw there pleased him more than a little: jealousy.

Before he could answer, Sandra did it for him. "I'm Sandra, a friend of Billy's. This is my daughter, Brianna." Sandra pushed her daughter forward, giving Samantha a clear view of the girl.

From anyone else, Adam would have assumed motherly pride the reason for displaying the girl. But judging from the malicious smile on Sandra's face, no maternal instinct motivated her actions. She hoped to rub Sam's nose in the fact that she'd had a child by Billy.

Turning to look at Sam, Adam knew the instant she recognized the child might possibly be Billy's. Her jaw dropped and she swayed slightly, bracing her hands on the wall behind her. "H-how old is she?"

Triumphantly, Sandra said, "She'll be four at the end of the month."

He could almost see Samantha's mind spinning, calculating when the child must have been conceived. While Sandra prattled on about her daughter, Adam watched Samantha. She smiled and nodded in the appropriate places, but he knew finding out about Billy's child in this way had rocked her.

"Come on, sweetheart. We need to get going." Adam grabbed Samantha's arm and steered her out the front door. She walked beside him woodenly, saying nothing. When he opened the car door for her, she sat, rested her forearms on the dash and laid her forehead against them.

He slid in behind the wheel and rubbed her back in a way he hoped she found soothing. "I'm sorry, sweetheart."

She lifted her head and sat back. "Does it ever end, Adam? Is there any end to the ways that man made a fool of me?"

He didn't know what to say to that, unsure of the answer himself. "You had no idea?"

She shook her head. "Even if I'd heard something about it, I probably wouldn't have paid it any attention. A man in Billy's position attracts paternity suits like a magnet attracts paper clips. You'd be surprised how many women are willing to come forward to claim that this or that famous man fathered their child. It's easier to pay them off and get them out of your hair."

She plowed her fingers through her hair, brushing it back from her face. "But I would have expected him to tell me, maybe not then, but one of those times in the last few months when he was supposedly trying to win me back."

He rubbed the back of her neck. "Are you all right?"

"Sure. What difference does it make now, anyway, right? Billy's gone. Whatever he did when we were together is ancient history."

Her flippant response didn't fool him, but he wasn't about to challenge her on it. "Are you ready to go?"

"Just a minute." She sat up and pulled the disk out of her back pocket and handed it to him. "I figured we might need this."

"You do realize that's theft."

"So arrest me."

Adam slid the disk into his breast pocket next to the photos and started the engine.

Sam's spirits sank even lower when they pulled up in front of the house to find Richard's car parked there. She glanced over at Adam. He didn't look any more pleased than she felt. Neither he nor Richard had been particularly vigilant about keeping their mutual animosity a secret.

"I'll be in my room," Adam said, getting out of the car.

"Oh, no, you don't." She got out of her side before Adam had a chance to open her door. "If I have to put up with him, so do you. Aren't you supposed to be protecting me?"

"From danger, not pompous, irritating windbags."

He took her elbow and led her toward the house. She knew

he intended to leave her on her doorstep and head around back, but she didn't want to face Richard alone. Undoubtedly Richard had heard about her appearance at Johnny Maxwell's last night. Most of the time she found his fatherly concern comforting, but right now she just wanted to be left alone.

When they reached the door, she turned to him. "Please, Adam."

A hint of a smile turned up one corner of his mouth. "I never could resist a woman begging."

She took a step away from him. "I'm not begging you for anything. I'm asking you."

He shook his head. "Sweetheart, it's a joke. Lighten up."

She licked her lips and preceded him into the house. She felt as light as a lead weight. She'd harbored some crazy notion that they'd walk into Billy's house and whatever might have gotten him killed would have jumped out at her immediately. They'd found absolutely nothing of any use, and she'd discovered Billy had sired a child, probably around the same time he'd proposed to her. She was over him, she knew that, but the knowledge still stung, still made her feel like the biggest idiot in southern California. At the moment she didn't think she could bear Richard's rantings without some sort of buffer. Adam Wexler was about as big a buffer as you could get.

She'd expected Richard to be angry, but his red-faced, glassy-eyed expression when she walked into the solarium bordered on fury. "Samantha Elizabeth Hathaway—what is this I hear about you cavorting at that . . . that . . . person's house. And drunk, no less."

Before she could respond, his gaze slid to Adam. "And you. What kind of policeman are you that you could allow her to visit such a place?"

She felt Adam tense beside her. Despite her anger at Richard, she didn't want to see him pounded into her carpet. She stepped in front of Adam.

"That is enough, Richard. You will not address me or anyone staying in my home in this manner. I was neither drunk nor cavorting, as you put it, but even if I were, it's none of your business. I have always appreciated your concern, but you are *not* my father."

"Maybe I should have been. No daughter of mine would parade around half nude, but then you always were your mother's daughter."

She cocked her head to one side. "What is that supposed to mean?"

"Theresa was a beautiful woman, but she had no idea what was good for her. Jack was my friend, but a man knows another man. I knew he'd hurt her. Like you, she had to find out for herself what kind of a man your father was. Obviously you're no better. First Billy, now . . ." His words trailed off, but he looked directly at Adam. "When are you going to learn, Samantha?"

She didn't know what to say to him. She didn't recognize the man standing in front of her, this Richard. Before today he'd never spoken one unkind word about either of her parents, though she'd always held the secret suspicion that Richard had been in love with her mother.

But that didn't excuse or explain his behavior now. She folded her arms in front of her and met his hostile gaze. "I don't know what your problem is, Richard. But I suggest you leave now, before *I* say something *I'll* regret."

For a moment, a belligerent expression came over Richard's face as he glanced from her to Adam and back again. "I'm only looking out for your best interests," he said finally.

"Good-bye, Richard."

She waited until he'd left the room to put her hands in her hair and make a sound of frustration in her throat. "Has everyone in my life gone nuts?"

"If you ask me, that one probably wasn't wrapped too tight to start with."

Sam snorted. She couldn't argue with him there. She turned to face Adam. "Thank you."

"For what?"

"Not butting in. Most men have this thing about taking over whenever it looks like a woman is in distress."

He chucked her under the chin. "If I'd thought he was in

any danger of getting the better of you, I'd have shown the little weasel the door, closed first, then open."

She smiled, imagining Adam doing just that. "Well, thank you anyway."

"If you want to thank me, go up to your room and rest. Your ankle is bothering you."

Her ankle throbbed and her shoulder ached, but she wondered how he knew.

As if sensing her question, he continued. "You get this pinched expression around your mouth when you're in pain." He turned her so that she faced the doorway. "Now go."

She didn't argue. At this point she wished she hadn't flushed the painkillers Jerry had given her. "See you at dinner."

"Maybe."

As she trudged her way up the stairs, she sensed Adam below watching her. Lupe came out into the hallway, anticipating her arrival. Lupe held a tiny kitten in her hands.

"Where did you get him?" Sam asked when she was close enough to pet the cat's soft fur.

"Joe. He wanted to thank me for fixing his car."

Sam gazed down at Lupe, who stared back with a tight-lipped, apprehensive expression on her face. Did she expect Sam to disapprove? Sam smiled in a way that she hoped reassured Lupe.

"Joe, huh?" Sam braced one fist on her hip. "And how come you get to have a kitten and I can't have a puppy?"

"Because this he's a she, that's why."

Sam had figured that already. She dropped her hand to her side. "Wake me up for dinner, okay? I'm going to take a nap."

Lupe nodded. "By the way, Fiorello's delivered some flowers this afternoon. I put them in your room."

"Who from?"

Lupe shrugged. "They got here five minutes before you did. I didn't have a chance to snoop and read the card."

Sam laughed. Lupe was probably too busy eavesdropping on her conversation with Richard. "Lupe, you're all heart." Sam found the box sitting on her dressing table. She carried them to her bed and sat down, placing the box on the bed beside her. She kicked off her shoes and massaged her ankle a moment before reaching for the card.

Sitting back, she slid the card from the envelope. The outside of the card showed a Model-T stranded by the side of the road, smoke coming out from under the open hood. What was that supposed to mean?

Shrugging, she opened the card and froze. Inside someone had pasted a message cut from newspaper articles: *I warned you to stay out of my way.*

Twenty-three

Adam took a swig of his beer and sat back in his chair. Twilight was making its descent, casting both darkness and moonlight on the azure waters of Samantha's pool. Citronella candles stationed in a semicircle around the small poolside table where they dined kept the bugs at bay and scented the air with a pleasing fragrance.

After finishing a perfectly grilled steak and most of one bottle of the beer from a local microbrewery that Joe had left with Lupe, he was feeling pretty mellow. He glanced from his clean plate to Samantha's. She'd barely eaten one bite. Ever since she'd risen from her nap she'd been skittish, displaying a nervousness that seemed alien to her. She hadn't said one word he hadn't prompted from her. She wouldn't even look at him. Her gaze centered on the pool and the play of light and darkness on the water.

He doubted her encounter with the gutless wonder she called her business manager had anything to do with it. After he'd gone, she'd seemed annoyed, not upset. But if not him, then what?

He nodded toward her plate. "What's the matter? Don't you like the salmon?"

She focused on him, a startled expression on her face. "I'm sorry. What did you say?"

"The salmon—don't you like it?"

She lifted one shoulder. "I guess I'm not very hungry tonight."

He couldn't believe that. They'd skipped lunch that afternoon, and as far as he knew she hadn't raided the refrigerator since they'd been home.

Pensively, he swirled the remains in his beer bottle before downing the last swallow. "Do you know this is only the second beer I've had since I've been in California?"

"Is that a big deal?"

"A couple of weeks ago it was." Though he hadn't wanted to admit it at the time, Jarad Naughton had been right about him. He'd been drowning himself in self-pity and hops until the other man had shown up at his door. If it hadn't been for his promise to watch over Samantha, he'd probably have come out here for Billy's funeral, gone back home, and done more of the same. He supposed he owed Jarad a thank-you for breaking him out of that cycle.

Most cops drank to cope with the pressures of police work, a pastime Adam rarely indulged in. Yet a few weeks off the job had him turning into a closet lush. Now, what did that say about him?

He set the bottle on the table. Not wanting to dwell on the machinations of his own psyche, he changed the subject. "How's your ankle?"

"About the same."

"Maybe you should get yourself into a nice, warm bath."

"I was thinking of hitting the hot tub. Care to join me, Detective?"

He shook his head. "We got ourselves in trouble the last time we tried that."

She tilted her head to one side. "So you're saying you have that little self-control?"

He had plenty of self-control, just very little of it where she was concerned. Though he knew he shouldn't, his mouth said, "Meet you there in ten minutes."

She nodded and rose from her chair. "Last one in's a rotten egg." He watched her as she walked away from him. The sundress she wore bared long, long legs and molded to the shapeliest backside this side of Jennifer Lopez.

Adam leaned back in his chair, closed his eyes, and groaned.

* * *

Sam waited the ten minutes Adam had given her before changing into a modest two-piece bathing suit. Obviously he thought she'd arranged their meeting for a repeat performance of the previous night, but she didn't care what he thought. She didn't want to be alone. The card she'd received, as well as the accompanying box of bloodred roses with the heads cut off, had sent a chill of alarm through her that still had her trembling.

She had no choice but to tell him now. She'd tried to broach the subject during dinner, but she'd still been too shaken up to put together two coherent words.

She put on her robe and tied the sash, then slid her feet into a pair of low-heeled slippers. She thought of the notes tucked safely in an alcove in the Angel Room. If worse came to worst, she'd simply show them to him and let him figure it out himself.

When she got to the hot tub, Adam had already settled into the water with his arms stretched across the rim. He looked up at her as she slipped out of her robe to lay it on the bench beside the tub. "If it isn't the rotten egg herself."

She stuck her toe in the water. Though cooler than the night before, warm water bubbled over her foot.

He stood and held out his hand to help her into the water. For a moment she stood in the dim surrounding light transfixed, her gaze skittering over broad shoulders, bulging pecs, a flat washboard stomach, and those strong arms that intrigued her. She swallowed. Lord, he was perfect, except for one jagged, healed scar along his left side.

She stepped into the tub and sat beside him. Sighing, she relaxed against the rim of the tub and closed her eyes. The water heated her ankle and bubbled over her shoulder, immediately relieving her of some of her discomfort.

"Better?"

Eyes closed, she nodded. "When I had this thing installed, I never imagined I'd be using it for medicinal purposes." She opened her eyes and turned her head to face him. "Is that where you were shot, your side?"

"That's a souvenir from a stint on a narcotics task force. Luckily, a very brief stint."

"Why luckily?"

"Generally, narcotics is one of the most dangerous duties you can pull. Your goal is to catch the bad guys with the drugs in hand, so you end up breaking into a lot of places, trying to take them by surprise. Their goal is to keep you out long enough to either escape or get rid of the evidence. Sometimes they're not so nice about their means of repelling visitors."

"Weren't you wearing a vest?"

"Mm-hmm. But somebody forgot to tell that to the bullet that hit me."

Sam bit her lip and stared off at the foliage that surrounded the tub. Despite all of the research that she'd done pertaining to police work, none of it had seemed real to her, not the way that one simple story did now.

She didn't understand him. Her one encounter with the wrong side of a gun had left her paralyzed with fear, and yet he faced that every day, or at least often enough to have been shot twice. What drive in him compelled him to go back day after day?

"Tell me what happened. How did you get shot?"

He rubbed his knuckles against her cheek. "Sweetheart, you don't want to know."

"Yes, I do." But she sensed he didn't want to tell her. From the newspaper reports she knew two people had lain dead at the end of the night, but the details had been sketchy and designed to make Adam look as if he were at fault for allowing his young, inexperienced partner to enter a dangerous situation unprotected. Knowing him, she couldn't believe he'd allowed that to happen.

Heaving out a heavy sigh, he looked up at the starlit sky. "Did you know that, aside from the obvious reasons, most cops hate working holidays?"

"Why?"

"Family gets together, a lot of times there's drinking, arguing, a gun or a knife handy. Somebody ends up on the wrong side of a dispute."

"That's exactly why I've always been against ordinary people having guns in the house. Too much potential for tragedy."

He shrugged, offering her a rueful smile. "Maybe you're right. I don't know."

"July fourth is a biggie on the cop holiday hit parade. All the usual nonsense, plus the yahoos who think Independence Day gives them the right to act like the Grucci family. My partner Josie and I get a call to investigate a homicide on Baychester Avenue. It had just stopped raining, one of those thunderstorms that make you wonder if you shouldn't have spent the last week building an ark. It's only five o'clock but the sky is dark enough for it to have been midnight. There's supposed to be a patrol car already at the scene, but when we pull up to the house there's nobody there but a couple of teenagers in a car a couple of houses down steaming up the windows.

"It doesn't happen often, but I figure we've got the wrong address. You can hit Baychester Avenue in the Bronx four or five different places and still be on the same street. Besides, this particular stretch of houses isn't known for much activity of any kind. I tell Josie to stay put while I radio in and find out where we are supposed to be.

"Hothead that she is, while I am finding out we're not supposed to be at a house, but an apartment building on the other side of the New England Thruway, she gets out of the car and walks up to the front door.

"At this point I'm annoyed, but I'm figuring the only light on in the house is in one of the bedrooms upstairs. The worst that can happen is she'll ring the doorbell and disturb some people making some fireworks of their own. I didn't count on the door being open, or that Josie would disappear inside before I had a chance to stop her.

"By the time I got inside the house the one light had gone out, so I knew whoever was in the house knew we were in there and didn't like it."

He fell silent. Sam pressed her lips together dreading what came next. "What happened?"

"In one of the bedrooms I saw a figure moving. Maybe it's the hormones in the milk, but these days your average thirteen-year-old looks more like a man than a boy. And when you see one holding anything, your first instinct is to do unto them before they do unto you. Kids get scared; they're unpredictable.

"He'd wedged himself between the bed and the wall. I didn't have to guess what he was holding. His hand shook worse than Muhammed Ali's. I told him I was a police officer and to put the gun down, but he just stood there. I realized he wasn't being uncooperative; he was terrified.

"I walked around the side of the bed toward him, hoping that if I got close enough to him, he'd let me take the gun from him. He let me get close, but then he started to back away. I think my size intimidated him. So I told him to give it to me, pointing it downward. He handed it to me so slowly it felt like slow motion. I kept thinking, 'Come on, kid. Come on.' I could hear Josie in the hallway, and knowing her record for leaping before she looked I wanted that gun in my hands before she did anything stupid.

"Two seconds later, Josie jumps into the room, shouting, 'Freeze.' The kid twitches, the gun goes off, and there's me lying on the floor with a bullet in my hip. I hear two more shots. The kid lands on top of me and now I can hardly breathe, much less move.

"I turn my head toward Josie just in time to see someone coming up behind her. Turns out the older sister's boyfriend isn't allowed in the house, so the girl meets him outside when the parents leave her to baby-sit."

"The two kids in the car?"

"Yeah. Well, they must have dragged themselves out of their pubescent hormone rage long enough to investigate why the light went out, the brother's signal that something was wrong in the house. Josie and the boyfriend wrangle over her gun and it goes off. A second later Josie hits the floor.

"So I'm lying there with one kid, his dead eyes staring up at me, a stunned expression on his face, another clinging to her brother, bawling her eyes out, and I'm bleeding to death. I felt like I was in the last act of *Hamlet* with everybody dying."

He let out a heavy sigh. "The next thing I knew, I was in a hospital bed. I ended up with little more than a flesh wound, but because of the angle of trajectory, the bullet glanced off my hipbone."

"I don't understand. Why would the boyfriend shoot your partner?"

"He didn't intend to; he just wanted the gun. We were in plainclothes. She never identified herself. What would you do if some crazy, gun-toting white woman showed up in your house?" He shook his head. "Believe it or not, they wanted to prosecute the father for having an unlicensed handgun."

"And you blame yourself for that?"

"Not blame, exactly. I keep turning the events over in my mind, wondering if I'd done this or that differently, maybe the situation wouldn't have turned so hopelessly bad. I was the experienced officer, not Josie. I knew how she was. She came from an old, conservative cop family, male cops. She always felt she had to prove she was as fearless as the men in her family. I should have taken better care of her. I should have handcuffed her to the damn car to keep her out of trouble."

He looked away from her, a pained expression on his face. Despite all she'd told herself about protecting herself from men who needed saving, she wished she could give him the peace that he so obviously lacked in his life. She wanted to feel connected to him.

She touched her fingertip to his cheek, and he turned to face her. She lifted her other hand to cradle his face between her palms. "Let it go, Adam. If you don't, it will eat you up inside." Her gaze lowered to his mouth, to the firm, sensual lips that made her tremble.

"Samantha, don't," he whispered, but he didn't pull away.

She ignored his warning and pressed her lips to his. She didn't have to wait long for a response from him. With a groan of surrender, his arms closed around her, pulling her onto his lap. His lips crushed down on hers as his tongue, hot, moist, and demanding, slid into her mouth. With one hand he cradled her head, setting off tiny sparks along her scalp. The other hand roved over her back, then lower, to cup her derriere in his palm.

She squeezed her eyes shut, acknowledging that this wild, erotic kiss was more than she'd bargained for. She sensed the passion in him, but more than that, she felt the need in him for absolution, something she couldn't give him. He could only give that to himself.

He broke the kiss and buried his face against her neck. He exhaled, sending his warm breath fanning out against her already heated skin. "I'm sorry, baby."

She wrapped her arms around him. He had nothing to apologize for. She'd been the one to push him when he'd told her not to. But she didn't regret it. She suspected that tonight she'd gotten a glimpse into the soul of Adam Wexler—more than he showed most people, certainly more than he'd intended for her to see. If she wasn't mistaken, beneath his persona of the jaded New York cop lay a more complex and sensitive man than she'd believed possible. She wanted to know that man.

Suddenly the grounds flooded with light. Adam's head immediately snapped up. Disoriented, she gazed up at him. "What's going on?"

He pushed her from his lap and stood. "There's someone on the property. Come on."

Twenty-four

"Come on, Samantha," Adam prompted when she didn't move. She stared at him wide-eyed, and he felt her tremble beside him. He'd never seen her this scared, not even the first time she'd seen his gun. "Sam," he snapped, and finally she seemed to come back to herself. She followed him out of the tub and to the path that could lead either to the main house or the guest bungalow. He started to lead her toward the latter when he sensed her resistance.

"Lupe," she said when he turned a questioning glance to her.

Adam groaned. If whoever had come onto the grounds intended her harm, he'd rather see her in the guesthouse. The smaller building had only one entrance, fewer windows, and a good strong dead bolt on the door. But he didn't have time to argue with her. He turned and took her to the house.

Lupe already waited for them at the back door, a worried expression on her face. He pushed Samantha toward her when she opened the door. Of the two of them, Lupe was definitely the more clearheaded. He told her, "No one gets in without a badge and an ID. Call Joe. And make sure she stays put."

Lupe nodded.

As he turned to leave, Samantha grabbed his arm. "Where are you going?"

"To offer the welcome wagon to our visitor. I shouldn't be gone long."

"Adam, please. Wait for the police to arrive."

He grazed her cheek with his knuckles. "I am the police,

as you are so fond of reminding me." He kissed her forehead. "Baby, I'll be fine." But the longer he waited, the more likely whoever had come onto the grounds would be gone.

Reluctantly she released him and stepped back. "Be careful."

He winked at her. "Now where's the fun in that?"

He slipped through the door and headed back to the guesthouse to retrieve his gun and a flashlight and to shove his feet into a pair of sneakers. The area around the house glowed like a thousand-watt Christmas tree, but the surrounding grounds were not so brightly lit.

In truth, he had no idea where to look. He'd had the repairman install the floodlights and motion sensors at the perimeter of the grounds the day he'd come to fix the alarm system. The woodland behind Samantha's house made a perfect cover for anyone wanting to get onto her property. It surprised him that no one had made the attempt before.

For all he knew, a deer or mountain lion or whatever other animals lived out there might have tripped the system, but he doubted it. Something in his gut and in Samantha's reaction gave the lie to that idea. She hadn't been merely afraid; she'd been terrified. Did she know something that he didn't?

He couldn't dwell on that now. The only thing that mattered was preventing whoever had gotten onto the property from getting to her.

A lighted path wound through the property, leading to a gazebo and beyond that the perimeter of the grounds. He stayed to the right of the path, figuring no one could be so stupid as to leave themselves out in the open at this point. He stopped and listened for a moment. At his size, stealth had never been his strong suit. In front of him and to his right he heard something rustle, almost like the sound of leaves underfoot, and the glint of something metal in the darkness.

A feral grin stretched across Adam's face. *Bingo.*

Alone and nearly frantic, Samantha paced the length of her room, waiting for the police to arrive. Logically, she knew only minutes had passed since Adam left out the back door, but it felt like hours.

She shivered, but the cold, damp suit she still wore had nothing to do with it. The chill was internal, spawned by her fear for Adam. She should have told him about the notes she'd received rather than procrastinating until it was too late. Now he was out there, probably figuring whoever had wandered onto the property was an autograph hound or someone else harmless, not someone who intended to hurt her.

She tugged off her suit and pulled on a thick satin robe and matching slippers, then went to the window to see if she could spot Adam. She couldn't see a thing, couldn't hear a sound, and she feared for him. Where the hell were the police?

Joe screeched to a halt in front of the Hathaway house. Luckily he'd been nearby when Lupe had reached him on his cell phone. The blood had frozen in his veins when he heard the normally laconic Lupe nearly hysterical on the phone. Before he got a chance to ring the bell, Lupe snatched the door open. "Joe, thank God."

She looked pale, fragile, and frightened. He wanted nothing more than to take her in his arms and comfort her, but now wasn't the time. He shut and locked the door behind him. "Where's Adam?"

"He went out back a few minutes ago."

He took her hand and led her to the back door. "Lock this behind me."

She nodded. "Get him."

He winked at her. "Just what I love, a bloodthirsty wench. Don't forget to lock the door."

She rolled her eyes at him. Chuckling, he slipped through the door and down the path that led to the guesthouse. In the distance he heard the rasp of someone breathing heavily, probably running. *Good.* He hadn't missed anything yet.

Just a few more feet. Adam focused on the small, wiry man in front of him. The guy strolled along, oblivious, as if he had all the time in the world. *Poor bastard*. He had no idea what was about to hit him.

And then something under Adam's foot crunched. He froze, but he already knew he'd given himself away. He aimed his gun at the intruder's head. "Police. Stay where you are." The guy took one look at him and took off.

For a moment he contemplated shooting the son of a bitch just for making him run. With a growl of frustration, Adam followed him. The guy was fast, and Adam's hip had ached even before they'd started this mad dash.

Suddenly the guy tripped and sprawled against the ground. Whatever he held in his hand skittered across the grass away from him. A large, sneaker-wearing foot on the back of the guy's neck prevented him from getting up. The beam of a flashlight flicked on, directed at Adam.

"Just what the well-dressed cop is wearing these days. A bathing suit and tennies. *Trés chic.*"

Adam leaned over, bracing his hands on his knees, breathing heavily. In the distance he heard the sounds of police sirens— the cavalry arriving after the battle had been won. "What the hell took you so long?"

"I just washed my hair and I couldn't do a thing with it. Who do we have here?"

"Someone with a death wish."

Joe chuckled. "Lucky for him the state of California frowns on police brutality." Joe flashed the light in the face of the squirming, helpless man at his feet. "What's your name, buddy?"

The man gurgled until Joe eased up a bit "W-William. My name is William Barrington Prescott the Third."

Sam stood at the solarium window trying to make out what was going on behind her house. Ten minutes ago the police had arrived and swarmed over her house like bees. One uniformed officer stood by the door to this room. From what she'd ˉˉered from eavesdropping, officers had been stationed at ˉˉ of the entrances. The remainder were divided between the grounds out back and the front lawn, where a bevy of reporters scenting a scoop had accumulated.

For the millionth time, she turned to glance at Lupe, who sat on the floor playing with that damn cat. Maybe she'd misjudged Lupe's burgeoning feelings for Joe. Lupe seemed completely unconcerned with the outcome of what played out in their backyard. Or maybe Lupe had simply shut down, closed herself off from it emotionally. If she had, Sam wished she'd share the secret, because Sam would give anything to shake the feeling of dread that pervaded her.

Sam glanced at the doorway as a plainclothes officer entered, a heavyset giant of a man with heavy jowls and thick, dark hair and eyebrows. He struck her as the human incarnation of a Saint Bernard.

He advanced toward her, a sour expression on his face. "Ms. Hathaway, I have news for you."

A chill of foreboding ran through her. If there was bad news, why didn't Adam tell her himself? Had Adam been injured or worse because of her? She pressed her lips together and cleared her throat. "Where's Adam? I mean Detective Wexler."

"He's still outside with Detective Martinez. An intruder was apprehended on your property. A man named Edgar Lomax. Does that name mean anything to you?"

Sam shook her head. "Should it?"

"Probably not. Despite the evidence in his wallet to the contrary, he claims he's Billy Prescott, your fiancé."

Sam covered her face with her hands as relief flooded through her. Some unhinged individual, that was all it was. Adam had never been in any real danger. Still, she wouldn't relax totally until she could see for herself that he was all right.

"Ms. Hathaway, do you want to press charges?"

"I-I don't know." She couldn't think beyond making sure they were all okay. And if the man was merely a crackpot, he might be better served by psychiatric counseling than a prison term. "I have to think about it."

"He's not going anywhere until tomorrow morning. But I urge you to come down to the station. Among other items in his possession, he was carrying a four-inch hunting knife.

High-profile cases like Mr. Prescott's tend to bring out every nut in a five-mile radius. Some of them can be dangerous if their delusions are challenged."

He walked away from her, leaving her chilled to her very bones.

Adam stood outside the guesthouse beside Joe as the swarm of police who'd invaded Samantha's house packed up and went home. Edgar Lomax had been shepherded into a patrol car a few minutes ago, and would become intimately acquainted with a padded room if there was any justice in the world. The poor bastard actually believed he was Billy. He'd even brought her a tacky crystal angel to prove it. Apparently Adam had been the only person in creation unaware that she'd collected them for years. The statue's silver base had been the metal Adam had seen in his hands. It wasn't until later that he found the bowie knife in Lomax's pocket. Every time Adam let his brain wander over what might have happened had this psycho actually gotten to Samantha, a shudder passed through him.

"Now that the show's over, you got a minute?" Joe asked.

"Only one." Adam's brain was too frazzled and his body was too weary to think much about anything right now. His whole being focused on getting back to Samantha and making sure she was okay.

"This may not be the time to lay this on you, but I found out something else today that might interest you."

Adam's ears pricked up and his eyes opened. "About who?"

"About this place. Samantha Hathaway's name isn't the only one listed on the title to this place. A Carmen Mendoza is listed as coowner. Now what do you make of that?"

Adam shrugged. "I'm sure you'll figure it out. And while you're at it, you might want to look at her business manager, Richard Russell, too. He was over here ranting today, something to do with Sam's parents. I'll admit I can't stand the guy, but something about him doesn't add up."

"I'll see what turns up."

Adam clapped his hand on Joe's shoulder. "Thanks, buddy. For a minute there, it felt like old times."

"Don't I know it. I hope you don't mind if I stick around for a while."

"I don't mind, but I don't think it's me you're hanging around for."

"Who says you're as dumb as you look?" Joe sighed and shoved his hands in his pockets. "If she doesn't want me here, I'll go."

Adam sighed. He hoped for Joe's sake—and maybe even for Lupe's—that he wouldn't have to.

Twenty-five

After the detective left her, Sam turned back to the window. She realized she was not only terrified for his safety, but angry with him for rushing off into danger alone. In that respect, she'd been unfair to him.

She should have known that was what he'd do. She'd had him pegged from the very beginning. Adam Wexler was a cop through and through, down to the marrow in his bones. He could no more have waited patiently for reinforcements to show up than he could have sprouted wings or grown another head. When his time here was over, he'd go back to his job, if they let him, if a moment's hesitation hadn't cost him everything he treasured.

She didn't know how any woman stood this on a regular basis—sending a man she loved into harm's way every morning, never knowing if he'd come back to her that night. Coping with Billy's flirtations with peril had been hard enough for her to take. She knew she'd never survive it if she had to worry about Adam's safety on a daily basis.

Sam sighed. When had she started to fall in love with him? Was it the night he'd held her after her dream? Or when he'd come for her at Johnny's house and made her dizzy with relief and wanting? Or maybe it was that first day when he'd told her softly that he wanted to help her?

She didn't know, and in the end, it didn't matter. When the time came she would let him go, but for now he was hers. All her other petty concerns paled to insignificance in the light of her need for him. If he wouldn't come to her, she intended to go to him.

And she didn't intend to stand around and wait for him anymore. She turned to Lupe. "I'm going to find Adam."

Lupe stared up at her wide-eyed. "Adam told me to keep you inside."

"Since when do you take orders from Adam Wexler?"

She moved toward the doorway, where a young, uniformed officer stood. He held up his hands to forestall her. "It's not a good idea, ma'am. You should stay inside until we get the all-clear."

"This is my home, Officer. I can go where I like."

She realized she was being unreasonable, but she didn't care. She also realized the young officer was in awe of her and unsure what to do about her uncooperativeness. She slipped past him into the hallway.

"Ms. Hathaway," he called, trailing behind her. He could come with her if he liked, but she wouldn't let him stop her.

Unfortunately, the officer at the back door was a bit older and more self-assured. "What's the problem, Ms. Hathaway?" he asked as they approached.

"I need to see Detective Wexler immediately."

"If you'll go back to your room, I'll call him for you."

Not good enough. "There's no need. I can find my way around my own property, thank you."

"Ms. Hathaway, our orders are to keep you inside the house."

"Who's going to stop me? Lay one finger on me, Officer, and I'll be wearing your badge as a brooch."

The man stepped away from her, which surprised her. She wasn't used to exerting her power as a Hollywood star to get what she wanted. After a moment's hesitation, she opened the door and stepped out into the cool night. She headed out to the guesthouse, hoping to find Adam there.

When she saw him she stopped midstride. He still wore only his bathing suit and a pair of sneakers, an ensemble that brought a smile to her lips. Lines of exhaustion were etched around his eyes and mouth. His five-o'clock shadow had long since passed a ten-o'clock burr. He probably didn't realize it, but a leaf was stuck to the side of his neck, probably by perspiration. Yet he looked so damn good to her that tears sprang to her eyes.

"Adam."

Adam looked up to see Samantha standing in the path in front of him flanked by two harried-looking officers. He could imagine what she'd done to put those looks on their faces. His own face probably bore a similar expression. If she'd pulled this stunt ten minutes ago, Lomax would have still been here. She seemed unaware of her own jeopardy and the other people she put in danger with her actions.

He should be angry with her for disobeying him once again, but he wasn't. Right now he didn't feel much like a cop. He felt like a man who needed to know that the woman he loved was all right.

He folded his arms in front of him. "What are you doing out here? I distinctly remember telling you to stay in the house."

"I would have, if you'd come back to me instead of hanging out here with your friend."

Joe motioned to the two officers still standing by, "Come on boys. I'll buy you a cup of coffee."

Chicken, Adam thought, as the three men moved off in the direction of the house. His gaze settled on Samantha. She looked beautiful and pale in that white gown. He shook his head. "What am I supposed to do with you, Samantha? You're too old for me to put across my knee."

She tilted her head to one side. "Why not? That might prove interesting."

He shook his head again. Always a challenge. "Come here," he said.

She walked toward him slowly, but with each step her pace quickened until she ran to him and threw herself in his arms. He caught her to him. For a moment the two of them simply clung to one another.

And then her mouth found his, or vice versa—he wasn't

sure which and didn't care. All that mattered was the warmth of her body against his, the soft scent of her, and the feel of her tongue mating wildly with his own.

He broke the kiss and buried his face against her soft, fragrant hair. She shivered in his arms, but he doubted her tremors had anything to do with the cool night air, or even the kiss. She'd been frightened tonight, truly frightened. And to some degree, that fear still had her in its grasp.

He ran his hands over her back in a soothing manner. "It's over, baby. It's over," he whispered against her ear. "Just some sickie who thought he knew you. But it's over."

She lifted her head and smacked him on the arm. "It wasn't me I was worried about, you big idiot. It was you."

He set her on her feet, but still held on to her. "You were worried about me?"

"Why does that surprise you? Big, tough New York City cops aren't supposed to get worried over?"

He shook his head. The only person who ever worried about him was his landlady, but that was because she expected the rent on time. "I can take care of myself," he said. But in truth, her concern touched him more than he wanted to admit. "It's time I got you back up to the house."

She shook her head, and her hands cupped his face. "I want you, Adam," she whispered. Desire, white hot and potent sizzled through him as she brought his mouth down on hers. He couldn't help himself, his tongue slid into her mouth. When she drew it further into her mouth and sucked on it, a groan rumbled up from deep in his chest.

Still holding on to her, he stepped inside the guesthouse and shut the door by backing them up into it. He broke the kiss and took a step back from her. She looked up at him, confused. "What is it, Adam?"

He took both of her hands in his. "Look, Samantha, I've seen this happen before. People get in a dangerous situation and the adrenaline goes into overdrive. Anger and danger and arousal all send the same chemicals through the body."

"Is that what you think this is?" She gestured in a way that encompassed both of them. "An adrenaline overload?"

"Yes. Maybe. I don't know." He couldn't take the chance. Regardless of his feelings for her, he recalled her tears of a couple of nights ago. He wouldn't push her into anything for which she wasn't ready.

She straightened her spine and brushed her hair back from her shoulders. "I want you, Adam, just the way I promised, with no strings, no promises, and more important, no recriminations and no regrets. We both know there's no future for us. Can't we have tonight?"

"Baby, are you sure?"

She smiled. "To paraphrase your friend Mr. Williams, I think we've had this date from the very beginning.' "

He felt it too, the inevitability of their being together. Even before he met her, he wanted her. And even though his feelings for her had deepened way beyond that, he was willing to take what she would give him. Taking his cue from the theater, he swept her into his arms and carried her to his bed.

He sat down and laid her cross-wise on the bed. Her hair spread out beneath her, an auburn counterpoint to the white satin robe she wore and the beige satin coverlet. Her eyes had darkened to a deep sherry color that wreaked havoc with his heartbeat.

His fingers found the sash to her robe and easily undid the knot. He pushed aside the fabric to bare her body to him. His eyes scanned her softly curved body, her long legs, her full breasts and slender waist. Lord, she was beautiful. Only in the most bizarre of universes did it make sense that he should be with her. He cupped her breast in his palm and gave the soft flesh a gentle squeeze.

In response, her back arched and she called his name. "Adam."

That one softly spoken word sent a thrum of sexual current through him. That and the sloe-eyed, hungry expression on her face. For the first time in his life he felt out of his depth with a woman. Given his size and occupation, most women expected a roughness or lack of sensitivity in him, some even sought it out. Sometimes, he even indulged them.

With Samantha, he wanted to take it slow, to please her, to

prove to her, and maybe to himself, that he was nothing like his brother.

But how was he supposed to maintain any sort of equilibrium when she looked at him like that?

In truth, he couldn't. He leaned down and claimed her mouth, sliding his tongue past her lips to sample the sweet recesses of her mouth. She moaned and hands rose to grip his shoulders. He groaned, knowing it was a losing battle. She'd barely touched him, and already he was fully erect and ached to be inside her. He broke the kiss lowered his head to take her nipple into his mouth.

She jerked and cried out as his tongue flicked against her sweet flesh. He nipped her with his teeth and she gasped. He loved that sound and the mixture of surprise and delight contained in it. He nipped her again as his hand roved downward, over her flat abdomen to delve between her legs. His fingers circled over her soft slick flesh, eliciting a throaty moan from her. Her hips bucked against his hand and her nails dug into his shoulders. "Adam."

He knew what she wanted, but he couldn't give it to her yet. He disentangled himself from her long enough to shed his clothes. He sat beside her and rummaged around in the nightstand drawer for the condoms he'd left there. He found one, but she took it from him, tore it open with her teeth and rolled the condom on him. He squeezed his eyes shut, as a shiver of pure pleasure racked his entire body, having her hands on him like that.

He pushed her back against the mattress and came over her. "Now, Adam," she moaned, guiding him into her body.

He thrust into her, and his body shivered again as hers enveloped him. Perspiration broke out on his body as she wrapped her legs around his waist and pulled him down to her. He braced one elbow on the bed beside her. The other hand cupped and lifted her breast to give him better access to her nipple. He touched the tip of his tongue to the tender peak. Her eyes squeezed shut and her hips arched into him as he drew her nipple into his mouth and suckled her.

He felt the restlessness in her, the tension in her legs

wrapped around him. He slid his hand between their two bodies to stroke her clitoris with his thumb. At the same time, he thrust into her, any control he'd had long since gone. She arched against him and called his name. Her nails scored his back as her orgasm overtook her. He thrust into her again, and his own release arched his back and tore a groan from his throat. He collapsed on top of her, and for a moment all he could concentrate on was getting air into his lungs and the small shivers of pleasure that still coursed through him.

After a moment he turned his head and kissed her shoulder. How could this be the same woman that Billy had slept with and found wanting? He couldn't imagine it. He couldn't imagine that her responsiveness and lack of inhibition were due solely to being with him. It was part of her character, essential to her make-up. Why would any man want to squelch that?

He lifted her and settled them beneath the covers. After a while, she lifted her head and folded her arms on his chest. "Why so quiet?" she asked.

Adam inhaled and let his breath out slowly. "I was waiting for my vital organs to start functioning again."

She smacked his shoulder. "Be serious."

He opened his eyes and glimpsed the uncertainty in hers. "I am. I think you short-circuited my nervous system. I may need mouth to mouth."

She buried her face against his throat, obviously not appreciating his humor. It should have occurred to him that she would want his reassurance and given it to her without her having to ask for it.

He pulled her on top of him and ran his hands down her body until he cupped her buttocks in his palms. One of his hands lifted then fell to administer a gentle tap to her behind.

"Ouch," she protested. She lifted her head and glared down at him. "What was that for?"

Though he knew he hadn't hurt her, he rubbed the offended spot. "For not waiting for me up at the house like you were supposed to. Besides, aren't you the one who said it might prove interesting for me to take you over my knee?"

"That's when you had me convinced you didn't have one single kink in your whole big body."

"So I lied." He lifted his hand and brought it down again. "That's for scaring me half to death at Maxwell's house." He ran his hand over her derriere before lifting his hand a final time.

"What was that one for?"

"Because you like it."

"I do not," she protested, but her voice was breathy and low.

"Really?" He brushed her hair from her face. "I have a confession of my own to make, Samantha."

She folded her arms on his chest and eyed him skeptically.

He nodded. "Tonight isn't the first time I've made love to you. I have been fantasizing about you for years. I haven't had a good night's sleep since I've been here. But never once did I imagine anything one eighth as mind-blowing as what we shared just now." He threaded his fingers through her hair and stroked his thumbs over her cheekbones. "If you're wondering if I have any regrets, the answer is no."

He saw her smile. Then she lowered her head and took his nipple into her mouth.

He jerked and his breathing snagged. She lifted her head and smiled down at him, a siren's smile. "What's the matter, Detective? You can dish it out, but you can't take it?"

"Oh, I can take it," he said. But as she continued making love to him with her teeth and tongue and hands, he wondered how much of her sweet torture he could stand.

In the kitchen, Joe took a last sip of his coffee, set his cup down, and focused on Lupe. She'd spent every minute since the uniforms had left pacing the floor or scrubbing imaginary bits of dirt from her kitchen. Joe wished he could get her to sit down, but he was afraid that if he pressed her she'd tell him to go home.

Lupe wrapped her arms around herself. "What are they doing out there?"

"Whatever it is, I'm sure it's legal and consensual. I'm not making any guesses on immoral, though."

Lupe gazed at him in wide-eyed horror, either at his answer or that she'd spoken her question aloud.

She turned away from him, leaning her back against the counter. He didn't see he had any other choice. He rose from his chair and went to her. Slowly he pulled her against him. He let out a long, relieved sigh when she didn't resist him or try to scratch his eyes out. She was so small the top of her head didn't reach his shoulder, but her cheek rested against his chest, and her fingers fiddled with one of the buttons on his shirt.

He rested his head on top of hers. "It's okay, *muñequita.*"

She pulled away from him enough to look up at him. "No, it's not. I feel like such an idiot."

"Why?"

She shook her head. "For allowing myself to be a victim."

"Sweetheart, you were only a child. You had no control over—"

She shook her head. "Not then, now. What my stepfather did was horrible, unforgivable, but I've been doing something to myself that's far worse. I've let fear rule me my entire life.

"While you were outside chasing down that lunatic I was sitting here thinking, How could I trust my life to a man I'm afraid to be alone with in the same room? Who I'm afraid to touch? I don't want to be afraid anymore."

Bracing her hands on his shoulders she rose on tiptoe and pressed her mouth to his.

Joe squeezed his eyes shut, reveling in the simple pleasure of her lips on his. He knew better than to react too much to her overture or she'd shut down on him again. But his heartbeat had gone wild and his body hardened in response to her.

She drew back and touched her fingertips to his cheek. "How was that?"

"N-not bad," he said, surprised his voice creaked like an adolescent's.

She pressed her mouth to his again, and this time her tongue darted out to touch his lips. He let her have her way, holding still while her tongue delved into his mouth, probing, tentative, and so damn erotic that she took his breath away.

With a sigh, she withdrew. "Kiss me back, Joe," she whispered against his mouth.

A shudder gripped him as her tongue found his. He wanted to hold back, to take it easy, but with her soft body pressed up against his and her hands in his hair holding him to her, he couldn't help himself. Cradling her head in one hand and her hip in the other, he kissed her like he wanted to. He half expected her to pull away, but she molded herself even closer to him, and a tiny moan escaped her lips.

He pulled away from her. She gazed up at him, obviously confused. He inhaled, trying to normalize his breathing. "We have to stop now."

"Why? It's okay, Joe. I can handle it."

She sounded proud of herself, and perhaps she should be. But her innocent explorations were driving him out of his mind. He took both of her hands in his and kissed the back of each. "I'm sorry, *muñequita*. Maybe you can handle it, but I can't."

She lowered her head, but not before he saw the dejected look in her eyes. "I see."

With a hand under her chin, he tilted her face up to him. "Being with you like this makes me want to do wild, wicked things you're not ready for."

She tried to suppress a grin, but he saw it. "Really?"

He ran his finger down the bridge of her nose. "Yes, really." He slipped an arm around her shoulders. "Walk me to the door?"

She nodded. At the threshold, with his mind a little clearer, the cop in him asserted itself. Maybe it wasn't wise to leave her alone after all that had happened tonight. Lord only knew when or if the two outside would come up for air. A patrol car had been assigned to guard the house, but it wasn't the same thing as having someone you knew and trusted in the house with you.

He took her hand. "Are you sure you're going to be all right? You don't need me to stay?"

"I'm fine."

"You have my number in case you need me, right?"

"Of course."

He didn't know what else to say to her, so he leaned forward and kissed her cheek. "Good night."

"Good night."

He waited until she'd closed the door and he'd heard her turn the lock before he got into his car. Once inside, he folded his arms on the steering wheel and laid his forehead against them. He needed a few minutes to collect himself before he'd be worth driving anywhere. He turned his head and saw Lupe standing at the window watching him. He sighed, wondering exactly what she felt for him. Was he merely a practice dummy for her newly discovered feminine wiles, or had some other, deeper emotion motivated her overture toward him tonight?

Expelling a heavy breath, Joe started the engine and drove away.

Twenty-six

At three in the morning Adam awoke to find himself alone. Samantha wasn't in the bathroom either. Immediately he knew where she'd gone. He tugged on a pair of jeans and a T-shirt and headed back to the house to the Angel Room. The door was open, and she didn't look particularly surprised to find him standing in the doorway. She lay on the divan, a crystal cherub sparkling in her hands.

"I didn't wake you when I left, did I?" she asked.

Stepping into the room, he shook his head. He picked up another of the angels and studied it. "What is it with you and this room anyway?"

She lifted one shoulder. "You had your Orchard Beach; I had mine." She sighed. "Like you, my childhood was less than ideal. To the rest of the world, Jack and Theresa Hathaway were the perfect couple, but life at home was a different story."

She sighed. "I suppose they must have been in love once, but by the time I came along, whatever good had existed between them had gone. Unlike most Hollywood couples, they decided to stay together for the sake of the kid—me. When they fought I would run down here to remind myself that even if they no longer loved each other, each of them still loved me."

"Why did you start collecting angels?"

"I didn't. My father bought the first one, this one, the day I was born. They'd had a tough time conceiving a child, probably one of the stresses on their marriage. When I came along they considered me their miracle baby, their angel. Whenever

I'd get good grades at school, or whatever, he'd buy me another one." She shrugged again. "Some reporter did a story on me once and mentioned the room. Then everybody and his mother started sending them to me."

"What did your parents fight about?"

"Mostly my father's habit of ending up in women's beds that didn't happen to be my mother's."

A vague suspicion coalesced in Adam's mind. "Was one of those beds Lupe's mother's?"

She nodded. "My father didn't know Lupe existed until the incident with her stepfather. Lupe's mother had been sick, hospitalized with Parkinson's. She trusted her husband to take care of her daughter. When she got out, she realized what was going on and called the police. She contacted my father because she knew she couldn't take care of Lupe herself anymore."

"What did your mother say to that?"

"She told him to go to New York and get his child. Lupe's mother even lived with us for a while until she died. I guess my mother found it hard to be jealous of a dying woman."

While he had her in such a talkative mood, he didn't plan to waste it. "Who's Carmen Mendoza?"

"Lupe. Carmen Lupita Mendoza. Her mother was also named Carmen, so everyone always called her by her middle name. When she came here, she didn't want anything from my father, not even his name. She called him Mr. Hathaway until the day he died. He got her in the end, though. He left everything to both of us in his will, although by that time most of what he left was debt."

"And then Lupe got sent off to live with her aunt?"

"I was too young to take legal custody of her. Jarad's parents would have taken her in, too, but her aunt went to court to get custody. That woman makes Andrea Dworkin look like Mary Poppins. She home-schooled Lupe, but mostly she filled her head with all sorts of horror stories about men. By the time I got her back, she was terrified every time the mailman showed up at the door. Believe it or not, the woman you know today is the new and improved Lupe."

"So why is she pretending to be the housekeeper?"

"Actually, it started out as a joke. She said if she was going to play nursemaid to me, she was going to look the part, but she could only find a maid's uniform in her size. Then you showed up."

She shrugged. "She didn't trust you and wanted to keep an eye on you. Who better than a servant, a nobody, to do that? Look at Teddy. He knows everyone's business because people say things in front of him they wouldn't tell their best friend."

Adam put down the angel he'd been holding and sat on the edge of the divan next to her. "Why did you come here now? To escape from me?"

She pressed her lips together and shook her head. "I knew I had to show you some things that I've kept down here." She reached into her pocket and pulled out two envelopes. "I got the letter the day after the news conference. The card came yesterday afternoon."

He read them both and returned them to their envelopes as anger mounted in him. The stamp on the letter had never been canceled, which meant a killer could have come as close as the mailbox at the end of Samantha's driveway. In as calm a voice as he could muster, he asked, "Why didn't you show these to me before?" He'd suspected she'd been jumpy about something at dinner the night before. Now he knew why.

"The first one I thought was probably sent by some crank. You wouldn't believe how many horrible letters I got from people right after Billy died, mostly from women, blaming me for Billy's death."

"Do you still have them?"

"Lupe does."

"I want to see them in the morning. And the card?"

"I was working my way up to telling you about it in the hot tub, but I got a little sidetracked."

"Didn't it occur to you that you should have shown these to someone? If you didn't trust me, then how about the LAPD?"

"It wasn't a matter of trust, Adam. I knew if I told you, you would go all-out to protect me. That would have worried Jarad and Ariel when they should have been thinking about delivering healthy babies, and Lupe . . . well, she was so worried about me after the accident, I didn't think she could handle any more. I'm sorry."

His anger faded as he realized she'd been trying to protect the people she loved. He would get Joe over here in the morning and sort through what this new evidence meant. If the notes could be believed, he now had proof positive that Billy's accident hadn't been an accident at all.

He leaned over her and touched his lips to hers. "Let's go back to bed."

She nodded and took his hand. "Thank you, Adam."

"For what?"

"For understanding why I didn't tell you. For taking care of me. You've been very good to me."

He didn't know how to take her praise. She sounded so solemn, as though something was ending instead of beginning. "What are you trying to tell me?"

"Nothing. I'm tired, I guess."

He took her to her room and settled them in her bed. She lay against him, her fingers weaving patterns on his chest. "Don't leave me, Adam." She gazed up at him, an imploring expression on her face. "The rest of your time here, stay with me, in my room. Don't go back to the guesthouse."

"Not even for my skivvies?"

She smiled and hit him on the chest. "You know what I mean."

"Whatever you want, sweetheart." He kissed the bridge of her nose, which led to kissing her mouth and all the other delectable parts of her body he'd discovered. She moaned and writhed beneath him, and when she climaxed, calling his name, it presaged the most intense orgasm of his life.

Afterward, she fell asleep with her cheek resting against his chest. Adam closed his eyes and held her, but it was a long while before he slept.

When the sun came up, Adam left her sleeping, got in his car, and drove to Johnny Maxwell's house. He had less trouble getting in now than he did the first time. When he pulled up the guard immediately opened the gate. Another man at the front door led him to a small room off the foyer. Obviously the little weasel was expecting him.

The room was decorated simply in shades of cream and white, the only outstanding piece being a coffee table inlaid with stained glass.

Johnny sat in one of the pair of wing-backed chairs that flanked the sofa. "Detective Wexler," Johnny said, placing the delicate cup and saucer in his hands on the coffee table. "Two visits from the police in two days. Couldn't that be considered harassment?"

"It might be, if you planned to tell anyone about it." He sat in the chair across from Johnny and propped his feet on the edge of the coffee table with enough force to make the cup and saucer clatter.

Johnny's eyes narrowed. "Take care, Detective; that glass cost more than you'll make in your lifetime."

Adam lifted one shoulder. "Really? Then I'd say someone overcharged you."

Johnny expelled a breath and averted his eyes, perhaps not as nonchalant about this meeting as he wanted Adam to believe. "So, what brings you here this time? Sam didn't send you here, did she?"

"She doesn't know I'm here. She doesn't know about these either." He took the envelope of photos from his pocket and tossed them onto the table, just missing the coffee cup. "Care to explain the little note attached?"

Johnny picked up the envelope but didn't seem surprised by either the note or the photographs. Adam didn't expect he would be.

Johnny slid the pictures back into the envelope and tossed it back to Adam. "Sam has a beautiful body, don't you think? I'm particularly fascinated by the little mole next to her navel."

Adam's fingers flexed on the delicate arms of his chair, but he said nothing. He refused to respond to Johnny's attempt at baiting him. "How much did Billy have to pay you to keep those photos a secret?"

"How pedestrian you make our little arrangement sound.

Billy never paid me a cent. He simply signed over the pink slip to his prized 'thirty-six Jag. I'd always admired it, but he refused to sell it to me."

"So you blackmailed him for it."

"Why not? He decided he wanted to get back into Sam's good graces and suddenly I wasn't good enough for him anymore. He should have remembered getting stoned one night and confiding that he'd taken those pictures of Samantha, pretending that the camera had run out of film. He even told me where they were. Can you imagine Sam's reaction seeing one of those snapshots on the pages of *High Society* magazine? The Internet? He would never have gotten her back, first because he'd lied to her and second for being stupid enough not to keep his mouth shut."

Johnny sat back in his chair, a feral smile tilting up his lips. "Nobody snubs Johnny Maxwell, Detective, not if they know what's good for them."

Adam picked up the envelope and returned it to his pocket. Johnny could afford to be forthcoming, as he had to know Adam couldn't prove anything he said, nor would he bother to try. He'd already spent more time in Johnny Maxwell's company than he cared to.

"Don't think this hasn't been fun, but I've got better things to do."

Adam stood and started toward the door, but stopped when Johnny spoke again.

"Did you notice that there were no negatives in the envelope, Detective? It was my message to Billy that I wasn't finished with him yet. Perhaps you'd like to take over payments now that you stand to inherit your brother's estate?"

What else had Billy told this son of a bitch in a drug-induced state? A stone paperweight on the table by the door caught Adam's attention. He picked it up and turned to face Maxwell. "Catch."

He tossed the weight toward the table, just out of Maxwell's reach. The weight crashed through the glass, shattering it into tiny colored pieces. The cup and saucer slid to the floor, spilling dark liquid onto the rug beneath.

Adam smiled, watching Maxwell sink to the floor as if he could salvage something from the mess Adam had created.

Maxwell turned to him. "You bastard."

Adam's grin transformed into a narrow-eyed scowl. "Don't threaten me, Maxwell. Or that won't be the only thing of yours that gets broken."

Adam turned and left the Maxwell estate for what he hoped would be the last time.

On his way back from Malibu, Adam called Joe and asked him to meet him at Samantha's. When Adam pulled into the drive, the Green Ghost was already parked at the curb. Adam suspected Joe had used his request as an excuse to visit with Lupe for as long as possible.

When he walked into the kitchen, he found Joe, Lupe, and Samantha all huddled around the small kitchen table, finishing up a lunch of shrimp salad and iced tea. Lupe grinned at him; Joe had the nerve to look sheepish. Samantha stared at him with such a hungry expression in her eyes that he wished he could banish the other two indefinitely.

Joe, who usually didn't miss a thing, took Lupe's hand and said, "Let's find out what my namesake is doing."

"She is not your namesake," Lupe said, but she took the hint and left with Joe.

Adam went to the refrigerator, found a bottle of water, and swigged half of it down in one gulp. It didn't help. He turned to Samantha, who regarded him with the same expression. "Baby, unless you want to christen your kitchen table, stop looking at me like that."

She blinked and stared down at her hands. "I'm sorry. I missed you this morning."

He sat on the table facing her. "I missed you, too." He kissed her mouth and slowly drew away. "I need to talk to Joe for a few minutes; then I need to see those letters, okay?"

"Sure. Teddy's due any minute anyway."

"Teddy?"

"Good grief, Adam. Don't tell me you're jealous."

Not that he'd admit, anyway. "Me? Never. As long as the man keeps his eyes closed and doesn't touch anything, we're cool."

She stood and kissed his forehead. "The man is my physical therapist and my masseur. Besides, I don't think Teddy likes girls, so you have nothing to worry about."

She picked up her plate and carried it to the sink. She was right: any proprietary urges he might be feeling were misplaced. In a few days he'd get on a plane and go home to his life, and she'd stay here with hers. He'd go back to his job, though he had to admit he no longer wanted it with same single-mindedness that he once had. At one time it had been his whole existence, all he'd allowed himself to care about. Thinking now about the life he had waiting for him in New York, it seemed empty and unfulfilling.

"Hey, Balboa, land is that way."

He blinked and realized he'd been staring into space. Samantha was watching him with an amused expression on her face. "What did you say?"

"Isn't Joe waiting for you?"

Adam rose from the table, went to her and kissed her cheek. "Tell Teddy I said hi."

"I'll be damned."

That was Joe's response to hearing all that Adam had learned since they'd last seen each other. Adam had taken Joe to the green room, where they could lock themselves in and, more important, keep the women out. "That's all you have to say?"

"Who do you think is behind the notes?"

"I have no idea." But in his mind they erased Lupe from the list of suspects. If Lupe had caused the accident, she'd have kept quiet about it and hoped no one investigated too thoroughly. Whoever sent the notes still wanted something. The question was, what?

"Break it down then. Who did Billy know who knew Sam who might want either of them dead?"

"The only name that springs to mind is Russell, her business manager. I can see him wanting Billy gone, but I don't think he'd hurt Samantha. On top of that, all that cutting and pasting might ruin his manicure."

"Speaking of him, I asked a PI friend to look into that one for me. A top guy, discreet. I had a feeling your interest in him was more personal than business."

"And?"

He tells me he got a call from a guy last week, a citizen who thinks Russell might be running some sort of scam with his clients' money. Seems Russell was crying poor, that a certain company he'd gotten his clients to invest in had gone bust, but said citizen walks into a high-stakes card game they got going up here in the Hills and who's there but Russell, losing money like he was pouring out water. He wants to know why Russell has money to burn if the people he works for are in the hole.

"It could be a case of sour grapes, but who knows? My guy is supposed to call me later if he turns up anything."

Adam pulled from his back pocket the disk Sam had lifted from Billy's place. "See if your guy can find something useful on this."

Joe nodded. "It's kind of ironic, though, don't you think? You've got two guys who are partners, no offense, but one is a degenerate womanizer and one's a degenerate gambler and the womanizer is the one who dies broke? Even if Sam's father had started to drink, so what? Drinking's not like blow or gambling, where your habit eats into your cash." Joe shrugged. "Unless her old man had a jones for Dom Perignon it doesn't add up."

Adam contemplated what he said. He would love to get a peek at whatever financial records had existed at the time to prove Samantha's father's debt.

Joe stood. *"Me voy.* I'm going to head out. What do you have on the agenda for today?"

"I've got a few things to take care of with Samantha."

"I bet."

"For once, try to lift your mind out of the gutter. Did you bring the things I asked for?"

"Of course. They're in a bag on the table in the hallway." Adam checked the bag first, then took it out back with him to find a suitable spot.

Twenty-seven

When he got back to the house, Samantha was still in the gym with Mr. Clean. She sat at the butterfly machine, struggling to bring her elbows together in front of her. Mr. Clean stood in front of her, an exasperated look on his face.

"Give it up, Sam," he said. "You're not ready."

With a sigh of frustration she let the paddles fall back. "I was doing fine until you started complaining."

Adam cleared his throat and both of them turned their heads to stare at him. Mr. Clean threw up his hands. "Maybe you can do something with her."

Adam suppressed a grin. Apparently she'd lied when she said he was the only one she gave agita to. "What's the problem?"

"Someone here wants to reinjure herself by doing too much."

She rolled her eyes at Teddy. "Some of us, like Chicken Little, imagine the sky is falling the minute there's a drop of rain. Three weeks ago, I could press five times this weight."

He sat on the weight bench across from her. He understood that impulse in her, the desire to get back to normal. He'd given up the cane the doctor had prescribed for him for the same reason.

Sam put up her hands. "Don't say anything, Adam. I'm acting like a two-year-old. I'm going to take a shower before I embarrass myself any further."

She stood and accepted the towel and bottle of water that Teddy offered her. "Thanks."

Adam expected her to walk right past him, but she stopped in front of him, braced one hand on his shoulder, and kissed him. "Just so Teddy knows you're taken," she whispered against his ear.

He thought about what she'd said about Mr. Clean knowing everybody's business. "Can I ask you a question?"

"Sure."

"What do you know about Richard Russell?"

Teddy lifted his eyebrows and frowned in an expression of disgust. "If you want my advice, stake out LAX."

"What do you mean?"

"Every now and again we have a wonderful scandal where some manager runs off with the majority of their clients' money. Although Russell's pickin's have gotten kind of slim. He's worked himself down to two or three clients, not including Sam. Even Billy Prescott fired him a couple of months ago."

Samantha must not have known that, but he couldn't think of any reason why Billy or Russell would have offered up that information. "Why is he such a flight risk?"

"I might consider taking the money and running if Johnny Maxwell had his hooks into me. Johnny doesn't know how to play nicely with the other children."

To say the least. "Gambling?"

"If Russell could get someone to lay odds on which hair on his head would grow fastest, he'd take 'em."

Adam recalled what Joe had said about the irony of Russell's and Samantha's father's financial standings. Joe had been joking, but an idea began to take root in Adam's mind. "Do you know anything about Samantha's father, Jack?"

"How old do you think I am, Detective? I was twelve when the Hathaway scandal broke."

"And?"

Teddy chuckled. "Jack was a friend of my father's, well respected, which in Hollywood terms means no one was too successful at trying to screw him over. When he died, it hit the papers that Jack had been siphoning money from his clients' accounts for his own use. I remember my father telling his wife at the time that no one could make him believe Jack Hathaway had cheated anyone out of anything, no matter what the papers said. He suspected Russell had stolen the money and forged the records to disgrace Jack."

Adam didn't have to search far for a motive if that had been true. Russell seemed obsessed with both Samantha and her mother, and his animosity toward his former business partner wasn't a state secret either. But did his hatred run deep enough for him to want to kill not once, but twice?

Teddy zipped his bag and slung it over his shoulder. "It's been real, but I've got to fly." He checked his watch. "Time and your average Hollywood starlet wait for no man."

Adam extended his hand. "Thanks."

"Anytime." His deceptively mild blue eyes bore into Adam as he shook his hand. "And don't worry about Sam. She always lands on her feet."

Adam rocked back on his heels. Though that might be true, in order to land, you had to take a fall.

After showering and dressing in shorts and a matching shirt, Sam descended the stairs to look for Adam. Hearing voices coming from the back of the house, she headed for the kitchen. She found him there with Lupe, she at the counter and he at the table, eating a late lunch of the shrimp salad. Lupe's head tilted lower toward the vegetables she chopped, while Adam's head lifted and his dark eyes surveyed her. She'd give anything to know what had been said two moments before she'd arrived.

"What's going on?" she asked.

If she'd looked away for a second, she'd have missed Adam's gaze dart in Lupe's direction. "Nothing much."

She tilted her head to one side, studying him. The intensity in his eyes belied his casual pose in the chair.

He stood. "Come for a walk with me."

"Where are we going?"

"Didn't I just say? For a walk. It occurred to me the other night that I'd never seen your property during the daylight."

"Really?" He wanted a tour of the grounds? He didn't need her for that. Besides, that comment about never seeing her property in the daytime had to be an out-and-out lie. How had he directed the man from the security company to place the sensors if he'd never seen the grounds?

With almost any other man, she'd probably suspect he'd set up some secret trysting place in her backyard. But Adam wasn't the rendezvous type. He was the get-over-here-and-let-me-make-love-to-you type. Of the two she by far preferred the latter.

He nodded his head in the direction of the back door. "Indulge me."

She decided to give in, because she figured it was the only way she'd find out what was on his mind. She also wanted to ask him something far away from Lupe's hearing.

Late-afternoon sunlight filtered through the trees that lined the path through her property. Sam took Adam's hand and laced her fingers with his. "How far do you think things have gone between Lupe and Joe?"

"She hasn't told you?"

Sam shook her head. "She's been avoiding being alone with me. Usually Lupe isn't secretive. She'll tell you to mind your business in a minute, but this is different. Did Joe say anything to you?"

Only that in spite of the fact that she'd left the kitchen with him earlier that day, Lupe seemed to have withdrawn from him, too. Joe planned to lie low for a while, to give her time to decide what she wanted.

As he saw it, that was between Lupe and Joe, two grown adults who could make their peace on their own. He understood Sam's concern for her sister, but Lupe needed to stand on her own two feet.

Since he didn't know how Sam would react to his telling her that, the best solution was to change the subject. "How did Lupe end up with the shotgun in the first place?"

"When they were trying to get the Brady Bill passed, I testified in front of Congress on my experience. I made the mistake of saying I would never keep a gun in my house. Some yahoo had the gun hand-delivered to me. The note inside the box read, 'Now you have a gun in your house.' I freaked out and told Lupe to get it out of my sight. I guess she figured hiding it in the bottom of her closet complied with my wishes, in the technical sense, at least."

He squeezed her hand in a reassuring way, which only made her more suspicious. "Where are we really going?"

"For a little target practice."

"You're joking, right?"

"No. I promised to help you get ready for your movie role, and so far I've done squat. Today I'm going to teach you about guns."

"Why?"

He let out an exasperated sigh. "Because I don't like seeing you afraid. Okay?"

She didn't know what to make of that admission, but considering she wasn't fond of being frightened herself, she had to give in to him. She nodded.

She followed him to the clearing around the gazebo. Several stone benches ringed the small white structure. They stopped at one of the benches, where a large black bag rested beside it. On the bench rested two black garments she recognized as bulletproof vests.

A shiver passed through Sam. The actuality of picking up a gun, a lethal weapon, even if it was loaded with blanks, had never seemed so real to her before. She swallowed, but her mouth had gone dry and her eyes burned. "What do you want me to do?"

"First thing, we put on a vest." He tugged the smaller one over her head and fastened the Velcro straps snugly, then put on the larger one himself.

She squeezed her eyes shut. She was not a coward. She was not. She could do this. Her selfpep talk did nothing to her anxiety. She decided to try humor instead. She opened her eyes and surveyed Adam. "Afraid I might miss the target, Detective?"

"Actually, yes."

Her mouth dropped open and her eyes widened until Adam shook his head and a droll smile turned up his lips.

"It was a joke," he said in a patient tone. "Baby, there's nothing to firing a gun. Any idiot can pull a trigger. The hard part is becoming skilled enough to hit a target where you want to. You don't even have that problem. You just have to look like you're aiming at the right thing. Special effects takes care of the rest."

His voice sounded so calm and his words so reasonable that she began to relax. "Okay, Adam. What next?"

He pulled the gun from the holster at his side. Her eyes widened and she backed away from him.

He grabbed her arm and pulled her back. "Sam, the clip is out and the chamber is clear."

"What does that mean?"

"In layman's terms, there aren't any bullets in it. Just look at it."

She focused her gaze on the weapon in Adam's hand. Without the bullets, all it was really was a cold, black piece of metal in his hand. It couldn't hurt anybody, but she shivered anyway. Revulsion roiled in her belly at the thought of shooting anything, even if it was only an illusion. "I don't like guns, Adam."

"I know, baby. Now concentrate."

She huffed out a breath. "All right."

"We're going to keep it simple, okay? Only the things you need to know. All right?"

She nodded.

"First off, treat every gun as if it were loaded. Never point it at anyone or anything that doesn't need to get shot."

She nodded. If she ever got up the nerve to touch the thing, she'd have to remember that.

"Second, never pick up a weapon that you don't know how to operate. This is a G-17 semiautomatic handgun. That means it fires one bullet and expels the cartridge every time you squeeze the trigger."

He pointed to what was obviously the trigger. "This is the trigger. Keep your finger off it unless you intend to fire. Keep it on the guard—the outer half circle—until you're ready to shoot."

"Shoot?"

"Samantha," he said in a voice meant to disguise his impatience. "this is one of the safest, most well-designed handguns in the world. You can drop it and probably the most exciting thing that will happen is it'll land on your toe. Relax."

He shifted the gun in his hand, as if he expected her to take it. "Besides, I'm not expecting you to morph into Annie Oakley. This is the wrong gun for you anyway."

"Why?"

"For one thing, I doubt your hand could make it around the handle. It should be a comfortable fit. For another, it's got a .357 barrel. Since you're not used to it, the recoil would probably knock you on your butt. Remember Newton's Law? For every action there is an equal and opposite reaction?

"For now, I just want you to hold it. Think you can handle that?"

She swallowed. She supposed more than anything he wanted to get that gun in her hands. It was what she wanted, too. To rid herself of the phobia that had plagued her most of her life. But she couldn't seem to get her arm to move from its position at her side.

"Come on, baby. You can do it."

She wet her lips with the tip of her tongue. Slowly she lifted her hand and wrapped her trembling fingers around the handle of the gun. The gun wasn't heavy, but the weight of it registered in her hand.

"Open your eyes."

She hadn't realized she'd shut her eyes until he'd spoken. He stood behind her, reaching around her to adjust her grip. Despite the warmth of his body surrounding her, she shivered.

"You're doing fine, Samantha."

She nodded, but she felt anything but fine. Her eyes burned and her stomach had tied itself in knots. She tried to swallow, but her throat had gone dry. "W-what now?"

"Do you see that doohickey on the end of the barrel?"

She nodded.

"That's the sight. You look through that to make sure you are aiming at your target. Unlike in the movies, you don't just point and shoot."

She lifted the gun and squinted to look through the sight. On the other side of the crosshairs stood a weeping willow tree that had been on the property since before she was born. But in reality, people didn't shoot trees; they shot animals or other people. Her mind zigzagged over what Adam had said. He'd called it not only a gun but a weapon—a weapon that's sole purpose was to kill.

She shut her eyes, and a picture of her mother superimposed itself on her consciousness—the instant their attacker's gun had gone off. The impact had sent her mother staggering backward to fall faceup on the ground. Sam had stood by, helpless to do anything but watch her mother's lifeblood spill out like a crimson scarf on the snow.

Tears welled in her eyes and seeped from beneath her lashes. "I can't do this, Adam. I can't."

The gun slipped from her fingers, but Adam caught it in one hand and drew Samantha into his arms with the other. "I'm sorry, baby," he whispered against her hair. Adam reholstered his gun and drew her closer, feeling like a class-A heel. He'd pushed her to confront a fear she might never be ready to deal with. If it weren't for that damn movie, she probably would never have to.

He brought her into the house, past Lupe, who watched them with a narrowed gaze. Once they got to her room, Samantha claimed to want a nap, so he left her by herself, though he didn't want to. He suspected she intended to indulge in a bout of self-pity rather than sleep. But he'd pushed her too far once today; he didn't want to risk it again.

When he got back down to the kitchen, Lupe was waiting for him.

"I told you not to do it," Lupe accused. "I told you she wasn't ready. What did you do to her?"

He didn't need her acrimony right now. He'd just watched Samantha turn from a bright, competent woman to a scared little girl. The image didn't please him. "I didn't do anything to her."

"Then why did she look so upset when she came in the house?"

He was tempted to tell her it was none of her damn business. "What have I ever done to make you think I want to hurt Samantha?"

She sputtered, but no words came out.

"Oh, that's right. All men are marauding beasts out to wreak havoc on women. I forgot for a moment there what my role in society was."

Seeing the stricken expression on her face, he knew he should stop, but he couldn't help himself. "Well, let me ask you something then. Who is the one here guilty of playing with someone's emotions? Joe told me what went on between you in this kitchen last night. And I saw the accusation in your eyes when you looked at him today. The poor fool feels guilty just for having touched you.

"But you want to know what I think really happened? You wanted to use him, and when he put a stop to it you took it out on him."

"That's not true." Tears glistened in her eyes, threatening to spill over any second. "I never meant to hurt Joe." She turned her back to him and swiped at her eyes.

"Look to your own house, Lupe," he said quietly. "Get some help before you let the past ruin any chance you have for a decent future."

Twenty-eight

Adam went out to the guesthouse and called Joe. With Samantha locked away in her room and Lupe furious with him, Adam didn't have much reason to stick around. Besides, his conversation with Teddy had gotten his brain moving in the direction of suspecting Richard Russell of worse things than poor taste in nicknames. Joe showed up looking as morose as Adam felt. Together they drove to Russell's house in Beverly Hills.

When they got there, Russell's housekeeper let them in and led them to the study on the first floor. Russell sat on the sofa with his feet propped up on a hassock. A tartan-plaid afghan lay across his lap. He appeared to be watching the screen in front of him, oblivious to their entrance. Without turning his head, he said, "Come in, Detective. I've been expecting you."

"Why is that?"

"Didn't you think I knew from the beginning that you were Billy's brother? Why do you think I tried to have Sam fire you? I knew you'd go snooping around and find out everything." Finally Russell turned to face him, seeming surprised to find Joe in the room with them. "A member of the local police force, I assume."

"Det. Joseph Martinez, LAPD," Joe said.

"Good evening, Detective." Russell raised the glass in his hand in salute. "Is this the point where I'm supposed to confess my sins and you take me off to jail?"

"If you wouldn't mind." Joe added, "Start with Samantha's father."

A look of disgust crossed Russell's face. "He took Theresa from me. The only reason I befriended him was to be near her, but that idiot was too blind to see that. He spent more time in other women's beds than he did in his own. That suited me fine, as Theresa turned to me for comfort.

"Do you know where he was when Theresa was killed? He was supposed to be with them, but begged off to spend time with some tramp. Jack didn't start drinking because he'd lost the love of his life, as everyone supposed. It was guilt. Guilt because he left his family alone and unprotected."

Adam rubbed his temples, tired of the other man's ramblings. "That's a tragic story, but what has that got to do with anything?"

Russell shot him a chastising look, which he ignored. "As I stood at Theresa's grave site, I vowed to her that I would avenge her, that I would get him back for all he'd done to her. When he started drinking, I had the perfect opportunity. He wasn't paying attention to his work, leaving me to cover for him. I got the idea to take money from his clients' accounts and burying it in his. All it would take was one pretty-boy actor to cry foul and disgrace him and send him to jail. Given his mental state most of the time, he'd never be able to defend himself."

"But your plan didn't work."

"No." Russell looked down at his lap and shook his head. "I underestimated little Samantha's influence over him. She begged him to sober up and he did. He figured out what I was doing. He came to my house one night to confront me with his suspicions."

Russell chuckled. "As luck would have it, I had on hand a little chemical that mimics alcohol in the bloodstream. That night I offered him a drink, tonic water. I knew he hated the taste of it without the gin to go with it. He'd never notice. I also knew he'd never make it home before the drug kicked in."

Russell sipped from his drink. "What I didn't know was

that he was picking Sam up from an event at school. You have
to believe me, I never would have done anything to hurt her.
When I found out she'd been injured in the car with him, I
nearly went out of my mind with fear. I made sure she got the
best care, the best doctors to help her recover.

"She should have been mine. She probably is mine. Jack
and Theresa had been trying for years. I wanted to adopt
Samantha. I would even have taken in that hellion sister of
hers, Jack's bastard, if I had to. But the Naughtons were her
godparents. Jack granted them custody in his will.

"What could I do? Legally I had no standing. I let the world
think Jack died penniless and in disgrace so they wouldn't get
their hands on her money. But I gave it back to her over the
years, every cent. And I was always there for her."

"How touching. Maybe Hallmark will make a greeting card
out of it."

Adam glanced at Joe. Usually Joe reserved the worst of his
sarcasm for his buddies, not for suspects who were likely to
clam up if you didn't do a good enough job hiding your disgust. Obviously Joe took Russell's actions as personally as
Adam did himself, as they affected Lupe as well as Sam. Jack
Hathaway's murder had cost Lupe her real father and her stable
home. It begged the question, How much different a person
would she have become if she'd never been forced to live with
her aunt?

"Go on," Adam said.

Those simple words mollified Russell. "I have a little weak-
ness, Detective." Russell shrugged. "We all do. I got myself
into a bit of trouble and used your brother's money and that
of a few others to get me out. I'm afraid HS Enterprises never
existed. I guess actors aren't quite as stupid as they used to
be. Billy figured out what I was doing. I blackmailed him into
remaining silent."

Adam shook his head. "I thought Maxwell was the one who
had the photos."

"It was his idea. Maxwell knew about the pictures of
Samantha and told me about them. It was Maxwell to whom
I owed the money. Those pictures bought both Billy's silence

and repaid Johnny. But the fool should have known I would never have exposed those pictures of Samantha. Just seeing them made me nauseated."

But he had looked. "What made you decide to murder Billy? He decided he'd take his chances with Sam if she found out the truth?"

"All I'll say about that is that your brother got exactly what he deserved. He had no business anywhere near her. I don't know why Sam didn't see that. I couldn't let her make that mistake twice."

Adam shut his eyes. An indescribable emotion washed over him. Was it anger at this lunatic for playing God with other people's lives? Was it a strange form of relief that it was finally over? Adam opened his eyes as Russell spoke again.

"Gentlemen, it has been a pleasure, but I'm afraid it's time I used this." He reached toward his lap.

Adam had his gun out of its holster and trained on Russell before Russell got the small silver revolver from beneath the blanket. In his periphery, Adam saw that Joe had done the same. "Drop it," Adam said. He wouldn't hesitate to put the man out of his misery if he had to, but he'd rather see him wasting the rest of his life in jail, the thing he dreaded. "Put the gun on the table and your hands on your head."

"This isn't for you, gentlemen. I have no intention of going to jail with those . . . people. And unfortunately the choice of disappearing has been taken from me. Some enterprising lawyer has managed to have my assets frozen."

"Put the gun down," Adam said, realizing his intent. He said the only thing he thought might reach Russell: "Think how Samantha will feel if you do this."

"Tell Samantha I love her." Russell turned the gun to his own temple and fired.

Twenty-nine

Midnight found Adam and Joe at the revolving bar at the top of the Bonaventure Hotel. Adam looked out the window at the mountains in the distance. Without the haze of smog visible in the daytime, the landmass seemed dark and majestic in the moonlight. Maybe L.A. was growing on him.

Adam sipped from his glass. The waitress had looked at them as if they were insane when they'd both ordered Cokes. To have ordered something alcoholic would have meant that Russell's suicide had gotten to them, something neither of them wanted to admit.

It was over. He knew Billy's killer. But still a feeling of unease gripped him. If Richard killed Billy, what was with the notes? One of the plainclothes officers had suggested Russell had sent them as a diversion, to make it appear that something Samantha had done had motivated Billy's murder. Adam didn't buy that. For one thing, the notes were the only real evidence they'd had that Billy had been murdered. If Russell had been trying to get rid of Adam, as he claimed, sending mash notes would have given him more reason to stay, not less—that was, if Samantha had shown them to him from the beginning.

But if Russell hadn't killed Billy, why would he imply that he had? He couldn't imagine that Russell could be protecting someone else. That would leave Samantha in danger. Maybe Russell didn't know about the notes. If it hadn't been for the intruder on her property, she might not have told him about them, either.

Adam shifted in his seat and sighed. Maybe he just couldn't let it go. Maybe Russell had sent the notes because subconsciously he wanted to get caught. It wouldn't be the first time a killer went out of his way to make himself a suspect. In any event, Russell had taken his secrets with him to his grave. Adam would never know if his suspicions were true unless someone else made another move on Samantha.

Adam glanced over at Joe, who sat slumped in his chair with his head back and his eyes closed. Adam tapped his shoulder with the side of his fist. "Are you falling asleep over there?"

Joe started and sat up. "Nah, I was just resting my eyes. Do you really think Russell did it?"

Adam inhaled and let his breath out slowly. "I don't know."

"You know, with this guy dead, the higher-ups will be satisfied. They'll pull the car from in front of the house. Watch your back, man."

Adam nodded. Maybe he should simply take her away from here for a while. Jarad and his wife had given him the perfect excuse to get her to New York: the babies.

And while he had her there, away from all this madness, on his own turf, he'd confess to her his real role in Billy's life. If he was lucky, she might even forgive him for lying to her.

"Let's get out of here." Adam tossed enough bills on the table to cover the drinks and stood.

As they rode the glass-enclosed elevator to the lobby, Adam gazed at Joe. Adam doubted the harshness etched in his features was due to the incandescent light overhead. "You sure you won't want to come in for a minute?"

Adam shook his head. "Nah. She'll be asleep, and besides, she don't want to see my ugly mug anyway."

Adam stared up at the light panel. If Joe could be this miserable after knowing Lupe three days, Adam wondered how he'd feel if Samantha shut him out of her life. And unlike Lupe, Samantha had a valid reason not to want to see him again.

Adam sighed. He'd have to cross that bridge when he came to it.

* * *

Sam was asleep when Adam finally returned home. He stripped out of his clothes and slid into bed beside her. She turned over and snuggled up next to him. He pulled her to him, needing her softness and warmth to comfort him, even if she was asleep. He kissed her temple and she stirred, lifting her head.

"What happened? Where were you?"

"Russell's house. He's dead."

"How?"

He told her everything, keeping nothing from her except that he was Billy's brother. At one point she dropped her head to her chest, facing away from him. As he fell silent, he realized she was crying.

He cupped her face in his palms and forced her to look at him. "I'm sorry about Russell," he said, figuring his death weighed heavily on her.

"I'm sorry, too. I'm sorry that he caused so much havoc in other people's lives. And I feel sorry for Billy, too. He was right: I would never have gotten back with him knowing about the pictures. I wouldn't have done it under any circumstances. I knew I wasn't in love with him and would never be."

She swiped at her eyes. "But these aren't sad tears; they're tears of gratitude. Thank you, Adam."

"For what?"

"Don't you understand? Despite his problems with my mother, I always loved my father. All these years I thought he loved the inside of a bottle more than he loved me. You see, I'd told him if he didn't stop, I'd petition family court to be emancipated from him. That I wouldn't live with a drunk. My adolescent idea of an intervention. I thought he'd made his choice and it wasn't me." She sniffled. "You've given me back the memory of my father."

She lowered her mouth to his to kiss him sweetly. He shut his eyes and let the sensations of her lips on his and her soft flesh molded to his blot away the violent images of the day from his mind.

* * *

Joe awoke the next morning to the insistent sound of his doorbell ringing. Why was it every time he had a day off, some joker had to show up on his doorstep? And from the way whoever was leaning on the doorbell, he'd bet it was those delinquents who lived two doors down from him. What were they doing home on a school day?

Joe had fallen asleep on the sofa watching a Spanish-language version of *First Blood* on channel forty-one. The hammy acting along with the poorly dubbed translation had taken his mind off the real bloodshed he'd seen earlier that day.

"I'm coming," he shouted when the doorbell sounded again. He padded to the doorway exactly as he'd slept, in his shorts and T-shirt. One sock had come off during the night, and the other was bunched down around his ankle. Whoever wanted to see him would have to take what they got.

He flung open the door and his breath stalled. Lupe stood on the other side of the door. She wore a pink sweater set over a pair of khaki pants and a pair of low-heeled sandals. For the first time since he'd known her, her waist-length hair was down and held back from her face on one side by a pink clip. Lip gloss glistened on her lips, and when she lifted her sunglasses from her face he saw that she was wearing mascara. "Hi, Joe," she said, as if she showed up at his apartment every day.

Joe closed his eyes and shook his head. When he opened his eyes she was still there, not a figment of his imagination.

She regarded him with a mixture of humor and anticipation. "Can I come in?"

Still a bit disoriented from having his sleep interrupted and Lupe's mysterious appearance on his doorstep, he rubbed his eyes. "Sure."

He backed up, opening the door wider. Early-morning sunshine washed into the apartment, illuminating the disarray of the living room. Among other offenses, the TV was still going, and he'd left his clothes from the night before puddled by the sofa. "Would you believe me if I told you it was the cleaning woman's day off?"

She folded her arms in front of her. "No. But I do love your outfit. Are those duckies or giraffes? I can't tell."

He looked down at himself and snorted. He'd never gotten around to doing his laundry. The day before he'd been reduced to wearing the boxers his sister had given him last year for Christmas as a goof. "They're Santa faces. I guess I'd better throw something on."

In his bathroom, Joe gave himself a quick sponge bath, brushed his teeth, and ran a comb through his hair. He contemplated shaving, too, but he'd probably nick himself to death rushing to get back to Lupe.

Why had she come here? The last time he'd seen her, she'd barely said good-bye to him. He didn't want to speculate only to be disappointed. He tugged on a pair of jeans and a T-shirt and headed back out to her.

He found her in the same spot he'd left her. That surprised and pleased him. Most women, when faced with a man's messy apartment, had the annoying tendency to try to clean up.

She must have read his thoughts, because she smiled indulgently. "I'm not really the housekeeper, remember?"

"Then what do you do?"

"I own a restaurant on Hollywood Boulevard. Mestizos. Maybe you've heard of it?"

"Heard of it? I tried to make reservations once. They told me to try back in two months."

"I'll see what I can do about squeezing you in when we open back up next week. We've been closed while I stayed home to take care of Sam."

Joe shook his head. He'd had enough of this inane conversation. He wanted to know why she'd come. He motioned for her to join him on the sofa. She sat, but at the opposite end of the sofa from him, fiddling with one of the buttons on her cardigan. All the confidence he'd sensed in her seemed to have fled.

He stretched his arm across the back of the sofa to touch her shoulder. "What is it, *muñequita*? Why did you come to see me today?"

"I wanted to apologize for the way I treated you yesterday. You didn't deserve that."

Maybe not, but she could have called him on the phone to tell him that. "And . . ." he prompted.

"I wanted to ask you a favor."

"What's that?"

She licked those luscious lips of hers and met his gaze. "I was wondering if you would make love to me."

Her lashes fluttered and she looked away from him. It had obviously taken all her courage to ask him that. It took all his strength not to leap on her and oblige her. "Why?"

"Well . . ." She went back to fiddling with the button on her sweater. "They say the best way to face a fear is to jump right in and do the thing you're afraid of."

Whoever said that needed to have their brain adjusted. He moved closer to her and took her hand in his. "Listen to me, *muñequita*. As flattered as I am that you would ask me, I have to say no. This isn't one of your romance novels, where a few minutes in bed solve all the world's problems. You need to speak to someone, to work out your issues with your stepfather. Going to bed with me isn't going to change anything."

"I know. Sam has been after me for years to go. I called the doctor this morning and made an appointment for next week."

He wondered what had prompted her to finally take Samantha's advice. "That's a start. So why are you in a rush to get to the bedroom?"

She shook her head and stood. "I don't know. I thought now that the case is over I wouldn't see you anymore."

And she'd lose her chance to shed her fear with a man she trusted. He got up and wrapped his arms around her from behind. He rested his chin on her shoulder. "Baby, I'm not going anywhere. I want to be with you, but we have all the time in the world to get to know each other. We'll take it slow, okay?"

She turned in his arms to face him. "Would a kiss be out of the question right now?"

"Did you think I'd let you out that door without one?" He brought his lips down on hers for a kiss full of tenderness and promise.

Thirty

Adam pulled up in front of the Prescott estate. He wasn't sure how he felt about coming here today. Considering that Russell probably was the one who'd killed Billy, it might be the last time he'd have need to. A new maid answered the door. Although petite and pretty, she exuded a no-nonsense attitude.

"Welcome, Mr. Wexler," she said.

"Hello, Adam."

Adam turned to see his mother descending the stairs. She wore a blue-and-white tennis outfit and pristine white sneakers. She carried a covered tennis racket in her right hand. She stopped at the base of the stairs.

"Hello, Mother."

For a moment neither of them said anything. In the periphery of his vision, Adam noticed the maid close the front door and disappear down the hallway.

"We can go into Barrington's study, if you like."

Adam gestured for her to precede him. She led him to the familiar room and offered him a drink. He declined. She dropped her racket onto one of the chairs and poured herself a tall glass of what looked like iced tea.

"What did you want to talk to me about, Adam?"

"I thought you should hear it from me that Richard Russell admitted to killing Billy last night, then took his own life."

"What?" A stricken look crossed her face. She sank into the seat behind her. "How is that possible? Why?"

"It's complicated. He was blackmailing Billy." He deliberately left out the part concerning Samantha, and she didn't question him.

Adam shrugged. For the time being, he'd said all he needed to say. He stood. "I'd better be going." He started toward the door.

"Adam, wait," she called after him.

He turned, but he didn't quite look at her. "Yes?"

"I know this probably won't mean anything to you, but I'm sorry."

He did look at her then. His normally unflappable mother stood with her fingers gripped together and her lower lip caught between her teeth. "What for?"

"For not being a better mother. For not fighting harder to keep you. For not showing you how much I loved you when I had the chance."

His brow furrowed. "What are you talking about?"

"I'm talking about mistakes, Adam. All the ones I've made where you are concerned."

Adam folded his arms in front of him. He'd never expected to hear his mother express any guilt about the way she'd treated him. If she wanted to unburden her conscience, he wouldn't dream of stopping her. "Really?"

"Yes." She picked up her glass from the table next to her and sipped deeply. She inhaled and let her breath out on a sigh. "Now that I have you here, I don't know what to say."

"Start at the beginning."

She shrugged and gave a rueful little laugh. "I guess it all started the day I married your father. We were a total mismatch from the very beginning. The only place we ever got along was in the bedroom. Looking back on it now, I realize most of his appeal came from the fact that my father detested him. Not only did my father consider him beneath my station, he couldn't intimidate your father, either.

"A year after you were born, I wanted to leave him. I'd learned that not only couldn't your father be intimidated, he couldn't be kissed, cajoled, or manipulated into anything either. The only opinions he valued were his own, his commanding officer's, and God's. As a wife, the only opinions that should matter to me were my husband's."

Adam snorted. He could remember his father telling him something similar. As a kid, he'd done what he wanted and prayed his old man never found out. He could imagine how maddening such an attitude would be for a grown woman with a mind of her own.

Adele sighed. "I went to my father and asked him if I could stay with him until I got on my feet. We hadn't spoken in years. He'd even refused to give me away at my wedding. Your grandfather told me that since I'd defied him by marrying 'that soldier,' as your grandfather referred to him, I could rot with him for all he cared."

She sniffled and looked away from him, but not before Adam saw the sheen of tears in her eyes. "I'm sorry, Adam. Even after all these years, when I think of how he slammed the door in my face, it still hurts."

He didn't understand her. If she knew how much a parent's rejection could sting, why had she abandoned him? "So you left me with my father?"

"Not the way you mean. I left you for three months. I came out here to find a job, a place to live. I had a girlfriend who lived out here, and she helped me. I wanted to be as far away from Jacob Wexler as domestic flight could take me.

"But by the time I went back for you, you didn't remember me. Babies have such short memories. When I tried to hold you, you cried. It broke my heart. What was I supposed to do? Drag you with me? I left you with your father, knowing that he would take care of you. He was a good man even if he was a lousy husband. I filed for divorce trusting that the courts would sort out the custody issue in my favor.

"But that was just the leverage your father needed. He was furious with me for leaving him and embarrassing him in front of his friends. He vowed no son of his was going to be corrupted by the sissified air in California. He told me that if I tried to get custody of you, he'd make sure I never saw you again. One thing you could say about your father—he always made good on his promises. The court awarded him sole custody, since he claimed I'd abandoned you."

Adam watched his mother as she turned to look out the window. He'd always assumed his father had sole custody because his mother didn't want him. His father had led him to believe that, even though neither his father nor his aunts had ever come out and said anything disparaging about his mother. It was innuendo, and the genuine anger he'd sensed in his father whenever his mother's name came up. He'd never imagined that she might be the one who'd been wronged.

"If he hated you so much, why did he let me stay with you that summer?"

"To taunt me. I met and married Barrington within six months of moving out here. Your father had it in his head that I'd really left him to be with your stepfather.

"Well, it hit the papers that Barrington was having an affair with some dancer. Of course, I knew about it. I knew about all his women, but always before he'd had the courtesy to be discreet. Out of nowhere your father calls me and asks me if I can take you for a few weeks. He sent you with a note for me. Do you remember that?"

Adam nodded. "Yes."

"It read, 'See what you gave up for a man who cheats on you? Was he worth it?'

"He sent you to me, but the whole time you were here, you stared at me with this cold, cold expression in your eyes. And I knew he had turned you against me. I couldn't even touch you. Every time I got near you, you recoiled."

Adam's stomach roiled, hearing of his own father's cruelty. Jacob Wexler had been a hard man, and even if he wanted to deny his mother's claims, he acknowledged that his father had it in him to do everything she'd said.

"Why didn't you ever tell me any of this?"

"I didn't want to ruin your memory of your father. I could never deal with him, but you seemed to get along with him, love him. Your aunt Sarah would sneak and send me pictures of you, and on your birthday and every Christmas, one of the presents she gave you always came from me."

She lifted her shoulders in a delicate shrug. "Truthfully, I was afraid you wouldn't believe me. You never missed an opportunity to show your contempt for me."

He couldn't deny that. Perhaps there was a little more of his father in him than he wanted to admit. "Why didn't you want Billy's death investigated?"

"At first, I honestly thought Billy's accident had been just that. When you have a famous son, you can't grieve like a normal mother. The world acts as if it has a greater claim on your child than you do. The papers criticized me for not crying at Billy's funeral. But why should I have to display my pain for public consumption? All I wanted was to be left alone.

"Then you came to me, telling me you thought someone might have murdered your brother, and you wanted me to fix things to put you in danger, too. I know you're a policeman, Adam, but did you really expect me to agree to that? When I told you my job was to protect my son, I was talking about you.

"But I should have known you would do what you wanted no matter how I felt. I figured I should do what I could to help you."

"Thank you."

And he decided to answer the question that she must still be burning to ask. "I'm going to accept Billy's money."

She smiled, seeming to have expected his admission. "Do you think I ever doubted that? Billy knew that your conscience would never allow you to give money to a criminal, and so did I."

He shook his head, realizing both his mother and his brother had known him better than he'd ever allowed himself to know them. He didn't know what else to say. He needed to get away from her, to digest what she had said. "I'd better get back. I'm going back to New York today."

"To get your job back?"

"Partly."

"Good luck, Adam." She walked toward him and braced her hands on his arm. He obliged her by bending down to let her kiss his cheek. "If that's what you want, I hope it works out."

The problem was, Adam reflected as he drove back to Samantha's house, that at the moment, he didn't know what he wanted.

Sam lay on Adam's bed as he packed the rest of his belongings in his bag. "Why are you so hell-bent on getting to New York today?"

"I promised Jarad I would bring you east as soon as you were able to travel."

She turned on her side, facing him. She doubted any promise he'd made to Jarad had anything to do with their flight plans, but she didn't challenge him. Actually, she was thankful to get away from L.A. and all the events of the last two weeks.

"Besides, I've been summoned back by my captain. Something to do with my getting back to work."

She was happy for him, because she knew that was what he wanted more than anything. At the same time, it signaled that her time with him was almost over. She'd have a few days with him in the Big Apple; then she'd come back to California alone.

The prospect sent a shiver through her, and a dull ache beat in her heart. Hadn't she been the one to offer no strings, no promises, no regrets? It sounded fine in the abstract. That was before she'd made love to him, fallen in love with him, started to hope for things that could never be. When the time came, how was she supposed to let him go?

"What's the matter?" Adam asked, scrutinizing her.

"Nothing. But if you don't hurry up, we'll miss the plane." Needing something to occupy her mind, she climbed off the bed to stand beside him. "Why don't you go put my bags in the car and let me finish packing for you? They're too heavy for me to bring down anyway."

He kissed the tip of her nose. "Sounds like a plan."

As Adam left she picked up the folded stack of clothes beside the nearly full suitcase and tried to stuff them into the bag. She tried to mash them down, but something hard at the bottom of the case prevented it. She pushed aside the clothes to see what it was.

A photo album stared back at her. On the cover it read, *My brother the cop,* and there was Adam's picture, an old one, but distinctly him. She pulled it from the case and simply stared at it. It couldn't be. It could not. A cold hand gripped her insides, but she had to know. She opened the album and saw a young Billy and a young Adam playing together. Like an observer at a train wreck, she couldn't look away. She turned the pages until she reached the end.

The last picture was by far the most striking. The black-and-white image, cut from a newspaper, showed two soot-covered men, one white, one black. One wore an NYPD T-shirt; the other wore a turnout coat stamped FDNY. Both had fallen into an exhausted sleep with their backs against a building.

She'd seen this picture before, taken in the first days of the recovery at Ground Zero. It had made the *Times,* among other publications, under a headline that read, *The Faces of Heroism.*

Visually, the image was captivating—opposite or disparate elements coming together in a poignant way. It also captured the sentiment of the nation at the time, a mood of unity and patriotism.

Sam didn't realize she was crying until a tear dropped onto the page. She closed the book just as she heard the door to the guesthouse opening. She glanced up to find Adam framed in the doorway. He gazed from her to the book, then back again.

"Samantha," he said. "Let me explain."

Thirty-one

When he saw the ravaged look on Samantha's face and the album in her lap, Adam wished he could turn back time to the first day he'd met her. He wished he'd told her then, because he wouldn't have to see the contempt in her eyes right now. He wouldn't have to feel lower than the carpet beneath his feet.

"Why didn't you tell me?"

At least she gave him a chance to explain himself. "Would you have had anything to do with me if you'd known?"

"No. I'll give you that. If you'd come to me and told me you were Billy's brother, I would have had you removed from my home. We both know that. But there were any number of times after that when you could have told me.

"How about when I asked you how you got involved in Billy's murder? How about when I allowed you into my bed? Did you get a kick sleeping with your brother's leftovers, or was that a turnoff?"

"Samantha, you know it wasn't like that." He took a step toward her.

She jumped up from the bed and moved backward toward the door. "Don't you touch me. Did you ever plan to tell me?"

"As soon as we got to New York. I wanted some space between us and all that had happened."

"I see. You planned to take me cross country, where I don't know anyone, to spring this on me."

Adam made an exasperated sound and covered his forehead with his palm. Nothing he said came out as he meant it. And aside from that, he really had no excuse, or at least none that made sense now, though his reasons had seemed perfectly rational at the time.

He dropped his hand to his side. "Look, Sam. I know I should have told you. But I knew how you felt about Billy's brother, about me. If I'd told you, I would have lost the ability to protect you. I couldn't risk that."

"You can tell yourself anything you want to. Rationalize it any way you want to. Sorry I didn't finish your packing. Have a nice flight."

She turned to go, but he grabbed her arm to prevent her from leaving. "Sam, come with me to New York. We'll talk. I can't tell you how sorry I am that I didn't tell you."

She seemed to soften for a moment, but when her gaze met his, all he saw was resignation. "What's the point, Adam? We both knew from the start that there was no future for us. If it makes you feel any better, I forgive you. Now go home. I don't think Joe would appreciate having to come out here to arrest you for trespassing."

She shook off his grasp and left. Adam sank down on the bed and put his head in his hands. He'd blown it—he'd blown everything with her—because he was afraid to tell her the truth. That was really what it boiled down to. All the other nonsense he'd told himself meant nothing. He'd been afraid of what she would think of him if she knew, and more than that, afraid that she was right.

He couldn't blame her for her anger, but neither would he leave her unprotected. He went back to the house to find her. He would come clean with her totally, and tell her his suspicion that Russell hadn't acted alone in Billy's death.

He didn't find her in the Angel Room or in the solarium. Lupe sat on the sofa in the front room. "Where's Samantha?"

"She left. She said she's not coming back until you're gone."

Adam ground his teeth together. He hadn't considered the possibility that she'd be so angry with him that she'd leave her own home to get away from him. After the break-in, anybody who owned a television would be wary about coming here. If there was a second actor, someone who wanted her dead, this might be just the break they needed to get to her.

A tightness settled in the middle of Adam's chest. "Where did she go, Lupe?"

Lupe shook her head. "Whose house should you be looking to, Adam?"

"Damn it, Lupe. She may still be in danger."

Lupe cocked her head to one side. "How stupid do I look? Do you really expect me to believe anything you say?"

"Then answer me this, Lupe. If I'm feeding you a line, why would I bother? Why wouldn't I just go home like she asked me to?"

Her dark eyes searched his for a moment. "Even if you're right, I don't know. Always before when she was upset, she went to the Angel Room. I don't know where she would have gone."

"I'm going to look for her. Stay here in case she comes back. If she does, call me." He pulled one of his cards out of his wallet and handed it to her. "The number is on there."

He went back to the guesthouse, got his jacket and his gun, and got in his car. He called Joe and told him what had happened.

"Where are you going to look?" Joe asked.

The last place he would expect her to go. "Billy's house."

Sam didn't know why she came here. After heading out on the freeway blindly, she found herself headed in this direction. She drove along the path up to Billy's house, and half of her wanted to turn back. There was nothing left for her here—no peace, no closure, only bitterness.

She pulled around the back of the house. Since Adam had taken her keys, she'd had to call George on the intercom to get in. He waited for her outside the garage door.

"Miss Sam, it's so nice to see a friendly face," he said as he helped her from the car. "That other one is up at the house. She's been here every day now, like she owns the place. Most times she comes with her little girl, so I let her in. But today she came alone."

"It's okay, George. I'm sure Billy wouldn't mind." She patted his arm. "You wouldn't have any of your patented iced tea around, would you? My throat's a little dry."

"I got some in the back. I'll get you some straightaway."

After he'd gone, Sam wandered through the rows of cars, appreciating the beauty of the well-maintained, shiny automobiles. To her knowledge, most of Billy's cars had never been driven by him. She'd never understood his need for acquiring things he never intended to use. Maybe because the people in his life had proved so profoundly disappointing. His parents, Adam, his friends had either abandoned him of taken advantage of him in some way.

Even she had deserted him. Long before that fateful car ride, she'd known why he'd suddenly reemerged in her life. She'd heard rumors that he was straightening out his life, and she hadn't wanted to hear it. She could have given him the benefit of the doubt. She could have offered him her friendship, even though resuming their relationship had been out of the question. She could have, at least in her heart, wished him well.

She closed her eyes and sighed. None of it made any difference now, except maybe this. "I'm sorry, Billy," she whispered. "Sorry that things didn't turn out better for you."

"How touching."

Sam opened her eyes and spun around in the direction of the female voice. Sandra stood in front of her holding on to George's arm with one hand. In the other she held a gun pointed directly at Sam.

Sam froze, her eyes riveted to the barrel of the gun. Suddenly she was fourteen years old again, and someone bent on madness held her life in their hands by a finger curled around a trigger. As if from somewhere far away, she heard George going on and on, apologizing for putting Sam in danger. He seemed as disoriented as she felt.

"Shut up, old man." Sandra pointed the gun at him. "Don't give me any reason to shoot you. It's Sam here I want." Sandra turned to face her. "I have to thank you for coming here today. It saves me the trouble of having to hunt you down. What happened to our friend the cop?"

By now Adam's plane would have taken off. She swallowed roughly. "He went back to New York without me."

Sandra puffed out her lower lip and frowned. "How sad. "I'll have to remember to cry later."

"What do you want from me?"

A malicious smile spread across Sandra's face. "We're going for a little ride. A little ride to see Billy."

Sam focused on George. His cap had fallen askew, revealing a fresh and bloody wound at his temple. No wonder he'd seemed disoriented. Sandra must have blindsided him, because under normal circumstances George would have had enough strength to overtake Sandra.

If Sandra truly meant to kill George, she could have done it while they were in the house.

"Then let George go. I'll go with you." She'd go with Sandra and pray George had the presence of mind to call the police once they'd gone.

"You got that right." Sandra pushed George away from her with enough force to send the old man crashing to the floor. While Sam's attention was diverted with George's well-being, Sandra came up beside her and grabbed her arm. She motioned toward Sam's Mercedes. "We'll take your car. Move."

Sam did as she was told, getting in on the passenger side and sliding over behind the wheel. Sandra slid in behind her and slammed the door shut. "Start the car," Sandra commanded.

Sam turned the key. In a few minutes they would be away from here, and George, at least, would be safe. The engine hummed to life. Suddenly Sandra pointed the gun in George's direction.

"By the way, old man," Sandra snarled. "Here's something to remember me by."

Sandra fired. Sam screamed as the gun's loud report echoed in her ears. A red dot appeared on George's plaid shirt, deepening and expanding as he slumped lifelessly against the garage floor.

Icy fingers of dread gripped Sam's insides as Sandra turned to her and barked one word: "Drive."

Thirty-two

Adam had been so certain that he would find Samantha at Billy's that when he pulled up and saw no sign of her or her car, he felt immediately disconcerted. There didn't seem to be any sign of George either. George would know if Samantha had been there and left.

Adam stepped out of the car and glanced up at the sky. The first overcast day since he'd been here. He hoped it didn't actually rain, as that would force him to do the one thing he dreaded where his clown car was concerned—he might have to put the top down.

He slammed the car door shut and headed toward the back room, where George usually stayed during the day, keeping an eye on the cars.

Adam walked toward the open garage door. As he advanced he noticed George's cap on the ground beside a pool of dark liquid. As he drew nearer, he recognized the metallic smell of it—blood. A deep puddle of it, then drag lines, as if someone had been pulled or pulled himself deeper into the garage.

Adam's heartbeat kicked into overdrive and a flush of adrenaline, like heat rising from the pavement, whooshed through his body. He drew his gun and followed the trail. He found George slumped against the office wall, unmoving. Adam went down on one knee beside him. "George," Adam called, while searching for a pulse at his carotid artery.

Relief flooded Adam as the old man's eyes fluttered open. "Samantha," the old man gurgled. "Gun."

Adam squeezed his eyes shut. No way had Samantha shot George. She couldn't even hold a gun, which meant she was at the mercy of someone who could. "Who?"

"Sandra. Went to see Billy."

"How long ago?"

"F-five minutes. Go."

Adam tried to wrap his mind around that information, but couldn't concentrate. His first priority was the man beside him. So much blood stained his shirt that it was impossible to tell where the bullet went in. He couldn't try to stop the bleeding if he couldn't find its source.

He ripped open George's shirt, and fresh blood bubbled up from a wound in his shoulder, but almost immediately the flow slowed to a trickle.

The old man grasped Adam's wrist in a surprisingly strong hold. "I'm okay," George whispered. "Go."

Samantha darted a glance at Sandra as they headed onto the freeway. Sandra held the gun on her lap pointed in Sam's direction. Sam swallowed. By now, Adam was on the way to New York, and George was probably dead. No one knew where she was or that a madwoman held her hostage. Sam was no less terrified of the gun Sandra held, or the knowledge that Sandra intended to use it on her. But she didn't see any way out of this situation, and her hopelessness made her bold. "Where are you taking me?"

"Keep your eyes on the road," Sandra barked. "We wouldn't want to have an accident on the way." Sandra laughed at her own private joke, the maliciousness in that sound lifting the hairs on the back of Sam's neck.

"Why are you doing this? I never did anything to you."

"Didn't you? You cost me everything. All my planning was for nothing."

"What are you talking about?"

Sandra sighed dreamily, as if she were about to make a confession to a girlfriend, not to a woman she intended to kill. "I wanted Billy Prescott from the first time I laid eyes on him.

On the screen, Billy is handsome, but in person, there's just something about him that draws you in."

Sam nodded. She'd felt it too. Now was only one of many times she wished she hadn't.

"I'd heard he was dating you, but all's fair in love and war, so I went after him. He resisted me at first, but not for long. I told him I'd do anything he wanted, become anything he wanted, and he succumbed.

"But I knew that sooner or later he'd get bored with me, like he had with everyone else. If I wanted to keep him, I'd have to do something special. I made up my mind to give him the one thing no other woman had—a child. That way, no matter what, he'd always be connected to me."

Sam glanced over at Sandra. In the dark interior of the car, Sandra's eyes seemed curiously luminescent, frightening, maybe mad. "You gave him Brianna."

"Yes. It wasn't too hard to poke a few holes in a few condoms." She laughed. "He never noticed. I gave him a beautiful daughter, the very image of him. And how did he repay me?

"He never forgave me for causing you to break off your engagement. He'd told me not to come to the hospital, but I didn't listen. The day you threw your ring in his face was the last time we were together that way. But I still had Brianna. If he wanted to see her, he'd have to come through me."

Sam swallowed over a throat devoid of moisture. Given Billy's weaknesses, he'd never stood a chance against this woman. In an odd way, she felt sorry for him. If Billy had possessed the least bit of self-control, he wouldn't have been such easy prey for Sandra's manipulations. That didn't excuse his behavior, but somehow the anger she'd felt for Billy dissipated.

However, none of what Sandra said explained why she'd killed him.

"Get out here," Sandra directed.

"This is the way to my house," Sam said.

"I told you we were going to see Billy. We're going to finish what I didn't get right the first time."

* * *

Adam sped past Billy's gate and turned onto the side road that would take him to the freeway. George had said that Sandra was taking Sam to see Billy. Where? Not the cemetery. Because of the number of celebrities buried there, the place was guarded more closely than Fort Knox. How did Sandra expect to make it through the gate holding a gun on Samantha?

Only one other destination popped into his mind. *Damn!* If he'd stayed home, he could have made it there in five minutes, but then he never would have known Samantha needed him. He gunned the engine and headed for the freeway.

"Pull over here," Sandra instructed. "This is close enough."

Sam pulled onto the same embankment facing the cliff edge where she had parked with Billy. From the moment Sandra had directed her onto the road behind her house, Sam knew what Sandra intended: she meant to reunite her with Billy permanently in the spot where he had died. How Sandra intended to get her down that cliff, Sam had no idea. But she did know one thing: there wouldn't be any rescue. No Good Samaritan to come to her aid. No one in their right mind would travel this road during a rainstorm. She was totally on her own.

"Why did you kill Billy? If you loved him, how could you send him to his death?"

Sandra laughed. "I never said anything about loving Billy. I liked his money and I liked what he did to me. Billy could be a real freak sometimes. Love was never part of the equation.

"He came to me and told me that he was going to propose again to you. The fool even showed me the ring he planned to give you, since he was certain you would accept. He told me he was going to his lawyer's office, too. That he'd asked Alex Winters to write up a new will leaving most of his assets to you."

"And you killed him for that?"

"I panicked. I had mistakenly thought he'd leave everything to me, or at least my daughter. He'd always told me that no matter what, Brianna and I would be taken care of. I had no idea he meant with a measly allowance and a house on the outskirts of Los Angeles."

Sandra shrugged. "That was my first mistake. I assumed that if I let him sign that new will, I'd lose millions. While Billy was playing with Brianna, I slipped outside to the drive where his car was parked. The only thing I could think of to do was sabotage his car. I'd dated a guy in high school who thought a hot date was me watching him rebuild trannies. I nicked the brake wires, so when they failed he'd be far away from my house."

"That was no guarantee that Billy would get into a fatal accident."

"The way Billy drove? It was virtually guaranteed. And even if he survived, it might give me more time to plan, maybe to change his mind."

Sam bit her lip. Meanwhile Sandra had sent a man out on the road in a faulty car with no regard for the fact that he might have taken innocent people with him.

"That was my second mistake," Sandra continued. "If I'd kept a clear head I would have realized that Billy wasn't the problem; you were. As long as he was obsessed with you, nothing I said or did made a difference. I should have gotten you out of the way. Even with Billy gone, you've been nothing but trouble. I tried to make a play for Adam—you know, follow the money trail—but you already had him in your bed."

Sandra lifted the gun. "I've had enough of true confessions. Get out of the car."

The moment had come. Sam had spent the last few minutes with half her mind on Sandra's tale and half on trying to figure out something, anything to do to extricate herself from Sandra's grasp—and she had come up with nothing.

Sandra seemed to read her thoughts. "Don't get cute. You know I'll shoot you."

The way she'd shot George—defenseless and unsuspecting. Sam opened the car door. She really had no choice. The confines of a car was no place to defend herself. Sam stepped out, and thick, heavy drops rained down on her, drenching her clothes and plastering her hair to her scalp. Sandra climbed out behind her. Before Sam could blink, Sandra was beside her, pressing the gun into her side.

"Walk," Sandra instructed, but both women froze as a familiar male voice shouted, "Let her go, before I blow your goddamn head off."

Thirty-three

Adam held his gun trained on Sandra, willing the rain to stay out of his eyes and his lungs to remain in his chest. When Sam's car hadn't shown up at the spot where Billy had crashed, he'd left his car and hiked back, hoping to catch Sandra by surprise. Another two minutes and he'd have been close enough to wring her scrawny neck. He'd made his presence known only because he feared what Sandra would do to Sam so close to the cliff's edge.

If the gun weren't pressed up against Sam he'd take Sandra down without thinking twice. But he couldn't risk that Sandra's gun would go off and hit Sam. "You heard me. Let her go."

Sandra raised the gun so that it was pointed at Samantha's throat. "On the contrary, Detective. Put your gun down before your girlfriend gets an emergency tracheotomy. Do it."

He glanced at Samantha. She looked pale and terrified, but she was shaking her head no. Did she honestly think he'd leave them both at the mercy of this madwoman? He only intended to let her think he had.

He lifted his hands as if surrendering and bent down as if to place the gun on the ground. As he'd hoped, Sandra slowly turned her gun away from Sam and toward him. In an instant he had Sandra in his sights. But before he could squeeze off a round, Samantha did the last thing he expected of her: she grabbed Sandra's arm, trying to wrest the gun away from her.

He stood by helplessly as the two women grappled for control of the gun. He didn't dare shoot now. Sam was taller, but still hadn't regained full strength after the accident. And Sandra was fighting for her life—the only way she could get out of this hole she'd dug for herself was to make sure neither he nor Sam lived to tell anyone about it. He ran toward them, realizing their struggle led them closer and closer to the cliff's edge.

The gun went off, freezing every nerve in Adam's body. For a moment it was impossible to tell which, if either of them, had been hit. As if in slow motion, Sandra crumpled to the ground.

Relief flooded him until he heard Sam scream his name. His chest constricted and his breath stalled in his lungs. Her eyes wide, her arms flailing, still holding the gun in her hand, she struggled for balance. He ran harder, trying to reach her before she fell, but the drenched earth pulled at his heels, holding him back. Before he could get to her, she fell backward, plunging out of sight over the cliff's edge.

"SAAAAAM!" He raced to the edge of the cliff and looked over, expecting to find Samantha's body way down in the valley below.

Instead she gazed back at him from a few feet down. She'd latched onto a Joshua tree growing out of the side of the mountain. "Adam, help me."

He threw himself on his stomach and reached his hand down to her. "Baby, grab my hand."

She did, and he hauled her and half the mountainside up with her. He lay on his back in the cold, wet mud and pulled her on top of him. Filthy and exhausted and emotionally drained, all he could do was hold Sam to him and try to breathe at a normal pace. From a distance, the whine of sirens reached his ears.

Much later, they lay together in Sam's big bed. Once the police arrived at the cliff, they hadn't spent one moment alone in each other's company. After the police had interrogated them, Sam had insisted that Adam take her to the hospital to check on George. Once they got home, Lupe fussed at the two of them for worrying her out of her mind. Joe, who had been in the car that found them, seemed to be the only one happy with the situation, as he got to comfort Lupe.

Sam snuggled closer to Adam and rested her shoulder against his chest. "What's going to happen to her?"

"Sandra? She's in police custody at the hospital. Once her leg heals, she'll probably be put in jail. I can't imagine a judge offering her bail."

"What about Brianna?"

"She's with my mother for now. If things play out for Sandra as I think they will, she won't be in any position to raise her daughter. I'm going to file for custody."

Sam lifted her head and looked down at Adam. He would make a wonderful father, stern but loving—just what a child needed. With one finger she traced the outline of his face, the bridge of his nose, the shape of his bottom lip. All the while, he watched her with a dark, unreadable expression in his eyes.

Sam inhaled, mustering her courage to ask the question burning in her. "Why didn't you get on the plane today? Don't you have to meet with your captain tomorrow?"

"I would, if I intended to go back to New York to stay."

"What are you saying?"

Adam sighed and brushed her hair back from her face. "I'm saying I screwed up, Sam. I know we agreed to no strings, no promises, no future, but I fell in love with you. There's nothing in New York more important to me than that. I want to make a family with you and me and Brianna and whatever other children you'd like to give me."

"You would leave the police force?"

"Maybe. Believe it or not, they've got a department out here, too. Or maybe I'll do the typical ex-New Yorker thing and write a screenplay. The next great cop drama."

She laughed and hit him on the shoulder. "If you do, make sure to pattern your hero after yourself. You are all the hero I will ever need. I love you, Adam."

"Is that why you reached for Sandra's gun?"

She nodded. "I was in the car with my father during the accident that took his life. My mother died in my arms after being shot. I couldn't watch another person I loved die before my eyes."

"I nearly died from shock when you went over that cliff.

Mr. Clean is right about you: you do have a guardian angel on your shoulder."

"And another thing, Detective." She poked him in the chest. "I distinctly heard you call me Sam as I was hanging on for dear life on the side of that mountain."

Adam shrugged. "What can I say? It was the heat of the moment. Samantha has too many syllables to be screamed at the top of your lungs."

"So I have to make you scream to get you to call me by my name?" Sam trailed a path of kisses down his chest. "This could prove interesting."

Adam jerked as her tongue circled his navel. "Only one way to find out."

Epilogue

One year later

Adam leaned back in his chair, puffed on his cigar, and enjoyed the heat of the fading Labor Day sunshine. Even on remote islands such as Martha's Vineyard, where Ariel's grandmother lived, Adam mused that a certain division of the sexes could sometimes be a good thing.

The women had retired to the house a half-hour ago, when the sun had started to set. The men were outside on the patio doing what men did best—sitting around the dying barbecue fire, drinking beer and puffing on imported cigars supplied by Jarad Naughton. The children ran between the two groups—shrieking, laughing, chasing after an Irish setter named Dudley that had to be the dumbest dog Adam had ever laid eyes on.

A hand clapped his shoulder. He looked up to find an older man, Charlie, staring down at him. He held a jug in his hands and wore a devilish grin on his face. "Who'll be wanting some of this?"

A collective groan went up from the men around him. "Don't look at me," Ariel's father said.

Dan, Ariel's cousin's husband, shuddered. "Once was enough."

Adam glanced at Jarad, who'd remained silent. Adam wasn't sure Jarad approved of him as a husband for Sam, but Adam didn't care much. In his opinion, Jarad had been testy since the day Ariel had made him get snipped since they didn't want any more children. Jarad gazed back at him and said, "It's your funeral."

"Give me a cup," Adam said to Charlie. Whatever Charlie poured into that cup smelled like an open grave and tasted like a Brooklyn sewer. Adam drank it all down, aware the four men watched him. He handed the cup to Charlie. "Not bad."

All four of them shot him disgruntled looks. What had they expected him to do? Foam at the mouth? Speak in tongues? If this were some sort of initiation into the tribe, had he passed or failed?

Jarad took pity on him and changed the subject. "How's Lupe?"

"Good." Joe had called that morning to inform him, among other things, that Johnny Maxwell had introduced the wrong father's daughter to things white and hallucinogenic. He'd received two shots to the temple at point-blank range for his efforts. Barrington had already agreed to defend the father. Word was he would probably get off on a Fourth Amendment violation. It was almost enough to make Adam believe in karma.

"Jo just had a litter of kittens."

Jarad chuckled. "I take it you mean Jo the cat and not Joe the husband."

"Yes, Joe the husband. He also says he's looking forward to meeting you next month when *Guardian Angel* premieres in L.A."

"I'll bet. Sam tells me he's working on a screenplay."

Adam shrugged. "What else have we ex-New Yorkers got to do?"

"Move back?"

Adam chuckled. Jarad had done just that when he'd met and fell in love with Ariel, who lived in New York. Adam understood the other man's motivation. When he'd married Samantha, he hadn't cared whether they lived in New York, L.A. or Timbuktu—as long as they were together.

The oldest of the children, Dan's son, came to stand by his father. "Aunt Sam asked me to ask you if you could make her a cheeseburger, well-done." The boy dashed off before his father had a chance to answer.

At first Adam got hung up on the ludicrousness of the appellation "Aunt Sam" to pay attention to what the kid asked for. Then his brow furrowed and he asked, "Did I just hear D. J. say Sam wanted a cheeseburger?"

"M-hmm." Jarad watched him with a peculiar expression on his face.

Adam shook his head. It couldn't be for Brianna, because she liked them like he did, blood-rare, not well-done. He tried to put it out of his mind and pay attention to the conversation, which had shifted to who would win the World Series that year. Since he couldn't care less, he decided to check on Sam.

Adam stood and the world around him swam. "What the hell did you put in that drink?"

"My secret recipe," Charlie said. "So don't go asking what's in it."

"I wouldn't dream of it." Right now his innards felt as if they'd been stapled on inside out. He shook his head and it cleared a little. He went into the house to the sitting room, where the women sat drinking wine and laughing.

While none of them noticed him, he let his gaze travel over them, from Gran, the family matriarch, to Diana, Ariel's mother, to Jenny, Ariel's cousin, to Ariel herself, who sat next to Samantha on the sofa.

The men in Ariel's family claimed the lot of them were witches who'd snared them all with their bewitching eyes. *Yeah, right.* But he did find it a bit unnerving that all the women in Ariel's family, even her daughters, bore the same sea-green eyes. Although the girls were identical twins, the boys were not, which led Sam to tease Ariel that although Jarad may have been responsible for the first set of twins, Ariel had done the second set to herself.

Adam focused on the owner of the lone pair of amber eyes in the room. A weekend in the sun had given her cheeks color and caused a smattering of freckles to rise on her nose. As always, her beauty took his breath away.

Brianna, who sat on Sam's lap, cocked her head to one side

and regarded him through narrowed eyes. "Mama, why does Daddy Adam look funny?"

In the one wise and unselfish act she'd committed, Sandra had given up parental rights to Brianna. When he and Sam adopted her, they'd told her she could call them whatever names she liked. Those were the ones she'd picked. Adam found it telling that the girl felt comfortable calling another woman Mama, but when she said Daddy she referred to Billy.

One day they would have to tell her the real story of what happened to her parents. For now, all she wanted was the reassurance that people loved her and would always take care of her.

He winked at Brianna. "What's so funny about the way I look?"

Sam gazed back at him with a narrow-eyed look. "Daddy Adam's eyes are red and as glassy as a fishbowl."

Adam huffed out a harsh breath. He knew how sensitive Sam was about drinking, given her father's addiction. That was why he'd spent the afternoon nursing the same beer. Yet he'd allowed himself to be drawn into some juvenile pissing contest with Jarad. Before he could say anything, Ariel put her hand on Sam's arm.

"I hope you will excuse the male half of my family. Their idea of having a good time is forcing some vile brew on unsuspecting guests and waiting to see how long it takes them to pass out or throw up."

"So how long has it been?" Jenny asked. "Dan lasted all of seventeen minutes."

He found Jenny's humor infectious, but no one else did.

"Come on, Mother," Diana said. "Let's give the children some ice cream."

Brianna wiggled off of Sam's lap to follow the others. He watched her scamper off, then turned to face Sam. The troubled look in her eyes had been replaced by a faint smile. "What's this about a cheeseburger?" he asked. "Who was that for?"

"For me," she said, her face the picture of innocence.

"For you? When did you start eating meat?"

"Not me, exactly. It's for the baby. The baby wants meat."

Maybe that drink really had gone to his head, but Sam wasn't making any sense. "What baby?"

"The one we're going to have in about seven months."

The world around him swam again, and this time it had nothing to do with Charlie's home brew. "What did you say?"

She laughed. "I said, we're going to have a baby."

"Excuse us," Adam said to the other occupants of the room, then grabbed his wife by the hand and led her to the bedroom they'd shared for the last two days.

Samantha entered the room first. Adam leaned his back on the door to close it. "Come here," he said.

She walked back to him, an anxious expression on her face. "You're not upset, are you? I know we said we'd wait awhile before having children of our own to let Brianna get accustomed to living with us."

He pulled her into his arms. For a moment he buried his face against her hair, overwhelmed by the gift she'd given him. He lifted his head to smile down at her. "I know what we said, but why would you think I'd be upset? I told you I'd welcome any children you wanted to give me."

He ran his hand down her body to cover her flat abdomen that would soon round with his child. He covered her mouth briefly with his own. "I love you, Sam."

"I love you, too, Adam."

"I have one question for you." He tucked a strand of her hair behind her ear. "If you're the one who's pregnant, why do I feel like throwing up?"

Laughing, she smacked him on the shoulder. "Because you, Adam Wexler, don't know how to hold your liquor."

"Nonsense. I haven't been drunk since I was thirteen and Andy Simpson lifted a bottle of Boone's Farm sour apple wine from his old man's liquor store. We downed that sucker in my aunt Sarah's garage and puked our guts out on her living room carpet."

She took his hand and led him over to the bed. "You should lie down before you fall out."

He lay down on his back and pulled her on top of him. "Never."

"Why not? Big, tough LAPD cops don't pass out at the family barbecue?"

"I'm not so tough anymore." He winked at her. "Now I ride a desk, and in my spare time I lecture school kids on gun safety."

She thought of all he'd given up to be with her. The question occurred to her often, but she had never been brave enough before to ask it. "Do you miss it? Do you miss the life you had in New York before me?"

He ran his hand up and down her arm in a soothing manner. "No, baby. You know I don't feel that way. In New York I had nothing but a job, a crummy apartment, and a chip on my shoulder the size of Wyoming. I didn't see it then, not until I met you and found I wanted more out of my life.

"Besides, I know it was my mother's influence that got me promoted to keep me off the streets. But even she couldn't have done that if I hadn't gone along with it."

She hadn't thought about that before. "So, Lieutenant, what are we going to name this baby of ours?"

Getting no answer, she lifted her head to look down at him. His eyes were closed and his mouth was slack, and a deep snore resonated up from his chest. She glanced at the clock on the bedside table. Exactly seven minutes had passed since they'd walked into the room.

"My hero." Sam leaned down and kissed his mouth. "You're secret's safe with me."

Dear Readers,

I hope you enjoyed reading Adam and Samantha's story. The book is a bit of a departure for me, in that I have never really delved into romantic suspense before. In all honesty, Holding Out for a Hero is a different book than I imagined it being when I started out. I was about a third into the book when September 11th hit.

For a long time after that, I couldn't touch the story. In the wake of so much loss, it seemed incomprehensible to me that it made one ounce of difference in the world whether I wrote or not. It was you readers who drew me back to writing. I got so many e-mails from readers asking me if I had a new book out (luckily, MIDNIGHT MAGIC was just about to hit the shelves). They wanted something to take their minds off the events in the world around them—an escape into the fantasy of romance.

I thank you so much for your support and encouragement and kind words over the years that have sustained me and given me a renewed sense of purpose. Please continue to write to me at:

P.O. Box 233
Bronx, NY 10469
or e-mail me at DeeSavoy@aol.com.

In closing, I offer a simple wish for the future: That we will not forget the spirit of compassion, unity and courage that was forged by the events of September 11th. I hope that each of us offers up a prayer for those who are gone and another one of thanks that we are still here, still able to make a difference in the world.

All the best,
Deirdre Savoy

About the Author

Native New Yorker Deirdre Savoy spent her summers on the shores of Martha's Vineyard, soaking up the sun and scribbling in one of her many notebooks. It was there that she first started writing romance as a teenager. The island proved to be the perfect setting for her first novel, SPELLBOUND, published by BET/Arabesque Books in 1999.

SPELLBOUND received rave reviews and earned her the distinction of the first Rising Star author of Romance in Color and was voted their Best New Author of 1999. Deirdre also won the first annual Emma award for Favorite New Author, presented at the 2001 Romance Slam Jam in Orlando, Florida.

Deirdre's second book, ALWAYS, was published by BET/Arabesque in October 2000. ALWAYS was a February 2001 Selection for the Black Expressions Book Club. ONCE AND AGAIN, the sequel to ALWAYS, was published in May 2001, and was also selected by the Black Expressions Book Club. MIDNIGHT MAGIC, the third book in the Thorne family saga was a 2001 Holiday release.

Deirdre's fifth book, HOLDING OUT FOR A HERO, features fictional hero, NYPD detective Adam Wexler and real-life hero firefighter Paul Haney, the winner of the 2001 Arabesque Man Contest on the cover.

In her other life, Deirdre is a kindergarten teacher for the New York City Board of Education. She started her career as a secretary in the school art department of Macmillan Publishing Company in New York, rising to Advertising/Promotion Supervisor of the International Division in three years. She has also worked as a freelance copy writer, legal proofreader, and news editor for CLASS magazine.

Deirdre graduated from Bernard M. Baruch College of the

City University of New York with a Bachelors of Business Administration in Marketing/Advertising.

Deirdre is a member of African American Authors Helping Authors (AA-AHA) and the founder of the Writer's Co-op writer's group. She lectures on such topics as Marketing Your Masterpiece, Getting Your Writing Career Started, and other subjects related to the craft of writing. She is listed in the American and International Authors and Writers Who's Who, as well as the Dictionary of International Biography.

Deirdre lives in Bronx, New York with her husband of ten-plus years and their two children. In her spare time she enjoys reading, dancing, calligraphy and "wicked" crossword puzzles.

BOOK YOUR PLACE ON OUR WEBSITE AND MAKE THE ARABESQUE ROMANCE CONNECTION!

We've created a customized website just for our very special Arabesque readers, where you can get the inside scoop on everything that's going on with Arabesque romance novels.

When you come online, you'll have the exciting opportunity to:

- View covers of upcoming books

- Learn about our future publishing schedule (listed by publication month and author)

- Find out when your favorite authors will be visiting a city near you

- Search for and order backlist books

- Check out author bios and background information

- Send e-mail to your favorite authors

- Join us in weekly chats with authors, readers and other guests

- Get writing guidelines

- AND MUCH MORE!

Visit our website at
http://www.arabesquebooks.com